MONSTER NATION

DAVID WELLINGTON

MONSTER NATION

A ZOMBIE NOVEL

RUNNING PRESS
PHILADELPHIA • LONDON

ACKNOWLEDGMENTS

THIS WAS A very different kind of book from what I'm used to writing. It was much, much more difficult and a little more fun. It was also very therapeutic. I'm coming off the most eventful year of my life as I'm writing this. A lot of great things happened. I got married for one, and had the best day of my life surrounded by our two families. A lot of dark things happened, too, though, and we lost some very good friends. I've taken solace in these pages, turning to my writing as a way to get my demons out. I don't know if it shows or not. I think on the whole this was a darker book than *Monster Island*, but I suppose that's up to the readers to decide.

Speaking of whom: I'd like to thank everyone who read *Monster Nation*, whether you read it on your cell phone, your PDA, your computer, or printouts you clutched in shaking hands as you read under the covers on a moonless night. I especially want to thank those who commented on the chapters. Adrian Padden, of course, was the sexiest cheerleader of all, yet again. Alnjo tried to keep me honest. The Laura(s), Digbeta, igame3d, Feral Fish (who started a fan site!), Marbo/Marbotty/Marb-something, Don, Donny D, DavidKayc929, Mendoza, Mel, Jacqui, Carlos, Shadowfusion99, Timmy, Baglegod, liam, Saketini and everybody else I'm forgetting, thank you so much. You kept me going, you kept me writing when I just wanted to curl up and go to sleep forever. Your role in this project has been far more dynamic and far more valued than you know.

There were two people who provided information without which I could not have written this book:

Raul Gallego provided information on topics military, architectural, and religious. Then there was Clint Freeman, who knew more about Florence, Colorado, and its famous prison than I had room to fit into the book. There are those who say a story like this is only as good as its research. If you enjoy *Monster Nation* you owe these two men a round of applause.

Also, let us never forget Alex Lencicki, of course, my intrepid business manager. And webmaster. And Halo 2 instructor (the man is unstoppable with an energy sword). And friend. Alex went so far past the call of duty this time I nearly lost sight of him. In 2004 Alex made this story available on cellular phones, PDAs, and iPods. Alex Lencicki is no Johnny Halfways.

Finally I would like to thank my wife, Elisabeth, who put up with all of this at a time when she had her own worries. During a time of great personal loss and grief she never stopped loving and supporting me and my zombie stories. Thanks, Pepper.

MONSTER NATION

PART
ONE

"MY BROTHER WAS ALREADY DEAD!" Clifton Thackeray made some outrageous claims while he was being held in a Fort Collins lockup on suspicion of involvement in a truly bizarre and grizzly murder. Last Saturday he attempted to hang himself with his belt. What really happened that night in the mountains? Our Harry Blount investigates: Page 17. [*Westword Weekly*, Denver, Colorado, 3/15/05]

HERE'S WHAT SHE had:

She was dressed all in white. Drawstring pants, halter top, linen jacket. Sandals and sunglasses, with her short blonde hair pulled back in a tight bun. A niobium stud in her nose and a tribal tattoo around her belly button, a sun with wavy triangular rays that flashed every so often as her top rode up and down with the rhythm of her walking.

She felt good: she was smiling, swaying her hips a little more than she needed to. She remembered wanting to slip her sandals off and feel the rough rasp of the sidewalk with her feet.

How much of this recollection could she trust? It was pretty threadbare and frayed around the edges. All the sounds she heard when she went back to this place were low and distorted.

Oceanic vibrations. She couldn't smell anything. The light seemed to hang in individual sunbeams, stray photons pinned to the air.

Worst of all there were no words. No names or signs. She bopped right past a stop sign but in this sunny space it was just a blank red octagon. Stop, she thought to herself. Stop, stop stop! The word wouldn't manifest.

Palm trees. Rollerbladers and homeless people competing for sidewalk space. The place had to be California, unless a million movies had steered her wrong. Not a famous part of California, just seedy and a little run-down in a charming multi-cultural way. A four-way intersection with a food market selling Goya products, a free clinic, a boarded up storefront with no sign, and some kind of bar. What she might be doing there she had no idea.

Time started up and the light moved again: with the scene set the action was ready to begin. At the intersection a Jeep Cherokee slurped up onto the curb and smacked into a stone bench with the sound of tin foil tearing and rattling. The car rocked on its tires, its windows the color of oil on water. Time hovered and danced around the scene like a bumblebee in search of nectar. Cubes of broken glass spun languorously in the air while clouds raced overhead in a fractured time lapse. She was frozen in place, in shock, in mid-stride. How much time passed? A minute? Fifteen seconds? The driver's door opened and a man in a blue western-style shirt tumbled out.

The look on his face made no sense at all.

He staggered a bit. Grabbed at the bench, at the hood of his car. He was having trouble walking, standing upright.

Of course she went to help him. She was supposed to—why? What was she? A doctor? A nurse? Massage therapist? The look on his face was just . . . slack. His jaw didn't seem to close properly and his eyes weren't tracking. Stroke? Seizure? Heart attack? She had to help. It was an obligation, part of the social contract.

He was dead when she got to him.

It didn't stop him from reaching for her.

The man was dead but he was still moving. An impossibility, a singularity of biology. The point where normal rules no longer apply. The recollection began to break down at this point into raw sense-data, fragments of information that didn't add up to a single memory. She could remember the synthetic fabric of his shirt where she touched it, the oils of his skin, the pure and unadulterated comfort of his arm as it crossed her back, holding her to him, hugging her—as if he were a brother—a father—boyfriend—husband—priest—something, some male presence, still welcome and good and wanted because she didn't know what was going on, just glad for the human contact in a scary moment when nothing quite worked the way it should.

Then pain, intense and real, far more real than anything else in her memory, as thirty-two needles sank into her shoulder, into her skin, his teeth.

That's what she had. Everything else was torn away leaving ragged edges, bloody sockets. Her head was full of grimy windows she couldn't see through everywhere else she looked. Her memory was dead and rotting and it had left her only these few scant impressions. Everything else was gone.

For instance: she couldn't remember her name.

FIVE FOUND DEAD NEAR ESTES PARK: Police Chief Suggests Links to "Meth" Production in High Country [*Rocky Mountain News*, 3/17/05]

Dick rolled to a stop on the shoulder and dug through old Burger King bags until he found the gas station map. It had a bad grease stain on it that spread slowly while he watched. *Shit, there goes Gunnison*, he thought, chuckling to himself.

He hardly ever used the map—he'd grown up in these mountains and the prairies beneath them and there were hardly a handful of roads in that part of the Front Range anyway. With a compass and a good idea of where he was headed he could usually get where he needed without straying too far. Still. Once you went off-road it was another story. There were a hundred canyons up in these mountains, little valleys like pockets on the sides of the big peaks, hollows lost in shadows or so overgrown with trees you couldn't see them until you were in them. He was somewhere near Rand, on the wild side of Rocky Mountain National Park, pretty far from anywhere civilized. The map showed an unpaved road or more precisely a track— a single dotted line branching off from 125 and zig-zagging up the mountain, ending nowhere in particular. He had missed it somehow. Not too surprising. March might have thawed out most of the Great Plains but up this high snow still glinted in every declivity and overhang and lingered under the shade of every stunted tree. An unpaved road at this altitude could have literally disappeared since the map was printed, ground out of existence by the winter snow squalls or the run-off from spring freshets. Dick frowned and checked the GPS unit bolted to his dashboard, then looked again at the map. If he was reading the scale correctly he was within a quarter mile of the track but he had seen nothing as he drove by at ten miles per hour.

While he sat there wondering what to do he nearly missed a flash of movement in the rearview mirror. He turned around as fast as he could and saw a teenage girl come flailing out of the scrub growth on the side of the road maybe two hundred yards behind him. Her hair was a mess—well, she had just emerged from a stand of juniper bushes—and she wore an over-sized parka that was too heavy for the season. She had some trouble getting out of the bushes, her sleeves tangling up in the mazy branches until she had to yank hard just to get clear. That sent her tumbling to the ground. She got up and without even brushing herself off started walking. She didn't even glance in his direction, just started stumping down the road to the south. He remembered seeing some parked cars back there. Just a hiker, he thought. Plenty of them got this far up and decided, between the ruggedness of the trail and incipient altitude sickness, that what they really wanted was to just go home. He even smiled at the thought. There was something strange about the way she was walking—like her knees were stiff with arthritis, maybe, though she was much too young for that. He watched her go until she had passed around a corner and out of sight and only then wondered if he should have gotten her attention, offered some help if she needed it.

He never really got a solid look at her face.

Whatever. Dick had been there himself many times. He knew that when he was that anxious to go home he personally never wanted to talk to anybody. Let her be, he decided. If she wanted his help she would come back and ask for it. He still had to find the track and now he had a pretty good idea where to look for it. The idiot girl was hiking alone, which was a pretty bad idea in general, but hell, Dick wasn't law enforcement. If people wanted to be stupid he figured they had a right.

Back to the problem at hand—the missing track. Nothing for it but to inspect the site on foot. He groaned as he unbuckled his seat belt and grabbed his gloves and coat from the litter-strewn back seat but in truth he loved this shit, always had. From endless hiking adventures as a kid to summer stints as a park ranger in his college years to his current post with the National Institute of Health he had spent more of his life outside and above ten thousand feet than anywhere else.

The second Dick opened the door of the white Jeep snow blasted across his face and hands in a fine crystalline spray, making him squint up his eyes until he got his sunglasses on. Outside he was trodding on snow with every step, crunching it down. When he stood still he could hear nothing at all. The shadows of clouds roamed over the mountains, startlingly huge. He never got used to that beauty, to the breathtaking way the clouds painted the mountains with shadows. He turned back to where the girl had emerged and took a long, hard look-see.

When he found the track he wasn't surprised that he had missed it. The juniper bushes had completely obscured it from the road and anyway there wasn't much of it to find. It looked like it had been gouged out of the slope instead of graded. Gravel had collected in spots along its length—maybe it had been a real path once but now it was hard to even think of it as an acceptable animal track. No wonder the girl had been so anxious to get off of it and back to the road. When you knew it was there you could follow it with your eyes as it snaked up the side of the mountain and disappeared around a bend. It didn't look too steep. Dick headed back to the Jeep to get his daypack and his cell phone. A nice walk in the mountains, nothing more. He just wished he could stop thinking about that girl and the crazy way she was walking.

UNEXPLAINED FIRE IN IDAHO SPRINGS CLAIMS RIVER GUIDE, SIX SONS: Gasoline cans found on scene and "the front door was nailed shut."
[The Coloradoan (Fort Collins), 3/17/05]

Bannerman Clark, Captain Bannerman Clark of the Colorado Army National Guard to be precise, placed his cloth napkin neatly on his thigh and lined up his steak knife next to his silver fork. Once a month he treated himself to a twenty-dollar cut of beef at the Brown Palace, Denver's finest hotel and restaurant, and he had a standard checklist of tasks to complete in the proper enjoyment of the meal.

First: a sip of a good, if moderately priced French wine. Next he took a pinch of sea salt from the cellar on the table and crumbled it liberally over the bloody red meat. Finally he blew out the table's candle so the light wouldn't dazzle his eyes and distract him.

He was the kind of person commonly referred to as "anal," and rather proud of it. The fact that he was aware of his nature and took steps to keep his behavior from becoming too extreme kept him from being mocked too openly in the ranks—or at least he believed so. He made it a point never to inquire too closely.

For himself he simply thought of himself as practical. As someone who chose to plan his day in advance and tried to stick to his plan. It was that simple. Life was best lived by those who were prepared for its contingencies.

Bannerman Clark had begun his adult life in the Army Corps of Engineers, serving an undistinguished but flawless term of service in numerous overseas theaters before choosing the closest thing to semi-retirement open to a man of his temperament: a lateral move into a post where he could do some good without having to deploy so often. He hated traveling. His post with the Army National Guard, one of the few full-time positions in that organization, allowed him an office on a military base. It allowed him to schedule his activities whole months and years in advance. It allowed him a routine that he found comfortable, while permitting enough variety in his assignments to keep him from growing moribund or, worse, bored. Bannerman Clark knew what he liked, and what he disliked, and he attempted to maximize the former and minimize the latter.

By way of example: he loved a perfect slab of rare steak, even though at the age of sixty-one his personal physician frowned on his ritual. He hated being disturbed in the middle of a planned activity. When his cellular phone began to vibrate in his pocket he was tempted to ignore it long enough to take at least one bite.

That was not really an option, though. He replaced the fork on the table and drew out the phone. He glanced up and saw the elegant white-clothed tables, the massive dangling brass chandeliers that suggested the shape of wagon wheels, the elaborate brass and marble work left over from when the Brown Palace had been the finest bordello in the Wild West. He saw the other diners, all of whom were paying extravagant prices to eat in the midst of such opulence. A woman in a red dress stared daggers at his phone. No need for her disdain, though. The phone was set to receive only text messages, not voice. The message Bannerman Clark received made him sigh deeply.

GOVCO + AGCOARNG RQST YR PRES INST RE ADX-FLRNC RIOT

In other words, the Governor of Colorado and the Adjutant General both wanted him immediately to respond to an emerging threat: a riot at the "Supermax" prison in Florence, just south of

Colorado Springs. He would go at once, of course. That was his role, the job he had sought out: Rapid Assessment and Initial Detection Officer in Charge. His business cards described him as the OIC, RAID-COARNG. It was his job to be the first man on the scene in order to get an overview of an emerging crisis and establish what level, if any, of response was required or recommended.

He rose immediately and took his cover (ARNG-speak for his hat) from the empty chair next to him. A red-vested waiter rushed up, a distinct look of concern on his face but Bannerman Clark shook his head in reassurance. His steak would have to be sent back, he feared. The Brown Palace could probably provide a to-go bag but Bannerman Clark didn't request it. He would be onboard a UH-60 Blackhawk within the hour and the meal, even if it were possible to eat it while airborne, just wouldn't be the same without his little rituals. Besides, where he was headed it was best to arrive with an empty stomach.

MYSTERY CORPSE FOUND ON MAIN STREET IN WOODS LANDING, WYOMING: Coroner Claims Dead at Least Three Months [AP Wire Service, 3/17/05]

Lilies: the scent of.

ch-ch-ch-chuhhh / Shwhuhhhh

Her ears vibrated with the soft moaning sound. Her nose felt painfully dry.

ch-ch-ch-chuhhh / Shwhuhhhh

She opened her eyes. The lower limit of her vision was obscured by clear plastic: something on her face. The world was turned sideways because her head was lying on a piece of wood.

ch-ch-ch-chuhhh / Shwhuhhhh

Her head was killing her. Everything smelled like lilies. Plastic on her face. She lifted an arm—far too heavy—and swatted at her nose but it didn't work. She tried touching the thing on her face and found that her fingers didn't work right. The fingertips felt numb, almost completely without sensation. She couldn't grab the thing on her face, couldn't get her fingers around it. Panicking a little she scrabbled at it with both hands until it fell away, hissing like a snake. She put her hands down on the wood of a bar and pushed until she was sitting up. Sitting up on a bar stool.

ch ch-ch-ch

A mask—a kind of oxygen mask it looked like but it was decorated with a sticker of a day-glo flower. Tubing ran back to a metallic white tank bolted to the surface of the bar. There were other tanks, other masks: chromium red, cobalt blue, toxic green. She looked up, glanced around (killing her head as it whipped back and forth) and nearly fell backwards off her bar stool. Bar stool—bar stool—so she was in a bar. But. Not a regular bar. An oxygen bar, obviously. Why would she . . . ?

ch-ch-ch-ch

She reached down and switched off the oxygen mask. The stench of lilies began to dissipate. It must have been mixed in with the compressed gas.

She put a bare foot down on the floor. And screamed. Or at least tried to. The sound that came out of her throat sounded more like a retch. She tried to lift up her foot to take a closer look at what she had just stepped in but found she couldn't raise it to her face. Of course she couldn't! Normal people couldn't do that. She was a normal person, she was pretty sure. She looked down. Her foot was covered in brownish-purple blood.

So was the floor of the oxygen bar. Blood everywhere, some of it still liquid and dark red. A slaughterhouse, she thought, you wouldn't see something like that outside of a slaughterhouse. It had splattered in a broad oval pool centered on her bar stool, maybe ten feet wide, staining the orange shag carpet, matting down the fibers. Oh God.

She wanted to throw up, wanted to throw up everything she'd ever eaten but she couldn't feel her stomach at all, it was just an icy void below her breasts and, and, she was trying very, very hard not to admit it to herself, but—

That was her blood.

She screamed and this time it worked. Blood covered her, dyeing her white clothes, sticking to her skin. It had poured down from a punctured vein in her shoulder, poured down in great gouts and she had run, she remembered now, she had run into the bar, she had run up to the bar but no one was around, the place was deserted and she was already having trouble breathing, her body unable to oxygenate itself because she'd already lost so much blood, she knew the symptoms, somehow she knew the symptoms of somebody about to pass out from anoxia, and the oxygen mask had been right there and . . .

And.

The memory ended as abruptly as it had begun. She studied it, tried to find details but details there were none. Just that she had been bleeding and she had run here and had trouble breathing so she had self-administered nearly pure oxygen. She tried to step down gingerly from the stool, knowing she was going to have to walk through the blood, trying not to scream again. Her throat was so dry it hurt.

Her leg slid out from beneath her, unable to accept her commands, and she clattered down to the floor, her bones bouncing off the bar, the stools, the carpet and she screamed again even though it didn't really hurt, not that much, but she screamed because it seemed like if you were ever going to have a chance to scream that was it, when you were lying collapsed in a pool of your own blood and your hair had fallen down over your eyes. She screamed until there was no more air in her lungs.

The door of the bar swung open and she stopped screaming. She turned wild eyes to the light off the street and saw two kids there, black kids in basketball jerseys. One was taller than the other, maybe older. She couldn't speak, couldn't call out for help. The older kid disappeared but the younger one just stood there, staring at her, his facial features lost in silhouette.

Help me, she thought, please, help me, but he just stood there and stared.

THE NEXT MAD COW? Massive Outbreak of Scrapie in the American West Inflames the Fearful, the Fretful, and the Beef Industry Flacks. [*Gourmet* magazine, February 05]

"It's going to be fine. Shh," the policeman said, squatting next to her. A wood baton, a pair of handcuffs and a gun that looked like a toy dangled from his belt. He reached into a pouch at his back and took out a pair of disposable latex gloves. "Everything's going to be alright. I just want to help you, okay?"

She nodded eagerly. Her eyes went wide when he touched her shoulder, probing painfully in the wound there. She could see herself in his mirrored sunglasses and she understood some of his reticence. Her tan was gone—just gone, her skin turned the color and consistency of old, mildew-damaged paper. Fine traceries of broken capillaries showed in her eyes and the skin around their sockets, a raccoon mask of dead blood. A prominent artery running from her jaw to beneath her left ear looked as if it had been painted on with eyeliner.

"You've lost a lot of blood," he told her. His name was EMERSON, according to the nameplate on his uniform, right above his badge, a bas-relief of a pair of pistols crossed over a stylized Spanish mission. "Normally I'd call for an ambulance but I think we'd better just take you in the squad car. Can you walk?"

She didn't know. Not in the same way she didn't know who she was or what city she was in. Those were abstracts, easily defined and pigeonholed in the category of things she definitively did not know. Whether she could stand up was an open question, which was kind of a relief. Something she could find out.

Her body shuddered as she tried to put some weight on her feet, hauling herself upright by holding onto the bar stool. "Easy now. You're probably feeling a little weak. Maybe a little light-headed too. That's pretty common with this kind of injury." Okay, enough, officer, she thought, but she kept her mouth closed. She needed it to grimace as she shifted her weight entirely onto her legs. Somehow she managed to stumble toward the door, sup-ported on his arm, even though her knees kept locking up. Her muscles felt stiff in a way she knew they'd never felt before. Not so much a memory as an instinct, that, but it was something, and she was glad for it.

Outside another policeman was directing traffic away from the intersection. She glanced over and saw a pile of something on the street—old clothes, maybe fallen palm fronds or the tread off of a blown car tire or—oh. No. It was a body, a human body with a blue jacket draped over its face and chest. "Heh," she gagged. "He's the—"

"Shush now, little girl," the cop said, trying to turn her away from the scene. There was more to it: chalk circles on the ground around pieces of brass. Spent shell casings. More police everywhere she looked—a severe-looking woman filling out a form on a clipboard. Others, mostly men, looking under cars and benches and potted palms, their hands gloved, tiny plastic bags in their hands. Gather-ing evidence. One cop sat on the hood of his car; his face in his hands while another rubbed slow circles on his back. "You only did your duty," he said, and the one on the car hood took his hands away from his face, showing a look of absolute bleak horror.

Emerson pushed her into the back of a patrol car, pushing down on her head until her neck started to spasm but then she was in. He and another policeman—PANKIEWICZ—got into the front of the car.

Pankiewicz looked at her through the grille between the front and back of the car. She could barely see his face through the mesh. "How are you doing, Miss? You need any water or anything before we get going?"

She shook her head. "Hungry," she croaked out. That was about what she could manage vocally. The word was disconnected from what was happening in her head but strangely not from her body. Her nausea had passed and her stomach growled audibly.

Pankiewicz grunted and turned this way and that as if looking for food. He opened the patrol car's glove box and took something out. He had to get out of the car and come around to the back to give it to her—a snack-sized box of cookies. She took it gratefully. Once he was back inside Emerson got the car going and they headed out onto a highway, the flashers on but not the siren.

She shoved a cookie into her mouth with numbed fingers and crunched down on it. She couldn't really taste it but a feeling of warmth and health swept through her with each swallow. So good. She thrust her hand into the box to get another, ripping the cardboard.

"Do you have insurance, Miss?" Pankiewicz asked her, picking up a radio handset. "We need to know which hospital to take you to."

"Doesn't matter," she mumbled, the words distorted by the three cookies she'd stacked up between her teeth.

"I'm afraid that until we get a democrat in the White House, it does," Emerson said, darkly.

"Jesus, would you stop it?" Pankiewicz said. "Now's not the time." He turned to glance at her again, appraising her. Looking for something. "Am I right, Miss? Not when things are still so fucked up in Iraq. You don't switch horses in mid-war. We need a strong leader more than ever."

"I agree," Emerson snickered. "Too bad we don't have one right now. So, Miss. What's your name, anyway?"

Her hands went automatically to a purse or a wallet but there was nothing in her pockets, nothing that could help her answer that question. Something told her to lie. Not a voice in her head so much as a rising tide of panic that came out of nowhere.

Unfortunately she had no idea what to say.

While they had been bantering she had devoured the entire box of cookies. She looked down at the empty package that she had reduced to bits of shredded cardboard and wax paper. She'd even sucked out all the crumbs.

"Nilla," she said. Nil. Nothing. She had nothing of herself left, after all. She would have to create something new and the box of cookies, the first purely good thing she'd found, made the pefect inspiration.

She wished she had some more. Not cookies necessarily. More food, real food.

Five minutes later they reached the hospital only to find the emergency room entrance blocked by two ambulances that had collided with each other. Nilla could see into one of them through its open rear doors. Nobody was inside but the interior lights were on. Blood dripped from the rear bumper.

"There must be something bad going down. This place looks swamped," Pankiewicz said. He popped open his door before the patrol car had even come to a stop. He opened her door and helped her out. She leaned on him as they made their way around the ambulances and into the emergency room.

"LARGEST EVER" MANHUNT IN NEVADA DESERT TURNS UP GRUESOME RESULT: Partial Body Found, Feared to be Shawna, Awaits Identification [CNN.com breaking story alert, 3/17/05]

One look at the blood on Nilla's shirt and they put her in an examination room right away—really just a cubicle, hemmed in by mobile partitions, barely big enough for her narrow bed. Outside the moans of the injured and the sick never stopped. Shadows crossed the fabric of the partition, the acoustic ceiling tiles above her head. A nurse in a jacket decorated with panda bears came in and attached a plastic clip to her finger but didn't have time to turn on the attached machine before she was called away. When she turned to go the back of her jacket showed a bloody handprint.

Nilla heard screaming a minute later and what had to be a gunshot. After a long, long time of holding her breath and waiting to hear what came next an orderly in a white uniform opened her partition and stormed inside. "I'm really sorry about this, Ma'am," he said. He spoke with a West Indian accent, syncopated

and musical. He had a shaved head and he looked exhausted.
Draped across his arm were countless loops of thick yellow nylon.
He tore one open by its Velcro closure and started feeding it
through the tubular frame of her bed.

"That's not necessary," she insisted as he fastened the loop
around her left wrist. A rivulet of icy cold ran down her back and
her body twitched. Her head was pounding.

He just shook his head. "Lots of people get them, Ma'am, I'm
just doing my job." He bit his lip before securing her right wrist, perhaps wondering if she was going to fight him. The thought hadn't
crossed Nilla's mind until then. "It's rabies, we think."

"Rabies? You think it's rabies?" she repeated, her voice shrill.
"What the hell is going on? I haven't even seen a doctor yet!" Fear
rattled inside of her emptiness, desperation at being imprisoned in
a ward full of slavering lunatics. This was a hospital, goddamnit!
They were supposed to help her. "Get away from me!"

"Ma'am, you've got a textbook pattern of bite marks on your
shoulder," he said quietly, with infinite delicacy. "Ma'am, I have a
gag here, too. That you don't have to get, if you cooperate."

It was a second gunshot, though, that convinced her. Together
they looked up—and then their eyes met and she knew he was
deadly serious. Something was happening outside, something very
bad, and the orderly didn't know any more than she did but he
intended to complete his task one way or another. He tied down her
ankles and then turned to go. "Thank you, Ma'am," he whispered,
as if he didn't know what else to say.

**"Tonight the 16th Street pedestrian mall is closed to
foot traffic. Police cars blockaded the popular
shopping destination after reports of dangerous
animals on the loose. Our action reporting team is
on the way to downtown right now, and we'll have
film as it becomes available. Meanwhile, here's
Chip with local pro team action. Chip?" [9News
(Denver) Evening Broadcast, 3/17/05]**

*   *   *

Long thin stratus clouds turned the air the color of burnished metal. As he rose toward the treeline the oxygen grew so thin Dick was panting as he crested the slope. Up top no trees grew at all, just scattered patches of lichen like greenish doilies glued to the rock. Thankfully the track went over the ridge just ahead and started downhill again, heading for a narrow valley below so thickly packed with pine trees that when the wind stirred them the valley looked like a bowl filled with shimmering green water. There were buildings tucked away amongst the trees, modest clapboard structures of a kind that had been built in the mountains for over a century. He could mostly see the roofs, warped ranks of split-wood shingles weathered by the sun until they were colorless, veined with silver and dry as picked bones.

Dick paused at the ridgeline to drink some water from his daypack and phone in to his field office. He reached a teenage intern who swore he was writing down Dick's GPS coordinates but who was probably just doodling on NIH stationery. Dick didn't suppose it mattered too much. It was standard practice to report one's position on a regular basis—the best way to die up in the mountains was to have nobody know where you were—but he was no more than a quarter mile from the road and even if a snowstorm came through in the next few hours he was certain he could make it back alright. He'd lived through some bad scrapes in the Rockies and always he'd come through alright. "Do we have a phone number for my next interview?" he asked, pretty sure the answer would be no: there were no phone lines or satellite dishes attached to the buildings down in the valley, his next destination.

"Uh, uh, no," the intern replied after paging inexpertly through Dick's own calendar. "Mrs. Skye, right? Yeah, uh, she said she, uh, I can't really read your hand-writing but it looks like she walked into town to use a payphone."

Dick nodded and hung up. He remembered now—he'd received the message himself from the field office's voice mail system. This was a scrapie call. Scrapie was becoming the lion's share of Dick's business. Scrapie: a fatal and nasty disease of sheep and sometimes goats. Named for its victims' habit of scraping their skin off against trees and rocks. Most ranchers never bothered to report it when they saw it—the disease wasn't traditionally infectious, spreading over a span of generations instead of months. By the time a shepherd finally panicked and called for help the illness had usually compromised an entire flock.

Those calls were coming more and more frequently, which was truly scary to someone like Dick who knew the numbers. Nearly ten percent of Colorado's sheep were potentially infected, and that was just the known cases. Mad Cow disease, a related illness, had decimated the livestock population in England a few years back and he fully expected a similar disaster in American sheep within the decade.

Dick knew enough to assume the worst and he expected to find that Mrs. Skye's sheep would have to be destroyed and the carcasses incinerated. He didn't exactly skip down the path into the sheltered valley. It was tough to be grim on that track, though, with the sunlight streaming down through the branches in long dusty shafts, with the musty smell of pine needles baking in the warmth of spring mingling with the fresh winter smell of powdery snow. He had a smile on his face when he approached the main house. "Hello!" he called while he was still a hundred yards away. "Hello there!" In this part of the West, in such a secluded spot, you made a point of announcing your presence well before you arrived. You had to assume that everyone you visited was heavily armed and unfond of intruders. "Hello! Mrs. Skye?"

The house had seen better days. Its clapboard walls looked sturdy enough but its windows had been broken in several places and replaced with butcher paper and duct tape. Pine needles littered the covered porch where a cord of firewood had collapsed and spilled out into the yard. Broken and rusted farm implements hung from the porch rafters—sickles and mallets and hoes as well as some nasty bits of iron specific to sheep herders, like a mulesing saw and a tooth grinder. The tools looked hand-made. "Hello!" Dick shouted, as loud as he could.

A woman holding a hatchet came around the side of the house and squinted at him. She wore a tie-dyed quilted jacket and her long white hair played around her shoulders in thin strands. Her face looked like a contour map of the mountains around her, filled with lines and blotchy shading. "You," she called out to him. "You from the Health department?"

"Dick Walters, NIH," he agreed.

"You do me a favor, Walters," she said, and pointed at a pine about twenty yards away. "You run over to that tree and back."

Dick laughed but then he looked at her hatchet. The sharp edge was filthy with blood and hair. This was a farm, and animals on farms got slaughtered all the time. Still the sight of it made him uneasy. He swallowed and dashed over to the tree, then ran back to where he had originally been standing.

The old woman nodded. "Fair enough. They don't move that fast." She dropped her hatchet on the carpet of pine needles and stomped into her house, her boots crunching in the snow. The door had no lock. Not knowing what else to do Dick followed her inside.

MORMON BISHOPS IN HARPERSVILLE FORBID POLICE INVESTIGATION: Small Town Tabernacle Could be Hiding Terror Cell, State Bureau of Investigations Warns [*Deseret* Morning News, Salt Lake City, 3/18/05]

They left her there for hours, strapped to the bed, unable to move. She didn't grow stiff or uncomfortable but she couldn't even reach over to turn on the television set mounted in a steel bracket above her bed. She tried to sleep but she failed at that, too: her body refused to truly relax, not when she kept hearing screams outside her room. No more gunshots, at least. She tried to calm down and failed.

Being strapped to a hospital bed left her with a lot of time to think. To try to remember. She pushed hard into the dark parts of her brain, like developments full of houses with no lights on at all and nobody home. In the abandoned suburbs of her mind she tried to piece together anything, anything at all: the faces of her parents, her lovers, her friends. Did she have kids? Did she have a home somewhere? She tried not to color her thoughts with half-hearted guesses, but failed: the clothes she had on, the piercings had to mean something, at least, that she wasn't homeless, that she didn't work in an office. At least that much. These superficial deductions got in the way, though. They summed up a caricature of a life with no detail nor any texture at all. She tried to put them out of mind and remember something. She dug for any shard of memory: a birthday party. A trip to the mall. Where she had left her purse. She tried to remember her own name, even her initials.

She failed.

WEIRD: Horse bites dog in Wyoming. Apparently the horse was sick and the dog was a jerk. Cats and dogs still not living together. [Fark.com news portal, 3/16/05]

The Blackhawk set down well clear of the prison fence. There were pressure plates and laser sensors and dogs trained to attack without barking in there. Searchlights stabbed out from the guard towers and bathed the helicopter in a brilliant glow. As the rotor spun down Bannerman Clark jumped down to the sandy soil of the outer perimeter and looked for the man he was supposed to meet.

Assistant Warden Glynne of the Florence Administrative Maximum Corrections Facility greeted him with a snappy salute he did not return. Military personnel were not supposed to salute civilians and vice versa and Clark already knew enough about Glynne to know the man had never been a soldier.

"Welcome to the Big One," the Corrections Officer said, unfazed. The man hadn't shaved in days and his tie hung loose from an unbuttoned collar. "I'm glad you came so quickly. Things are degenerating and we could really use some help."

"I understand you have a riot on your hands, Mr. Glynne, and that it's been going on for three days. I'd appreciate knowing why I'm here, though. Surely this is a problem for a SWAT team or the State Bureau of Investigations. The National Guard shouldn't be called in unless—"

Glynne spoke over him with the assurance of complete exhaustion. The tone of a man who doesn't have the energy left for deference. "This isn't a riot, Captain. This is a complete protocol failure. It's been going on for seventy-nine hours. You're here because this is something we've never seen before. Follow me, please."

They passed through the main gate of the prison and into a well-lit series of rooms painted and repainted so many times the light switches and doorknobs had taken on a softened, rounded look. Glynne led him through a series of tight passages with heavy iron doors that had to be unlocked manually and which snapped shut and locked with an electronic buzz once they were through. "There are ten thousand doors in this facility, Captain. In an emergency lockdown all of them close and lock automatically. Nobody ever gets in or out unless we know about it. We've got eyes everywhere, even in the CO areas. That's the good news."

"All I see here is bad news," Clark said, glancing around in distaste at the dusty corridors.

"This is a supermax prison, Captain Clark, where the real dead-enders go. Violent inmates who can't be allowed to mingle in a normal prison environment. We impose twenty-three hour per day solitary confinement. Prisoners have to wear leg and wrist shackles when they go to eat. They get one four-inch-wide window in their cells. The toilets are designed so you can't fit a human head in them. They do that, you know. If you give them an opportunity to do something, no matter how sick or perverse, they'll do it. Just to fuck with us. The only control they have over their lives is to make things worse for each other, and they take every chance they get."

Clark made a grunt of understanding. Beyond one last door lay a control center, a red-lit claustrophobic space filled with computer monitors and desks and half-empty coffee cups. A dozen men and women in corrections uniforms sat slumped in uncomfortable chairs, most of them gathered around one dimly flickering monitor. Two other men stood before what looked to Clark's eyes like a black wall until his vision adjusted and he saw it was a slab of transparent polycarbonate plastic. A bulletproof one-way viewport. The men watching the view wore image enhancement optics—AN-PVS 7B night optic devices—and were rapt by what they saw on the other side of the window.

When Glynne spoke again it was in a whisper as if he were afraid something on the other side might hear him. "Directly underneath us," he said, gesturing at the window, "is where the real bad guys go, one of our special housing units. The inmates call it the Black Hole. There are a hundred and forty-eight punishment cells down there which we keep darkened and sound-dampened at all times. Nobody can stay violent for long in an environment like that. It's been psychologically proven."

Clark picked up a set of night-vision optics from a desk and strapped it onto his head and chin. He switched on the unit and looked down into the SHU. It took his brain a moment to make sense of the false-color images the goggles created but quickly enough he saw what was happening. The cells were completely closed off from one another but they had transparent ceilings so the guards could look down into them at any time. In the cells prisoners lay motionless on their beds or paced endlessly around their tiny rooms. Some stood at their doors patiently as if waiting for them to open while others smashed at their walls with arms and heads and shoulders. He looked straight down at the center of the unit and had to gasp in disgust. Two dozen inmates were milling about in a central open area, many of them naked and clearly injured. He saw arms and legs that hung limp, faces contorted by lacerations and swollen bruises, fingers and eyes missing. Another ten or so inmates lay in a pile in one corner, their bodies wriggling like fat worms. "What are they doing?" Clark demanded.

"They're eating each other," Glynne said, his voice flat. "Some of them . . . some of them eat, and some get eaten." The last bit of energy had gone right out of the Assistant Warden.

"Good God! Where is your staff? Where are your guards? You need to get them in there and stop this at once!" Clark demanded.

"You don't understand, Captain. The inmates are never allowed out of their cells in this unit. The men in that open area you're looking at? *Those* are my guards."

"The chickens are coming home to roost, everybody. Coming home to roost. You see all this violence—what? No, the chickens is what I said. This violence in the western states, just out of control, which is what happens when your prison system is like, it's like, it's a country club, you know, it's the cotillion ball for felons. They've got cable, they've got porn. Porn! I want to go to prison! Somebody arrest me! They have swimming—no, no, no! I said chickens! The chickens are coming home to roost!" [Ted Thiokol, "Ted and Andy's Morning Zoo" radio show, WNCI 97.9 (Columbus, OH), 3/18/05]

One whole wall of the mountain house had been converted into a mural painted in bright psychedelic colors. It showed a girl, perhaps thirteen years old with blonde hair exploding outward from her head. She had a pair of butterfly wings and she was hovering over a swirling galaxy of bursting stars. The colors had faded over a period of decades but someone had tried to touch it up periodically.

Mrs. Skye banged a half-full bucket of water down on an old, scarred table and started washing her face and her gnarled hands. The water came away dark with grit and dirt and dried flecks of blood. She shook as she rubbed at her eyes and her ears. "You're too fucking late, Walters, but I won't hold that against you. You help me slaughter them and we'll call it even, yeah?"

Dick sat down in a hand-made chair and tried not to look at her. "Mrs. Skye, I'm sorry we took so long to get back to you after your call. You have to admit though that you're kind of secluded here. It took me six hours to drive here from my office and then I had to climb over a hill to find you. How many sheep are we talking about?"

"Sheep," the old woman said. She peeled off her jacket and threw it on the floor. She had a bad cut on her arm that looked infected. With a dishrag she started cleaning out the injury. "You're here about the sheep. Ain't that a shit sandwich." She took a bottle from a dusty shelf and poured clear liquid down her arm. She winced visibly—it must have been rubbing alcohol or maybe even bleach. "The sheep are all dead. I slaughtered them myself. Next you're going to tell me you came up here unarmed." The look on his face must have convinced her that this was, in fact, the case. "I called this morning, I called your office and then came right back here. You didn't get my message? Fuck!"

"Maybe," Dick said, holding his hands up for calm, "we should just start over. You reported a case of scrapie a couple of weeks ago—"

"Yes, I did. And yesterday I called again, and said it was really urgent this time. Goddamnit! I make two phone calls in three years and you don't even bother to listen to the important one!" She stomped to a window and stared out at the trees. "Well that's as it is," she said, running her nails across her scalp. "I can't do this alone, I'm tired—I haven't slept in two days, I haven't eaten today. We're just going to have to . . ." She stiffened visibly. "What's that? Come here and look at this, Walters."

Dick rose from his chair and started over to the window. Before he got there he jumped back at the sound of broken glass and screaming. A human hand covered in blisters had come in through the shattered window and grabbed Mrs. Skye by the bottom lip, broken fingernails sinking deep into her skin, tearing her flesh.

Instead of panicking she got her teeth around the fingers and bit down hard enough to snap them off. She reeled backwards and Dick rushed to catch her before she could fall. She sank into his arms, then reared up and spat the fingertips into the corner of the room.

"Uh gud," Mrs. Skye wheezed, her mouth covered in blood. "Thur utt!" Dick had no idea what she meant but she could only seem to repeat over and over, "thur utt! Thur utt!"

He heard a thud on the side of the cabin, the sound of bone hitting wood very hard. It came again a moment later and then he heard boards creak as someone stepped up onto the porch.

"Shut thuh dur!" Mrs. Skye screamed but it was too late. Dick laid her down gently on the floor and stood up, wiping his sweaty palms on the backs of his pants. By the time he reached the door the assailant was already there.

He looked like a mountain climber—the purple ballistic nylon jacket, the rock boots, the ice axe hanging from his belt gave that away. He also looked like a sculpture of a human being made out of butter and left out in the rain. The flesh of his face had dripped away from the bone, revealing bare yellow skull in some places. One eye was completely obscured by collapsed skin, while the other had the white cast of glaucoma. A few long black hairs dangled from the climber's face but none were left on top of his head.

He didn't speak. He didn't turn his head to look at them. He just lurched forward, toward Dick, his mouth cranking open and his teeth biting at air. The climber moved slowly, so slowly Dick thought he must be running on adrenaline himself as he dodged the climber's clumsy advances. He ducked under an outstretched arm and tried to knock the climber's legs out from under him, amazed at how quickly he was reacting, at how instinct just took over.

The climber grabbed his belt and clambered up onto Dick's back, forcing Dick down to the floor with his weight. Dick could hear his own explosive breathing but the climber made no sound at all. The weight on him shifted a little and he tried to get out from under but then he felt teeth digging into the roll of fat at his waist. The pain was bright and intense: a vibrant horror splashed across his desperate senses. Dick heaved and the climber rolled off of his back.

Blood seeped into Dick's pants as he roared for breath, sucking down the rarefied mountain air to sustain his panic. Dick saw the ice axe hanging from the downed climber's belt and he wanted it, wanted it like a sixteen year old wants a new car. No—he wanted it like a sixteen year old wants a girlfriend.

The climber got one knee under himself and thrust out one

arm for support. He was taking his time about getting up. Dick grabbed the axe and yanked. It came free of its quick-release buckle. The rubberized grip felt *so good* in his hand. Dick swung.

The pick end of the axe went right through the climber's jacket and into a hollow space that must have been his lung. Dick expected to get sprayed with arterial blood but only a little dry brown powder billowed from the wound. Dick yanked the axe back out but by the time he was ready to swing again the climber had regained his stance.

The next blow hit the climber in the shoulder, hard enough to make Dick's own arm vibrate with the impact. The climber didn't appear to even feel any pain. With his free arm he reached for Dick's throat. He would have gotten it, too, if Mrs. Skye hadn't chosen that moment to cave in the back of the climber's head with a ball-peen hammer. The skull collapsed like cracked pottery and the climber slid to the floor, limp, seemingly boneless. Dick brandished the ice axe, ready to strike again but the climber didn't so much as twitch.

"Huh's dead, Wultuhs," Mrs. Skye said, clutching her lip. She took her hand away and spat blood at the corpse at her feet.

"Call me Dick." He felt no guilt, no remorse, just a high singing lightness in his stomach and a tension in his shoulders. He couldn't let go of the axe.

"Alrutt. Call muh Bleu. Layk thuh chis."

PRESIDENT CANCELS SKI WEEKEND: No Reason Given [*USA Today*, 3/19/05]

"Can we get some lights on? Surely there's emergency lighting in there. Let's get it on." Bannerman Clark stood rigid before the polycarbonate window, not sure what he would see once the lights were on in the Special Housing Unit. The Special Horror Unit, more like. Whatever could possess a man and drive him to cannibalism—possess rational men with good jobs and families, no less, like the prison guards—wasn't going to look pretty.

The Assistant Warden shrugged when his underlings looked to him for confirmation of Clark's order. "I've been relieved of command. Do what he says."

It had taken six phone calls to have Bannerman Clark assigned as the Local Incident Commander for what had yet to officially become an Incident. It used to be next to impossible to get around civilian chains of command, even in an emergency. After September Eleventh the system had been considerably streamlined. Clark's Captain's bars hardly warranted the kind of power and influence he was then authorized to wield but this was an OOTW (Operation Other Than War) and the normal priorities and niceties were overturned. Somebody needed to be in charge. Somebody needed to start giving orders.

"We thought it had to be drugs," Glynne said. "That's what we're trained to look for. I sent in men who don't even take aspirin when they have a headache. They didn't make it back out."

It did not surprise Clark at all that Glynne would look no further than the end of his nose. In 1997 an inmate had been murdered at ADX-Florence and the body wasn't found for four days. The prison was so tightly circumscribed and controlled that any deviation from the standard timetable—even a dangerous one— just didn't register. He flipped open his phone and thumbed a quick text message to a First Lieutenant at the Buckley Air Force Base with the 8th Civil Support Team, the Guard's WMD task force. It was quite clear to Clark that the men in that holding area were not under the influence of drugs. Only some kind of virulent disease could cause this cannibalistic behavior. Perhaps a mutated strain of meningitis. Or rabies.

"We had men go in there in full riot gear with electric prods. We filled that room with CS gas, we turned high-pressure hoses on them. Whenever I sent a man in there they just ripped off his armor and tore out his throat. I personally fired six rounds from a .357 into the chest of one of those assholes. He spun around like a top but then he just kept coming. He's still down there, walking around. Eating."

An emergency lamp near the ceiling of the Black Hole turned orange in the darkness as it started to warm up. It was designed to do that—if the inhabitants of the SHU were exposed to bright light without warning they could be temporarily blinded. Clark took the image enhancement optics off of his head and laid them neatly on his desk as the lamp ramped up to full power.

In the new illumination Clark saw one of the afflicted stumbling across a mound of trash—unspooled rolls of toilet paper, torn newsprint, pieces of ripped riot armor. He moved like a frog in a terrarium, his legs extending slowly to find purchase, his upper body motionless. The rest of them wriggled in their pile, naked and unashamed as they fed. The men in the cells looked up at the light but they didn't blink. Clark grunted despite himself. The victims were in bad shape. One inmate had lost his ears and lips. Another had most of his midriff torn away, everything between his rib cage and his pelvis. How could anyone get up and move around after sustaining such an injury? How could anyone survive it? Clark shuddered and recovered himself. He had a job to do.

"I need your entire staff here. Wake them up if you have to and bring them in. The next twenty-four hours are going to be crucial in containing this. We need everyone who might have been exposed to stay locked down here in quarantine until we know we aren't going to spread it." He turned to the technician who had turned on the lights. The man at least knew how to do something useful. "Glynne here was described to me as an Assistant Warden. Where is the actual Warden while all this is going on?"

The technician glanced at Glynne.

"On vacation. He went to visit his family in California," the Assistant Warden announced.

Vegans Go Home: This is Meat Country! [Billboard outside of Grand Junction Colorado, leased by the Colorado Beef and Buffalo Cattlemen's Association, 2005]

The nurse in the panda bear coat came back, finally, wheeling an EKG machine into Nilla's cubicle. She looked tired, near exhaustion, and sweat had soaked through the armpits of her coat. Without a word she dragged her cart to Nilla's bedside and started tearing open plastic bags and unsealing tubes of gel. When she pulled Nilla's shirt up, nearly exposing her breasts, something had to be said.

"What's going on?" Nilla demanded. "I've been lying here for hours in these restraints. Surely if I was rabid I'd be foaming at the mouth now or something."

The nurse stared at her with a pained look. "Rabid? Who said you had rabies? This is ridiculous. I'm in the middle of a double shift I got assigned with no warning and no lunch break. I'm hungry and tired and I want to go home and now I have to listen to patients who've seen one episode of ER and think they can diagnose themselves. Rabies, for fuck's sake. Can I just do my job, huh? Do you think I can just do my job? I don't have time for this."

Nilla couldn't help but be chastened. She understood what it was like to be hungry and tired, after all. She was pretty much nothing but. "I'm sorry," she said.

The nurse just shook her head. She squeezed a tube over Nilla's stomach and icy cold gel dripped on her skin, making her wince. Next came a series of electrodes that had to be patted down. Finally the nurse switched on her machine and turned a few knobs.

"Come on. Come on," the nurse muttered as the EKG warmed up. "Come on already."

The screen of the EKG finally lit up and simultaneously an alarm tone sounded. On the screen a flat line etched its way from left to right with no deviation whatsoever.

"Jesus," the nurse swore, and thumped the machine hard. Nothing changed. She switched off the alarm. "Another malfunction!"

"What—what did that mean?" Nilla asked, suddenly terrified. "I don't have a heartbeat? What's going on?"

The nurse swore again and yanked the electrodes off of Nilla's body. "It means my machine is fucked, and now I have to get another one from the other side of the hospital, and that I don't get my smoke break for another half hour! That's what it fucking means. Jesus, would you calm down?" She grabbed for Nilla's bound wrist and shoved her index finger into the pulse point. After a few seconds her mouth jerked in bewilderment and she shoved her palm underneath Nilla's nose, trying to feel her breath.

The anger drained out of her face, taking all the color with it. Her eyes softened and her mouth trembled a little.

"Oh, God. Doctor!" she screamed. "Code blue, code blue!" She turned to run out of the cubicle just as one curtained wall twitched back. The two police officers who brought Nilla in—Emerson and Pankiewicz, she remembered—stood there. They didn't look so good. Their skin looked positively blue in the fluorescent light and their eyes were vacant, all but rolled up in their heads. Emerson's shirt was badly torn and Pankiewicz was missing his hat.

"Please," the nurse said, "please get out of my—"

Emerson grabbed her by the head and bit off her nose. Pankiewicz staggered forward and into her stomach, knocking her against the bed. The three of them fell to the floor in a heap, a writhing, spasmodic heap that screamed sometimes, but not for very long.

This station is conducting a test of the emergency broadcast system. This is only a test. [KCNC-TV, Denver, 3/19/05]

In her bed Nilla imagined she was about to die. She felt as if her soul had already left her flesh. She screamed and her consciousness fluttered above her body, her mind detaching to spare itself from the shock. She writhed on the bed, her muscles convulsing wildly as she watched her arms and legs flex and release, kick and shove and shake trying to get free of her restraints.

From the foot of the bed she heard a sound like air being let out of a balloon and then a noise of bubbles forced out of a soft enclosure. Occasionally she heard teeth gnashing together.

They were going to kill her, they were going to eat her, too. Any second now.

Above herself, floating where she could see her tattoo and the bite mark in her shoulder and the greasy mess her hair had become Nilla felt very little fear or concern. She did notice inefficiency. For instance, her arms were in danger of overextending themselves and possibly tearing ligaments the way they kept straining and pulling at the restraints. If she just arched her back so, and brought her forearm up as high as she could, like this, it would be so much easier. She could simply use her teeth to pull at the Velcro closure of the strap. It would be easy.

No, no, no, her body told her. Limbs and backs don't bend like that. Normal bodies can't. Was her body not normal? Was she different somehow?

A jet of hot blood shot up and splattered the soles of Nilla's feet. She could see Emerson's back bobbing up and down—seizing, moving spasmodically as it might during the moment of orgasm. She understood what that meant. He was swallowing chunks of meat whole, the way a snake does.

Her mind grunted in exasperation and ordered her body to move. Twisting on the bed, forcing sinews that were far stiffer than they should be, she managed to get her arm up, her back twisted around so she could just turn her head and touch the end of the restraint with her mouth. Just a little further, she demanded, but her body complained: any further and she'd tear a muscle in her back. Her mind pointed out what the alternative would be.

She jerked her head forward and got her teeth into the nylon strap. She felt the smoothness of it, the texture of the weave with her tongue. She shouldn't have been able to do that. Had she been a yoga instructor before she lost her memory? She didn't have time to think about it. Her head jerked back, unable to maintain the awkward position, and the strap tore open with a noise as loud as a lawnmower starting up.

Pankiewicz looked up, his blood-soaked face peering over the edge of the bed, clearly alerted by the sound. A moment later he disappeared again, distracted by his feast. With one arm free Nilla grabbed at her other wrist and tore away the binding there, then hastily did her ankles, too. She was free, she was out, her mind flew right back into her body and she realized she had achieved very little. The cops were still eating the nurse alive right in front of her. She was still in danger.

Get out—her mind and body agreed—get out! She pulled her feet underneath her on the bed and swiveled up to a kneeling position. She expected a head rush but instead it was her entire body that convulsed, her muscles vibrating like plucked rubber bands. She was not in good shape and these gymnastics weren't helping.

Just one more stunt to pull, though, she told herself, and leapt right over the heads of the cops. She hit the cold tile floor on the far side, rolled to a stop, and looked up, her arms sheltering her head, her legs tucked as best she could.

Emerson didn't react at all. He kept feeding, his face buried in the mid-section of the nurse like a vulture looking for entrails. Pankiewicz noticed her, however. He turned around, still on his knees on the stained hospital floor, and stared at her. Only his eyes were visible. The rest of his face was dripping gore.

He stumped toward her on his knees, his head drifting to one side. He moved slowly, so slowly but she couldn't stop shaking with fear, couldn't get up. She closed her eyes, not wanting to see her own death creeping ever closer.

She could still see him. Right through her eyelids.

Maybe . . . maybe seeing was the wrong word, more like she could sense him, maybe the hairs on the back of her neck were shivering—maybe it was just like the phosphor afterimage you saw when you looked at a bright light and then closed your eyes but . . . she saw . . . right through him, saw the inside of him. A kind of x-ray vision. She saw a darkness in him, a roiling cloud of dulled energy that fumed away like fog coming off of dry ice. It filled his shape, made him a figure of shadowy smoke floating on a background of pure white.

What the hell? She glanced over at Emerson and the nurse. The other cop had undergone the same transformation, his body rendered into a boiling silhouette of hazy dimness that sizzled and spat.

Nilla saw the nurse, too, but not the same way. The nurse's energy oozed from her and ran away across the floor in wide rivulets. It wasn't dark, either, but a beautiful radiant gold that shimmered and gleamed and dazzled Nilla's eyes so she almost had to look away. She didn't want to, though. Whereas before the nurse's rent and bloody body had horrified her, in this perspective the dying woman had been transformed into a thing of almost perfect beauty. Nilla wanted to get closer, to touch the nurse. To bask in that warm effusion of light. To drink of it. To consume it.

She realized she was salivating. She quickly looked down at her own hands, needing to know. Somehow she wasn't surprised to see darkness there, filling the shapes of her fingers, swirling madly in her palms. She looked up at Pankiewicz again and showed him her hands.

No words passed between them. She was pretty clear the policeman would not have understood if she spoke to him. Still, a kind of communion was possible. He could see her dark energy as well as she could see his, she knew that without questioning *how* she knew it. They shared an awareness. She sensed his mood, his hunger, his confusion. He moved closer to her, half a step, but then sat back on his haunches. He radiated indifference at her. Irrelevance. She was neither food nor threat. He turned around and headed back to the nurse.

Nilla sat very still, holding her head with both hands, and watched as they feasted. As she watched the nurse's energy changed, the golden fullness dimming out like a dying candle, shifting through a last flaring shade of blue. Her flame went out and dark smoke billowed up inside her.

The horribly mutilated woman sat up with a wet tearing noise as she unstuck herself from the floor tiles. She looked around for a minute and then pushed the two policemen away. They had lost interest in her the moment her energy changed anyway. Rising on legs of slaughtered meat and gnawed bone the nurse slumped against a wall and started walking, leaning against the wall for support, dragging a bloodstain along the plaster. The cops followed close behind.

Where they were headed Nilla didn't know. She didn't dare follow. There were too many questions left unanswered.

What did it mean? What did the different kind of energies signify? What, most importantly, did it mean that her energy was dark? Reluctantly she circled one hand with the fingers of the other and pressed her index finger against the vein in her wrist, trying to find a pulse.

"He's crawling toward me . . . no, on his arms, his legs don't seem to work anymore, listen, I don't have time—oh my God—his eyes—his eyes—please! Please tell them to hurry!" [911 Emergency Response System call, Gabbs, NV, 3/20/05]

In the shadows of the spruces and the firs Dick and Bleu Skye (her legal name, she assured him) crunched through snow that would never melt even in high summer.

"I suppose that some people would call us freaks," Bleu said, the words distorted by her lip wound but he could at least understand her now. Not that he was really listening. Her voice was a rough melody in harmony with the scrunching down of snow and the squeak of pine needles he made with every step. "And I suppose I don't mind so much, we were trying to build something, is all. A quiet life in a pretty noisy world. Me and Tony, that was my husband, and our boy Stormy."

Dick's feet were numb with the cold. His brain was numb with implications, meanings, ramifications. He'd just participated in the butchering of another human being. Oh, it had been self defense, sure, and no, Dick was no peacenik. He owned guns, just like half of Colorado. A couple of target pistols and a hunting rifle and yes, he had used it to kill. To kill white-tailed deer. The idea of hurting a human being intentionally, of true violence, of murder . . . that he'd never even contemplated before.

"That was nigh on twenty years ago, back when Stormy was just a passenger, you know, when I was carrying him. We built all this with our hands and we loved it, just loved it, no matter if we were hungry. No matter if we didn't know how to do something—we could learn. And all we had to do was walk outside and look up and we knew why we came up here and why we didn't want to go back."

A half-visible path, a little clearer of snow than the surrounding terrain, went snaking through the trees and they followed it. Dick was lost on that path as he followed Bleu and he couldn't let go of the ice axe. It was like a talisman, some proof that he wasn't an evil man, that he wasn't a killer. Exhibit A in the trial going on in his head. Bleu's voice was just the soundtrack to that groundbreaking bit of courtroom drama and when she started sobbing it was just another instrument in the orchestra. On some level he realized that he wasn't thinking straight.

"I always worried that I couldn't teach Stormy enough. I worried he wouldn't know enough to make it in this life and now . . . oh God, now . . ."

She stopped, and so did Dick. They'd reached their destination, a wooden structure that had to be a century old. Just a shack really, with one wall open to the elements. Inside the trail lead downward, into the earth. An old abandoned mine entrance. The mountains were riddled with them, leftovers from the gold rush. The wind tore out of it, colder than the outside air, and it made a hollow sound. Dick stepped closer and Bleu took his arm, holding him back. There was something moving down there.

"He died quick. My son died quick. Tony took his time about it. And now . . . I guess maybe . . . maybe you should just look. Here." She handed him a flashlight. He clicked it on and peered down into the darkness.

"How many do you see?" she asked, her voice flinty again. He couldn't see anything.

Then he could. The beam caught on something wriggling, something dark but recognizable. A pair of human legs in snow pants and tan Timberland boots. The legs kicked fitfully. Dick scanned upward with the light, saw a heavy winter jacket. Arms and a head. The face tilted upward and he felt vomit rush up his throat. The skin of the face was red and black and white and yellow. The eye sockets were empty and half of the skin was missing from the jaw. The hands clutched at the slope of the tunnel, digging in until the knuckles stood out like walnuts. The person, because it was a person, yes, was trying to climb out of the tunnel but it was too steep or something.

"How many?" Bleu asked again.

"Two," Dick said, sweeping the light back and forth. "No, three. And—are those bones? Skulls. Hu." He cleared his throat. "Human." He clicked off the light and shoved it in his pocket so he could wipe his palms on his jeans. "I saw two—two skulls."

"My big strong men," Bleu rasped. "They just wanted to help and they're torn to pieces."

It took her a while to collect herself before she could speak again. "We found them two days ago and didn't know what we oughta do. We thought they were dead at first, well, why wouldn't we? They probably got caught in a storm and went in there looking for shelter. Climbers get themselves lost up here all the time. Nobody ever finds them till summer. When they started moving we decided they were just hurt. They don't never talk, not even when you yell questions at them." She took a pistol out of her pocket and cocked it. "There were more yesterday. Maybe six, and maybe seven." She pointed her weapon down into the tunnel. "They're getting out." She fired and the high-caliber shot echoed all around the valley, rolling along the mountains like an endless series of doors slamming shut.

"Wait!" Dick shouted, scampering backward, away from the gunshot. "Wait! They need medical assistance, you know, like a doctor, you can't just—" She fired again and he winced. "I've got to— I've got to call the police," he stammered. He had his cell phone in his hand.

"Good idea," she said. She aimed carefully, lining up her shot with the forehead of the third—the third person—the third creature? Dick didn't know what to call them. She pulled the trigger and then let her arm drop, the pistol still in her hand. "We can use the help. We should head back to the house before dark."

He followed her back, not knowing what else to do.

BAD MOON RISING: Top Psychologists Explain the Recent Outbreak of Violence in America [*Home Front* magazine, March 2005]

Nilla scrubbed at her hands and her throat, scraped at her skin with rough paper towels, trying to get the blood off of her body. She had discarded her white clothes. They were hopelessly stained. She had found a doctor's white coat that smelled like disinfectant and some loose-fitting scrub pants. It would have to be enough.

She kept staring in the women's room mirror though she told herself to stop.

Her teeth were coated. She ran a finger around them, wished she had some toothpaste and some dental floss. She stopped in mid-rub. Dental floss. Most people never bothered with it. Clearly she had. It wasn't quite a recollection, more like muscle memory or the pain of a phantom limb: she had used dental floss in her former life. It hurt to think about it. The broken stubs of memories were attached to the idea. I used to floss, she would think, and she could feel her brain trying automatically to find examples, to remember amusing anecdotes about flossing, to even remember flashes of her mouth in a bathroom mirror, to remember curls of floss between her fingers. The search came back with blank pages, dead links. She felt for some reason like her head was full of ice cubes that rattled together every time she moved.

She looked up again at herself in the mirror. The blue lines under her skin hadn't gone away. Those were her veins. They had never been that visible before. Under her eyes she saw dark spots. Blotches, really—not just bags under her eyes, more like tattoos. Or bruises. She looked like she'd been battered.

She looked back down at the sink and the blood swirling in the drain, not wanting to look at her face anymore. She had no pulse. She wasn't breathing.

Nilla knew what that meant. She had become the biological singularity. The thing that doesn't happen made manifest. She was dead, but also obviously alive. Dead. Alive. Alive. Dead. Undead.

SLEEPY YANK TOWN WAKES TO MURDER!
Selkirk, KS "Scene of Carnage" as Motorcycle Enthusiast Retreat Attacked by Locals
[thesun.co.uk, 3/22/05]

Three helicopters keeping station around the prison seemed to hover on pillars of radiance as their searchlights scanned the terrain around ADX-Florence. Their shivering noise had replaced the normal night sounds of cicadas and frogs. A fourth helicopter, bigger and darker, came in for a landing and Bannerman Clark was waiting.

"Welcome to Colorado," he said, saluting the young men and women who emerged. These were researchers from USAMRIID, the Army's primary biological weapons defense facility at Fort Detrick in Maryland. They looked as if they'd rather lick each other's boot soles then come any closer. Clark had removed his cover and replaced it with a plastic shower cap. He had latex gloves on his hands and a surgical mask dangling around his neck. "We don't know our parameters yet so we're being careful," he explained. "We have to assume everyone in this facility is compromised. Please follow the sergeant here."

The researchers dutifully filed through a sallyport defined by two barbed-wire fences and into their new home. The 8th Civil Support Team hadn't wasted any time setting up temporary lab facilities for the biowar people, taking over the prison grounds to set up ten double-wide trailers swathed in positive-pressure tents and installing decontamination stations at every access point. The USAMRIID contingent was used to this kind of confinement, all of them being certified for level four biosafety precautions, and they kept their heads down as they were taken through basic orientation.

One man remained inside the big helicopter and Clark looked to see who it might be. "Hello, Bannerman, is that you, my old buddy?" he asked, stepping into the illumination of the vehicle's exit ramp. He wore an army uniform with a turban and a bushy black beard and his eyes twinkled in the half-light.

"Vikram, Vikram, how have you been?" Clark laughed, happy despite the grim setting to see an old friend. Major Vickram Singh Nanda and Bannerman Clark had come up through the ranks together, starting in the Engineers during Vietnam. They had gone from Green to Gold together, as the saying went, receiving their commissions in the same ceremony. They had fallen out of touch over the years but Clark had heard that Vikram had ended up at Fort Detrick and he'd been hoping they would have a chance to resume contact. He'd never expected his old partner to show up personally.

"I heard you had a very, very serious problem here in your Colorado, so I have come. How could I do less? I requested this duty." Clark couldn't believe his luck—to get Vikram Singh Nanda in charge of the biowar team was a definite card up his sleeve. His smile must not have lasted, though, because a moment later Vikram's face fell. "It is bad, isn't it?"

Clark shook his head. "I'll tell you all about it en route. I'm running out to California tonight and you can come with me if you don't mind the jet lag. It's a virus, we think. The symptoms are ataxia, aphasia, and severe dementia. Victims manifest aggressive behaviors . . . including cannibalism." Vikram gasped and Clark nodded in agreement. "To put the cherry on the top, it's also got an incubation period of just a few minutes. Yes, it's bad."

Vikram shook his head vigorously. "I have never heard of such a thing happening in nature. That kind of effect should take months to manifest. God simply does not create something so virulent unless . . . unless you think it has been weaponized."

Bannerman Clark nodded discretely, because he didn't want to say it out loud yet. He'd come to the same conclusion. A pathogen that could destroy a man's mind and turn him against his friends and co-workers with homicidal intent in a span of minutes would be the ultimate terrorist weapon.

"We've got a lid on this place and it's tight enough for now," Clark said, pointing out the double-layer cyclone fence the 8th CST had erected around the entire prison compound in addition to the prison's own fences. "I've got digital topographic imaging and satellite support so vigilant I can see every acorn hidden by every squirrel in a twenty mile radius. I've got air and ground troops watching every corner of this site."

"Then why, my friend, do you look so frightened?" Vikram asked quietly.

Clark kicked the dirt in frustration. Not a terribly efficient way to get out his anger but he was running on twenty-four hours without food and it was starting to get to him. "Because the warden of this prison may very well have been carrying the virus when he took off on vacation three days ago. All of this," Clark said, gesturing around at the fences, the helicopters, the mobile labs, "might just be my way of locking the barn door when the horse has already run away."

Where is your family's Emergency Meet-Up Point? Where is your personal Go Bag, at work, at school, in the car? How many days worth of water do you have in the house right now? [Emergency Preparedness Update #7, published by the Federal Emergency Management Agency (FEMA), 1/05]

The kerosene lamp whoofed into life and threw some yellow around the bare plank walls of Bleu's root cellar. Dick could still see moonlight coming through the slats and he wondered how long it would take one of the homicidal climbers to break in. Bleu didn't seem particularly scared. Just anxious to get the job over with. "What happened to them?" Dick asked. "What makes people act like that?"

"I was going to ask you the same thing. It has to be some kind of government germ warfare thing gone wrong, doesn't it?" Bleu lifted the lantern and clomped down a narrow flight of stairs cut into the earth. They came into a low space with bowed walls and Bleu hung the lantern on a four-by-four that held up the ceiling like a toothpick holding open the mouth of a predatory cat in a cartoon. Stacks of cardboard boxes and bags full of potatoes and radishes filled most of the space. At the far end from the stairs sat a door wrapped in black plastic of the kind contractors use. Bleu went to the door and stopped. "I reckoned if anybody would know about that it would be you. Hell, kid, that's what I called you down here for."

Dick's eyes went wide. "Me? I'm just a low-level bureaucrat. A livestock inspector! I don't know anything about biowarfare." He thought about it a second. He was with the government, which must be all that mattered to Bleu. "Look, I'm on your side," he said, trying to remember what hippies stood for. Flower power, sure, and they didn't like the Vietnam War. "Um, peace and love, right? Love is all you need."

Bleu opened the waterproof door and light spilled over its contents. Five racked hunting rifles, most of them .22 caliber rimfire weapons but also a good old-fashioned thirty-ought-six. Even more insane: one was a heavy-duty big game rifle, a centerfire, bolt-action Weatherby Mark V Safari Custom, something Dick had only ever seen in gun magazines. An elephant gun, to be blunt about it, though most likely the Skye family had planned on using it against bears when they bought it.

Below the rack of rifles hung three shotguns in various gauges and below that pistols and revolvers, high-powered enough to cut a man and half. At the bottom of the closet sat box after box of ammunition, cleaning supplies for the weapons and sheaves of paper targets, some of them used. On the back of the door someone had taped up one target showing a human silhouette with the bull's-eye where the man's heart would be. Dick saw an almost perfect grouping, six narrow holes right in the center. In the white space of the target someone had written **NICE SHOOTING STORMY!!!** and **OCTOBER 17 2002, STORMY'S BIG DAY.**

Dick couldn't help but stare. He was looking at an arsenal, a survivalist's wet dream, enough guns to hold off an invasion of ATF and FBI agents for a week. He had thought he had been sent back through a time warp to Woodstock. Instead he'd wandered into Ruby Ridge.

What the Government Doesn't Want You to Know: RATE OF CATTLE MUTILATIONS SPIKES! [*UFO Insider* magazine, February 2005]

Nilla was standing in the hospital's cafeteria, devouring sliced beets out of a tin can she'd found sitting open on a counter when she heard a violent squawking noise coming from outside. She swallowed and went to the window. It was dark outside but blue and red light kept flashing across the slats of the Venetian blinds. With her clumsy hands she pushed open two of the slats and looked out.

Oh, God, no, she thought.

FEMA MOVES HEAVY EQUIPMENT THROUGH ILLINOIS AT 3 AM: What are they preparing for? [ctrl.org, 3/20/05]

"There are SWAT teams ready to storm the building. You still have a chance to come out of this in good shape if you're willing to release some hostages." The words blasted against the brick face of the hospital and rebounded off into space. No answer was forthcoming. The sheriff's deputy switched off his bullhorn and turned to shake hands with Clark and Vikram. He was a big man, clearly a weightlifter in his off hours. He had a blonde crew cut and dark deep-set eyes. "You're from the army, huh? I didn't know we rated that kind of attention." The deputy looked dazed. He was out of his element here—his town had always been a quiet place, one of a thousand Californian hamlets between San Francisco and Los Angeles where nothing ever happened. Now he was overseeing an actual hostage crisis. A complete breakdown of the social pecking order.

"We're just here as advisors," Vikram soothed, giving his biggest smile. He asked about the boy's tattoos. The deputy seemed grateful for the diversion but was too riled up to give more than one-word answers.

Clark wasn't particularly frosty himself. He very, very much wanted this to be a wasted trip. He wanted to go back to Colorado safe in the knowledge that the thing, the bug, the virus or whatever it might be was wholly contained in Florence.

He forced himself to relax by grabbing his keys in his pants pocket until the jagged edges bit into the ball of his thumb. The discomfort helped him focus. He studied the layout of the denied perimeter the sheriff's office had created. The hospital was a three-story building studded with windows. On the side that faced the street it had only a single entrance, a wide lobby of automatic doors leading into the emergency room. Blue and red light flashed across the glass: the deputies had formed a wedge with their patrol cars, a covered forward position for the negotiation phase of the hostage event.

Beyond the doors darkness filled the building like a fluid. Clark saw occasional flashes of motion in there but he could never make out any details. Just inside the emergency room, illuminated only by the police lights, he could see what looked like a leg—the wrinkled sole of a foot, the bumpy shape of an ankle—as if someone had collapsed in the shadows. "There," Clark said, pointing it out. "Do you see that? It looks like a man down. Can you get someone in there to retrieve casualties?"

The deputy glared at Clark but then he looked away and lifted his radio handset to his mouth. He uttered a few quick strings of police code numbers and after a moment three SWAT troopers in full armor emerged from a truck behind them. Two of them took up station in short range of the entrance while the third conspicuously put his weapon down on the ground and advanced. He kept his hands in plain view as he ducked under a flapping cordon of caution tape and advanced on the doors. No weapons fire or any other indication of resistance came from the hospital so the trooper moved in closer and then slipped quickly and silently through the glass doors.

Clark couldn't see him after that. "This is SWAT Two, 10-97," he heard crackling over the deputy's radio. "11-44." Clark knew that code—it meant "possible fatality." "Oh, man," the trooper said, his breath heavy as it roared out of the radio. "Oh, man, it's just a leg, it's been torn off . . ."

"Is there anyone else in there?" the deputy asked. "Anybody alive?" He looked like he might be sick.

"Stand by, please. I see six, maybe more males—it's very dark, they're approaching my position."

Clark stiffened. He squeezed his keys until the pain made him wince. "Get your man out of there now," he demanded.

The deputy waved at him is dismissal. "SWAT Two, are they armed?"

"SWAT Two here, negative . . . woah, shit! Okay, it's okay, one of them tried to grab me . . ."

The radio crackled with silence. Vikram put a hand on Clark's shoulder and he realized he'd been about to jump up and run inside. He let out a deep breath and then sucked in a new one when the door of the hospital slammed open.

"Fuck, fuck, fuuucckkk!" SWAT Two screamed as he came barreling out, the severed human leg clutched in one hand. The trooper dashed to cover as the doors slid open again and three badly wounded men came staggering out.

Blood covered one's face. Another wore no shirt and Clark could see he'd been disemboweled. The third's left arm dangled at his side, the skin flayed off down to the elbow. They made no sound at all as they limped toward the fleeing SWAT trooper. They didn't even look up when the deputy demanded that they halt.

A firearm went off very close to Clark's head and he instinctively ducked. When he looked again the three injured men were spinning in place, the dark craters of bullet wounds tearing open their flesh. "Hold your fire!" Clark shouted but the deputy bellowed over him, demanding that the SWAT team fire at will. "What are you doing?" Clark demanded. "Those men are unarmed! They need medical attention!"

The deputy set his mouth in a hard line. He studied Clark's face for a moment, then turned away to spit on the ground. "I have had just about enough of this shit," he said. "I don't care if they've got rabies or ebola or what the fuck ever—six of my men are in that hospital right now and who knows how many civilians and I know just one thing. This. Ends. Here." He pointed at the ground to emphasize his point.

Clark shook his head sadly. This was where it would truly begin.

In the red and blue light the three men jittered and danced toward the SWAT team, their eyes vacant as they tried to walk forward through the hail of gunfire. Their faces were completely slack, emotionless. Clark knew that look. It was the same one he'd seen at ADX-Florence.

"He was just leaning against the . . . standing there, he looked kind of confused and every once in a while he would knock on the door. With his fists, you know, maybe he was trying to break it open but . . . he wasn't my husband, not anymore . . . I didn't know what to do!" [Caller on the "Buzz Linklee Show", 1290 AM KKAR, Omaha, 3/19/05]

On the snowy roof of the Skye house Dick sipped at his coffee and tried the police again on his cell phone. When that didn't work he tried his office and finally his sister in Montana. No signal, not even a bar. It had been that way since the first time he'd tried but he couldn't seem to just put the phone away.

"Remember," Bleu said. "You have to go for the head. The brain. Otherwise they don't so much as feel it."

They had some moonlight, which was good, and plenty of guns, also good, and they were up on the roof and had pulled the ladder up behind them which was the best idea ever as far as Dick was concerned. It was also freezing cold and they couldn't go down until all of the climbers were dispatched. Bleu had a leg of mutton on a string that she dangled over the edge of the roof. Fishing for dead people.

The thought made Dick laugh and he wiped at his face as he chuckled, rubbing away the paste of dried saliva there. His mouth had dried out like a piece of jerky. "Gnugh," he moaned as he scratched at his leathery tongue. She stared at him and he realized he was being inappropriate. "Sorry," he mumbled.

He wasn't doing so well with the fear.

"Don't be sorry. Be ready." It sounded like something she might have told her son. Her dead son. Her dead survivalist son—well, he hadn't survived the walking dead, had he? Dick wanted to giggle again.

"When I say 'be ready', that means you should check your weapon there, sport." Bleu clomped over to the other side of the roof. Her hobnail boots had cracked some of the shingles and Dick was afraid to follow her over there. Instead he worked the breechblock of the Weatherby rifle and checked that there was a round ready to fire. Of course there was. He'd put it in himself under her supervision. Everything was according to her plan. He was the shooter because supposedly his eyes were better but she knew all about guns and she didn't really need him. He could just leave. His car was waiting for him just over the ridge. He just had to get past two or maybe three horribly mutilated cannibals who might or might not have supernatural powers of survival.

"There! Come on already, get your shot lined up!" Bleu was pointing out into the sighing pines, one boot stamping repeatedly on the shingles. Dick tried to bring the rifle up to his face and nearly dropped the heavy weapon in the process.

Okay, okay, he told himself, *calm down. Just calm the fuck down.*

"Do you see him? He's leaning on that tree. It's a perfect shot."

Dick nodded—he did see something kind of human-shaped—and brought the scope to his eye. Let his night vision adjust until the image cleared. Yes. A human figure, dark against the snow. The climber in question had been a woman once, judging by the shape of her hips. Now she looked like a rotting pumpkin perched on top of a sportswear mannequin. The scientist in Dick rose to the top, trying to understand what he saw and it made sense, in its way. Being

45

frozen all winter hadn't preserved the climbers as much as liquefied them: when ice crystals formed in their muscle cells the sharp apices of the crystals had shredded the cell membranes, turning the flesh flaccid and gooey. He remembered the one he'd fought with. It had been slippery with putrefaction.

They were dead. The climbers were dead, no matter how active they seemed. They had to be dead.

He grimaced to clear his head. The scientific observation was immaterial. The only thing that mattered was the shot. He tried to remember his time in the Boy Scouts. He had aced the requirements for the marksmanship merit badge. Seat the rifle, line up the shot, adjust for windage—

"Take the shot al-fucking-ready!" Bleu howled.

Dick fired spasmodically.

The magnum round hit the tree a few inches above the climber's head. The wood exploded, showering the dead woman with pulpy fragments and splinters of bark. Bleu didn't credit the climbers with too much mental wattage but it looked like they understood what it meant when the tree you were leaning on exploded. Without looking back the climber slumped off into the darkness.

It had taken them three hours to pick one shot and he missed. Dick wiped at his mouth again. He didn't feel so good.

New Flux Generating Step Identified in the Metabolic Pathways of Human Prion Protein (PrPsc) [*New England Journal of Medicine*, 11/6/04]

Nilla watched the three men get cut down by the SWAT team through the Venetian blinds in the cafeteria. Her blood wasn't circulating in her veins anymore but it went cold anyway. They weren't asking questions down there. They weren't trying to help people. The police were just slaughtering anyone who came out.

Maybe not just anyone. Maybe live people got a pass. Nilla was undead and she knew she would be on the short list for the firing squad. She had to get out—she had to escape the hospital somehow.

She tried to run but her legs cramped up instantly when she started to sprint. In pain she hobbled past a room full of nurses and orderlies bent over a bed. She didn't look too closely—she could hear what they were doing.

Out in the hallway she saw heart rate monitors and pulse oxygen readers mounted on IV poles, she saw bad art on the walls, pictures of kittens and houses in New England and, ugh, a streak of blood pointing towards the stairs. She leaned up against a wall, her leg muscles screaming at the workout she was giving them, and sank to the floor below a line of windows that let cold black night air burst in.

"This is the police! We're coming in! Everyone needs to be on the floor, now, with your hands in plain view!" someone shouted outside, his angry voice electronically amplified. He made it sound as if they would shoot anyone they found inside the hospital. Fear made Nilla's hands shake so much she shoved them in the pockets of her stolen coat.

She got up. She found the courage to stand up. She followed the blood trail only to find a dead guy in a jumpsuit blocking the doorway, motionless, his head tilted back a little. As if he was expecting to receive transmissions from space.

"Move!" she said, trying to shove at him. He had a foot on her and maybe fifty pounds. He wouldn't budge. Slowly, excruciatingly slowly his jaw began to drift down and his eyes started to focus on her.

Outside of the hospital she heard rapid gunfire. Short bursts of it that didn't let up: **B-B-BRATTT-B-B-BRATTT-B-B-BRATTT.** She tried shoving the big guy again and finally he looked down at her, saw her. His mouth opened as if he might speak.

A glassy rope of drool spilled over his lower lip. He shot out one hand to push her away and knocked her to the floor. She slid over onto her side on the glossy linoleum. He leaned down over her and tried to grab her with enormous hands. She slipped out of his grasp with more grace than she'd thought she possessed but she knew he would get her eventually.

Something whistled as it came in through the open window and took off the top of his head. Dried-out brain matter showered down on her as fragments of his skull plinked off the wall. Before he could even fall down she ducked around him and into the stairwell. A sniper had shot him without warning—maybe they had seen him attacking her, maybe they were trying to defend her. Or maybe she was the next target.

She took the stairs downward as quickly as she could manage. She kept tripping and having to grab the handrail because she was constantly looking back over her shoulder. She was halfway down when the door at the bottom of the stairwell opened and yellow light streamed in, dazzling her. Something black about the size of a soda can bounced off the floor and she slid to a halt. The canister clattered to a stop and started spewing white smoke. It smelled weird, truly weird and then it made her nose itch. Tear gas? She didn't know what tear gas smelled like. She couldn't go out that way, though— they would be guarding the door. She turned around and started heading back up, back to where snipers lay in wait just outside the open windows.

Nilla only made it a step or two before the lights went out. The police had cut the power.

"This was a test of the Reverse 9-1-1 Emergency Notification System. You do not need to reply to this call. Please hang up now. This was a test . . ."
[Phone Message received in Butte, MT, 3/21/05]

"That's it, you idiot. You take the fucking meat!" Bleu jiggled the bit of string and the leg of mutton danced in front of the dead woman's ruined eyes. The ghoul scrunched up her face and part of her cheek fell away, dangling by a flap of skin. Dick could see the pureed muscles beneath and a hint of bone.

The dead climber reached up and sank her fingernails into the leg. Her hunger vibrated through her, spasms of need pushing her on far more than Bleu's taunt. She sank yellow teeth through the wool and blood dripped on the pine needles below. "This is the last one," Dick said. He'd said it so many times it had to be true.

Bleu let go of the leg and the climber fell to the ground rather than let her prize go. She curled around the meat, protecting it from interlopers with her body.

Dick leaned over the edge of the roof. The rifle hadn't worked out so well so he'd switched to a pistol, a .38. He fired five shots into her head and neck. Powder burns darkened his pant leg but he didn't care. He was too busy coughing and snorting, getting ready to be sick. When he was done he sat down hard on the roof and breathed heavily, washing out his mouth with stale coffee. "That's it, then," he said. "You got three of them. At the mine. Then the one we killed in the house. This poor sucker. And the girl I saw. On the road." He nodded. "That's six."

"I said there might been seven when we found 'em," Bleu clucked.

He shook his head. "But you don't know. You couldn't count them so well in the mine. You said they were crawling all over each other. There might have been seven, but there might have been only six. You don't know."

"I sure don't." She stared out at the trees as if by peering hard enough into the murk she could see right through it. *Come on,* Dick thought. *Come on, come on, come on.* Any euphoria or giddiness or adrenaline he had felt earlier was long gone. He just wanted to go home, to get somewhere safe. He studied Bleu's face like a kid waiting for a teacher to dismiss class on the last day of school. Finally she nodded and helped him lower the ladder over the side.

They climbed down as quietly as they could, the pine needles muffling their footfalls. The moon laid down sharp-edged shadows as they made their way between the tree trunks, Dick putting out one hand to slide along the smooth or rugged or rough bark. After the noise and light of the gunshots the world seemed wrapped up in cotton and hidden away somewhere dark. His muscles were jumpy under his skin. He didn't know if there had six or seven either. He just had to get out, all of his excitement turning to cold dread sweat on his back, making the shoulders of his shirt cling to him.

Where the valley turned to hillside and then to the thrust of the ridge Bleu crouched low and put her guns in her belt. The slope came up pretty suddenly and they had to climb their way up instead of walking. It had been easy to get down the track—gravity had helped there—but going up proved far more difficult. Halfway to the top Bleu leaned forward and grabbed at a tree root to steady herself on the broken rock. "I don't know we should leave just yet. What if the police want to—" She stopped and looked down.

"What's wrong?" he asked.

"I just stepped in something sticky." Dick looked down to see a moldy hand reach up and grab at her ankle. She screamed as the last climber yanked her downward on top of him. She rocked back and forth trying to get free but he got one near-skeletal arm around her throat and pinned her down. "Walters!" she shrieked.

"Bleu!" He pulled out the ice axe and readied himself to strike but he couldn't see any way to hit the dead man without impaling Bleu too. He danced back and forth looking for an opening—and suddenly his feet were sliding on loose shale. Thin sheets of broken rock skittered down the slope, pebbles bouncing and flying as he tried to keep his balance.

"Walters!"

Dick threw out his arms to catch himself, letting go of the axe. He shouted out, half in surprise. "Bleu, just, just hold on—" His feet fell away from beneath him and the hill rolled over as he fell, colliding with the loose rock, sliding, skidding as Bleu and the dead man flew upward, away from him. He was sliding downhill and he couldn't stop himself. He got a good view of the dead climber finally and saw why there'd been so much confusion as to whether there were six or seven of them. The climber who had Bleu was nothing more than a torso, his legs and abdomen torn away leaving a ragged, stringy wound. Dick reached out, trying to grab Bleu's foot, trying to grab tree roots or solid rocks or anything. He had to save her—he had to get back up and save her, but then his head smacked something hard and cold and his vision went all sparkly.

He opened his eyes without remembering ever having closed them. His body rang like a bell. His mouth tasted stale and white—white? Was that a taste? He was pretty sure he'd wet himself. Above

him the stars burned hard and cold. He recognized the symptoms
of a bad concussion but his thoughts were swimming through him
like fishes. Like . . . fish? No, that was . . . that was wrong. He had
to stop—

Stop. Stop and rest.

Yes. Just lay there for a while in the soft snow. It didn't feel cold
at all. Something noisy and terrifying had been happening and he
was pretty sure he had the details written down somewhere if he
wanted to look them up but just then he only wanted to look up at
the stars. Such a beautiful night in the mountains. Something furry
brushed against his hand and he reached out to pat it, to pet it. A
dog? No, too fleecy.

He managed to tilt his head so he could look and found himself
staring into an eyeball with a horizontal pupil. A sheep's eye. Even
after years of working as a livestock inspection agent he had never
gotten used to those eyes with their sideways-elongated pupils like
something out of H. P. Lovecraft. Still. A sheep was nothing to worry
about. He gave this one a professional once-over. He recognized the
breed: Barbados blackbelly, although she seemed slightly off. Yes . . .
her rear legs were tucked in too tight and there were pink patches
in her coat where she'd rubbed herself raw. The principle symptoms
of scrapie. She had it, alright, just as Mrs. Skye had suggested. That
was a damned shame—she looked like a strong animal and she
would have to be put down so she didn't infect the rest of the flock.
The sheep put out her tongue and licked his hand. He laughed until
she nipped him, hard.

"Hey there," he said, "come on," and he sat up so suddenly the
blood rushed right out of his head. He groaned and tried to rub
at his temples. It didn't work. The sheep still had his fingers
clenched in her incisors. She choked up on his hand and started
crushing his fingers with her premolars. Her herbivore's teeth
couldn't tear his skin very well but she clearly meant to grind his
hand to paste.

Dick yelled and tried to get up but another sheep, this one missing part of her hindquarters, sprawled across his chest. She weighed

two hundred pounds, easily, much more than he could lift—he was trapped. A ram with broken horns got his mouth around Dick's shoulder and clamped down hard. He felt the bones there flex with the pressure. Soon enough they would snap. More sheep arrived. Maybe a dozen. A full flock, all of them showing signs of scrapie. And something else, too. Something worse.

Bleu had slaughtered all of her sheep—she'd done it herself. She had . . . she had cut their throats. Bled them. She wouldn't have decapitated them or destroyed their brains, though. Too messy.

Now they were back. Bloody wool obscured Dick's view but as the ram crushed the skin and muscle of his left arm he saw Bleu herself standing before him. Massive chunks of meat were missing from her neck and throat so that her head seemed to float above her body like a balloon on a string of vertebrae. She didn't say anything as she bent over him, pushing her way in amongst the sheep. She didn't say anything at all.

DOES AMERICA HAVE ENOUGH GUNS? Assault Weapons Bans and the Congressmen Who Hate Them [*The Economist* magazine, 1/05]

Stuttering flashes of light lit up the hospital's windows as the SWAT teams moved through room after room searching for hostages and shooting anyone who looked suspicious. Bannerman watched from the back of a squad car, trying not to look up every time he heard sub machine gun fire.

It was hard. "They're in there shooting people, Vikram. *Sick* people. This isn't law enforcement. It's eugenics. And I can't do a thing about it—I'm way out of my jurisdiction here and the local RAID-OIC isn't taking my calls. FEMA doesn't want to hear it until I've got a verified one hundred fatalities and the Governor's office is doing its own investigation. They promise they'll get back to me. So in the meantime I sit here and listen to people getting slaughtered. The alternative is to run in there and try to stop them with my bare hands, in which case they would decide I was a threat, too, and take *me* down." The sheriff's deputy had been quite clear on that last point. "I have never felt so helpless in my life."

Vikram Singh Nanda held up one hand. The other clutched his ruggedized cell phone to an ear hidden beneath his turban. "Okay, okay, okay," he said. "Okay." He finished his call. "I am sorry, Bannerman. What were you saying just then?"

Clark looked up at the hospital and saw tear gas streaming from a line of open windows. "Forget it." This was what happened when you put law enforcement teams in charge of what should be a military situation, he thought. It didn't matter how much training or discipline they had—they just weren't ready to psychologically handle a true combat experience. Just ask the Branch Dravidians at Waco. Even federal units were ill-equipped for a real fight.

"So I have news," Vikram told him, trying to move on. "News you will not like."

"We've found our warden?" Clark asked. This could be crucial. He had set his friend with the task of tracking down the elusive man but he hadn't expected results nearly so quickly.

"He left an immaculate paper trail. And why not? He had nothing to hide. He was a man going away on vacation. He took a flight from Denver International Airport that arrived at LAX at 3:22 on a Thursday. He rented a car, a Jeep Cherokee, from the Hertz counter and was later recorded purchasing gas at a service station in Petaluma. Two hours later he was seen biting a young woman on the neck and was subsequently gunned down by an officer of the law. His body was brought here, to this hospital."

"Jesus fucked a duck," Bannerman said. The first time he'd sworn in a month, probably, but well deserved. You couldn't ask for a cleaner timeline, for one thing—Vikram had always been thorough—but their luck in getting such a clear picture of the warden's movements was far and away eclipsed by the story's sheer horror.

The warden had been infected in Florence. Of that Clark had no doubt. He had flown through two major international airports, spreading his contagion to everyone in both terminals—and by extension the passengers and crews of every flight that left those airports. The germ could be on its way to hundreds of destinations by now. No, Clark reconsidered, the warden had a head start on them. The germ would already be at hundreds of destinations. Not every passenger on every plane would be infected, of course—no pathogen was that insidious—but if just one person on every flight had it . . . well, it had only taken one infected individual to turn a prison—and then a hospital—into a war zone. Bannerman Clark had been operating under a protocol of containment, intending to quarantine every known location where the new disease manifested itself. That was impossible now. What had happened here, at the hospital, would already be beginning in cities around the planet. Starting with Denver. And Los Angeles.

Jesus fucked a duck, indeed.

Clark grabbed the bridge of his nose and pinched. He was trained for this. As part of his being named the RAID officer for Colorado he had been required to complete an eight-week course in crisis response to biological warfare incidents. It was time to manage this thing. Time to prioritize. Time to stop feeling helpless and start doing things. He ran down a checklist in his head. What did he need?

"I need flight schedules," he said weakly, and Vikram pulled a PDA from his pocket. "We at least need to start looking at epidemiology. I need crew lists and passenger manifests, we'll track down as many people as we can—God, I hope none of those flights were headed to non-aligned states, we'd never catch them. I need to talk to the administrator for FEMA region IX and the local Guard CO, not just the AG, I—"

A flash-bang concussion grenade went off right inside the Emergency Room and Clark stopped in mid-sentence. He looked up to see SWAT teams pouring out of the hospital, their black Kevlar and their iridescent blue-blocker goggles making them look like demons pouring out of a crack in the side of Hell. Something major was happening.

"Naam," Vikram breathed, taking his God's name in vain but Clark thought maybe the time was right for that.

Clark opened the door of the patrol car and stepped out into the hospital's loading zone. The sheriff's deputy came marching toward him but he held up a hand for patience. He watched the SWAT teams fall into close ranks in two lines facing the emergency room doors at forty-five degree angles. They moved flawlessly, as a unit. As crazy as they might have become, as desperate, they had not forgotten their drills. They were forming a perfect firing formation. A kill zone. They expected something big and bad to come out of the hospital at any second.

The doors opened and a skinny blonde girl walked out.

She had her arms up, trying to surrender. She looked terrified. She also had a truly gruesome wound on her neck and what looked like bloodstains on her chin and chest. Her lips were shaking. They were blue.

"Please," she said, her voice thick with fear. "Please, don't kill me."

The SWAT team leader threw a hand signal at his men and the troopers swarmed her, some holding back to keep her in their weapons' sights, others streaking in with riot control batons to knock her legs out from under her. They got her hands behind her, fastened together with a thin plastic zip-cuff. Expert hands frisked her, pulling open her white lab coat to show she wore nothing underneath. When it was established that she was unarmed two troopers grabbed her by the arms and yanked her away from the glass doors and over to a clear patch of ground by some shrubbery. The sheriff's deputy loped over to look at her while the SWAT teams shifted position again to keep the doors covered.

Clark couldn't help himself. He stepped in between the deputy and the girl. "The infected persons I've seen couldn't talk. They were physically incapable of it," Clark insisted. "You have to take this woman into custody, sure, she needs to be monitored. You don't need to hurt her. At the very least that's going to end in a lawsuit. At worst it'll mean criminal charges filed against you."

"I've seen enough of them. I know what they look like and how they act. We can't let even one of them get away." The deputy nodded at his underlings.

The girl shivered and sobbed as a SWAT trooper leveled his weapon at her forehead.

"Who are you?" Clark asked her, trying to humanize her in the deputy's eyes. He wouldn't give up until she was actually dead—he owed her that much, after standing by and just watching the bloodshed all night. "What's your name?"

"I . . . I don't know," the girl said. "I've lost my memory, I can't remember!" She sobbed again. Mucus leaked from her nose and eyes. It was dark and thick with congealed blood. Oh, no, Clark thought, oh, no. He'd been wrong—she was one of them.

"Do it," the deputy coughed. He turned away. The SWAT trooper clicked off the safety of his firearm and steadied it with his free hand.

The girl vanished. Right before Clark's eyes. Or rather . . . he felt as if a particle of dust had fallen into his eyes and he tried to blink it away and when his vision cleared she was nowhere to be seen. She must have made a break for it. Yet when he looked around he saw only confused-looking men in riot gear. The SWAT trooper fired a few desultory rounds at the bushes where she'd been kneeling but clearly he didn't know what to target. The deputy's face was set like stone. Behind it his brain chugged along trying to figure out what had happened.

She had vanished into thin air.

IN THE BLOOD: A good-looking young woman named Marisol Gonsalvez wastes her time and ours by starring as an ass-kicking nun with, you guessed it, the stigmata. This mildly offensive gore romper is opening in "selected cities" which means it isn't going straight to video, but it probably should have (**, rated R for excessive religious violence and graphic nudity, 81 min). [Roger Ebert, One Minute Film Reviews, suntimes.com, 3/22/05]

The gun had been used recently and it was hot and it stank with a sour reek that poured down over her face and made her gag with fear. The SWAT trooper stood as still as a stone with his finger on the trigger. She couldn't see his eyes—they were hidden behind thick goggles. What was he thinking? Was he questioning this at all? He could wipe out her life—her un-death, she supposed—in a heart's beat if he chose. If she died there with no memories of her past it would be like she hadn't ever existed at all.

Maybe that would be for the best.

She was already dead. Did she really want to face a new un-life in a decaying body? A new lifespan of uncertain duration, without any knowledge of who she was or what she might have lost?

Then one of the others, the one in the military uniform—she could see his eyes and they were full of sadness—had to spoil it all. "Who are you?" he asked, "what's your name?" In the tone of voice you used when speaking to a frightened dog.

She sputtered out something, an answer, a negation and suddenly it was all too real. The possibility that she might have a name, lost out there somewhere but still intact, reawakened in her the sense of what she had to lose. She had something still, some breadth of time, and the fear of losing it could cripple her. Her brain rolled over inside her head as the dread overwhelmed her, completely took her over. Her body shook and spasmed and heaved as if she was going to cough up her own skeleton, spit it out on the ground. She felt something clotted and nasty leak from her, from her mouth, her nose, her eyes. She tried to cough it up.

She heard the gun click, heard a bullet inching through its oiled metal mechanism, getting ready for the shot. Her eyes squeezed shut, terrified of what they might see. Oblivion evaded her, however.

With her eyes closed she could see the men like torches in a snow-storm. Their radiance, their golden tasty goodness glow that she wanted so badly to get close to, to consume, burned and roared inside their bodies. It was their life force, she realized. She could feel the energy, the heat of it turned on her, focused on her and she knew they could sense somehow her own dark energy—that horrible perversion of life—God, she thought, if only she could hide that away from them, if only she could make them see her as one of them or even just see her as nothing at all, as invisible, transparent—

Something grated in her head, the bones of her skull sliding across one another like continental plates. The agony of it was unbearable—being shot in the brain couldn't hurt any more.

An icy shudder went through her. Her eyes shot open. She looked up and saw the men and every one of them had the same vacant look on his face.

"Where did she go?" the SWAT trooper asked. "I can't see her!"

It was impossible but . . . she had gotten her wish.

It couldn't last: her body felt drained, her mind hazy. The bare space of existence she'd bought for herself had cost all of her energy and in a moment she would lose it, that control. In a second they would see her. The man with the gun would see her again and nothing would stop him from shooting.

She had to escape.

Her hands were locked behind her with a loop of plastic, so she rolled over on her side and thrust upward with her back, with her shoulder against the concrete until she was sliding upward onto her feet, a move she didn't think human bones should allow but it worked for her. She must have been a yoga instructor in her past life—how else could she explain how limber she was, even with stiff, dead muscles? As fast as her feet could carry her (which wasn't fast at all, damn it, she needed to *move*) she ran right toward the men, slaloming between them, careful not to touch them because that might just break the spell. Already they were starting to blink and look around, their eyes unfocused when they glided over her but that would change in a hurry. She had to get away. There, she saw a gap, a narrow space between two parked police cars, their red and blue light splashing across her white coat, run, run, run, okay, just a fast walk, anything, she squatted low, her body stiffening and complaining about it. She pushed her way into a stand of bushes. Behind her she heard shots fired, gunshots much louder than she expected and her torso winced painfully, her stomach clenching.

They were moving then, searching for her. She picked a direction and just moved, no conscious effort required, pure flight reflex taking over. But where to run to? Every direction seemed equally fraught with danger. Hide—she could hide. She found a hole to crawl into, a dry drainage pipe at the bottom of a ditch, wide enough for her to curl up inside. She tucked herself away, desperate to remain undiscovered. She scraped her zip tie against a rough lip of concrete until it snapped: the noise petrified her, made her think they would be on her in a moment.

They didn't find her.

Dogs howled for her as she lay motionless and coiled. A helicopter buzzed overhead, its searchlight spearing the scrub grass right outside the mouth of her pipe, bleaching it of color. Men ran past with their guns jangling, excited for the kill, lusting for her blood. Hunger grew inside of her   it was the only way to measure the passage of time. She wanted to crawl out and away, to go look for some food but she couldn't dare. Instead she chewed on her fingernails, which just made her hungrier. She lost track of the seconds, the minutes, the hours. The night flew away from her on bat's wings.

Dawn came, a hallucinatory vibrant blue on the grass that slowly turned to a pale lemon glow. There was silence around her. There had been for hours. She'd been waiting for something, some signal that it was safe to come out.

Nothing presented itself. Still. She couldn't stay in the pipe forever. She had to get out. She had to get away. She harbored no illusion that the men had given up. They would still be looking for her. She was a monster. Something that had to be hunted down. She had to run as far and as fast as she could to avoid them. Definitely she had to get out of town. Where could she go, though? She might have family somewhere, people who would hide her, but she had no recollection of anyone. She didn't know where she lived herself.

Stiff with cold and moisture she unraveled herself in the pipe and climbed out on all fours, every inch costing her jolts of pain up and down her spine. Once she was fully out of the pipe she stood up with infinite care and caution. The motion made her head buzz. Exhaustion and the ever-growing hunger made everything around her jittery and sharp. She rubbed at her eyes with her knuckles and something dark flared in her mind's eye.

She gulped and choked on a shriek, keeping it inside of her but just barely. There—up on a hill above the hospital. Just a silhouette, a man-shaped darkness framed against the first orange smudge of the rising sun. She squinted hard and saw a naked man, his skin covered in blue curlicues and arabesques. Tattoos. He didn't look like one of the dead. He looked perfectly healthy. He had a thick bushy beard and his hair was pulled back in a tight ponytail. He wore nothing but a piece of rope around his neck and a band of fur around one bicep.

The man looked right into her head and she knew he was not just aware of her but psychically inside of her. He was probing her, studying her. She sensed some things about him, reciprocity for what he was taking from her. Not words, nothing so complex—just buzzing, distorted sensations, feelings, images. He was old, very old, and very much undead like herself, he let her know. He was a friend.

He turned away from her and pointed at the sun. She understood.

In a moment all of it was gone. He was gone. She was standing on wet grass, alone, defenseless. Hunted. She had something, though. There was somebody else—somebody like herself out there. She had no idea if she could trust him or not but what did it matter?

She had a direction. East. Go east, the naked man had been telling her. She had to go somewhere. Go east. *Okay*, she thought. Okay.

PART
TWO

DIESEL FUEL RESERVED FOR AUTHORIZED USERS ONLY! Please forgive the inconvenience. [Sign posted at a Petaluma, CA, gas station 3/23/05]

DICK WOKE UP different. Simplified.

Silvery moonlight lit up the world. It dripped from the branches of the trees and played on the surface of the snow. Dick was a shadow in the lee of that light. There were other shadows surrounding him. One huddled near him, her long white hair dyed with blood. She curled tight around a treasure that glowed dimly like a dying ember. It had a knob of bone protruding from one end. It had fingers on the other. It was a human arm, but Dick was beyond concerns of taste or decorum. He tried to grab it away from her only to find that he had no hands anymore. His shoulders ended in gore-caked nubs. The female shadow's prize was part of Dick's body. His arm.

The sheep had the other one. They were working hard at grinding it down to paste so they could swallow it. It would take them hours to finish it.

This was immaterial to Dick. There were lights and there were shadows and he was one of the latter. He was no longer capable of feeling loss or regret.

Only hunger.

The Homeland Security Advisory System today raised the level of threat awareness to Orange, or High for the following areas: Anaheim, Glendale, and Oakland. The level of threat awareness has been raised to Red, or Severe, for the following areas of the Southland: Atwater, Brentwood, Century City, Granada Hills, Los Feliz . . .
[DHS bulletin for the media, issued 3/26/05]

Back to Colorado. Four days had passed and so little had been accomplished. They had tightened the cordon where they could but the pathogen was already out.

A staff car took Bannerman Clark and Vikram Singh Nanda out to Commerce City, where the new detention facility had sprung up like a ring of fungus after the first rain of spring. Commerce City: not so much a town as a zoning error, a sprawling ex-prairie north of Denver full of chemical tanks and dusty weeds and long-haul truck agents and rusting railroad tracks. Ancient farmhouses that had been spruced up with particleboard and unpainted dry wall and turned into light manufactories. The prettiest thing in Commerce City was a petroleum cracking plant, a stack of steel intestines that was lit up at night like a carnival.

"The CDC has quarantined blocks of Atlanta, New York, and Detroit," Clark said, scanning his email on a Blackberry as the car bounced. "It's hard to tell if it's the same thing or some unrelated problem. What little intel I have is confused at best. The victims are all over Chicago. What kind of force do we have on the ground in Illinois? We need to cut the CDC out of this, take over." The Centers for Disease Control was a civilian group. Civilians lacked the discipline and devotion to protocol that marked military operations, and all they could offer in exchange for their chaos was intuition—guesswork. This was a time for action, not committees. Vikram nodded and made a note on his own handheld.

The car slid to a stop in a spray of gravel that made a noise like hailstones striking the gleaming car. The captain and the major got out and walked the rest of the way. "I have ten workgroups in California but nothing between here and Las Vegas. Maybe we can shuffle some people around. Let's liaise with the WHO as soon as we can. We need to think of this as global, now. If we haven't seen any cases in China or Europe yet we will, sooner rather than later. The rest of the world can't be allowed to think of this as a purely American problem. We need overseas support teams trained and ready to go."

The prison, with its ten thousand doors and its state-of-the-art prisoner control system, was a terrible place to store the infected. The Supermax at Florence had been overcrowded before the Epidemic began. It forced the ill and the healthy together, made them all breathe the same air. The detention facility in Commerce City, by way of contrast, had been set up to take the infected and keep them away from the general population. It mostly comprised a double-layered chain link fence and an open-pit latrine that so far sat clean and unused. The Guard brought in new cases of the mysterious disease every day. Clark had teams working round the clock, looking for ways to improve conditions for the detainees but the main thing was to warehouse them.

"We need to bring in regular Army squads to police up Los Angeles, there needs to be door-to-door catching. We need a declaration of emergency for at least four states."

Clark stopped talking and put his Blackberry in his pocket. He had reached the fence and he could feel their eyes on him. They looked pale and poorly fed. Most of them had visible wounds. They did not have the depressed and surrendering look of refugees, though. They looked more like junkies staring at their next fix.

None of them made a sound. They reached for him hungrily through the wire, their fingers twined through the links, their faces pressed close up against the fence as if they could push themselves through.

One of them slapped the chain link with the flat of a broken hand

and it rattled, watery, plinking echoes rolling up and down the length. The center was built for five hundred detainees. It was already at twice capacity and they were adding new pens daily.

"We need . . ." Clark stopped, unable to think for a moment. He pinched the bridge of his nose. "We need that girl, Vikram. The blonde. She could talk."

The Sikh Major looked up from his handheld—he'd been avoiding the gazes leveled at him through the fence. He pursed his lips as if he was about to speak.

"We need her. She's the answer." He had it. Soldiers, Bannerman Clark ruminated, sometimes possessed intuition too.

As of twenty-three hundred hours tonight in the UTC-8 time zone, parts of three highways in California will be closed to civil traffic. The Governor has called for all citizens to cooperate with this necessary step in maintaining the public health. The affected highways are the State Route 1 (Pacific Coast Highway), State Highway 27, and State Highway 74. [CalTrans press release, 3/28/05]

The dead can't drive. At least Nilla couldn't. She had tried stealing a car to get east only to abandon it before leaving the parking lot. Her hands when she tried to grip the steering wheel felt like thick mittens covered them. The wheel slid away from her and she tried to stamp on the brake, only to find that her leg was beyond such precise movements. If she had gotten up to any speed she would probably have broken her neck.

So she resorted to hitchhiking, because she didn't have any better ideas.

Nilla stood by the side of Route 46 and screened her eyes with one hand as she watched a plume of dust approaching her from the west. It would be her first ride all day if she actually made this one. She was ready to bolt at the first sign of green and nearly did—but it wasn't Army green, this was the bottle green of a civilian car. A little Toyota, it looked like. She was pretty sure the police only drove American-made cars.

It rolled up to a stop next to her but the window didn't come down at first. She could understand that. She'd been eating out of trashcans for a week, sleeping where she could. She had scrounged some clothes out of a dumpster, a pink baby tee a size too small for her and a pair of ratty chinos long out of fashion. Together they made her look like a prostitute. Her stringy hair and the unnatural pallor of her skin made her look like a junkie. People didn't pick up hitchhikers who looked like her. Not often.

She smiled through the window anyway, bending down to try to make eye contact. There were two people in the car—two kids. White suburban teenagers, going by looks. He had a little wispy facial hair and an Oakland Raiders baseball cap pulled low over his eyes. She had a gold cross around her neck. They both wore black T-shirts, band T-shirts.

The window came down, cranked by hand. This had to be the boy's first car. He probably scrimped and saved to buy it used. He had probably installed the spoiler on the back himself—the paint didn't quite match. Nilla knew she had to be careful with what she said, with what she asked for.

"I'm heading east, to, to Barstow," she suggested. She remembered to smile and put a hand on the windowsill. They were less likely to take off if she was already in contact with the car. You learned these things after a week on the road.

The boy looked her up and down, studying her clothes. Her breasts and her hips.

"I don't know, Charles," the girl whispered, as if Nilla couldn't hear her. "Look at her." Nilla gave the boy her best high wattage smile.

"Damn, Shar!" the boy shot back. "Shut up! I guess we got room for one more," he offered. He wasn't sure, no more than his girlfriend, but he had teenage hormones to contend with.

Nilla opened the back door and climbed in.

Limit: Two Gallons of Water per Person, due to Emergency, Please! [Handwritten sign posted at a CVS Pharmacy, Carefree, CA 3/28/05]

Nilla nestled back in the upholstery of the Toyota's back seat and chewed on a candy bar when she really wanted to swallow it whole. It was the closest thing the kids had to food.

"We were heading down to Hollywood, but the radio said you shouldn't." The girl, Shar, craned around in her seat to look back at the hitchhiker. "You're, well, you're not supposed to pick people up, either. You're not even supposed to drive unless you have to."

It was a sort of apology. The girl felt guilty for not wanting to pick her up. Nilla's mouth was full, so she gave Shar a closed-mouth smile.

"Damn, woman, if I want to go somewheres I'ma gonna do it," Charles swore, striking the steering wheel with the flat of his hand. "I got my mind on my drivin', and my drivin' on my mind, you know what I'm saying? Shit, that's just what freedom is all about. For reals. Now see if you can find something on the FM."

"I just get scared, is all," the girl said, slumping down in her seat again. She didn't touch the radio. "They say there's sick people down there. They say they're violent."

Nilla gave a polite shrug. The girl was still looking at her in the rearview mirror.

"They say they have glowing red eyes," Shar finished, and then looked away. "I get scared, is all."

"Unh-uh, no way, I told you already, woman. I'm psycho-killer crazy. I'm mad gangsta dangerous. I'm a *hard* man, baby, hard enough for both of us. I'll keep you safe, Shar. I already *told* you that."

He grabbed her around the shoulders with one arm and held her close, kissing the side of her forehead before he let her go again. He switched the radio on himself and they couldn't talk anymore, not and be heard over the blare of hip-hop that came out of the speakers by Nilla's head. It made a strange soundtrack for what she saw out her windows—flat land covered in spotty green and yellow vegetation in the perfect rectangular fields of big truck farms. They passed the occasional abandoned oil derrick like a tired animal bending down for a drink of water and unable to get up. Nilla saw a couple of houses that had collapsed down the middle. It looked like the ground itself had fallen away from beneath them. Nobody had bothered to repair them. She was a long way already from the bustling little town by the sea where she died and came back.

"There's a town up ahead," Shar said, sitting up in her seat. "Are you still hungry?"

Nilla nodded hopefully. "I don't have any money, though."

Shar sat back down. "Can we stop, Charles? Just for a minute? I need to pee."

They rolled in over the sudden shockingly blue ribbon of an aqueduct and into a tiny town bleached by sun into a uniform brownish-grey. There was no sign welcoming them to town but judging by the names of half the stores they had arrived in Lost Hills, California. As they glided through the cracked streets Nilla got a bad chill down her back and she realized that everyone they passed was staring at them. They were normal people—she saw faces with bad acne scars, old women with hair like frozen cumulus clouds, mothers carrying babies and brushing dark hair out of their eyes to see better. She got another shock when she realized that it wasn't the car garnering all that attention. The eyes didn't track the counter-rotating hubcaps or the handmade spoiler on the back. They were looking in the windows. In the back windows.

At her.

They knew. The people of Lost Hills knew what she was. They could sense it. If she closed her eyes she could see them all, their golden auras, and she knew they were all looking back and seeing her darkness. Surely not as vividly, certainly not consciously but they could sense her energy just like she could sense theirs.

She wanted to get out, but she didn't want to leave the safety of the car. She wanted Charles to just keep driving, to speed up, even as he began to maneuver into a parking space on the town's dusty main street. She wanted to make herself invisible—but that would surely spook Charles and Shar and she couldn't risk that, not when they were her only way out of town.

Charles switched off the ignition and the three of them got out. The stares intensified and on the corner a woman in a red cardigan called out something in Spanish. Nilla had no idea what she was saying. Well, at least she knew one more thing about herself than before: she couldn't speak Spanish.

They headed into a little convenience store—the sign out front said "bodega" in amongst the signs advertising cheap cigarettes and powdered milk. A little, narrow room with a low ceiling of stained acoustic tile and metal racks full of off-brand merchandise. The candy was all Mexican, the newspapers up front were full of words and even punctuation Nilla didn't recognize. The proprietress, a middle-aged woman in a blue print dress, could barely be seen behind an enormous lottery terminal and a display of artificial roses each sealed in its own plastic case.

Charles headed over to talk to her while Nilla and Shar roamed the aisles, looking for snacks. Nilla had a pretty good idea of what was going on and she kept her mouth shut. "So excuse me, ma'am? Do you sell condoms? No? Ma'am, I need some help here. What about the flavored kind, do you have any of those?" The woman behind the counter couldn't conceal her horror at the question. For the first time since they'd entered the store she looked away from Nilla. "What about those ones? They have little bumps on them, you know, excuse me, Ma'am? They're ribbed for her pleasure?"

"Boomps?" the woman asked, her eyes hard.

In the aisle just out of view Shar grabbed a link of plastic-wrapped salami and handed it to Nilla. "In your pants," she whispered, "there's plenty of room. Five-fingered discount."

"Yeah, bumps. Ribs, I guess," Charles suggested. He held up his hands about a foot and a half apart from one another. "In this size?"

"Boomps," the woman said again. "Ribs?"

"I think they call them French ticklers."

Shar sputtered with laughter even as she handed Nilla a block of cheddar cheese and a bag of potato chips. She just couldn't help herself. It was all over as soon as the laugh came out of her, though. "Thieves! They are thieves!" the woman shrieked. She started to crawl up onto her counter, clearly intending to seize them in the act of shoplifting.

"What do we do?" Nilla asked, but Shar had already dropped half the things she was carrying and was at the door. Nilla followed as close behind as she could, unable to move as fast as she might like both because she was, well, dead but also because her pants were full of cold cuts. Charles came up behind her and pushed her bodily into the door of the bodega until it flew open and they spilled out into the sunlight. The proprietress was still coming for them, her knees already up on the counter. They headed for the car, intending to make a clean getaway.

"*¿Que estas haciendo? ¡Ai! ¡Malvado fantasma, es peligroso!*" a man on the corner shouted and Nilla pulled up short, guilt flushing through her body. Shar and Charles kept running. The man came closer— an old, weathered guy in overalls and a baseball cap. What could she do? She felt pretty lousy about shoplifting but she would feel worse, she knew, if she were caught. The people of Lost Hills wouldn't give her a chance. *They knew.* She bolted for the car.

"*Hice por ayudar,*" the old man said behind her. She got maybe three strides down the road before she realized he'd been trying to warn her. Charles and Shar were behind the car, huddled in its shadow.

A crowd of men had gathered in the middle of the street. Some of them had farm implements—pitchforks, shovels, she saw a long-handled trowel—and others just had steel-toed boots. They had gathered around a girl who was maybe fifteen years old, lying curled up in the street, and they were kicking her to death.

No. Not death. When Nilla got closer she closed her eyes and saw the golden fires of the men in a ring around a huddled shape of fuming darkness. The girl was already dead. The blows the men rained down on her weren't stopping her from reaching for their ankles, trying to grab them and tear them apart.

No wonder the people of the town were so sensitive to her energy. The sickness had already come upon them.

The Under Secretary of Emergency Preparedness and Response has asked that all physicians and medical technicians register with their nearest Emergency Services Provider. [FEMA ListServ Message, 3/30/05]

The hunger swelled inside Dick, turned inside him, threatened to consume him. It was bigger than he was and he lacked any kind of willpower or ego to fight against it. Sometimes it seemed to speak to him in a low, moaning language more primitive than words. It told him what to do. It told him where to go. Up. Up into the mountains, up the winding course of the highway toward the light. What he would find there he couldn't know, but he couldn't resist the pull, either.

He lost one of his boots along the way, snagged under a protruding tree root. He pulled and pulled until the laces creaked, until the leather stretched and tore, until his foot came out red and swollen. He moved on, bouncing up and down with each step, up on the boot, down when his naked foot hit the gravel, or the concrete, or the loose rocky soil. He didn't let this hobbling gait slow him down.

The hunger drove him on.

At ten thousand feet above sea level he saw something white and low ahead—a car that had stalled out in the rarefied air. He moved in with a little caution, unsure if he was wasting his time. He wasn't. There was someone inside, a woman, a middle-aged woman in pearls and pantsuit. Her hair was like gossamer, like the silken strands of a spider's web. In Dick's altered vision her hair glowed like a fine tracery of gold. He wanted her. The hunger had to have her.

She screamed but he could barely hear her through the safety glass. She tried to get the car moving but failed. He came closer and lunged for her. His face smashed against the glass of her window. Pain sang a single low note in his nose and his cheek but the hunger roared louder. He struck again. She bounced across the front seats of the car and pushed her way out of the passenger door, out into the air.

The smell of her hit Dick like a storm of longing. His jaw stretched wide and his eyes rolled back in his head. She tried to run but she'd already made her fatal mistake. She would have been faster than Dick if she'd been wearing tennis shoes instead of high heels. She could have outrun him at sea level where she could catch her breath. That high up in the mountains she could barely run a dozen yards before she got winded. The air was too thin to properly fill her lungs.

Dick didn't need to breathe at all. He was dead. She would run a ways and have to stop to puff and gasp and wheeze. He just kept coming. It took most of an hour but in the end he closed the gap between them. He got his teeth in her flailing arm and just refused to let go. He couldn't feel any mercy or compassion anymore. To Dick she was just meat, a meal, something to snack on. He couldn't understand her pleas for release.

The hunger owned him. It didn't leave room for pity.

When he was done with her and her blood had dried on his chin and his vest, when the hunger was sated for a while (just a while, it would come back soon enough) he lay sprawled across her cooling body, his esophagus heaving with peristalsis, and he watched the gold filigree of her hair tarnish and turn dark. When she woke up she joined him, what was left of her. Together they headed up the highway. The hunger pulled her along too, and when they crested the mountain together they saw where it was leading them.

Public transportation is running on a reduced/holiday schedule. It is expected that normal schedules will be resumed shortly. [RTD Denver, CO service announcement, 3/31/05]

A new structure had been erected on the grounds of the prison overnight. The biowarfare people from Fort Detrick called it "the Bag." The biosecure research facility the 1157th Engineers

Company had built on the site of Florence-ADX comprised a series of interlocked Conex shipping containers lined inside with several thicknesses of transparent mylar. These envelopes were kept at varying levels of negative air pressure so that if one was punctured pathogens would be blow inward, not out. The Bag qualified as a Class II Biological Safety Cabinet.

To get inside the Bag you had to pass through a series of flaps that had to be unzipped and then resealed behind you. Clark had already been decontaminated and had his clothing (including his underwear and socks) replaced with disposable paper modesty garments. His name and rank were stenciled on the chest and sleeves. He felt humiliated. What Vikram had to tell him didn't please him either. "There's no word on the girl because there's no one there to answer the phone."

"Everyone is gone, all of them. Everyone with a telephone," Vikram shrugged in apology.

"What do you mean, gone?" he demanded as they ducked through yet another flap. "The entire town? Not just the sheriff's office?"

"The town has been officially deserted. The people to a soul evacuated, the surrounding roads sealed and barricaded. It was done on FEMA's order."

"Nobody over there has authority to evacuate an entire town! That's not supposed to be possible without my countersignature." Clark knew what this meant. The incident had grown too large for one lowly captain to be in charge anymore. Someone upstairs must have relieved him of duty and the papers were still in the mail. It was hardly surprising but he didn't like it at all. "Did those trigger-happy deputies ever find out her name? I mean before they ran away. At least tell me they didn't kill her."

"There's still an all points bulletin out for her. They wish to take her to protective custody. That at least means she still lives, certainly." Vikram grabbed his beard in a tight fist. "I am afraid though their description, is not so good. Age eighteen to forty-five. Blonde. Tattoo on the stomach."

"That describes half the women in California," Clark said,

scowling. "They didn't get a single photograph of her?" Of course they hadn't. The debacle at the hospital parking lot had been completely FUMTU (Fucked Up More Than Usual). He came up to the final envelope of the Bag and peered in. Through the cloudy mylar he could make out a figure like an obese white grub with stubby arms and legs gliding along a series of instrument trays, touching each tool in turn. That would be First Lieutenant Desiree Sanchez, the woman he'd come to talk to, dressed in a one-piece biological safety ventilated garment. A space suit, in biowarfare lingo. There was another occupant of the innermost reaches of the Bag and he wore nothing at all. Shriveled, grey, mutilated—one of the original victims from the prison. He was held to a gurney by four-point restraints but Clark could see him writhing and jerking even through the translucent wall. "Good afternoon, First Lieutenant," Clark said into an intercom box dangling by a cable from the ceiling. "I trust you've completed your initial assessment." He let go of the talk button and looked at Vikram. "They evacuated the entire town? That's madness." Vikram opened his mouth to respond but Sanchez's voice grated out of the speaker first.

"Sir, no, sir." Sanchez put down the aural thermometer she'd been holding and came closer to the wall so he could see her better. She snapped to attention and they exchanged salutes. "I have not completed my assessment because I was unable to sedate the patient. Sir, your orders clearly stated that no biopsies or invasive procedures were to be performed on a non-anesthetized individual."

Clark nodded silently. He wanted the infected patients to be as comfortable as possible. In their confused state they could hardly agree to medical examination but at least he could manage their pain. "Perhaps you'd care to elaborate, Sanchez," Clark suggested, gritting his teeth.

"Sir, I applied a narcotic sedative, namely morphine, in increasing doses at four hour intervals. I continued to up the dosage well past the safe human level. No matter how much I injected into him however his behavior and affect remained unchanged. A few minutes ago I applied what should be an instantly lethal dosage and as you can see the patient remains fully motile. I'll reiterate: that should have killed him. It didn't."

Clark tried to thrust his free hand into his pocket so he could reorganize the small change there. That usually helped him keep his cool. Unfortunately he'd left his coins with his uniform back at the entrance to the Bag. "Do you have an explanation for that?"

"I do, sir. The patient is already dead."

Clark said nothing and eventually she continued.

"The patient demonstrates no vital signs at all. No respiration, no pulse. I can't measure his blood oxygen levels because from what I can tell his blood has coagulated and dried up in his veins. He's dead, by pretty much any medical or legal definition I can think of. What we have here is not a human being anymore, but a zom—"

Clark stabbed the talk button on the intercom. "That will be enough."

"Sir, with all due respect, we are no longer dealing with an out-break of a traditional virus. A virus can't survive in dead tissue! We need to completely rethink our strategies and—"

Vikram leaned in close to the intercom. "You are under my direct command, Doctor, and I will not have this kind of insubordina-tion! I am shocked and appalled that you would talk back to—"

"He's dead! He's not faking it! Sir, I've run everything short of an MRI on this man and—"

Clark cleared his throat. The others fell silent and waited while he composed his thoughts. The only sound in the Bag was the crinkling rustle of mylar stirring in a ventilated breeze. He ran a hand across his forehead and then spoke in a soft, low voice he reserved for quieting panicked underlings on the battlefield. He stared hard at Sanchez, trying to find her eyes through all the plas-tic. "Soldier. What is your official report going to say? Have you thought about that?"

"Sir," Sanchez began, but Clark merely held up a hand for patience.

"Is it going to say you spent the last thirty-six hours trying to sedate a man who was already dead?"

Burning defiance erupted behind her eyes. It stayed there and didn't reach her voice. She was, after all, a soldier. She knew when she was receiving an order. "Sir, no, sir. It will not."

THIS AREA UNDER QUARANTINE—Trespassers will be subject to detainment and decontamination [Signage posted in Brentwood, CA, 3/30/05]

In the irrigated fields outside of Lost Hills they saw people moving sluggishly through the crops. Never more than one or two at a time, all of them headed toward town. None of them looked up at the passing car.

Shar stirred restlessly in Nilla's arms. The sight of the undead girl being beaten to death had really shaken her. "They're going to come for me next," she had kept sobbing, though Charles and Nilla had both pointed out there was no reason to think such a thing. Nilla had a very good reason to be frightened for her own well being but she kept it to herself.

After a few minutes of sheer hysteria and Charles constantly telling her to shut up Shar had demanded that he stop the car right in the middle of the road. There was no traffic. She had come around to the back of the car and crawled in with Nilla, who could hardly refuse to put her arms around the frightened girl.

"I need to call my mom," she said at one point. Sitting up in the seat she stared out the window at a man wearing nothing but a baggy T-shirt. He was wandering through a stand of avocado trees, the branches smacking him in the face but he paid no attention. "Do you think—is he one of them?" Shar asked.

"Holmes is just loaded, Shar," Charles chortled over the back seat. "He's all crunked up, you know what I'm saying?"

"I need to go home now, Charles," Shar said so quietly he couldn't have heard her. The windows of the little Toyota rattled whenever he took the car over forty miles per hour and he refused to turn down the radio so any conversation between the three of them had to be shouted. Nilla opened her mouth but Shar shook her head in negation. "No. No, I'm just practicing. I could make him take me home if I really wanted. Charles wanted to go to Hollywood, but I talked him out of it," Shar said, looking up into Nilla's face.

The girl was scared shitless and a little traumatized. Nilla wondered how she would react if she learned that she was seeking comfort in the embrace of a dead woman. Best not to find out. "Yeah?" Nilla asked, her voice a soft purr. Maybe she had been a nurturing person in her life or maybe it was just natural instinct but she knew what it took to comfort the girl. She brushed Shar's hair away from her forehead. Hunger stabbed her in the stomach and told her it was time to eat but she sucked in her belly and refused to entertain the notion. "Why did he want to go there?"

"He thought we could find some movie star, or maybe a singer, and save them from the sick people and then they would be so grateful they would let us stay with them and we wouldn't have to worry about money."

Nilla nodded as if this made perfect sense. "But then you heard on the radio that you should stay away from Los Angeles."

Shar nodded and rubbed anxiously at her nose. "I think maybe I should sit up now. Up front, I mean." She stared deep into Nilla's eyes and shot her a microsecond smile. "Thanks," she said. "I got so scared."

"It happens."

Charles pulled over on the side of the road so Shar could get back in the passenger's seat. As she was climbing out of the car the girl brought her face close to Nilla's ear. Nilla closed her eyes to better hear what Shar might say.

"Don't hate me, okay? But you really need some deodorant."

They didn't stop for Bakersfield, though Shar and Charles argued about whether they should until long after they'd passed through the sprawling downtown. Charles got them onto Route 58 after only a few tries and before they knew it they were in the middle of farmland again. Nilla breathed a sigh of relief. She really didn't want to stop anywhere populated again but even so Bakersfield looked untouched by the dead. Maybe it was just a local phenomenon.

Maybe if she got far enough east she would be safe. Was that what her mysterious benefactor on the hill was trying to tell her?

About ten miles past the last houses of the city they started seeing cars coming from the other direction, headed west. A station wagon flashed its lights as it sped by them and Charles looked pensive. "Yeah, fuck you too, grandma," he said, and chewed on the hair of his lower lip. When they started to see exit signs for Tehachapi it happened again, this time with a Mazda Miata. A third car honked its horn at them repeatedly.

Nilla stared through the windshield and saw the driver emphatically shaking her head and waving a hand to tell them to stop. "Charles, maybe we should slow down," Nilla suggested.

"Yeah, and maybe you should just sit there and not talk to me right now," he said, turning in his seat, the seat belt tugging at the skin of his neck. She had a momentary pang of desire—she really wanted to put her teeth in that throat of his—but she fought it down. "I'm kind of busy, and you wouldn't like me when I'm angry, okay, ho?"

Nilla crossed her arms and looked away.

They started to see more traffic heading east and Charles had to slow down anyway to match the prevailing speed. The lanes heading west grew packed and drew to a standstill. Charles switched off the radio and squinted at the road.

Many of the cars they passed honked their horns now and occasionally someone would lean out their window to shout at them. Nilla couldn't understand what they were saying—they were moving too fast. She found a map in the pocket of the seat in front of her and pulled it out. She tried to make sense of its colors and symbols. Just east of Tehachapi brown blotches surrounded the road on either side. She studied the tiny print.

Edwards Air Force Base. China Lake Naval Weapons Center. Fort Irwin Military Reserve. Twenty-nine Palms Marine Corps Base. It looked like the Armed Forces owned all the land between them and Nevada. She remembered the man in the Army uniform, the one who had almost presided over her execution.

"Charles, listen to me—we have to get off this road!" she shouted. The boy sneered and put up a fist as if he would punch her from the front seat. Clearly he was threatening her but she was far more worried about falling afoul of the Army. "Charles! There's a road-block, that's what's happening. Do you really want the Marines to ask you why you're running away from home?"

He started to grumble again but Shar sat up straight in her seat and looked right at him. It stopped his growling, anyway. The girl put a hand on his arm and stroked it gently. "They'll split us up. They'll find out I'm underage."

He lowered his head and refused to look away from the road. Nilla didn't have time to argue anymore. "There's a road—Route 14. We can turn off at a town called Mojave." It wasn't a great solution—it would take them along the edge of China Lake—but it would get them out of immediate danger.

Charles still refused to respond and she had to content herself with staring at the back of his head and imagining what would happen if the Army found her. They wouldn't fall for her trick again, would they? Even if they did there was no way Charles and Shar would let her stay in their car once they knew her secret.

Come on, Charles, she thought. *Come on.*

The big green signs for the exits at Mojave came up on the side of the road and Nilla had never wanted anything so much in her life. At least as far as she could remember.

It is recommended that travelers arrive at the airport four hours in advance of departure time to complete the required medical examinations before boarding. [FlyDenver.com "Tips for Travelers" page, updated 3/31/05]

A star had fallen to earth and gotten lodged there, still burning bright.

Its silver radiance illuminated the ridge, sending out long streamers of brilliance that made shadows on the facing slopes, shadows like the clouds made during the day, impossibly big, always moving. Like ocean waves of light and darkness washing across the spine of rocks and trees at the top of the world.

He headed toward it, drawn by it—physically pulled in. Death had not been kind to his eyes but he could make out more details as he got closer. There were buildings on the ridge, low concrete blocks. There were other shapes there as well, like titanic lizards eroded by rain and wind until their shapes were soft and smooth. They occluded the light, their silhouettes thrown across him, over him.

Others—other dead people—had gathered in the scree below the ridge. They stood apart from one another on ground crawling with lichens and dwarf pine trees that throbbed with energy but they weren't trying to devour that life. They stood motionless, their faces tilted upwards to catch the sleeting luminosity of the fallen star. As he came among them they made no sign of noticing him. They were too busy studying the endlessly changing glow. Feeding on it. One of its beams touched Dick and though he was mentally incapable of surprise anymore his body could still feel the shock. It felt like something had been torn from him, burnt out of him perhaps. The hunger was gone. When that light reached him it drove the hunger away. It fed him a constant, steady stream of energy, the energy he needed to continue his existence. More than enough.

It was like the glow of the woman in the car, like the golden aura of human life. Except . . . no. Better to say that the human aura was like the light of the fallen star. The radiation that shot through him was altogether more pure and more real. It nurtured him, warmed him. He wanted to run up the slope and jump inside of that light. Surrender to it—become one with it.

As he got closer though, the warmth he felt turned to heat. Real heat. He could feel it singing him, scorching every cell in his body. He took a step closer and tasted smoke at the back of his throat. He could see dark shapes ahead of him. Charred, burnt-out corpses, lumps of blackened meat in tattered remnants of clothing. He understood, in a wordless, primal way. The very thing that nourished him could consume him if he got too close. He was in a gray zone, a realm between comfort and instant annihilation and staying there meant pain.

No matter. He stepped backwards. It was enough to stand a respectable distance away and let the fallen star comfort him. It was enough to rest. To rest and watch the light show. It was all he ever wanted, the most beautiful thing he had ever seen in life or in death.

He was so absorbed in the coruscating patterns of the light, transfixed like an acid freak staring into the depths of a lava lamp that he barely noticed when a yellow rectangle appeared up in the buildings above the star. It was a door opening, letting out human noise and movement. A man, a living man, appeared there with a microphone in his hand. Dick bared his teeth by instinct but he felt no real need to attack the man. The light of the fallen star had given him that, a kind of serenity.

"Good evening," he told them, his voice amplified by loud-speakers strung on poles in the circle of statuary reptiles. Some of the gathered dead, like Dick, looked up. Most did not. "I see some new . . . new faces tonight. Welcome. I wish there was more that I could do for you. I truly do. You'll never know how sorry . . ."

The voice broke off in a choking noise. A sob. The man went back inside his house. Music played over the loudspeakers, light Classical music—Mozart, although Dick could not have made that distinction. The music meant nothing to him. He already had everything he wanted.

The man came back the next night. Every night. The music changed. The pleas for forgiveness didn't. Dick grew irritated with the man for a while. Eventually he learned to ignore him, to not even look up when the lights went on up there.

It was a kind of perfect existence. He felt warm and sated. Dick could have stayed there forever.

In a dawn time without time, long after the music had finished, Dick stood rock still where he'd stopped the night before though dew ran down his face and his muscles were stiff and sore. None of it bothered him. The rising sun couldn't overpower the rays of life and happiness that shot through him. Yet something had changed, something simple, easy to miss. He studied the fallen star to try to detect what it might be and felt the star looking back at him.

It was more than aware of him. It was actively looking at him. It had a consciousness and even a kind of voice, though its words were made of light. Dick had been unable to understand the living man's address the night before but these words made perfect sense to him. In time the consciousness of the star took shape, a certain fulgent form that conveyed the sense of a human body while being made entirely of rays of light. It reached out fingers that stretched across the slope and brushed the ruins of Dick's shoulders.

Yes, it thought, and Dick heard it sigh. There were others, it told him. Others that were closer or perhaps better equipped to perform the task (what task? It was a question, and Dick was beyond questions). Yet Dick possessed a certain quality of appearance. A supreme ugliness, a horror of aspect. His ruined body could inspire fear, much more fear than any whole corpse.

Dick could hardly be offended by the thought. He was more honored than anything else, honored to be picked by this perfect form at the heart of the fallen star. In the middle of the Source.

The form said it could use him. It told him to leave the valley of the star. Dick lacked the will to refuse the request and anyway the form wasn't asking. He would do its will. Even the concept of choice was beyond him.

Some part of him, some deep part felt regret and longing but it didn't stop him from turning his back on the beautiful healing radiance. Without a word, without complaint, he turned and left the ridge and headed down into the valleys below.

Bottled water will be available free of charge. You are also entitled to pick up pre-cooked foods at your local grocery store. Menus and options will be chosen or approved by your local FEMA representative. Please let us know about any dietary restrictions. [FEMA Supplemental Broadcast for Relocated Individuals, 3/31/05]

"Great fucking plan, Nilla." Charles grabbed the map out of her hands. One corner ripped off in her grasp. "Look, now it's torn. This is so whack!"

Nilla looked forward through the windshield. The road they'd been following—one lane, only partially paved—ended in a T intersection. There were no street signs or any kind of indication of where they were. The level cultivated land around Bakersfield had given way as they traveled north to trees and mountains and the roads had become sparser. They hadn't seen a human being or a car for half an hour and now, officially, they were lost.

East, Nilla thought. They should head east. Except that she couldn't see anything through all the trees. Sparse scrub pines and towering aspens crowded together on both sides of the road. East. Except they had turned around so many times and switched roads so often she had no idea which compass direction she was facing, much less which way was east. She felt something stir in her belly. Hunger, yes, of course it was hunger, it was always hunger. But the familiar pull was drawing her in a particular direction. It was telling her to go left.

Nilla had taken advice before from a naked man she had probably just hallucinated. A message from her stomach was just as good. "That way," she said. One of the few compensations of having no memory whatsoever was that you couldn't remember how many times your gut feelings had steered you wrong. "Seriously. That way."

No one will be allowed into or out of the quarantine area without official written permission. Violators will face criminal charges and possible lethal force for non-compliance. [FEMA Travel Advisory for Las Vegas, NV and Salt Lake City, UT, 3/31/05]

Three hours and change in an Airbus from DIA to Ronald Reagan National on an empty flight, just Bannerman Clark and a pair of exhausted Air Marshals who took one look at him and started ordering drinks. When was a flight to D.C. ever empty? He realized that he hadn't been watching much CNN since the incident began but he'd had no idea people were scared enough to stay off of planes.

At least the quiet flight gave Bannerman Clark some time for the paperwork that had been piling up since his interrupted dinner at the Brown Palace. He couldn't concentrate, though, and barely made it through a single Incident Account Report before he had to give up and snap shut his laptop. In the vibrating, rumbling cabin of the airplane he couldn't seem to shut off his brain and things kept occurring to him, things he'd forgotten, phone calls he needed to make, to-do lists he needed to write. Through it all one image never left his mind's eye. The girl's face kept jumping out at him, the look of terror in her eyes. The stuff that dripped from her nose. The fact that she could talk. She had to mean something. She was less affected by the pathogen than any other victim he'd seen or heard about. Did she possess some natural immunity? Or maybe she'd been infected with a different strain of the virus or bacterium or whatever it was.

He'd been putting together a requisition for some troops to go looking for her. He couldn't just grab men and women out of their barracks willy-nilly, even a Rapid Assessment and Initial Deployment officer had to formally request personnel from their commanding officer. He had a line on some really promising folks, veterans from Iraq who'd been pulling weekend warrior duty ever since they got back and should be rested and ready for a new adrenaline rush. Then Vikram had come in to break the news. He was wanted for a breakfast interview in Washington with a DoD Civilian.

It was all over. Initial Deployment was his Military Occupational Specialty, his MOS, and the initial deployment was complete. His role in the crisis was finished. He didn't resent it, really. There were other people, people far more qualified in dealing with widespread medical emergencies waiting to take his place. He just wasn't sure what he was going to do next. The world was on fire and he was holding a bucket full of water and he didn't know where to throw it.

When he touched down at D.C., a limo was waiting to take him right to an office building in Foggy Bottom. He was a little surprised he wasn't going to be debriefed in the Pentagon but he had a life-time of not questioning orders to quell his unease. After passing through a metal detector and an inspection by a nosy dog and a man in a uniform shirt that simply read CANINE SUPPORT he was allowed inside. Moments later he was alone again in a fourth floor office of lacquered cherry wood and office chairs wrapped in plas-tic. A stack of multi-line telephone units with no handsets had been shoved under the conference table. At the head of said table stood a chilled bottle of water and a cellophane-wrapped box of Marshmallow Peeps. Clark knew they weren't for him. He decided not to sit down and instead stood by the window, peering through the Venetian blinds as businessmen in dark suits or dress casual jeans rolled toward their various offices like Pachinko balls falling into their appropriate holes.

"Bannerman. Great name."

The man in the doorway had the sort of heavy body shape and steel-blue freshly scraped jaw of a desk officer with the CIA but he wore the dark suit, red tie, and American flag pin of someone who regularly appeared at press conferences. An under-secretary, surely, one of the Department of Defense's leading lights but nobody Clark would be expected to recognize on sight. He didn't offer his name. He sat down in one of the wrapped chairs, not bothering to remove the plastic, and cracked open his bottle of water. "Look at you. Veteran of multiple wars. Well decorated and commended. Thirty-five years on service and you're still just a captain. I think we both know why."

Clark moved his cover from one hand to another. He didn't care for the civilian's easy familiarity. "I've never questioned my lot in life. I simply serve at the pleasure of my governor."

"You never married, that's why. The Army likes to promote married men. It means they're not gay. Sit down, will you? You're annoying me with your conspicuous body language." The civilian tore open his box of marshmallow treats and stuffed one into his mouth. "My big weakness," he intimated when he'd swallowed the yellow goo. "It's less than a week since Easter, right? Anyway, I don't care if you were screwing Freddy Mercury in the seventies. I don't care if you dig sheep. Sit down, I said."

Clark did as he was told.

"They're in Chicago now, did you know that? We're keeping a lid on it but it's bad there, very, very, very bad." The civilian inhaled a long, slow breath and then laid down the law. He looked almost apologetic. "Look, you're off the case, you know that. FEMA is taking over in California. We need the flexibility and the ability to make snap decisions out there you only get with civilian agencies. The Army's great for doing the same thing a hundred times over and getting it right every time. This time, though, we need some new ideas. Don't get me wrong, you did a great job and nobody questions your loyalty but this, this . . . thing. This is serious."

"FEMA gets California, I understood that much. What about Colorado? That's the state I'm sworn to protect."

"Yeah, the Adjutant General of the COARNG gets to keep Colorado, whoop-dee-doo. He's got full-bird Colonels to put on that and you're not on the short list. But who cares about Colorado? I don't know if you've heard this or not but these dead fuckers are taking over *Los Angeles*. I care about Los Angeles. The president cares about Los Angeles. That makes Los Angeles important. Am I right?"

"No." Clark placed his hat squarely on the table and turned it so the brim was facing the civilian.

"I beg your pardon?"

"No, you're not entirely right. You've fallen for what I hope will very soon be classified as an urban legend. The infected are not dead. They've undergone some kind of basal metabolic change, something that depresses their vital signs but they're not dead. I have a team from Fort Detrick looking into it right now. If I'm being reassigned I just wanted to get that fact on the record." He began to stand up.

"Sit down. You're off the case, yes." The civilian stood up instead. He peeled one of his Peeps away from its fellows and held it in his hairy hand as if he were cradling an actual baby chicken. "But you're not done. I like you, Bannerman. I like your first name, I think it's funny, and I like people with funny names." He walked over to stand behind Clark and slowly, deliberately, placed his yellow candy on top of Clark's cover. "I also think you're a wonk and the President loves wonks. You were the first responder, the early adapter on this mess. I want you to be my go-to guy."

Clark inhaled slowly and folded his hands in his lap. "In what capacity?" he asked.

"As my wonk, I just said that. I don't care what you're called. The president doesn't care what you're called. You can make up your own MOS for this. You can have what you need—I'll rubber stamp anything because I know you, I've read your dossier so many times I know you would die, physically die before you would requisition a Bic pen that wasn't job-vital. What do you say, Bannerman? Are you my wonk or are you my wonk?"

It would mean reporting to this civilian. It meant operating as a free agent, without standing orders—something unthinkable to a career soldier like Clark. It also meant he would have carte blanche to find the girl and maybe bring resolution to the biggest public health crisis since the influenza of 1918.

Clark reached forward and picked up the yellow sugar bomb sitting on his cover. Without hesitation he put it on his tongue as if he were taking communion and bit down. The answer was yes.

Infectuated individuals are known to be of a highly dangerous nature. Under no circumstances should you, as civilians, attempt to subdue or take them out. I mean, come on. The police are trained for this. Let's let them do your job. [Televised speech delivered by the president of the United States, 3/31/05]

Kirsty Lang on the BBC World News channel, looking grave while a xylophone played a rising crescendo: "Growing fears in America tonight as the Epidemic spreads to the Pacific Northwest. Our Reginald Forless is in Spokane tonight where city officials and law enforce—"

A reporter with his head down in front of a line of cars, their headlights washing out his features as they passed in slow motion: "—scene of chaos behind me, this small town where nobody ever went anywhere has been mobilized tonight. Evacuees are heading south, toward San Diego, and—"

Two balding men faced each other in oversized chairs, their ties undone: "—can't just disregard what the Army is saying, they have the people and the equipment to—"

"Bullshit! That thing we just saw was dead!"

Emeril Lagasse came running down a set of stairs, his fists pumping in the air, a towel over the shoulder of his chef's whites. "Tonight we're talking tenderloin, we're talking beef bourguignon, and look at this cabbage, huh? Look at it! I'm makin' a slaw!"

Charles sprawled across the bed, with his shirt off, one foot waving back and forth in an agitated rhythm. "Nothing fucking on," he moaned, but he didn't switch off the television. "How do you get the porn and shit? You know what I'm saying?"

In a corner Shar squatted against the wall and held one hand over her ear. The other held the handset of a princess phone. "Mom? I can't get through to Uncle Phil. Well how many times have you tried? Me? I'm safe, I'm in some kind of motel—"

"Don't you fucking tell her where we are!" Charles shouted. His skinny arms raised like sticks to bat at her but he didn't sit up.

Nilla sniffed one of her armpits and winced at the stale smell there. Not body odor, necessarily. Something fouler. "I'm going next door," she said. She stepped out into a night full of bugs that batted suicidally against the one light over the motel's parking lot. Charles' Toyota was the only car parked there—the owners must have deserted the place and turned on the NO VACANCY sign on their way out. If they hadn't been so lost Nilla and the kids would have passed right by it.

Luckily the owners had forgotten to lock the doors when they left.

The whole place was wide open for their use. In the peace and quiet of an empty room Nilla sat down on the bed with its over-starched coverlet and stared at the useless telephone, wishing she had someone to call. There was no point in dwelling on that, she decided, and pulled the baby tee off over her head. The sleeves stank and she wondered if she could rinse it out in the sink with shampoo. She looked down, checking her skin, and noticed a green discoloration on her abdomen, right above her tattoo. It must be dye from the cheap shirt, she thought, even though it was the wrong color. She got up and went into the bathroom and turned on the shower. She stepped out of her baggy pants and saw that the discoloration was on her crotch, too. With a handful of soap she tried to scrub it off but it wouldn't budge. She moved into the shower and tried again with the motel's washcloth. Nothing.

There was a fog-resistant shaving mirror mounted in the shower and she studied her face. The bruising under her eyes had spread until she looked like a raccoon or a goth wearing too much kohl. She had a bad pimple on her cheek but it wasn't ready to pop. She wondered if she should shave her legs and realized that the hair there had stopped growing. That couldn't be a good sign.

She was still checking herself out when she heard the door of her room open and Charles came trooping in. He had a can of soda in either hand. "Hey," he said, "Shar thought you might want some—"

He stopped in mid-thought. His face opened up in a kind of half smile that made him look very, very stupid. He was staring at her but not in the malevolent way the people of Lost Hills had stared at her.

She looked down and saw that she had come out of the shower to greet him but she had forgotten to put her clothes back on. Water dripped from her elbows and her chin and splashed darkly on the ivory shag of the carpet.

What the hell? Had she forgotten all about modesty when she forgot her name? Or was her brain just breaking down, was she not making the necessary connections?

She suddenly felt very alone and very afraid.

"I guess I should . . ." he grinned, "I mean Shar wouldn't . . ."

He was stalling. He wanted something. He wanted her and that meant everything. It meant she was still whole and healthy and desirable. It meant he didn't see a monster when he looked at her but a woman, a human being full of vibrant life. She took a step closer and grabbed his hand. She couldn't believe what she was doing but she needed it so much.

She guided his hand to her breast and let him cup it. He immediately tweaked her nipple in a way she normally would have found more irritating than arousing but it just didn't matter. He was human and male and if he reacted to her she could be normal again.

He swallowed hard and moved closer to her, as if unsure of what to do next. Was he a virgin? Nilla was pretty sure she wasn't. She would use every whorish trick she could think of if she could just have this simple reassurance. She reached across the space between them and brushed the backs of her fingers across the front of his jeans.

Nothing. She felt nothing down there—no hardness at all. He looked down at her breast like someone who couldn't understand what he was seeing. "So cold," he said, his voice small and afraid.

She winced backward and it was the signal he'd been waiting for. He rushed out of the room, his sodas rolling across the floor where he'd dropped them. Nilla went to the door and shut it, locked it tight and fastened the chain.

She wanted to break down, to cry, but that was a human response and her body refused to let her have even that. She wanted to cut herself to pieces but there was nothing sharp at hand. She looked around the objects of the room—bed, TV, lamp, nightstand, Gideon bible—and none of them made sense, they'd been torn out of context and left hanging in a meaningless space. It was too much.

She undid all the locks on the door and ran out into the night, down the stairs and across the parking lot. The dark trees there accepted her without a murmur.

PLEASE BE ADVISED: Foreign nationals will not be allowed into the United States unless they carry up-to-date and authorized medical papers. Otherwise you are subject to incarceration! [Signage posted at Customs, John F. Kennedy International Airport, 4/1/05]

"This civilian knows talent when he sees it, yes, sir, that is what is happening," Vikram said, clutching a nylon handloop as the Black-hawk lifted up and banked away from the prison.

"He's hedging a bet." Back to California. Bannerman Clark hated flying. Washington to Denver on another empty airbus. Switch to a Blackhawk helicopter to Florence to pick up Vikram—now officially attached to Clark's nascent Action Team—and take the two of them back to DIA. Then a military transport, probably an old DC-10 judging by Clark's recent luck, then another helicopter to spirit them off to a place called Kern County where someone might possibly have seen the blonde girl, according to a tip phoned in on the APB.

It didn't matter. None of the wasted time or the jet lag or the bad food or the recirculated air mattered. "I looked him up in Nexis when I got airborne out of DCA. He's an up-and-comer, playing at being a young Turk at the tender age of fifty-two. He's angling for a Cabinet post. He wouldn't meet with me in the Pentagon—I didn't ask why but I can guess. He wants to keep me on the books but off the charts."

"He has you for his wild card. This man, he is playing games while the house is on fire?"

Clark laid one finger alongside his nose. Vikram had got it in one. "Don't forget we're talking about DoD civilians here. Arm-chair generals." He need say no more. For the last thirty years Vikram and Clark had been touring the world at the whim of men with Big Ideas and Foolproof Plans. Soldiers and even entire countries were just tokens on a game board when you looked down on them from those lofty heights.

"I'm his wonk, he calls me. His idea man. Somebody with experience in a brand new way of making war. After September Eleventh people like him wrote their own ticket because while the Old Guard were sputtering and pointing fingers at each other, trying to place the blame, the neocon philosophers were ready for the new paradigm. He hopes to do the same here."

"He is making political capital out of this horror."

Clark sighed and lifted both hands. 'Twas ever thus. "I can't help but thinking there's more to this than I get, but then I never understood politics. This guy most certainly does. If we can find this girl and if she is what I think she is this man will be appointing Cabinet posts, not filling one."

"Unless we are eaten, all of us, before then."

"Yes, that would spoil his gambit." Clark tried to laugh and found he couldn't.

CALIFORNIA, INFECTIOUS DISEASE OUTBREAK: This is a notification of the Presidential declaration of a major disaster for the State of California (FEMA-1899-DR), dated April First, 2005, and related determinations. [FEMA/DHS Federal Register Notice, 4/1/05]

Under a rising sun that looked like a ruddy impostor now a freight train full of emergency medical supplies shouldered its way westward through raw cuts in the mountain side, its rusted cars rattling and swaying on the tracks as it rattled through switchbacks, its horn a plaintive subsonic tone that seemed to rise up out of the ground like vapor in the heat of day.

It had to slow down to a bare crawl as it crested a ridge. Dick was waiting on a spur of rock just above. Behind him the Source called to him with its infinite love but he didn't look back. He was on a mission he could not refuse, a mission to faraway places he could not dream of. At just the right moment the voice in his head called *Now* and he leapt, spinning off his feet into space to come crashing down with a clatter on the roof of a boxcar. He dug in with his feet the best he could, unable to literally hold on. The vibration of the rumbling train made his teeth hurt but he was incapable of complaining.

He was a soldier now. He had his orders.

"No, I don't think people should panic. What kind of question is that? Look, just be ready to move. We've already had some evacuations. I think it's fair to say that you should expect more." [San Francisco Chief of Police Heather J. Fong at press conference, 4/1/05]

Nilla wandered through a landscape the colors of bleached bone. The rock beneath her feet looked white, whiter than her pale skin. The aspens and sequoias of the forest behind her had given up on the stony ground. From horizon to horizon all she could see were bristlecone pines, leafless, twisted things that looked undead by starlight. Their branches wrapped around their trunks like hurt people hugging themselves for comfort or speared upward in accusation at the frozen sky. Some were dead outright, cracked and splintered. They didn't rot, it seemed, so much as erode.

She was cold. She'd been cold before and never really cared but now, naked, soaked with dew, exposed in the chilly mountain night, she felt it in her skeleton. She could feel the frost getting into her individual ribs, into the creaky joints of her kneecaps and elbows.

She wanted to go back but she didn't know what that meant. Charles would be huddling with Shar in their room, wouldn't they? Terrified of her.

Charles had to know. He must have suspected before and now he knew.

The smell on her was the stink of death. The discoloration on her abdomen was the first sign of putrefaction. Her body and her mind were breaking down and there was nothing she could do about it, nothing anybody could do about it and why would they, anyway? She was dead, a corpse! She *should* be rotting away. Her flesh would sag and fall off in gobbets, her skin would slough off in greasy strips. Her face would melt away until her bare skull grinned out at the world—would she feel better then?

A prickling of the skin behind her ears made her look up. Something—something living nearby. She would turn her face from it, flee it, whatever it might be. It was big. She closed her eyes and saw it, not a hundred yards away. Two, maybe three times the size of her, its energy brighter than any living energy she'd seen.

She had to get closer. Damn it—the hunger in her had become a solid mass, a tumor in her stomach that had control of her feet. She wanted to run away, to hide herself but the hunger had other plans. She got closer.

Her nose picked up the smell of death right away. It was like her own smell but sharper. Her foot blared with pain as she tripped on something. Bending down she felt metal and wood. A gun, a shotgun. She looked up and saw a human body with no head dangling from the colorless branches of a bristlecone. Its lower extremities were missing and its life, its energy was dull and motionless. It was just dead meat. The corpse might be the owner of the motel, maybe, who had come out all this way to kill himself. She had no way of knowing for sure.

Something massive shifted behind her and she turned as fast as she could. The energy she'd seen, the bright source was right there. It came off of a black bear weighing maybe three hundred pounds. A female, old and grizzled, her pitch black fur ending in white tips that glistened with the reflected light of stars. The bear made no sound—she didn't growl.

She was beautiful. She stood on her hind legs, her eyes looking directly into Nilla's. There was something there. Understanding? Recognition? Impossible. Nilla was undead and unnatural while this gorgeous animal seemed carved out of the very earth she stood on. Was this some kind of spiritual awakening, Nilla wondered, was she meeting her spirit animal? Maybe this was the moment when everything would make sense.

The bear swiped one paw across Nilla's stomach, the claws digging great bloodless gouges through her midriff, slicing up her tattoo. The blow had enough force behind it to outright kill a full-grown deer. It knocked Nilla off her feet and sent her falling into the body in the tree. Looking up at the corpse Nilla finally understood. The bear had been having a midnight snack—breakfast after a long winter's hibernation. Nilla had just gotten in between the bear and her meal.

Relocation camps are now open at Cathedral City, Winterwarm and Oceanside. A map to these facilities is on the back of this handout. When entering a camp you may bring with you: personal (PRESCRIPTION) medication, TWO changes of clothing and ONE small toilet kit. All weapons, illegal items and communication/recording devices (laptop computers, PDAs, CELL PHONES) will be confiscated. [Flyer handed out at bus and train stations in Los Angeles, emphasis as per original, 4/1/05]

The bear didn't growl or roar or make any sound at all as she advanced. Her fur shivered in the breeze and her eyes glowed with fire as she pressed her snout wetly against Nilla's leg. She had to be seven feet long and her legs were all muscle. Hot breath jetted up Nilla's thigh and she cringed.

The bear looked up at Nilla and panted for a second. She stepped closer, her mass making the ground shake and Nilla cried out as she rolled away. Slowly, keeping her hands in plain view she got back to her feet. If she just walked away, backward so the bear wouldn't think she was running, well then, surely the bear would leave her alone. Right? The bear didn't want to eat her. She was undead—rotting flesh, full of toxins.

Nilla glanced at the corpse hanging from the tree. Oh. Bears must eat carrion, she decided.

It wasn't food the bear was after, though, she could see it in the animal's eyes. The bear knew what she was. It was the same look she'd seen in Lost Hills—the same look she'd gotten from Charles less than an hour earlier. The bear was intelligent enough to recognize an abomination.

Nilla turned and tried to run, her bare feet slapping on the slick rock, her arms pistoning as she—

The bear tore past her at a gallop, not even exerting herself. She rolled one shoulder and slammed into Nilla, sending her sprawling down a slope of loose shale. The pain was intense as she bounced from one sharp rock to another, her skin bruising and tearing as she rolled. When she finally stopped she could only curl around herself, her body screaming.

The bear came lumbering down the hill, a black shape that obscured half the sky, headed right for her.

No, she thought, *she didn't want to . . . to die like this, not alone in the dead wilderness. No.*

No.

The bear stopped not three feet away from her and sniffed the air. She lifted her head and opened her mouth, then moved in, her paws smacking the rock. She would have stepped on Nilla if Nilla had still been there.

Nilla was invisible. The cold bit her with renewed force but the pain melted away. She looked down at her hands with eyes closed and saw nothing—no dark energy, just nothing. She stared at the bear and knew the animal couldn't sense her at all. Whatever power Nilla possessed, whatever strange ability, it allowed her to cloud all the senses of the bear just as she had clouded the eyes and ears of the SWAT troopers back at the hospital. She had become invisible. As far as the bear was concerned Nilla had vanished in thin air.

She was momentarily safe. The danger wasn't over, though. Nilla had to end this or eventually she would run out of strength and become visible again—she had a span of time measured in seconds, maybe—and then the bear would be on her with rending claws and vicious teeth. Nilla had to defend herself if she wanted to walk away.

She reached over and grabbed a handful of loose flesh at the back of the bear's neck and squeezed through the fur, squeezed as hard as her fingers allowed, digging her nails into the pliant skin beneath. The bear made a noise, a titanic, warbling yell that almost sounded like human language.

Nilla's teeth entered the bear's neck. She could see the artery throbbing there. She could smell the blood. When she broke the loose skin the blood coursed out and over her, a red flood to carry her away. What happened next didn't involve thinking at all. She bit and tore and gouged as the bear screamed. A chunk of meat came loose in her mouth and she swallowed it effortlessly. The skin tore open and she thrust her face deep into the bear's body, into its hidden recesses. Blood clotted and stuck in her hair. It washed across her open eyes and she didn't blink. She bit and chewed and swallowed and bit, desperate to steal the bear's energy before it ran out. The bear couldn't resist her—shocked by the suddenness and the pain of her attack it could only scream and try to run but she had it, she had it down, down for the count.

Its life flowed into her, through her. Warm as blood, rich and sweet as the bear's flesh it thrilled in every cell of her body. It felt like being on fire. It felt like being alive again—there she was, all dressed in white bopping down the street, shaking her hips in the sunshine because it felt so very good to be alive and healthy and beautiful. It was almost too much.

She fell to the ground on her knees and swayed with it for a while with her eyes closed, watching the bear's golden energy degrade. When she opened her eyes again she saw the bear looking back at her with that same expression of recognition she'd been so startled by before. Then she did a double take. Her benefactor was sitting on the bear's back as if he planned to ride off into the sunset.

"You—" Nilla looked up at the naked man. His beard looked newly-trimmed and the blue tattoos that covered his skin glowed with their own light. "Who—"

"Mael Mag Och," he said, thumping his chest. He looked down at his mount, at the expression on her face. "She knows you. She knows what it is to be *gruaim air le acras.*"

Either he was speaking in two languages at once or Nilla's hearing was shot. It didn't matter what he said, though. It was just noise when she wanted information. "What are you doing here?" she demanded.

He ignored her. Slipping down the bear's furred flank he stepped onto the slick rock and looked straight upward at the stars. "In the salmon moon, she wakes from winter and eats, and does not stop. She swallows a river of fish if she can, a *cliath bhradan*. In summer she takes moths—forty thousand every day. They are so many they fill the forest air and they fly right into her mouth."

"How do you know that?" Nilla demanded. The bear's life energy was flickering out. She felt a pang of guilt like a rippling in her stomach muscles but—wait a minute. Stomach muscles. She look down and saw the four deep gashes there where the bear hit her first.

"I know many things. I know some English, now. Before, *chan fhaigh mi lorg air na facail!*" He grinned sheepishly. "Sometimes I slip back. I know you. I understand hunger, but do not know it. I talk to dead, you see. I learn."

Nilla frowned. "What are you? I know you're not really here. I thought before you were a hallucination. You aren't though. You're real."

He ignored her. "I know what you are. You are shadow, like so many shadows. Different, though. I see all the lights, like fires in a longhouse, except . . . this one, it goes out. Covered fire. Then it comes back. Reappears. I know it is only possible it is you. Sometimes no fire is better signal than fire, yes? You are stronger, and you are smarter than the rest. I must use you."

"What are you talking about?"

"A job, for you. A *cam borraig*. Work. Purpose. You want something more than that?"

"What kind of job?" She brushed hair out of her eyes.

He smiled. "Be yourself."

She opened her mouth to speak then closed it again with a click. "Be myself."

"Be the darkness. Be a shadow. You first come east, come to me. To my body. It lie in some place that is called—New York. We talk there. No more commerce with live things, though. No more of the living. They are not allies. They are food for you."

Nilla shook her head, confused. "What? I—what?" She thought of Charles and Shar—and everyone else who had stared at her, condemned her, hated her. She didn't like where the thought headed (into her teeth) so she threw it away. "I need them. I can't drive. I don't remember how."

"Then you walk to me."

The bear died. She made no death rattle nor did she go into convulsions. She simply flickered out, the last of her vital fire gone. Darkness began to fill her up instantly. There was no transitional zone, it seemed, between life and death, or at least between life and undeath. It was a change of state, not form.

Nilla pulled her hair back in a ponytail but had nothing to tie it with so she just held it. It felt less greasy than before, strangely enough. It had more body, too. That was weird but she had no time to consider it. "Screw this. I don't need a job, guy. What I need is to stay alive. If that means consorting with living people, I don't mind that at all. You want me to walk east, with no idea where I'm going."

"Yes," he nodded happily.

"To talk to some guy who may or may not be a figment of my imagination."

"Yes."

"And for this I get a sense of purpose."

"Oh, yes," he said, and opened his arms as if to embrace her. "Let us begin." He bowed and gestured toward the east with one arm. The first pale glow of dawn was surging there. "You begin, now."

"No. Not tonight." She turned on her heel and started walking away, up the slope and back towards the motel. Whatever the future held it started with a shower. She was covered in the bear's lifeblood, thick gobbets of it coagulating on her skin. She could imagine a better time to conduct a job interview.

A wave of humanity ran through her and her stomach tensed. She felt as if she were seeing herself from outside, as if she saw with human eyes once more. A naked beast covered in gore walking under the light of the moon. The image faded quickly but it left behind a cold horror that ran through her veins, stealing a little of the good feeling she'd had.

She refused to let him see what she was feeling. She straightened up and reached for a joke. Yes. That was how she responded to fear—with humor. That hadn't been taken from her. "When we're talking about full dental and three weeks paid vacation, then you get back to me," she said.

Behind her she felt the bear stir, her energy smoky and dark. The bear was undead. Nilla had spread her curse. She didn't turn around. She didn't want to look back and see her own handiwork.

"Very well," he said to her back, "I'll give you what you want, though *is fhasa deagh ainm a chall na a chosnadh.*"

"What the hell does that mean?"

"You drive a hard bargain, but it may be worthy. Lass, you come east, to my body, and I will tell the name you lost."

He was gone when she turned to look. Only the bear remained, inching her way up the slope toward her interrupted meal. The look of recognition on her face was gone. Nilla saw nothing there but hunger.

KNOW THE SYMPTOMS OF CHOLERA! Diarrhea. Abdominal cramps. Nausea and Vomiting. Dehydration. [Hospital Bulletin published by the Centers for Disease Control, 4/1/05]

Clark heard Vikram just fine but he wished he hadn't. "I don't see enough lights down there. It's only what, 2200 hours? There should be lights on, people should be watching primetime television. Get us closer and hit that target with the main light," Clark said over the headset built into his helmet. He could barely hear himself think over the noise of the helicopter's engines.

"I am sorry, Bannerman, do you copy me?" Vikram asked from the next crewseat over. "I will repeat. Doctor First Lieutenant Desiree Sanchez is requesting that she be allowed to euthanize some of the victims, so she can dissect them. I am as discomforted as you, but I think it is the only way to—"

"I copied you the first time, and I still won't allow it." Clark peered down at the unlit streets of Lost Hills, California. He couldn't see a damned thing. The pilot wore NODs to see in the dark but the passengers had to make do with their naked eyes. The town looked deserted. The people were scared, sure, he didn't blame them. He didn't see any vehicular traffic at all, though. What was going on? There were supposed to be people down there for him to interview, people who might have seen the blonde girl as she came through. Clark had gotten a truly lucky break—traditional channels had actually turned up something useful. The Kern County Sheriff's office had flipped the girl's description on a trivial shoplifting investigation at a local convenience store. The owner had described one of the thieves as blonde, maybe forty years old with a black tribal tattoo of a sun with wavy rays on her stomach. The Sheriff had recognized the description of the tattoo from the APB. The girl had been in Kern County, maybe a day or two before at the very most. It was Clark's best lead.

"Bannerman, Captain, I must implore you! Destroying a few of the specimens may be the only way! What if by doing this she finds a cure?"

"And what if she doesn't? How do I explain to the families that their dad, their grandma, their twelve-year-old son had to have his head cut open while he was still *alive* because we thought it might help other people with the same illness, except it turned out not to help at all? Let her use the bodies those SWAT butchers at the hospital gave us."

Vikram stared at him. In the dark cabin his eyes gleamed with frustration. "Their heads were all shot to pieces. Not much use when studying a brain ailment."

Clark grimaced in distaste. He stared through the polycarbonate canopy of the Blackhawk at the square shadows of buildings below. "Okay, get the lamp on that structure," he demanded. The pilot flipped a switch.

In the overwhelming white light of the Blackhawk's main searchlight everything was the same flat gray, distinguishable only by ultra-black shadows blasted away by the lamp. The infected swarmed across the broken windows of a feed store like enormous maggots, their faces slack as their twisted hands reached upward to try to snag the helicopter.

One of them held a broken piece of bone. He threw it hard and it bounced off the metal skin of the helicopter with a resonating clang.

Breath puffed out of Bannerman's lungs. Not in surprise, not anymore, no, this was just nervous exhaustion. *Jesus*, he thought. Another one. Another town overrun. That made six in California, three each in Utah, Wyoming, and Texas, twelve in Colorado. More of them, certainly, that he didn't even know about yet. The infected had taken over the streets of Lost Hills. "Did we receive any kind of distress call from this place before it went down?"

The pilot answered on the helmet circuit. "Negative, sir. These little farm places, they're full of illegals. Probably more afraid of *la Migra* than they are of the infected. Do you want me to initiate a search pattern of maneuvers and look for survivors, sir?"

"Yes," Bannerman Clark said, his fingers working nervously at the cap in his hands. He found a loose thread and started to pull. "Yes, I do."

"You've got dead—or infected, or whatever— people wandering into streams and reservoirs and rotting there. You've got healthy people being shuttled around like livestock to camps where they don't even have basic health services. We've got sanitation breaking down all over the west and with that comes cholera, with that comes typhoid, and giardia on a scale you can't imagine. In Arizona, in New Mexico dirty water is going to

kill us faster than these cannibals." [The Surgeon General in a briefing for NIH Field Agents, 4/2/05]

Dick did not know why he'd been brought to this zone of naked blood-red rock. The sun was intense. It dried him, leached the moisture out of his most hidden orifices. He chafed and blistered and the skin of his thighs wore away in red patches but he didn't stop. The dead don't stop for pain.

The voice in his head that was no voice knew what needed to be done. Dick did not question his instructions. He marched with his two-step gait—bare foot, then the boot, bare foot, then the boot— and devoured the miles beneath him.

Dick lacked any kind of sense of time. He could not have determined how many hours or how many days passed when he finally came to the edge of a cliff and looked down on white, foaming water. His dry body cried out for the smooth kiss of that moisture and the thing that steered him agreed. Dick toppled forward and fell, an ungainly diver, into the hissing silver of the river, heedless of rocks, uncaring of his clothes. He surrendered himself to the current and for a while he drifted along the bottom, his toes brushing the stony riverbed, his eyes closed. When he opened them again he had washed up on the far bank and water poured from his wet clothing, rolling back down into the stream.

He did not know how many times he had done this before, or how many bodies of water he was yet to visit. Someone else, some other force kept track of those things.

Time to move on to the next errand. Dick pushed his face into a crack in the rock and dug out some ants with his tongue. Just enough to give him strength. Then he headed forward, once again into the excoriating sunlight.

STAY TOGETHER! Know your group number by heart! [Signage posted at Evacuation Centers in Los Angeles, CA, 4/2/05]

Nilla couldn't help herself. She knocked on the door of the little apartment behind the motel's registration desk. No one answered, of course. She stepped inside into a faint smell of mildew and a lot of dust that jumped up out of her way everywhere she moved.

She found a dresser in the cramped bedroom and touched the smooth wood of its drawers for a moment before opening them. It wasn't so much that she felt bad about stealing another person's clothes, though there was that. It was more the lack of familiarity. She couldn't remember her own dresser, if she had one. She couldn't remember her own bed, the smell of the sheets, whether they were starchy or silky or even what color they were. It felt less like she was intruding on someone else's domain than as if she were inventing each gesture—this might have been the first time she ever opened a drawer, the first time she ever pulled on a pair of simple cotton underwear. Things she must have done thousands, tens of thousands of times before in her living life.

Every single thing was new. Maybe that was a good thing. Maybe her life had been tragic and horrible. Maybe even that didn't matter. Maybe getting a second chance, one where you didn't have to be aware of the old life you'd lost—maybe that was something valuable and good by itself.

The clothes in the dresser were men's clothes. Maybe the man on the tree, the one who blew out his own brains with a shotgun—

The airy light coming in through the apartment's windows wouldn't let her dwell on thoughts like that. The little apartment was too cozy, the day too bright. She brushed the image right out of her head. It wasn't hard. She felt good, amazingly good. Maybe not as exultant as she'd felt in the middle of the night with her hands steeped in the blood of the bear. But good.

She zipped up a pair of low-riding jeans around her hips and buttoned down a soft white cotton shirt, rolling up the sleeves because they were too long. She caught her reflection in a mirror hung behind the door and had to stop a while and just take it all in. Her skin was clear. Pale, still, but her eyes were big and warm and bright. No dark circles, no bags, not even crow's feet. Her hair looked like it had just been styled. She pulled up the shirt to check her abdomen, standing on tiptoe to see it in the mirror—a man's mirror, it only showed her from the neck up—and saw there was no discoloration there anymore. Even the wound on her belly had settled down to a few thin lines of scar tissue that looked old and well healed where they bisected her tattoo. The only real injury she retained was the one that started it all—the circle of tooth marks on her neck and shoulder where she'd been bitten to death. They were red and fresh but there was no inflammation around them. The wound didn't look infected at all.

"How about that," she breathed, a smile folding her lips. Pinkish lips, not blue. She laughed out loud, just a single *ha* but it was natural, spontaneous.

She looked great. She sniffed her armpits—nothing.

She was still admiring herself in the mirror when she heard a door slam nearby and someone come clattering out onto the motel's breezeway. Charles and Shar.

Now what was she going to do about them?

It is imperative, especially now, that facilities for worship and religious observance are made available for the use of relocated persons. In the interest of saving space a standard multi-faith chapel may be erected, as long as it follows military guidelines on diversity and tolerance. [FEMA Supplementary Notice No. 74: Relocation Camps: Facilities, issued 4/2/05]

From the Bakersfield checkpoint cars were standing three miles back, most of them with their motors switched off. The marines from Twenty-Nine Palms were Iraq War veterans and they knew how to perform a vehicular search quickly and efficiently. They also knew the danger of letting anything at all slip by uninspected.

"Sir, with all due respect." First Lieutenant Armitrading, United

States Marine Corps bit off what he was about to say. He gestured at the soldiers arrayed around the checkpoint. They wore the new ACUs with digital camouflage, something the Marines had invented and the other service branches were starting to adopt. The grey and black uniforms looked pixilated up close as if the marines were characters from some violent video game. "I get five thousand thumbsuckers a day through here, headed for the camps at California City. Most of them are blonde."

Bannerman Clark watched, only mildly indignant on her behalf, as a fifty-nine year old woman was subjected to a DNA swab from the inside of her cheek by a nineteen year old girl in pigtails, freckles, and Interceptor body armor complete with CAPPE plates. The woman's four children, the oldest the same age as the marine, stared through the windows of their stopped car as if they never expected to go anywhere again, as if they assumed they were going to set up housekeeping right there at the roadblock. The test the marine performed was the creation of Desiree Sanchez, Clark's main medical investigator in Florence. She claimed it was foolproof. A few epithelial cells taken from the cheek could be examined under a microscope. If they looked vital and healthy the person was not infected. Easy.

"You heard me about the tattoo, correct? This is important. I need you to start looking for her—she could be the answer to this thing." This was the place, it had to be. She was heading east, toward Nevada. Clearly she wanted to get out of California. From Lost Hills Route 15 was the easiest way to do that. If she went too far north or south she would be trapped—every road around Los Angeles and San Francisco was locked down and she would be picked up in minutes. Route 15 was the only way out. There were smaller roads, more circuitous paths but they all lead right through hell on earth. She'd be a fool to go that way and infected or not she had some intelligence left.

Down the line someone honked his horn three times in rapid succession. A marine dashed across the heat-smeared blacktop and smacked the hood of the offending car with the butt of his SAW.

The honking stopped but the driver and the soldier had more than a few words to exchange.

"Sir, I will reiterate my respect for your rank," Armitrading sneered. "However this is not a joint operation, sir. You are far from your jurisdiction right now, sir. I promise I'll keep my eyes open for her. Now, if you don't mind?" The First Lieutenant turned and dashed off, his M4 held at low ready, barrel pointed at the ground, finger on the trigger guard.

Up the line a car door opened—the sun flashed off of it like a warning beacon. A twenty-odd-year-old man holding a little girl in his arms got out and just walked away, leaving his car chiming plaintively behind him. Clark wondered where he thought he was going to go.

Others in the line must not have shared Clark's insecurity. A family of four followed the young man out into the shoulder on foot. A trio of college-age boys in sweatshirts came next. Soon a small crowd had gathered at the checkpoint, their cars forgotten, intent on crossing on foot.

The marines were there before them, falling into perfect formation. A single line of men and women, weapons in plain sight but not pointing anywhere in particular. There was a lot of screaming and gesturing going on but none of it came from the soldiers.

What were these people fleeing from, Clark wondered, that would make them face off with marines armed with automatic weapons? He pondered going inward, to Los Angeles, to see what was becoming of California. He was stopped from actually planning such a move by Vikram who came running over from the helicopter waving his arms in distress.

"Bannerman!" he shouted. "Come quickly!"

LOOTERS WILL BE SHOT ON SIGHT! [Signage posted in Los Angeles, CA, 4/3/05]

Nilla was sitting in the back seat when Charles and Shar arrived at the car. When they saw her they stopped and didn't open the doors.

They stood there very close to each other for a while and then Charles climbed in.

"Damn, woman, you clean up nice," Charles said, looking at her over the back of his seat. His eyes searched her face, looking for something. He didn't find it.

Shar stood perfectly motionless outside the passenger-side doors. Nilla couldn't see her face from that angle, just the fists she kept clenching and releasing, clenching and releasing. Nilla wondered what the two of them had said to each other last night.

Eventually Shar opened the front door and got in. She buckled her seatbelt very carefully.

All citizens unable to reach the evacuation staging area at Loma are implored to stay in their homes and only open the door to law enforcement personnel with appropriate credentials. Please do not use your telephones: this will only tie up vitally-needed lines of communication. [Emergency Broadcast for Grand Junction, CO 4/3/05]

The afflicted had broken out of their containment facilities.

There was no time to go to Commerce City, even if it wasn't denied territory. What would he find there anyway—some ruptured cyclone fencing? A latrine pit that had never been used? He landed in Denver, near the airport, and headed straight for the heart of the city. He had orders.

"We've never seen organized behavior from them before," Clark kept telling people. It felt like he was making excuses. He had to pass through any number of clerks and military police before he finally reached the Esplanade south of City Park. There was a high school there, a big brick pile with a clock tower. Alvin Braintree, the Adjutant General of the Colorado Army National Guard had turned it into a forward command post.

In a classroom set up for chemistry experiments—big black fiberglass tables, a row of sinks and exhaust hoods along one wall, periodic table of the elements on the wall—Bannerman Clark stood at attention and waited while the AG received the same report that Clark had heard twenty minutes earlier.

"The infected then formed what I can only describe, sir, as a human pyramid." The chief warrant officer giving the report steepled his hands. "Some individuals went over the top, over the razor wire. Others simply pressed their bodies against the chain-link perimeter fence until it gave way. We attempted to contain the situation but we lacked sufficient force to subdue the detainees. They headed southwest, toward the downtown area. We gave pursuit but again, we lacked the manpower to overcome them and eventually had to break contact. Had we been allowed to aggress on them I think we could have done something but we had strict orders not to endanger the infected."

Clark felt the temperature in the room drop about twenty degrees. Those had been his orders, of course, that the infected should not be harmed. The chief warrant officer was suggesting, in a not very politic way, that Bannerman Clark was personally responsible for what was happening to Denver.

Namely: it was being overrun. They had lost small towns before, all over the West. This was the first time a real city was endangered. It was the biggest setback of the Epidemic.

The AG put his feet up on the teacher's desk and looked at the two soldiers before him. "That order is rescinded as of this fucking minute," he said. His mouth, under the white stubble of a long day, was as straight as a ruler. "You will shoot the infected on sight and no more of this willy-wogging. Do I make myself clear?"

"Sir, yes, sir!" Clark shouted, his voice echoed by that of the CWO.

"You both need to hear me on this, because I'm putting you in charge of platoons today. It looks like I'm short on real officers." It was a slight—a soldier of Clark's rank should be in command of a full company, as many as two hundred warriors. Instead he was being given thirty. "Chief Warrant Officer, you're dismissed. Go get your men and sort out what vehicles you can commandeer. Captain, you're with me." The AG stood up and headed for the door. Clark hurried to catch up, staying a step behind his commanding officer at all times. The AG was the highest-ranking member of the COARNG, answering only to the Governor. As far as Clark knew this was the first time in the man's life he'd ever worn camo.

Now he wore the full battle rattle—body armor complete with shoulder-mounted flashlight, protective gas mask stowed at his belt, a tank commander's CVC helmet with Nomex liner under his arm with a clip for his nods—and he clattered as he hurried down the hallway lined with students' lockers. "This is your mess, Clark. I don't particularly care to know what you were thinking but now I know you're a real barnacle on the world's backside and at least that's something. You were supposed to keep this thing contained in the prison. You were supposed to give us appropriate guidelines for how to proceed when that failed. You were supposed to find a cure. Have you done anything but watch this mess ignite right in front of your face?"

It wasn't a question requiring an answer. Clark stayed at attention and fought the urge to explain himself. Making excuses in the face of such wrath would be seen as cringing if it wasn't treated as outright insubordination. Clark had been a military man long enough to know the drill—when you were being chewed out you shut up and took it. Anything else was unacceptable behavior. He and the AG stepped to one side of the hallway to let a file of enlisted get past, their sergeant keeping them in step with obscene jody calls. "Don't feel too bad, Captain," the AG said to Clark as the men stomped past, even their footfalls in unison. "You're going over Niagara Falls for this, yes. I have my own career to consider. But maybe your friends at the Pentagon can find you a job when this is all over. I think you'd make a perfectly capable dog catcher."

Clark clamped his teeth shut, ashamed more by the AG's lack of professionalism than his own complicity in the breakout. The rules said he was supposed to keep his mouth shut. They also said the AG was supposed to keep his temper under control and refrain from personal insults when addressing his inferiors. It was a leftover of *noblesse obligé*. Clark didn't say a word as he was led into an impromptu armory set up in the gymnasium. The AG selected a sidearm for him, an M9 Beretta, the standard weapon for the officer corps since the mid-eighties and a definite step up from the old traditional Colt .45. It felt heavier than Clark remembered—he hadn't hefted one since his last visit to the pistol qualification range nearly a year past. He'd never been a shooting soldier, really. At least never before. He fed his belt through the weapon's holster and checked the safety before putting it away.

"You'll at least have a chance to redeem yourself," Braintree told him. Clark kept his eyes front so he didn't have to look at the man. "That's more than I can say for the three troops who were eaten alive during the breakout."

Clark felt his knees turn to water and he consciously forced his spine to stiffen. He hadn't heard about those casualties. He had dozens of questions to ask—what were their names, had their families been notified, were they weekend warriors or heroes from the fighting in Iraq—but he hadn't been given permission to question his superior officer.

Vikram was waiting for him in the school's lobby when he was dismissed. The Major belonged to the Regular Army and had no standing in the command post and in the interest of base security he shouldn't have been allowed inside at all but Clark was truly glad to see his old friend.

"He chewed out my fourth point of contact," Clark said, surprising himself a little. It was a euphemism he hadn't heard or used since the earliest days of his career. "I'll be lucky not to be court-martialed after this."

Vikram shook his head to brush away the negativity. "We can do good in this world or we can be miserable over the bad that is already done. What would you have me do?"

Clark inhaled sharply. Vikram was a balm for the soul, all right. He tried to think clearly, to prioritize. That was something he was good at. "Get up to Florence. Sit on the prison, clamp it down. We cannot let the work there be delayed, no matter what else happens. You may receive new orders while you're there. You may be reassigned to somebody else. I can hardly ask you to countermand direct orders, but make sure before you leave that Florence is airtight."

Vikram saluted by way of response. Clark dismissed him and headed down to the parking lot of the school where a convoy of RTD buses was headed out. They were stuffed full of civilian evacuees. A motor pool staff sergeant assigned him the last military vehicle in the lot—an enormous lumbering eight-wheeled M977 HEMTT (Heavy Expanded Mobility Tactical Truck) that was built for hauling cargo. Before Clark could even inspect the two-man crew he received his platoon, too, a scared-looking group of warfighters who fell into ranks behind their sergeant major without a word.

"Sir, platoon reporting for duty, sir!" the platoon sergeant barked. He looked like a prospector with bushy white non-regulation hair spilling out of his helmet and eyes like embers set at the bottom of dark pits. He had his men in line, though. Judging by the way they snapped to attention there was no question of his ability. He gestured and a specialist ran up holding a soft boonie hat a fisherman's hat in desert camo—as if it were a crown. Soldiers in the field—in Iraq—wore such hats to keep the sun out of their eyes. Clark understood the gesture and knew what he was being offered. These were veterans and they were acknowledging that he was one of their own regardless of his service record or any mistakes he might have made. The sergeant was telling him he was in command and that any orders he issued would be followed to the letter. Clark took off his own cover and put on the boonie hat. The specialist took his peaked cap and returned to the line. Clark had no doubt he would get his cover back dry cleaned and reblocked. Clark gave the sergeant the briefest of glances in way of thanks. The sergeant major nodded discretely and turned to face his platoon. "Attention to orders!"

"Drive on, chief," Clark said. It was the traditional order to keep up good work. The platoon leapt up into the HEMTT's boxy cargo compartment. Clark rode up front with the crew in the much more comfortable shovel-nosed cabin. The driver got the prime mover roaring and shuddered out onto a deserted Colfax

Avenue, threading the needle between big tent churches and peepshow parlors, fast food franchises and gas stations.

That was how Bannerman Clark went to war.

Downtown Denver is considered a safe zone until 9:00 PM tonight or until further notice. Medical care and food distribution centers on the 16th Street Mall will remain open until that time. [Emergency Broadcast, Denver, CO 4/4/05]

"Shar, turn the AC up. It's getting' all sweaty up in heah." Charles wiped at the back of his neck. Nilla studied the small thin hairs there, the way they lined up where his hand had plastered them down. She could see his pores opening up in the heat, the tiny droplets of sweat gathering together, turning into rivulets that ran down into his collar. Every cell in his body burned like molten gold.

"It's all the way up already," Shar complained, but she played with the controls anyway.

In the back seat Nilla felt the heat but she stayed perfectly dry. Her sweat glands didn't work anymore. She tried rolling her window down a crack but the air that came pushing in felt like the exhaust from a blast furnace. Too much. She was tired of riding in the car, tired of being hot and cooped up.

Charles and Shar shared a coke—the last of the sodas they'd pilfered from the motel—but they didn't think to offer her any. They had barely spoken to her since they'd started out that morning. When Charles had stopped to refuel at an abandoned gas station at a lonely intersection high in the mountains Shar had gotten out with him, as if she didn't feel safe in the car without his company.

She could hardly blame the girl, Nilla supposed. Not with the kind of thoughts she'd been thinking. Mael Mag Och had told her the kids weren't her friends. She'd seen for herself the way the living looked at her—like she was something unclean. The enemy. Why should she think of them any other way? She didn't belong among them anymore. That should have been clear to her from the start.

Mael had said she should abandon Charles and Shar. That she should make her own way east. He'd said some other things that she didn't even want to think about but he'd been quite clear on that point. No more fraternization with the living. Something in her responded to that message and she longed to strike out on her own. No more dirty looks. It would be so much easier than the silent game the three of them were playing.

Still—he was in New York, he'd said. Thousands of miles away. She could hardly walk across the country. She needed the kids. If she wanted her name back she had to have a ride. Surely he would understand. He seemed to have a pretty poor grasp on the English language and he had kept lapsing into another language, one she didn't recognize. Maybe he wasn't from New York originally. Maybe he didn't know how far his body was from her. He would have to understand.

Just to get out of her head for a while Nilla nudged the back of Charles' seat. He tried not to flinch. "So when are you going to tell me what you're running away from?" she asked, intentionally cryptic, a little ashamed of what she was demanding when the two of them had clearly intended to keep it amongst themselves. She was just bored enough to prod in spite of herself.

"Charles," Shar said, soothingly, as if she expected her boyfriend to lurch into violence at any moment. Maybe that was what Nilla expected, too, or even hoped for. It would be a great justification. The boy didn't say anything, though.

"Seriously, I want to know. Why did you run away? Were you getting beaten by your parents or something? That would make sense."

"I know you didn't just say somethin' 'bout my moms," Charles muttered. There was no force in the words, no anger. He was scared of her now. It angered her more than anything. She had turned to him for a little human contact and now he was scared of her. What the hell was up with that?

"Please don't," Shar said. It sounded like she was saying it to herself.

"Was it school? Were you having a hard time at school? Come

on. Just tell me. We're all friends now, right?" The neediness in her voice annoyed her and in frustration she slid across the back seat, putting the soles of her bare feet up against the window. The sun felt like a blowtorch on her skin and she yanked them away. When he maintained his stony silence she sat up on the warm seat and stared out at the mountainous land that flew by, its folds and creases etched into the side of a barren, unfinished planet. "Were you just bored?"

"Shar," he said, but Nilla knew he was speaking to her, not his girlfriend.

"Huh?" she asked. "What does that mean? Why did you say 'Shar'?"

Just saying her name had a strange effect on the girl in question. "Shut up! Oh my God don't you say it!" Shar scrunched down in her seat and buried her face in her hands.

"Her name—" Charles began, keeping his eyes on the yellow line running down the middle of the road.

"My fucking name is Sharona, okay? Is that what you wanted to know?" The girl whirled around in her seat, her eyes huge and sharp. "You know. Like 'M-m-m-my Sharona,' like in that stupid song! That should tell you a little about my parents. You know the song."

Nilla had no idea what the girl was talking about.

"They thought it was funny. I would come home from school and I would be crying, bawling my eyes out for fuck's sake. And they would laugh at me. Then they would sing that stupid song, over and over again."

"I don't understand. You came along with Charles when he ran away because of a song?" Nilla fanned her face with one hand. Had it gotten hotter in the car?

"No! I'm the one who's running away! They don't care about me. I called my Mom from that hotel and you know what? She was so fucking stoned she didn't even ask if I was okay. I tried, I tried so hard but when they closed the school because of this Epidemic I just could not face them anymore. I used to go to school to get some peace, can you believe that? I used to love school and the government took that away from me. So I went to Charles and I talked him into this. Into running away with me. He cares about me. He loves me."

Nilla couldn't process the girl's outburst. "I don't understand," she said. "You ran away because of a song?"

"Holy shit," Charles shouted. "Holy shit!" He pointed through the windshield as he stepped on the brakes, throwing Shar forward against her seat belt. The sign read **DEATH VALLEY NATIONAL PARK, 2 MILES.**

He pulled to a stop just at the top of a ridge and got out. Overheated air instantly pushed out the air-conditioned comfort of the car. Nilla could taste how dry the air was as it buffeted her face and hands.

She grabbed the map and rolled out of the car to join him. Together the two of them looked down the slope of craggy rocks at a depression in the landscape that seemed to go down forever. The view shimmered in a blast of heat that burst up at them, not so much like a hot wind as the shockwave of some terrible fiery cataclysm.

"I knew it was getting hotter," Charles said.

"We have to keep going," Nilla said. He laughed at her but she shook her head for patience. "No, seriously. We have to keep going east. Look, look here," she said, pointing at the map. "It's not as wide as it looks and on the other side we'll be in Nevada. We'll be safe there."

"It's called 'Death Valley,' " Charles told her. " 'Death Valley,' " he repeated as if that alone would change her mind. "It's the hottest place on earth, I think. We learned about it in geography class. People who go there get lost and they die. You don't go in there without water or you die. We don't have any water, in case you didn't notice. So if we go in there—"

"You're not going to die!" she protested. They could not just stop. Not when Nevada was so close. They couldn't go back, either. California was one big trap for her. The entire U.S. Army was probably looking for her back there. If they found her they would shoot her and she wouldn't have a chance to turn invisible or run away. " 'Death Valley' is just a name! We can cross it in a couple of hours. We can stop for water in just a couple of hours." He started heading back to the car. A wavering shadow caught her eye. "Charles, wait—look. There's somebody else here."

He looked where she pointed. She was right, there was a pickup truck parked on the side of the road just a couple of hundred yards away. Dust and grime besmirched its sides so thoroughly that it had taken on the colors of the desert. In the shimmering air it had been all too easy to miss but once you saw it its reality struck you forcibly. Something moved in the cargo bed. It looked like there were two people lying down in the bed of the truck, moving against one another. Lovers parked in the middle of nowhere for a little afternoon fun, she guessed. It felt too hot for that but she supposed hormones could overcome heat exhaustion if they were strong enough.

"Oh, dude," Charles said, his face falling. "That's two *guys*."

"Yeah, well," Nilla said, getting desperate. They couldn't turn back now—her name was waiting for her and death was close behind. "Maybe they have some water."

Charles didn't move. She smiled weakly at him but she knew very well he wasn't going to go ask for water from the truck's occupants. *Fine*, she thought, she would do it herself. She covered the distance between the two vehicles as quickly as she could, her feet slipping on the loose gravel of the shoulder. It was so hot. When she reached the pickup she cleared her throat a couple of times to try to warn the two men that she was approaching. They didn't stop what they were doing so she stepped closer. "Hello? Excuse me?" She took another step and smelled blood in the air. Despite the heat a chill rolled down her spine. She closed her eyes, knowing what she would find. There were two people in the back of the truck, yes. One of them was rapidly bleeding to death. The other one had beat him there.

The ghoul must have felt her regard. He reared up, a mouthful of flesh tumbling from between his lips and got to his feet so that he towered over her, his stained face ten feet up in the air. He wore a torn-up padded vest even in the intense heat and his legs looked as thick as tree trunks. That wasn't what she noticed first, though.

He didn't have any arms.

The I-25 Corridor is completely backed up, all the way to the Tech Center, it looks like there was a multi-car pileup somewhere down there—please, once again we have to urge everyone not to try to get out of the city by car, it will only increase the chaos. [Traffic Report from Denver's 7, Special Emergency Bulletin 4/4/05]

A spill of them came up the bed of the Platte, maybe two or maybe three dozen, their feet splashing wildly in the muddy water. Among the dead Clark saw a couple of orange jumpsuits—those would be the original infected prisoners of Florence—but also one or two Battle Dress Uniforms. Military personnel. He raised his pistol but didn't shoot.

Behind him the platoon sergeant howled at the troops. Chief Horrocks waved his arms like a demon as he urged his soldiers on. "Put your fucking back into that, Mendelsohn! Get some of that 550 cord down here, we need to secure this end."

Clark lined up his weapon with the forehead of the leading assailant. A middle-aged woman in a sweatsuit, her face wide and open and blank. Clark had never fired on a civilian target before. He hadn't fired at a human being in decades. He would have to cover a lot of mental terrain and pull a complete shift in perspective before he could pull the trigger. It had to happen in the next few seconds.

"Come on, come on, you all get lazy since we came home? You been sitting around watchin' cable, eating Burger King every day? It's MREs on the menu tonight unless we stop this thing here and now!"

Clark knew better than that. The infected had not stayed together as a unified force against which he could run flanking maneuvers and surgical strikes. They had spread out, thousands of them heading in thousands of directions and everywhere they infected the civilians they found. In a few hours there would be more infected than healthy in Denver. This was a holding action, a way to buy time until the relocation buses were out in convoy, headed for safer climes. Clark lowered his weapon.

"Now now now, go go go, move it, move it," Horrocks boomed and finally, yes—the two lengths of orange detainment netting lifted like the sails of a day-glo ship. The plastic netting formed crowd control barriers lining the narrow channel of the river, keeping any of the enemy from climbing up the sides. The netting snagged a few of the infected, their clumsy hands snarled up in the plastic but the rest just surged forward, trying to get through the gauntlet the soldiers had erected. They were being funneled straight toward Clark and the ten best shots of the platoon.

Clark raised his weapon again, sighted. The middle-aged woman in the front lifted one hand toward him and she stumbled, going down to her knees in the muddy water.

"We're a go, sir," Horrocks bellowed, not ten feet away. "Firing on your order." The chief knew better than to question Clark's hesitation in shooting but Clark could feel it, a hot, hard stare boring into his back. If he didn't shoot now he could never ask the men and women of the platoon to follow his orders. If he didn't fire he would be in direct contradiction of the AG's standing instruction to shoot on sight.

He lined up the end of his firearm with the woman's forehead. She was no more than fifteen yards away. She was somebody's mother, somebody's sister maybe. There were people who loved her and wanted her to recover from this.

"FIGMO," Clark said. Language unbecoming of the officer's corps, something he hadn't said since his time in Vietnam.

Fuck it, got my orders.

"Fire at will," he said. He squeezed the trigger and the flesh of the woman's forehead erupted, fragments of bone exploding from her temple. To Clark's left the marksmen opened up with a sustained volley, the noise rolling around the front range of the mountains and echoing on forever.

The president has been moved to a safe location, where he will remain until this is all over. Thank you, that's all. [White House Press Briefing, 4/4/05]

She heard gravel squealing under Charles's sneakers, knew he was racing to help her. She started to turn around, to tell him to stop. She didn't need his help—the dead man wouldn't attack her, not one of his own kind.

She knew she wouldn't get the warning out in time.

Charles spun in the gravel beside Nilla even as she reached to push him back. He had his arms twisted around for a nasty punch right to the dead man's genitals. It connected with a sound like a side of beef being dropped from a height.

The armless dead man didn't even flinch. Instead he put one bare foot up on the side of the truck and propelled himself into space. Nilla dodged to one side but he wasn't aiming for her.

"Get him off, get this fucker off me!" Charles wailed as the dead man collided with him, knocking him flat to the road. Nilla grabbed at the dead man's matted hair to yank his head back and keep him from getting his teeth into Charles' neck. "Get him off!" Charles screamed again, but Nilla couldn't hold the dead man, his hair was too greasy and even when she dug her fingers in it just came out with a noise like a zipper opening up. "Get him off!" Charles begged as the teeth sank deep into the fleshy part of his throat. Blood spilled out onto the roadway like a bucket of water being upturned.

Nilla kicked the dead man as hard as she could in the cheek, in the ear, in the eye. She fell down to her knees and pulled with both hands on his vest, on the nubs of bone at the ends of his shoulders. "You don't want him," she protested, trying to haul him off of Charles bodily. "You want me," but she knew it wasn't true.

"Get him off," Charles sobbed. "Get . . . him . . . off, please."

Nilla got her shoulder into the narrow gap between the dead man's chest and Charles' back and heaved, pushed and pushed, tried to brace her feet against the asphalt for leverage. The armless corpse shifted but not enough— his teeth were chewing at Charles' skin, digging in deep. Nilla grunted and heaved one last time with all her strength and somehow dislodged the ghoul. She wasted no time yanking Charles up to his feet. With her shoulder in his armpit she hurried him back toward the Toyota. Behind them the corpse staggered up to its knees.

"Just a little further," Nilla told Charles, her arms around his waist. He clamped both hands against his throat. His legs shook violently and she dragged him for a second until he could get under his own power again. "Just get to the car," she told him. They were barely moving forward, inching along, Nilla's slight frame no good at carrying Charles' weight.

The dead man got one foot up and started rising, only to lose his balance and tumble backwards. Nilla's mind surged with hope. Just a little further. Just a little . . .

Charles' hand fell away from his neck and a pencil-thin jet of blood shot out ahead of him. He wheezed and choked and Nilla shoved one of her own hands against his wound. Her hand was soaked with blood instantly. It started to run down her forearm, into her shirtsleeve. She felt a visceral desire to lick the blood off her hand but she fought it down. She would not let Charles die, not now.

The armless corpse rolled back against the pickup truck and levered himself upward on its bumper. This time he ended up on his feet. He began staggering toward them. They had a head start but the dead man stumbled forward faster than Nilla's dragging pace.

Nilla looked forward again—and nearly collided with the Toyota as it came screeching up to her. It bounced on its wheels as it braked to a halt. In the driver's seat Shar looked stunned, paralyzed, her fingers white on the wheel, her face narrow and wrinkled with fear.

Behind them the corpse had nearly closed the gap. In a few seconds he would be on them. Nilla let Charles fall across the side of the car and wrenched open the back door. She pushed him inside and jumped in on top of him. She grabbed a bundle of fast food restaurant napkins off the floor of the car—they were filthy and probably covered in germs but it didn't matter—and stuffed them into the crook of Charles' neck. She yanked the door closed behind her.

The dead man stumbled up to the side of the car and lurched forward, his face slamming against the window only inches from Nilla's nose. She fell backwards in terror as the corpse stumbled back for another strike.

"Shar!" Nilla screamed. "Shar! Drive!"

The teenaged girl threw the car into drive just as the armless guy slapped his face against the window a second time. Glass erupted into the car in a green cascade, tiny cubes of safety glass spilling down across Nilla and Charles, bouncing off the car's upholstery. Nilla spun around as the car lurched forward and saw the corpse standing in the road, his face a blurred distortion of human features. As the car raced away from him he stumbled after it, unable to stop coming for them even though it was hopeless—he would never catch them now.

There are too many of them, Archie. No, I don't mean . . . there are more of them than we thought, than our, our models showed. I'm talking about your computer model, the one you . . . it's like they're multiplying, reproducing but . . . Yeah. That's exactly what I mean. It's time for Warlock Green to come out of the closet. [Telephone conversation between the Adjutant General of the Colorado National Guard and an undisclosed second party, 4/4/05]

A hazy cobweb of vapor trails filled the big sky over Cherry Creek, scar tissue on the blue sky left behind by planes and helicopters full of refugees headed in every possible direction. The aircraft were all gone but they left their tracks behind.

There were more infected coming up Third Avenue from the country club. Maybe two dozen. Clark gestured for the nearest squad to handle them, then spun around when someone behind him shouted "Target spotted, in that window!"

"Somebody kill that motherfucker for me already!" Horrocks

screamed, his eyes huge and white. A squad of soldiers carrying M4s broke off to assault the entrance to a copy shop with wide windows overlooking Fillmore Street. A young man in a blue apron was in there pressed up against the glass, his hands white blobs against the window, the muscles of his face completely slack. Like something stuck to the wall of an aquarium. One of his cheeks was dark with torn skin and dried blood.

Clark backed up against the side of the HEMTT and reloaded his sidearm. It had been a long, haunting night and it just kept getting worse. He thought about countermanding the order—the infected boy wasn't a danger to anybody stuck inside that store. It would demoralize the troops though to leave even one of the cannibals standing.

Keeping morale alive was pretty much all Clark could hope to accomplish. For every one of the infected they cut down ten more seemed to appear out of thin air. They were making no progress at all toward their stated objectives.

"Come on, come on, let's not lose our operational tempo here," Horrocks insisted.

The soldiers were still crisp, still professional. Maybe it was only Clark who was wilting after a night of violence and cold food and no sleep. They kicked the boy away from the window and butchered him and were back to the HEMTT inside of sixty seconds. On the roof of the big truck a crew-served M249 kept them covered the whole time.

The HEMTT was full of scared survivors, people they'd picked up along the way. Every time one of the troops discharged a weapon a collective moan of shock billowed out of the back. The sound got on Clark's nerves—he felt guilty enough already. He didn't need the infernal howling of the survivors to remind him he was slaughtering innocent civilians.

"Comms," Clark called out and a specialist with a satellite cell phone came duck-walking up to him. Keeping low, just like she'd been trained—it made it less easy for a sniper to hit her. Nobody was shooting at them in Denver but she'd had proper cover procedure drilled into her so hard it stuck. She knelt down by the side of the truck with Clark and threw him a salute. "What do we have?" he asked. "Did you get through to the Adjutant General?"

"Sir, no, sir, nothing since the last transmission." That had been half an hour before. A column of light armor (Hum-Vees with mounted weaponry) was supposed to come down Speer Boulevard any minute and relieve the platoon. Clark wasn't holding his breath. The AG wasn't responding to his calls, which couldn't mean anything good. "Alright, get back to the vehicle," he told her. He called for Horrocks and the sergeant appeared instantly. "It's time to break contact. We're holding our ground here but that's not exactly the same as making progress. I want squad three on rear security."

The sergeant set about making it happen while Clark hauled himself up into the cab of the HEMTT. A laptop on the dashboard showed a GPS map of the neighborhood. It showed the country club and the Cherry Creek shopping center tinged in red. That made it denied territory, a place deemed too unsafe for soldiers. Blue was for places being actively held against the infected. Clark had to zoom out on the map to see any blue at all. The closest was a Stryker group sitting tight on a stretch of Federal Boulevard. "How old is this product?" he asked.

"Sir, about thirty minutes," the comms specialist replied. She was blushing under her helmet. The best data she had must have come in with the last download from command.

"Alright," he said, and rubbed the bridge of his nose. "What is CNN saying?"

She played with the laptop for a while, collating text reports from the news channel's Web site with the map's imaging software. When she showed it to him again the Strykers were missing and whole new districts of the city had turned red. The Epidemic was spreading, far faster than any infectious disease had a right to. And where did those Strykers go? He couldn't find them anywhere on the map at all. Had they retreated?

The HEMTT started up with a roar and got under way. The driver kept it to a crawl—the cargo unit in back was stuffed full of survivors so the soldiers had to run alongside carrying all their equipment with them.

The infected seemed to sense that Clark was withdrawing. The soccer fields of Congress Park were crawling with them and they stretched out bloody arms to try to grab the truck as it went past. They came out of every street the HEMTT passed, streamed out of half the buildings. The soldiers wanted to aggress on the enemy but Horrocks kept a tight rein on them—fighting would just slow them down. Clark wanted to get back to command and find out what the hell was going on before he committed to another combat effort.

On Colfax somebody had opened up a dumpster and spread trash across half the street. It looked like some of the bags had been torn open by animals. Clark buckled and unbuckled the holster of his sidearm for something to do with his hands.

The driver took them straight up the Esplanade, crushing the grass and bushes there in the interest of speed. "Try the AG again," Clark told the comms specialist and she dutifully called home but got no response. Maybe the Joint Tactical Radio System was down again—it had a bad reputation. As the driver brought them into the school's parking lot Clark leapt down from the cabin before the vehicle had even stopped.

There was no one around.

Nobody guarded the rear entrance. Nobody staffed the motor pool. The big TROJAN SPIRIT II signal vans on the playing fields were standing vacated and alone. Clark told Horrocks to send two squads into the school and report back at once but he already knew what they would find, and he was pretty sure he knew where the Stryker group went, too.

They would have turned into more red dots on the screen. There was no way to save Denver, Clark realized. It just couldn't be done. There were too many infected, and not enough bullets.

The Pentagon is dispatching troops to help us right now—units of the 82nd Airborne Division, ah, you may have heard of them and also the 10th Mountain

**Division, they're trained in high altitude work.
Whether they can get here in time we don't know
. . . wait, what? No, we'll stay on the air until we're
ordered to leave. Well, I don't care, Marty. I don't
care, you can go, that's fine. Just leave the camera
running. [Denver's 7, Emergency Bulletin 4/4/05]**

Nilla wanted to laugh, to whoop for joy at their escape. Except
that in her hand the bundle of napkins was already soaking
through, a spreading red stain growing in the center of the
makeshift bandage.

"Shar," she said. The girl kept staring straight ahead. The car
jounced through a pothole and Nilla's hand flew free. Blood sloshed
out of Charles' neck. "Shar," she said again. "Look, we need to get
Charles some help now or he's going to die."

Shar sped up; the mountains falling away on either side, dead and
barren desert consuming the view through the windshield. The Toyota screamed with heat prostration and stripped gears. Through the
broken window a gritty wind battered Nilla's face and ruffled the
napkins in her hand. There was glass everywhere but she couldn't
spare a hand to brush it away—her free hand was needed just for
holding on.

"If he dies—I know you don't want to hear this—but if he dies
on us he's going to come back. He's going to come back hungry."

WELCOME TO DEATH VALLEY. The sign whipped past
them, almost too fast to read. Through the rear window Nilla saw
nothing but their own plume of dust.

"You have to accept this, Shar. There may be no way to save him.
I know what I'm talking about. Would you just say something,
please? Shar—if he dies, and comes back, he'll be as dangerous as
the armless guy back there. He won't hesitate to, to attack you. Shar,
can you even hear me?"

The girl stepped on the brake and the car shuddered as it decel-
erated, throwing Nilla against the seat back. When it came to a complete stop dust surrounded them like a brownish fog. It came in

through the shattered window and filled Nilla's already dry mouth, making her gag.

"I'm so sorry."

Shar's voice was tiny in the car, almost lost in the sound of the engine pinging and the chiming cascade of glass spilling off the backseat.

"What was that? I don't understand," Nilla said.

"I'll take care of him. Look, I am so, so sorry." Shar was weeping. She reached up and smeared the back of one hand across her nose. "Please, Nilla. You were really nice to me. I want you to know I feel bad about this. But I can't—I can't take you any further."

Nilla stared at the back of the girl's head as it shook with emotion. She made no attempt to start the car back up again. Nilla understood, of course. She pushed the napkins into Charles' wound as best she could and fastened the seat belt across both of his arms, just in case. Then she pushed open the door and stepped out onto the fractured surface of the desert. The car pulled away from her as soon as she had closed the door, Charles and Shar heading east without her. In a minute they were lost to the heat shimmers coming off the burning sand.

PART
THREE

TonguesOfFire92: I read you can send care packages of clothes, and foodstuffs if they're in cans, or dry foods like soda crackers, Pepperidge Farm Goldfish, beef jerky, you know. I'll try to find the link, those poor starving Californians really need our help. [Christian Love: Singles Chat Room Transcript, 4/8/05]

EARS FLICKING BACK and forth, nose up and into the night breezes, the kit fox trotted to the back of a creosote bush and pawed at the ground. Something didn't smell right, but she was hungry after a long day curled up in her den and she needed to hunt. She looked up, around, her black eyes drinking in the tattered dribs and drabs of starlight available. Far, far away from city lights this night, this moonless desert was one of the darkest places on the surface of the earth.

The vixen dipped her head and sniffed at the ground, at a narrow pit in the sandy soil. Grains of mica and dust spilled down into the hole as she nosed it. In an instant, far too fast for human eyes to discern, her forepaws were inside the hole, her claws sunk into the tiny body of a shrew. She hauled the animal up to her mouth and set out for the safety of her own den where she could feast at her leisure.

Without bothering to make herself visible again Nilla reached down and scooped up the fox with her numb, chapped hands and shoved her face deep into the animal's throat. She had bitten through the jugular vein and consumed the fox's slight flicker of golden life before the animal could even begin to fight.

She made a point of destroying the fox's skull before she threw away its remains. She felt guilty enough about the bear she had consigned to a life of wandering undeath. There was no need to spread her disease any further. When she was done with her meal she sat down hard on the sand and let her brain relax, let herself become visible again. Every time in the past she had used her trick Mael Mag Och had appeared to tease her with riddles but not this time. She waited an hour but he never showed. That saddened her—she would have been glad for his company. Loneliness gnawed at Nilla, though she was hardly alone.

For one thing she had the desert all around her. Death Valley had failed to live up to its name. It might be a dangerous place for unprepared campers but it was hardly dead: in fact it crawled with life, with animals in startling abundance. They didn't exactly announce themselves and with normal human eyes she rarely caught sight of them. With her eyes closed, though, the desert sparkled with their energy, like a vast field of stars but far more active and mobile. She would sit and watch for hours sometimes, especially at night as the life-lights of the desert played out their endless game, chasing each other, devouring each other. Predators were big bright blotches of light that flowed toward and absorbed the smaller, dimmer sparks of prey animals. The shrubs and cacti around her flickered dimly but under the ground their massive root systems, ten times as large as the parts they showed above the ground, made a tapestry of interwoven bright radial lines and curves, a fabric with a radiant warp and a luminous weft. It was the most beautiful thing Nilla had ever seen.

For another thing she couldn't say she was alone because she was being followed. Followed and watched by the armless dead thing that had killed Charles. She had become aware of his continued presence during her first torturous afternoon in the valley, when she had walked so far and so hard she wore holes in the fabric of her too-tight jeans and her lips had split open with dehydration. The sun had started playing tricks on her early and had never let up—she saw heat shimmers in every direction that looked like pools of water rippling on the horizon, felt the shadow of every wisp of cloud on her back like a blast of icy breath.

He stood at the top of a rise, his face distorted by glare, his ravaged body full of dark, smoky energy. She would have liked to write him off as yet another hallucination but she couldn't. She knew he was there. She was pretty sure he had instructions to follow her, though how anyone could make a dead man do their bidding was an open question.

He dogged her footsteps no matter how far or how fast she moved. On foot she was slightly more mobile, more agile, and with better balance, but he had longer legs. He never got any closer than five hundred feet from her but he never receded over the horizon either. As she headed east, walking night and day, stopping only to feed her body or to give her mind a momentary rest, he was never too far behind.

She stopped looking back, eventually. His presence became a fixed thing, a necessary piece of the environment. If he had stopped or turned away she would have felt it, she knew. She ignored him the best she could and kept trudging.

More of the same. Bushes no higher than her knee, some as low as her ankle. Soil cracked and broken by evaporation gave way to sharp-edged sand dunes gave way to rock scoured as smooth as a billiard ball by trillions of individual grains of sand, each of them rolling, tumbling, microscopic jagged edges catching on the tiny defiles in the stone, tearing and breaking, wearing the rock face smooth a nanometer at a time over eons. The world had plenty of time to rot away in quiet. She begrudged it that serenity, that quietude. It seemed she was destined to never rest again.

After three days she came to the place where desert ended and mountains began. She bore no illusions about what lay ahead—she still had the map she had taken from Charles' car and she knew there was another desert on the far side of this new mountain range. Not just another valley but a high plateau of desert that went on forever. Still she was glad to be climbing upward, even when her legs complained, even when her thighs burned with the unrelenting effort. Getting up into high country meant the nights were cooler and the daytime sun less punishing.

In the absence of anything else the mind grows to fill the landscape it observes and in turn it takes on the aspects thereof. After days of walking nearly non-stop she had learned to stop thinking about every individual thing she saw, the swaying branches of every Mormon tea bush, every tiny yellow flower of a brittlebrush. Instead she had come to understand everything as process. In constant motion she began to see the world in terms of movement and change, and any change for the cooler, the wetter, or the rockier was for the better.

She used her hands and feet to pull her way up the Amargosa mountains and into Nevada. There was nothing to mark the border—she had to guess, based on what sense she could make of the map in a place with no unique landmarks. She was well off the paved roads that cut Death Valley into quadrants, and the gas station map had very little physical detail to guide her.

Did it matter? If you walked across the country, from one ocean to the other, did it matter at any point what state you happened to be in? She had been holding Nevada in her mind as a goal, an escape—a place where she would be safe from the military and the police and everyone else who wanted to destroy her. Had anything really changed, though? It would be truly naïve to think that the sickness, the plague of undeath, stopped at the border between the two states. Surely the people of Nevada hated the walking dead as much as the Californians. The desert was providing for her, it was a safe place for her. Maybe she should just stop. Maybe she should ignore Mael Mag Och's offer, forget about finding her name. She could just . . . *exist* underneath the cottonwoods; spend the rest of time getting more and more crusty and dry, eating kit foxes and tortoises and coyotes in the smell of sagebrush and baking rock. Maybe that would last forever.

She stopped to ponder that and just to sit down for a second. Her feet were mostly numb but her legs were killing her. When she perched on a rock her body stopped complaining so loudly and her mind began to settle, to gather itself back up. Returning to concrete thought she slowly became aware that the armless corpse was gone. She felt his disappearance as a sudden shock of absence, the way she might have felt on having a tooth knocked out of her head.

Why had he gone? Where had he gone? She spun around, searching the high ridge then closed her eyes and tried the same search again but . . . nothing. He was just gone. She turned and faced eastward—maybe he had gotten ahead of her somehow? No. No, but there was something. She stood at the top of a wandering canyon, the imprint of some ancient mazy river. At the head of the canyon stood a simple wood-frame house. Smoke dribbled out of the chimney to be torn apart by a gusting wind.

Where there was smoke there had to be people, didn't there? Living people. People who would make better company than the armless freak. She hurried down toward the house, her legs screaming but her hands reaching out.

CDC almost certain they can be pretty sure about one thing . . . maybe:
So the Centers for Disease Control says here that it's not a virus. Which builds on what we already knew from this spectacularly useful press release from the National Institute of Health, which claims it isn't a bacteria. So what the hell is it? In the meantime, here's your conspiracy theory of the week from Romenesko's: Man in Oklahoma claims rapture happened, only no one was fit to be saved. [blog entry, DiseasePlanet.org, 4/8/05]

Clark ordered the HEMTT to a stop and leaned out his window to listen. In the distance, past a line of trees he could hear something. A noise like paper being crumpled, over and over, interspersed with sharp bangs. He knew that sound. It was an automatic grenade launcher blowing the hell out of a city block. "That's the Stryker group," he told the driver and comms. After three days of hard fighting they both just looked numb.

It was a strange kind of conflict where the noise of automatic weapons fire meant safety, while unarmed civilians were your prime target. "Firefight ahead, chief," he shouted back at Horrocks. The sergeant snapped to attention. "Get your people squared away."

Horrocks snapped into action. "Alright, everybody find your battle buddy, we've got trigger time coming up. You, you, you, take point—you six spread out and keep your eyes open. Look out for negligent discharge!"

In the truck's cabin the comms specialist spoke in a monotone into one of her cell phones. "Stryker group three, this is assault element six. Assault element six calling, Stryker group three. Do you copy, please?"

"Five by five, Assault. We are holding onto a golf course approximately one-quarter kilometer north and east of your location, taking heavy fire ... scratch that, not fire, you know what I mean. We've got air support coming in from Buckley ANG to remove friendlies, can you assist?"

"On our way, Stryker group," comms said, but they were already in the middle of it. The HEMTT crept forward into a leafy residential street and grumbled to a stop. Ten or so infected stood in the intersection, stumbling around aimlessly on ravaged legs. One of them turned to look directly at Clark through the windshield. He heard Horrocks shouting at Squad Two and the infected man's head erupted like a volcano. An infected woman in a bright red sweater came hurrying toward the truck, her long black hair floating behind her, still silky and full of body even though her face was grey and pitted with sores. The squad cut her down, too—and an old man in a pair of coveralls, and a teenaged boy wearing a sweatshirt. There were more of them and more coming down the street, perhaps drawn by the combat noise.

"Chief, we need to get through here," Clark yelled out the window.

The sergeant was on it, shouting for his platoon to deploy themselves in a semicircular formation before the truck. Clark addressed the HEMTT's driver. "Specialist, take us in as slow as you can—let these men do their work without having to be afraid of getting run over."

Inch by inch they pressed forward. The troops took their time, lined up their shots. There seemed to be no end of infected citizens for them to mow down but they had a sizeable advantage—they could think, for one thing, rather than just running blindly into a crossfire. They had the advantage of being able to strike from a distance. They had their training and discipline to fall back on.

"Stryker group, we are converging on your location," comms said, holding her phone tight against her cheek. A bloody hand smacked against the window beside her face and she screamed. Clark drew his sidearm but the squads had already pulled the infected man off of the side of the truck and blown open his skull.

Out of the cab, beyond Clark's line of sight someone let loose with a sustained burst of automatic weapons fire—a pointless waste of ammunition and a sign that somebody had lost his or her cool. Clark climbed over the comms specialist and jumped down to the street to see what was happening. Infected crowded around on every side, more of them coming out of every side street, every alley, every garage and doorway. *The noise of the gunfire must be drawing them,* he thought. There was nothing for it but to fight their way through. Clark loosed his weapon and shot down a bald man with no skin on the lower half of his face. Another victim reached for him from fifteen feet away and he gunned her down, too. His hand was turning numb from all the recoil.

Motion on the edge of his vision startled him. More of them— how? How had the pathogen spread so quickly? Clark was sick of asking himself questions but he was constantly confronted with new variations on the theme. How did this start? What enemy, what nation, what terrorist faction would let this happen? He fired again and a naked woman spun off her feet and landed in a heap. He lined up his next shot and pierced her cranium.

He was putting them out of misery, he told himself. Yes, they were sick people. Yes, they were citizens of the United States. But if the pathogen spread this quickly there just weren't enough doctors to treat them all. Especially since half the doctors in the country were probably already infected themselves.

"Chief, do you think we can just ram through this?" he asked, his voice low. The unwritten rules allowed him to ask his sergeant questions but it was better if the troops didn't hear.

Horrocks spat noisily. "They'll get stuck in the wheels. We'll get bogged down and eventually we'll run out of ammo, sir."

"I was afraid you'd say that. Open me up an escape corridor. We need to reinforce that Stryker group. Get the men on the truck." He caught himself. "The men and the women." He wasn't fresh. That was all. Normally he would never have made such a mistake but he had been too long without sleep or real food. "Get the troops onboard, and clear me a path with the SAW, with the small arms, whatever we have."

"Sir, yes, sir!" Horrocks shouted and made it happen. The SAW crew on the roof of the HEMTT opened up with an unholy rattle and the infected fell before the truck like corn at the harvest. The troops clung to the sides and top of the vehicle and slaughtered anything that tried to get into the gap the SAW made. The driver got them moving, both arms clutched around the steering wheel as the HEMTT drove up and over the pile of bodies and they popped through the crowd like a cork out of a champagne bottle. In under sixty seconds they were spinning out on a perfectly manicured golf course, fighting to keep traction.

The infected came at them from behind but Squad Three kept them at a distance with harassing fire. On the grass the driver opened up his throttle and they raced over and through bunkers and greens. The soldiers on the outside of the truck hung on for dear life as it bounced and shook on its eight wheels. Clark could see the Strykers up ahead. He counted three vehicles. There should have been five. One of the light urban warfare tanks looked badly damaged as well. They had been parked in a triangular formation that allowed the group to cover enemy action from any angle. The golf course around the armored vehicles was pockmarked with dark, smoking craters. Clark saw civilians, perhaps seventy-five of them and many badly wounded, huddled inside the loose perimeter. Added to the shell-shocked survivors in the back of the HEMTT that made nearly a hundred.

One of the Strykers deployed a spread of grenades from a roof-mounted MK-19 and smoke and fire tore through a stand of trees, shattering the wood and sending clouds of leaves twirling down through the air. As they pulled up to the Stryker group Clark heard the vehicles' .50 caliber machine guns roaring in tight, controlled bursts, chopping down clusters of the infected as they emerged from the surrounding streets and buildings.

The comms specialist's phone chimed and she answered it, "Copy that Buckley, we are five by five. Captain, sir, there's a helicopter coming in right now to upload these friendlies and they can take ours, too."

"Yes, finally," Clark said. Finally something was going right. He squinted against the sun and saw an MH-53 Pave Low coming in just above the tree tops. The Pave Low, a double-wide chopper studded with instrument and weapon pods, was the biggest rotor-wing aircraft the ANG possessed. It could easily carry the survivors to a safe place, wherever that might be.

The helicopter dropped its ungainly bulk onto a putting green and started loading civilians onboard. A copilot wearing a gold Second Lieutenant's bar dropped out of the crew hatch by the nose and came running up to throw Clark a salute.

"I admire your timing, airman," Clark said, returning the salute. "We just arrived here ourselves."

"Sir, permission to inquire whether I am addressing Captain Bannerman Clark, sir?"

"Granted, and yes, you are. What's going on? Speak candidly, son, I don't have all day."

"Sir, I have special orders for you, sir, straight from the DoD." *The Civilian*, Clark thought. The man with the marshmallow peeps. What was he thinking, issuing orders to a military unit during combat operations? That broke pretty much every one of the unwritten rules. "We're supposed to track you down and send you home. You should take your platoon and head somewhere fortified, they told us. Hunker down and wait for further instructions."

Clark sputtered in surprise. "That's preposterous. There's still work to be done here and I'm not leaving until that work is done and it isn't done until I say when it is done!"

The Second Louey looked down at his flight boots. "Sir, begging your pardon but I'm just the messenger and . . . sir, I've been flying over this town back and forth all day. I'm truly sorry but when you say there's work to be done—there's not. We haven't seen any sign of real survival since this morning."

Ice cubes trickled down Clark's spine. "That's," he said softly. "That's not the kind of attitude I like to hear," he continued but he couldn't finish the rebuke. He tried to remember when the last survivor had climbed aboard the HEMTT. The last time they'd seen anyone else opposing the infected. It had been during the previous night, the endless, sleepless night. He took a second to think about what that meant, but only a second.

"Sergeant Horrocks," he called, "did you hear what this man had to say? It's time for us to make a tactical withdrawal." Which was Army speak for what had formerly known as a retreat. Which meant the National Guard—and the Federal Government—had written Denver off as irredeemable. A complete wash.

"Get your asses in gear, my little babies," Horrocks screamed, walking away. "We're popping smoke!" At the news some of the troops offered up a weary cheer.

Dear Sis:

The elms outside my window are dying, which hardly seems like a big deal now, does it? And yet I can't help but look at them, at the sickly leaves and the branches that just aren't budding. Someone came by today to paint them with medicine but

stopped before he was half done, everyone is so
distracted right now. Heard San Francisco was
gone, now how could that be? How do you lose an
entire city? The nurses turned off the television
before I could find out. Please visit soon, if you can.
Love, Irene [Letter delivered to an abandoned
house in Minneapolis, 4/8/05]

The tiny shack stood on short stilts above the floor of the box
canyon. A narrow row of stairs led up to a weathered wooden door
that didn't quite fit its frame. Behind the house stood a white cylin-
drical tank, probably the fuel supply for a generator or a gas stove.
Nilla spent most of an hour checking the place out, climbing the
rocks all around. No road, not even a path led to the misshapen
door. As far as she could see in every direction lay nothing but desert.
Who would live in such a desolate spot?

She was asking herself that question when the door swung open,
revealing a rectangle of cool darkness beyond. Unable to move fast
enough to find cover Nilla did what was starting to come natural—
she hid away her energy, made herself invisible.

A man stepped out of the house and onto the first of the steps.
He wore nothing but a pair of boxer shorts and a white beard that
descended in bushy curls to the middle of his chest. His head was
shaven or perhaps just bald. His skin had the sallow shade of
untanned leather and he looked like he might be a hundred years
old or perhaps only sixty. He scratched the back of one thigh and
stared right at Nilla. "That's pretty good," he said. "You can make
yourself invisible. Please, come inside. We need to talk."

"I heard a guy on the TV today, I think he was an
evangelist or something."
"Yeah."
"He was talking about the end of the world.
Saying—"
"Yeah."

"—right, saying maybe this, you know. Maybe this is it. Judgement Day? And we're being punished because of our sins. And that got me to thinking . . ."
"Yeah?"
"Well I mean if we've already been judged, right? If God has already decided who's good and who's bad and all that shit . . . then what we do from now on just doesn't matter. Like this is kind of a grace period. Like we could, I don't know, maybe you and I could. Well."
"Yeah."
"Yeah?"
"Yeah."
"I'll be right over."
[Telephone call between two local customers in Boise, ID, 4/8/05]

The infected kept coming in slow motion. As if they were swimming through the air. "Fuck you!" With a baby screaming in the crook of his left arm the survivor lifted his shiny pistol and fired again. Bannerman Clark wondered if the man was even aiming. He certainly wasn't hitting anything. "Fuck you," he yelped with every shot. His voice had gone hoarse with it.

With a hand signal Clark sent Squad Three forward to back the man up. The soldiers dropped to one knee and fired on the enemy before they could reach the survivor. The infected citizens of Fountain, Colorado spun and dropped and beat their heels against the sidewalk, one after the other. After the fall of Denver the soldiers knew to take their time and line up perfect head shots. Anything else was a waste of ammunition.

The man with the nickel-plated revolver couldn't seem to bring his arm down. It stood out from his shoulder like half of a crucifix. He wore a blue buttoned-down Oxford cloth shirt, a loose tie, and tan chinos smudged with what might have been engine grease. Clark was pretty sure it wasn't. "Somebody . . ." the man rasped, "somebody take this baby . . . it's not mine, oh, fuck." He closed his eyes and Clark rushed up to grab the infant before the man dropped it. He knew that look, had seen it hundreds of times before. "Fuck," the man screeched, and started to fold up, as if his knees had turned to gelatin.

"Someone get this man a survival blanket. He's in shock," Clark shouted but before anyone could obey the order Clark heard the chittering spring-loaded sound of a cheap firearm being cocked. He looked down and saw the revolver pointed up at his face. He could feel the heat coming out of the barrel, smell the spent powder.

Nobody moved. The members of Squad Three were too smart and too well-trained to point their weapons at an armed assailant. Sudden movements and implied threats could spur on a desperate man instead of convincing him to stand down.

"I'm Rich Wylie. I lived over there." The barrel of the revolver dipped to the left. "Nice place, you know? I kept the yard nice, fertilized it, watered it all the time. You have to in this climate. I paid my taxes. Do you understand me? I paid my taxes every goddamned year. I paid your salary and you were supposed to come rescue me."

"We're here now," Clark suggested, his tone as soft and even as he could manage.

Bannerman Clark had a full board of medals on the breast of his dress uniform. It didn't mean he could look into the barrel of a loaded gun without quaking in his boots. He was about five pounds of pressure away from being dead and he knew it.

"Not acceptable," the survivor told him.

Clark stayed perfectly still. He didn't raise his hand to calm the man down. It might look like he was reaching for the pistol. Absurdly the main thought in his head was not that he might die but that he hoped he wouldn't soil his BDUs in his fear. If he shit himself someone would see it, which would mean everyone would know about it within twenty-four hours and the jawjacking would go on forever. Clark knew—he'd once been one of those kids with nothing better to do than trade scuttlebutt about the CO. Even if he survived he would never command the respect of his soldiers again. For that reason alone he needed to keep it together. "If you'll put that weapon down we can—"

"If I put this down you won't listen to me!" Wylie looked tired. Exhausted, even, but that could just make him unpredictable. "As soon as I do it your guys are going to tackle me and we both know it. I'm not a complete moron. You need to hear this. You're coming from Denver, right? Yeah, I saw all about that on the news. You're coming from Denver. You were up there trying to do fuck knows what. You shot some dead people, ooh, how exciting but down here we didn't have any military to help us. Down here we had two cops and one of them had diabetes! He didn't do so good."

It wasn't so much news to Clark as the variation on a theme. The Adjutant General had drawn every troop we could get into the defense of Denver, leaving the rest of the front range without a military line of defense. Reinforcements from the east were supposedly on their way but for three critical days the rural population of Colorado had stood alone.

It was hard for Clark to fault the AG's reasoning, though. Four million people inhabited the state of Colorado. Three million of them lived in or around Denver. Or at least they had. The choice must have seemed clear at the time.

"I want my life back, but you can't . . . you weren't here in . . . in time . . ." a plaintive, high sound came out of Wylie's throat. He didn't have a lot left. "You can't . . . stop this. You can't stop this," he said. His face had gone white. The revolver drifted downward and then fell from his hand to clatter on the street. In an instant Squad Three pushed in, knocking Clark backward, away from the assailant. One of them took the baby from him—it wouldn't stop screaming. Two men grabbed at Wylie's shirt and arms and neck, pulled his arms behind his back, restrained him. It was over in seconds. Clark swallowed though there was nothing in his mouth.

"Fucking spaz," a troop said, and filled his mouth to spit on Wylie. Sergeant Horrocks stepped up into the soldier's face and stared him down until he swallowed visibly.

Clark adjusted his boonie hat and turned away. "Sergeant, please find a place for this civilian in one of the vehicles," he ordered over the sound of the baby's cries. "And find . . . find someone to take this. This infant." He couldn't hear himself think. Alone, he strode away from the vehicles to stand on the shoulder of the road. He stared up over the tops of the quaint Victorian mountain town buildings, at the snow-covered peaks, until his stomach muscles stopped flip-flopping beneath his uniform shirt. It had been a long time since someone pointed a gun at him. He had served in two major wars and nearly a half dozen small conflicts and he'd never gotten used to the feeling. He had believed that he would get through the current crisis without it ever happening. The infected had sharp teeth and grabbing hands and he had seen how they killed but somehow it took a fifty dollar revolver to teach him true fear.

The convoy got moving again before Clark was ready to go. He watched the HEMTT go by and two of the Strykers. Then the line of minivans and panel trucks and school buses—anything they could find, anything civilian that could hold a few people. The last of the Strykers pulled rear security. Clark swung up onto its back compartment and sat down on the turret, feeling better with the wind in his face.

The Civilian had ordered him to get to a hardened location and wait. Clark had chosen Florence—the best-fortified site he knew—and he would get there eventually. But not before he'd rescued every survivor he found between Denver and the supermax prison.

US slouches toward Martial Law, Conspiracy Nuts Everywhere Cream their Jeans:
The Att-Gen asking for extra powers, well, what else is new. But with the Army pretty much owning half of the Western US already and security inside the Beltway making every trip to Starbucks into a fun-filled lightning round of "name that gun" this is starting to look like the real deal. Brr. [blog entry, wonkette.com, 4/9/05]

Nilla perched on the edge of a hand-made wicker chair, her hands on the table. The bald man twisted the can opener a final time and put a tin of potted meat down between them. It looked like cat food.

"I'm, uh, I'm Jason Singletary." He showed her an expanse of brown and ugly teeth. She supposed it was a smile or something.

"Nilla," she said.

"I know." He stepped back from the table and moved his hands in front of him, touching his fingers together as if he was counting. "I know a lot of things about you. I know what your purpose is, I think. There's a lot to discuss."

Nilla frowned at him. This was nonsense. How could he know her name? She'd never seen him before. At least not since she'd died and lost her memory. If he'd known her during her life he still wouldn't know the name she'd chosen for herself. He was lying.

Then again he could see her when she was invisible which meant that maybe he had sources of information that weren't readily available to her.

She ran a fingertip across the puce surface of the potted meat and touched it to her tongue. She couldn't deny it was tasty. It had been flesh once, after all. She dug in with a much-dented spoon he provided and started eating. "Why do you live—" she began, intending to ask him why he lived in such a lonely place, but he reacted as if she were shouting right in his ear, wincing away from her words, clutching at his head with both hands. He dashed into the tiny house's kitchenette and grabbed a roll of tin foil, which he wrapped around and around his head until it formed a tight, shiny skullcap.

"Sorry, what was that?" he asked.

"I . . . was going . . . to ask," Nilla said, trying to keep her words soft and slow, "why you lived all the way out here. In the middle of the desert."

He smiled again. "Nevada has the lowest population of any of the fifty states," he told her, reciting something he'd read in a book in school by the sound of it. "There's a lot less chatter. I call it chatter, like the background transmissions they pick up on their radios, radio operators, they call that chatter."

He stepped backward, colliding with the wooden wall of his shack.

"I'm, well, psychic," he told her.

"No, really," Nilla said, digging with her finger for the last shreds of meat in the bottom of the tin. She couldn't remember eating it, frankly, it had gone so quickly and—

Yes, really, she thought, interrupting her own train of thought. Which should have been impossible, she pondered—after all, nobody could think of two things at once, and therefore, *I really am psychic. This is me you're hearing. It just sounds like your own inner voice.* The thought was papery and soft, barely audible in her head. As he had suggested it sounded exactly like her own interior monologue. As if she were talking to herself.

Nilla stared up at him, trying not to think of anything. *That's impossible, I'm afraid. You're always thinking about something, no matter how abstract or banal. The mind can't just stand still. It has to keep moving or it dies. Like a shark. Sharks suffocate if they stop swimming.*

"Don't do that again," she told him. "It's very disconcerting."

"Imagine how I feel," he said out loud. He held up his hands to show her how badly they were shaking. Then he bent and half turned away from her as if he couldn't stand to look at her. "I have that—all of that, that noise in my head, except, it's all the time, it's, it's, it's . . . it's very difficult having you here. I'm sorry but it has to be said. I thought, well, with your memory condition maybe, maybe just maybe you'd be less, oh God, less noisy, but but but but you're just full. Full of questions. I've been living here a very long time. I get everything I need through the mail. You're the first visitor I've had in twenty years." As he spoke he kept scratching the skin around his eyes and the top of his nose as if something in his head was trying to get out. Nilla stared at his hands and he dropped them to his sides.

She looked around the one-room shack for the first time, really, actually studying how Singletary lived. She saw his bed in one corner, a utilitarian cot covered in old, tattered magazines and a box of tissues. She saw his stove, a rusted white box that sat well away from any of the walls. She saw the shelves above it filled with tin cans. She saw the orange bottles that pills come in everywhere, scattered underfoot, lined up neatly on the edge of the table, interspersed with the stored food. She picked one up and studied its label.

TEGRETOL (Carbamazepine), 1600 mg. Take three times daily with food.

"That's for the, the, the seizures," he sputtered, taking it away from her. "I have some canned tuna fish, would you like that?"

"Yes," Nilla said. She studied him as he moved around the side of his house that might be considered his kitchen. "I guess that explains how you were able to see me, even with my aura hidden. Were you born like this?" she asked.

His shoulders tightened as he worked a manual can opener. "Yes, I think so. I saw . . . saw ghosts, ghosts sometimes, when I was, little. Still do. It got so much worse during puberty. I couldn't take it, just couldn't . . . they sent me around to the hospitals but the drugs, they just . . . there's something very wrong with my brain, I know that. I know that! It leaks. It leaks and it, it doesn't always. It doesn't always work, the tin foil doesn't always . . . I'm so terribly sorry. I'm stuttering, aren't I?"

"You saw ghosts," Nilla said.

"Yes." He set down the can of tuna in front of her and she knocked it back into her mouth as if she were drinking a shot of whiskey. It curbed her hunger for a few seconds but then it returned as strong as ever.

He went on, his hands clutching the edge of the table. "Dead people, the, the memories, the memories of dead people that get stuck here. In this world. Nothing ever gets forgotten, see, it, it's like a vibration, a vibration in a kind of, well, a string, and it keeps vibrating forever, it gets fainter over time. You know. Like a violin string, if you pluck it. It'll keep vibrating and even though you can't hear it after a while it's still . . . it's still . . ."

She knew her eyes had gone very wide. She couldn't help it.

He was saying that memories were never really lost. For instance, her memories.

He wouldn't look at her. He took down a can of spam from his shelf and peeled back the lid. He set it down on the table in front of her. When she didn't touch it he shifted it toward her an inch or so. She lifted her spoon.

"No," he said, answering the question she hadn't asked.

"Why not, damnit? Why. The fuck. Not?"

"I can't return your memory to you because I haven't seen it. I haven't seen your ghost, Nilla." He had calmed down considerably. Maybe he was afraid of her and his fear was keeping him quiet. "I don't . . . pick and choose. They just come to me. If you were still alive, maybe I could look for your ghost or . . . or your memory. But then you wouldn't need your memory back. And you wouldn't be here."

The can before her was empty. She couldn't even remember the taste of the spam.

He sat down on the edge of the table. "There are things you need to know. You didn't come here by accident. I led you here myself."

Nilla placed her hands in her lap. "Maybe if you just tried really hard. Or you just kept yourself open to the possibility. If I stay here, for a while, maybe my ghost will come here. Maybe it will come looking for me."

"It doesn't work that way, and we have more important things to talk about," he told her, dismissing the notion in a way that made rage bubble inside of her. What could be more important than recovering her memories? "Please, we don't have much time! I guided you here—the occasional thought I put in your head, telling you to head down this valley or to skirt that road. There's something you need to know, Nilla. There's a man up in the, the, the mountains east of here, I've touched his mind many times. He's done something horrible. Something truly terrible, like, I see a fire, this fire that will burn up the world. He knows what he's done. He's consumed with guilt and—and—and—"

"Just answer me, alright?" she said. She stood up very fast—fast enough to have given herself a head rush if her blood could actually move anymore. "You know so much about me—my new name, the fact that I'm undead, what I like to eat. Why can't you just look inside my head and find out who I really am?"

"I told you, it doesn't . . . Nilla—Nilla, you need to, to . . . . This guilty man, he." He shivered violently and she wondered if he was about to have a convulsion. A low, mooing sound rattled up and out of him. She could smell the fear on him—the adrenaline breaking down in his sweat, sour, acrid. "You, you you—"

"Just calm down!" She moved around the table and grabbed him by the shoulders. The hunger rolled through her innards and she really, really wanted to take a bite out of his neck, out of his golden energy. "Just—I know I'm scary right now, I know I must be monstrous to you but you have to calm down!"

She let go of him in disgust when his eyes rolled up into his head. He slumped down to the floor. She felt a desire to help him, to move him over to his bed but it would probably just rile him up more. There were a lot of questions she needed answers to but she was just going to have to wait for his seizure to pass.

On the shelf above his stove she found a tin of sardines she thought she could open even with her numb fingers. She went back to the table and sat down, more than willing to give him the time he needed. On the floor near her feet, Jason Singletary moaned plaintively and wrapped his arms around himself as if he were very, very cold.

JESUS IS COMING to eat your leg [Graffiti in an Arby's men's room, Grand Rapids, MI 4/8/05]

Florence-ADX sat in the middle of a bowl filled with scrub grass. No trees grew in the fields around the prison, just rocks and weeds. Nothing had been allowed to get tall enough to hide a fugitive. The prison itself sat low on that empty hollow, most of its bulk hidden under the ground like an animal digging itself into the soil against the threat of all that empty blue sky. The clouds overhead shot past on winds that tore them to pieces as they came howling down out of the mountains.

Clark rolled into the Supermax prison at the head of a convoy sixty vehicles strong. The place looked spookier than he would have liked—the refugees in his minivans and big rigs had been through a lot already and he hated to deliver them to such a frightening place but there were no alternatives. As far as he knew the prison could be the last safe place in a three-hundred-mile radius.

While he had been gone much work had been done on the place to harden it against the ongoing disaster. Clark nodded in approval when he saw what had been done in his absence— the inmates had been evacuated and the prison had been cleaned up, the dogs put back to work controlling the perimeter, the sallyports reinforced and well-guarded. The trailers that constituted Desiree Sanchez's domain, the Bag, had been moved inside the second tier of fencing where they would be safe.

Vikram Singh Nanda waited for him at the main gate of the prison. Clark detached Sergeant Horrocks to square away the soldiers and get them started on their AERs. He greeted his old friend with a brief hug. Something clattered against the epaulets of his uniform and he lifted Vikram's wrist to get a good look. The Sikh Major wore a hammered steel bracelet on his left wrist. Not regulation, not by any means.

"It is my *karra*, a sign of my bondage to the teachings of the ten gurus," Vikram explained, looking almost sheepish. "I do not normally wear it, though I should."

"Trying to get right with your God, I see," Clark muttered, and clapped his friend on the shoulder as he headed inside to the warden's office. It would be Clark's office for the time being. As requested someone had installed a cot and a dedicated communications terminal, a laptop that connected with Washington via satellite network. He intended to spend a lot of time in the small room.

Vikram closed the door behind himself. Clark was suddenly and unexpectedly alone. It had been a long time since he'd been left to his own thoughts.

He sat down in the leather chair behind the desk and placed his sidearm in a top desk drawer. He steepled his fingers in front of him and stared forward across empty space. Something was coming, some horrible realization. He could feel it building in the back of his brain, in the oldest part where fears lurked like lizards in a swamp. The realization was being patient. Waiting for him to acknowledge it. He sighed a little, a brief release of the pressure in his chest. And then it hit him all at once.

Bannerman Clark had gone for a week with little more than catnaps and cold MREs for sustenance. In that time he had fought a war.

He had butchered civilians.

Innocent, sick civilians who desperately needed medical care and basic services. He had fought and strived against the unarmed citizens of the United States.

And he had lost anyway.

A cold emptiness like the void of space between galaxies opened up in his stomach and it went all the way down. He was empty, physically empty so that a slight wind could have come along and blown him away. The weariness in his arms and legs turned to paralysis and the buzzing in his head, the grinding, whining buzz-saw headache he always felt during combat operations unfolded into an entire machine shop of torment. Every moment of the battle for Denver waited there, separated and dissected, awaiting his careful analysis. He would spend the rest of his life, he knew, going over these factoids, these isolated decisions from the fray. Just as he continued to think through and re-think every battle he'd ever participated in. Most of them he had won, with relatively little loss of life. Those were easy, just logistics reports, lists of numbers and names, so many men deployed to this location, so much materiel consumed there. The ones he had lost were the same except the lists of names had ghosts paper-clipped to them.

Something other than a ghost came with this action. The girl. The blonde girl who had to be the key to the Epidemic. She had escaped while he was busy with the WOFTAM of trying to defend a doomed city.

Vikram was suddenly standing before the desk, looking anxious but smiling. Always smiling. Clark had not heard his friend come in, did not know how long he had been standing there. Vikram was a veteran, though. He would understand the intensely personal malaise one fell into following a bad action.

Clark stared at the bracelet on his friend's wrist. The current calamity had driven Vikram closer to his deity. "You've never doubted the existence of God for a moment, have you?" he asked, the words swimming out of him as if he were at the bottom of a cold, dark lake.

Vikram straightened up to a considerable height—he'd already been at attention but he found some more backbone somewhere. "The teachings of my faith require me to never have dealings with one who has no faith in some manner of god," Vikram said in a proper, clipped tone. "This could prove difficult in our line of work. What should I do if my commanding officer was an atheist? I have asked myself this question many times. In the end I have chosen to follow a strict policy where it comes to religion." The smile broadened a fraction of an inch. "Don't ask, don't tell."

Clark grinned and it felt very, very good. A half-formed chuckle came out of his mouth like a cough. He didn't examine why he wanted to laugh so much, he just went with it. "I'm way outside of my jurisdiction, here. This has become a joint duty assignment. Because of my special position as a subject expert," he couldn't bring himself to use the Civilian's term: *wonk*. "I've been prevailing on your good counsel despite the fact that you outrank me. If you want to jump ship now you'd be well within your rights."

"Not until the hurly-burly's done, my friend," Vikram said. "Let me rephrase: not until it is done, sir." And that was that. "I have a situation report all in preparedness, should you care to hear it."

Clark did not care to hear it. He had feasted on enough bad news to choke him. *No*, he thought, *not now*. "Alright," he said. "No time like the present." Sometimes you had to keep going in life no matter how awful you felt. Sometimes sheer obstinacy was the only thing for it.

"Colorado is under martial law. The cadets of the Air Force Academy were armed and mobilized. They have not fared so well. Reinforcements of regular Army troops, namely the 82nd Airborne and the 10th Mountain Division, are doing what they can to secure the state. This amounts in the most to blocking all the highways leading out. The interior of the state, by all accounts, is without governance."

Clark had pretty much seen that for himself. He nodded.

"Nevada and Utah have both declared state-wide disasters but the relevant authorities remain in control. I spoke with a very nice radio operator in Las Vegas and he told me that large parts of the city are quarantined but they believe they can hold the infected back from the central region. We have lost contact with California."

Clark opened a box of pens he had found in one of his desk drawers. He had been arranging them in a penholder while he listened. He stopped and set down the pen holder carefully on the edge of the desk blotter. "What does that mean? Los Angeles or San Francisco?"

"I mean that the entire state has stopped communicating with the outside world." Vikram didn't shift on his feet, didn't so much as blink. "It was a gradual process, of course, and did not happen all and at once. Until this morning there still were units of the Marine Corps in Sacramento who I could speak with, though they were very busy. The last I heard was that they were expecting reinforcements from the sea—a carrier group, called in to help maintain order. Then silence only."

Insanity. What could a fleet of warships do against common anarchy? Had they shelled the cities, carried out anti-infrastructure operations to destroy the roads and create choke-points? Certainly they hadn't just armed the sailors and sent them in to the fray on foot. Had they? Clark wondered if he could have come up with anything else.

Thinking about tactics helped him ignore the fact that Vikram had just said the state of California had been overrun. It didn't help him in any way to wrap his brain around that particular factoid.

"The infection has spread as far east as Ohio. We expect to hear about Pennsylvania in a few hours—there have been isolated reports of infection as far east as New York City, where whole neighborhoods are under quarantine. The overseas picture is murky at best but we know that both Mexico and Canada have mobilized troops and that they are asking for help we cannot currently provide."

Clark nodded. He picked up the pens again and started sorting them by color. "Bad, bad, bad, worse. So. We need to find out what to do next. Are you in contact with the Governor right now?" He dropped the pens in their cup one after the other. "Normally I would take this time to liaise with the Adjutant General of Colorado but he, I happen to know, is dead." They had found him in the high school chemistry room. He had been infected, with the meat of his right leg entirely torn away. He had been crawling on the floor, turning in endless circles. Clark had personally put the AG out of his misery.

Vikram shrugged. "The Governor is not available, I'm afraid. His current whereabouts are unknown."

Clark just nodded. "Alright, so find me a General somewhere. Or a Colonel. Somebody who can give me an order." Vikram shook his head. "A Lieutenant Colonel?"

Vikram was silent for a moment before he went on. His eyes searched Clark's face, looking for something. Some last shred of strength to take a new shock, perhaps. "Bannerman, sir, I am saying that in the whole of the COARNG, I cannot find an officer that outranks your good self. I think you are it."

Clark pursed his lips. That wasn't possible and yet . . . many of the best officers in the Guard, and therefore the highest ranking, were deployed still in Iraq. Many more had died in Denver. Was it possible that not even a single Major had survived? Well, there hadn't been that many to start with.

The implications, however, were devastating. If a mere Captain was in charge of the Colorado Guard, if he was to be the supreme authority at the state level, then surely everything was lost. Clark had never been trained for that kind of autonomy. Then he thought of something. He still had his master in the DoD. Not every link in the chain of command was gone. In the morning he would call the Civilian and figure out what to do next. "Alright," he said. He placed the pen holder at the top of his desk, on the left side, then moved it to the right. It looked better there. "Alright, we're tucked in here. If I have to be in charge I'm going to at least get a night's sleep before I start barking at people. Unless there's something more you need to tell me," he added, seeing the look on Vikram's face.

"Bannerman, there is more to tell but I think it is better if you should see it for yourself."

Clark raised an eyebrow.

"First Lieutenant Desiree Sanchez could use a moment of your time. Down in the Bag," Vikram explained. "She has learned something."

Mood: Pissed Off!
Listening to: Slipknot, Wait and Bleed
yo 'sup, we're still here cause the road south is closed and brian thinks its no good in Canada, either, he's so fucking smart, he thinks excep then wheres his girlfriend? . . . I would have protected my woman, true dat, I would lay down all I had for her I dunno. We got three big water jugs, and I filled up the tub last night, its not clean I guess, maybe well leve before it comes to that, if brian gets off his stupid ass. [Livejournal update for user PiramidHed, 4/9/05]

The infected patient on the gurney had been cut down to an obscene minimum of humanity. His face had been carved off as well as the front of his skull. His brain sat like a shriveled piece of fruit in a bone bowl. Much of his chest had been removed—skin, sternum, musculature—to reveal his heart and lungs. Neither of them moved. Yet his fingers twitched and clenched, his toes writhed as the First Lieutenant prodded a long white curve of nerve tissue with a pair of forceps.

"They aren't using most of their organs. Their blood is dried up in their veins. They digest their food . . . somehow, and they excrete wastes." Desiree Sanchez looked up at Clark. "Noxious waste." She scratched at her chin. "What you're looking at, sir, isn't human. It's a nervous system that has failed to die."

The good doctor had doffed her level four biosafety suit. Inside the Bag she wore an apron and a pair of heavy work gloves over her uniform. She had a pair of plastic goggles for eye protection but they were pushed up on her forehead. Splatters of human tissue and clotted blood covered her from head to toe but she wasn't even wearing a filter mask.

"Lieutenant, I believe we spoke before about the patient's hypothetical morbidity." Clark held onto the intercom box, ready to interrupt her if necessary.

"Sir, yes, sir," Sanchez said, and blew a stray hair out of her eyes. "I just don't know how this man could live through what I've done to him. I mean, this isn't an alternative lifestyle. This is a complete physiological change." She dropped the forceps into a bloody instrument tray. Clark heard the clatter even through the multiple layers of thick plastic curtain between them. She leaned on the gurney and closed her eyes for a moment before going on. "I'm at the end here, there's nothing I can do short of torturing this man pointlessly in the name of science. There's another avenue of research I'd like to pursue, though—the epidemiology of this thing. I think . . . that . . . that . . ."

Sanchez' face went blank and a pained croak belched out of her mouth. Alarmed, Clark reached for his firearm even before he knew what was happening to the woman. The weapon wasn't there, though—he'd put the Beretta in his desk drawer and forgotten about it.

"Get—get off," Sanchez mewled. Clark looked down and saw

that the infected man had wrapped grey fingers around her wrist. "Get off me," she shouted, and grabbed with her free hand for the instrument tray. It was just out of her reach. Her eyes sought his through the plastic.

Clark lacked so much as a pocket knife. He couldn't get through the safety plastic with his fingers—he would have to go around. "Hold on, Lieutenant," he said through the intercom box, then dashed out of the room. He whipped out his cell phone and called for help—for anyone.

Outside the Conex trailer the sun was very, very bright. Clark hurried around the side of the shipping container and pushed in the other end through a zippered wall, then through a decontamination station. An automatic shower pelted him with scalding hot water and he threw his arms up around his face, his eyes burning with antiseptic. Behind him he heard boots crunching gravel—too far away, he was the only one close enough to respond. He pushed through the inner air lock, heedless of the whooping alarms that told him he'd failed to close the outer door.

Inside in air that smelled of decay and horror he wiped soapy water out of his eyes and tried to get his bearings. He found himself standing next to the gurney, on the far side from Sanchez. The infected man had torn loose his wrist restraints—he sat upright on the table, both of his hands clutching at the squirming scientist. The exposed brain slouched forward across the decimated face, dangling on its spinal cord. *My God*, Clark thought, *how is that possible?* He grabbed for the instrument tray, looking for anything that might be a weapon. He came up with a gore-caked scalpel and tried to stab at the infected man's wrists but Sanchez kept writhing around, trying to break the iron grip. There was no way to guarantee that he wouldn't stab her instead.

"It's—it's alright," she said to him, "I'm sorry I scared you. He can't hurt me—he doesn't have a mouth, so how can he bite me? Really, Captain, I—"

The infected man released her wrist and plunged his fingers

into her throat, the thick, jagged nails sinking deep into her flesh. Clark jabbed at the specimen's wrist, trying to cut the tendons there. Hot, red blood sluiced down his forearm. Sanchez's blood. The infected man had found her jugular vein.

Clark dropped the scalpel and rushed around the side of the gurney, intent on getting his own hands around Sanchez' neck to stop the bleeding, knowing it was too late, unable to stop himself anyway. He caught his hip on the metal edge of the table and felt pain blossom through his thigh. The infected man let go of Sanchez and she staggered backwards, blood pouring from her throat like wine from a bottle.

She didn't look so much frightened or pained as curious. Clark wondered—was she a good scientist right up until the end? Was she approaching her own death with a burning desire to know what it felt like, to see what happened next? She slumped to the metal floor of the Conex without a sound.

Something in Clark's body contracted as if he were having a heart attack or a stroke. No—it wasn't him at all. The infected man had grabbed him in both hands and was trying to pull him close. He whirled to face Sanchez's killer and saw two MPs come rushing into the room. They raised their pistols to shoot at the specimen. "No, no!" Clark ordered. "Hold your fire!" The firearms dropped at once.

The infected man tightened his grasp, his fingers cold against Clark's arm and stomach. The determination in his arms was nothing short of extraordinary. Clark stared into the gray folds of his brain and wondered where he got that resolve. He reached out with his own hands and took hold of the man's frontal cortex. It was softer, much softer than he'd expected it to be and far less slimy. With a single two-handed motion he shredded it like a head of lettuce.

The fingers weakened where they touched him and then they stopped moving altogether. The cut-down man fell backwards, what was left of his skull colliding noisily with the metal edge of the gurney.

The MPs came closer and Clark waved them away. They huddled

over Sanchez, probably trying to determine if she was actually dead. Clark staggered toward the airlock, intent on getting some fresh air. He could barely believe what had just happened. Florence ADX was supposed to be a fortress, an impregnable stronghold in this new and horrible war. If death could come for them even inside of its barbed-wire fences and dog-patrolled perimeter, then where was safe? Did such a thing as safety exist anymore?

Before he could switch off the automatic shower in the airlock—he was already drenched with soap, suds filling his mouth and nose—he heard one of the MPs grunt from just behind him and the other one took his arm. What was happening?

"Beg pardon, sir," one said. His eyes were very, very blue. Clark blinked. Why were they holding him up? "You looked like you were about to fall."

Legs—Clark's legs—stretched out before him, connected to him only in the most metaphysical sense. His body reeled, his head was wrapped in felt. He had hit the wall. There was only so much fear and exhaustion a man in his sixties could handle. Fighting himself he regained control. He was more afraid of further humiliation than he was of exhaustive collapse.

"Yes, soldier, I see that . . . I'm fine now, though, so—"

Metal clashed to the floor behind them, a bright, jangling, piercing sound. Clark turned his head and saw Desiree Sanchez standing up. Her neck had ragged holes in it. She had knocked over the instrument tray: one scalpel had fallen into her foot and stood there quivering, sticking out of her uniform shoe. The goggles had gotten themselves wrapped around her ears in such a way that they occluded one of her eyes. The other one was blank of expression. Her mouth opened, showing teeth stained with blood.

Clark reached down and grabbed at the belt of the blue-eyed MP. He came up with the soldier's weapon and fired one shot right through the middle of Sanchez' head. For the second time in as many minutes she fell to the ground, lifeless. "I'm going to retire to my room now," he told the younger men standing with him. "I think I need to get some sleep."

I'm sorry, but the number you requested is not answering. If you'd like, I can keep trying, and your phone will ring when I get through. This service will incur a seventy-five cent surcharge. Press one now. [Automated telephone message, 4/10/05]

Nilla picked at a curl of paint on the side of the shack. It came loose in her hand and she rattled it around in her fist, then threw it away from her, out into the scrub brush by the propane tank. She couldn't stand just waiting around but what else did she have to do? Eventually Singletary would give in. Eventually he would tell her what she wanted to know.

She heard him whimpering in her head, even through the wall of the shack. Begging her to go, to stay, to listen to him. They were in constant communication now, attached to one another by a mental link she didn't understand. He had important things to tell her, he claimed, but she kept fighting him off. He kept prattling on about his guilty man and some place up in the mountains—probably a hallucination he'd had from being out in the desert too long. She didn't give it much credence since he was obviously crazy. Her presence was terrorizing him but she knew she couldn't just leave. Not without getting something first.

Nilla, the guilty man . . . you are the one he's looking for . . . please, it's all up to you . . . he moaned. *The fire . . . it will burn up the world.*

Rage spiked up inside of her and she felt him curl like a moth in the middle of a bonfire. Her emotions pained him, excruciated him, she had discovered. Normally she tried to get control of herself, to consciously calm down when he screamed like that. This time was different—she had run out of patience. She fed her rage, stoked it until it blazed.

"I'm not working for anybody!" she shouted out loud. Her words rolled around the canyon, echoing like rippling explosions but they were far louder in her head. "Nobody but myself." "I am my own . . ." she struggled for the right word. Boss? Master? "My own . . . woman!"

The word you're looking for is 'weapon,' she thought. No, somebody else thought that. It didn't sound like something Singletary would have said, though. The voice was loud, almost deafening. When Singletary spoke into her mind it was always in a soft whisper.

It wasn't me! he howled. *Nilla! Don't—don't go up there! You have to listen to me first!*

Images unfolded in her head. A landscape of rugged mountains topped with snow. A herd of huge animals—enormous beasts, lumbering across lichen-ringed rock. A ring of fire that spread outwards, rippling, engulfing the entire world.

It made no sense.

Singletary had been sending her those pictures for days but he didn't have an explanation for them. He had received them in what he claimed was a prophetic dream and somehow, never mind how, he knew he was supposed to pass them on to her. Because she had some duty, some sacred mission to perform relating to those mountains, those animals, that fire. Nilla had no idea what they meant. She lacked even a frame of reference to begin to piece together their significance, if they had any.

"Stop that! You tell me what I want to know and then we can play any game you want. Stop mucking about in my head and concentrate on finding my name!"

His suffering leached into her and she felt her body shiver in the eighty-degree heat. He was twisted on his plank floor, one arm constricted under his body, the circulation cut off. His back arched, drool spilled from between his lips. The pain was awful. She couldn't watch it, couldn't stand it at all.

Then stop it, lass. Stop it forever if you find it so distasteful.

"Singletary, shut the fuck up already!" she screamed. The psychic was beyond understanding her, though. In his pain he didn't even hear her. "Listen to me," she shouted. "I'm talking to you!"

I hear you just fine, love. Look up here.

She turned, slowly, beginning to understand, and shaded her eyes.

On top of a ridge, not two hundred yards away, Mael Mag Och sat with his long hair blowing in a breeze she couldn't feel. He raised one hand and waggled his fingers at her.

Nilla crossed the bottom of the canyon and clambered up the rock face beyond. She kicked off her shoes and used her bare toes to dig for footholds, clawed at the weathered sandstone. She didn't sweat, nor did she pant for breath as she climbed upward, always upward, but she felt the strain in her dead muscles, the pull in her back as she hoisted herself bodily to where the naked man sat waiting for her, not moving an inch to close the distance between them.

When he spoke she actually heard the words, the only audible sound she'd heard in hours. The strangeness of an actual human voice struck her and she flinched. "So brutal you can be." He tsked her, looking like he had just dropped by for a social chat. She clambered up to him on her stomach, crawling like an insect, and just collapsed. "So angry. I suppose it's understandable. The living have been so cruel to you, haven't they? And now you're willing to torture them just to find out a name that doesn't mean anything anymore."

She stared at him for a moment, unsure what to think. She was pretty sure that Mael was not at all what he appeared to be. "You have a better plan?"

"I do, lass. Would you like to hear it?"

She rolled over onto her back and lay staring up at the intensely blue sky, so rich in color it nearly turned to black at the zenith. "Your English has improved," she told him.

He took it as a yes. "End all the anguish, finish all the sadness. Wipe out the violence and the depravity and the suffering in one fell swoop. It is a tall order, I'll admit. Perhaps we can go one better: get them to do it for themselves."

She hadn't cared for Singletary's nebulous refusals. She liked even less when Mael talked in riddles. "What are you?" she asked, sitting up, facing away from him. He wasn't really there, of course. He was still a more pleasing illusion than Singletary's reality. It was pleasant to be away from the madman for a while.

"I was a musician, once upon a time. And a politician. I was a sorcerer and a hunter, too. I wrestled with monsters in my day. I conversed with what you would call gods."

She smiled weakly. Great. A Jesus freak. Or no, he had said gods, plural. Maybe he was a Hare Krishna. "Oh, I see. And what did the gods tell you?"

His voice softened. "Shall I be plain? They whispered to me in the dark and the stillness at the bottom of a pond. They told me that humanity is wicked. That men are evil in their hearts, and must expiate their sins by deeds. By sacrifice. Blood sacrifice. The longer we went unredeemed, the more drastic the payment must become. They told me that should the necessary rituals go unfulfilled and the good works left undone for too long it might eventually be necessary to wipe out the human race altogether. For the good of the world."

"That's . . ." Nilla started, but she knew better than to finish.

"Crazy? I know you think it so. Your generation *knows* better. Your land doesn't believe in gods. You believe everything just sort of happens for no reason, isn't that right? You call that belief science. In my day we knew better. When the old ones spoke, especially when the Father of Clans spoke, we listened."

Nilla stood up on the top of the rock and stared down at him. "Did you start the Epidemic?" she demanded. "Did you? That's what I'm feeling here. You brought the dead back to life so they could kill all the living for you. I swear—"

"Lass, you're confusing the author with the agent. I didn't make this apocalypse. I *serve* it. As will you."

She shook her head violently and started away from him, moving as fast as she could, walking flat-footed on the uneven rock. The sun's heat, stored up all day in the rock, burned her feet but she kept moving. She wanted to get away from him, away from—

"You might as well as not have existed before the moment you woke to find yourself thus. You were created to be the sword in my hand. My weapon." He stood before her. She hadn't seen him move, hadn't even seen him blink into existence there, he just . . .

was there. She stopped short before she collided with him. "Why do you think your name was taken away from you?"

"That's easy. Brain damage. There was no oxygen going to my brain so part of it died."

He grinned at her. "That sounds *crazy* to me. Why would the Father of Clans bring you back only to leave you damaged? He had his reasons for taking your memory away, I can assure you. He wanted to make this task easy for you. You have no attachments to any human. The living hate you—you may safely hate them because you don't remember what it is like to be one of them. You can do violence without guilt. You don't ever need to question your own motives. What a gift you have been given!"

"Christ! I'm not some kind of evil undead warrior! I don't want to hurt anyone!"

"Except Jason Singletary." Mael place a hand on her shoulder and squeezed. The touch felt good despite what he was saying—it had been a long time since anyone had touched her—but she shrugged it away. "I've seen through you, Nilla. You would have shaken him till his teeth rattled in his mouth if it would have gotten you a name. And what about those children in the car? You led them right to their deaths, even after I warned you to stay apart from them."

She took a swing at Mael, her hard fist tight as a muscle cramp, but her arm met no resistance. She felt a clamminess in the air but there was no connection. She reached out and grabbed for his throat but her fingers just disappeared into his flesh as if she had stuck her hand into a column of smoke.

Nilla threw her hands up in disgust and turned around, heading back the way she'd come.

"Singletary's life has been one of torture. He's been in pain since he was a child. Your heart didn't go out to him, though. You were willing to use his pain. You wanted to make him hurt more."

"And that's a good thing?" she demanded. She was not surprised when she found him standing in front of her again. She tried walking right through him but he grabbed her shoulders and stopped her dead in her tracks. "You want me to do that, to hurt him?"

"Lass, you haven't been listening. I want to stop his pain." Mael glanced down into the canyon, toward the weathered shack. "I want to take it all away."

Nilla looked too and her eyes nearly bugged out of her head. A dead man stood on the doorstep of Singletary's little home. The dead man with no arms. With his head the corpse butted open the door and stepped inside.

She nearly broke her neck racing down the side of the rock.

Virgin desperately seeking help before world ends, T/Th 5:00, tap foot [Graffiti in a bathroom stall, O'Hare International Airport, 4/18/05]

Dick stumbled through the door into cool air and just swayed there for a moment, glad to be out of the punishing sun, glad to have a soft wooden floor under his bare foot. For a moment, just a moment he felt the comfort of being in a place with square corners again. There were no memories in his head to be awakened, no thoughts of any kind but this perfectly simple, perfectly harmless pleasure.

It was a game. Dick's universe had become a sort of game. It had prizes to be won like this moment of comfort. It also had rules that had to be followed.

"No—no, not now," someone said from below him and his moment was over. The hunger raced up his spine and into his brain and he swung his head around, sniffing out whatever had made that noise. He stumbled against a table and metal crashed to the floor, bright sounds banging and crashing in staccato rhythm, turned and spun, he stepped forward and nearly trod on the very thing he sought.

Rule One: Dick will eat what Dick finds.

In a heap on the floor a nearly-naked man lay curled around one leg of the table, his head in his hands. "I didn't hear you come in," he said, a sad, gentle smile in his voice.

Dick didn't understand the words—words as a whole were lost to him. It was a relief more than anything. When people spoke to him he knew that they were trying to get his attention, that they were trying to communicate. That was pointless, however—no amount of pleading would get through. Dick felt no frustration when he failed to understand the people. There were rules in this world to be followed, but no decisions to be made.

Dick sank to his knees. The food in front of him whimpered quietly but didn't try to get away. Dick felt no pangs of conscience. Sometimes food ran and you had to chase it all day, the hunger dogging every footstep, every moment that passed an agony of want. When the food just laid there perfectly still that was best.

He bent lower, bringing his mouth down toward the glowing energy of the food. It looked a little thready, a little dulled as if this food was already wounded but that made no difference. Dick bared his teeth and aimed for the food's throat.

Stop now. Wait for my command.

The voice did not startle Dick even though he understood it perfectly. The message was not made of words at all but of pure neural voltage. It slotted into his nervous system like a computer program loading from a disk.

Dick could more easily have stopped a moving bulldozer with his face than he could disobey that command.

Rule Two: Dick obeys the Voice. The Voice is the Voice of the Source. No further explanation is required.

The door opened again and another came in. A shadow like himself, different in some way that didn't matter. In every way that counted they were one and the same and that meant she was competition for the food. Dick had seen her before but he was incapable of creating new memories and uninterested in connecting the dots of any old ones. He stayed where he was.

The competitor moved around the tiny room in a flurry of action, faster than Dick could move, much more agile. She picked up something heavy and metallic from a shelf and came at Dick, her hand held high, her weapon ready to smash in his head.

You want to destroy *him* now? A perfect innocent? The words were not meant for Dick. He ignored them.

The competitor snarled and held her hand in place, ready to bring the weight down on Dick's skull. Dick felt no fear, though he understood what was happening in his own dim way and that he might die in a second. That was okay.

Rule Three: Dick and death are old friends.

"He's a killer! A monster with no mind left!"

You have more in common with him than you do with that sick, living thing on the floor. The only difference is that my friend here can't be held responsible for his actions.

The other said nothing but she lowered her arm.

This is a test, lass. A test for you. No one will leave this dwelling until Jason Singletary is dead. You have some choices to make now, and I'm so sorry to force your hand but I have my duty. You can let my friend tear out the psychic's throat. Or you can do it yourself.

"No," the competitor sobbed, a blurred sound like a shake of the head, like the sound of an avalanche starting to let go. "No."

Nilla, someone said. It sounded like the Voice but even Dick knew it wasn't. Did it come from the food? That made no sense. Luckily for Dick's sake it didn't matter. Only the rules mattered. *That place, the fire in the mountains. Don't get distracted now!*

"No—I won't," the other demanded.

You have to go there—you are the only one who can!

Ignore him, the Voice said. **You have to understand this, lass. I would turn away if I could. I cannot. My friend and I have done some things . . . some terrible things. Together we poisoned the waters, lass. We have sown a savage crop. But it's not over yet, and we can't rest. You are one of us. We need you for what comes next.**

"The end of the world," the other breathed.

We are that end. You, myself, and my friends. It has

**been decided by powers I am compelled to serve. You
must serve them as well. Can't you see it now? We've
been given this work by forces larger than ourselves.**

"No, not me . . ." The other sounded pained. What could be
bothering her so? There was food. She would be hungry, as Dick
knew all too well. Why would she not eat? Even the Voice agreed.
She should eat!

Rule Four: Questions run from Dick like the ripples on a pond.
They were gone before anyone had a chance to speak again.

Nilla! The snow-peaked mountains! The fire!

**Everything happens for a reason. You were made for
a reason. You were allowed to keep some portion of
your wits in your head. That makes you special. It does
not make you free. The Father of Clans has judged
mankind and mankind has been found wanting. Someone must carry out this decree. Someone must wipe the
slate clean. When it is done, Nilla, the world will be
healthy again. It will be clean and as beautiful as it once
was. Do the humans deserve to remain in a world they
have polluted? Do the powerful have a right to despoil,
simply because they are powerful? There must be limits, lass. There must be a vengeance. A justice. Without
the threat of a penalty why would a man not commit a
crime? This burden is ours. We died so that others may
be purified.**

"This isn't my purpose. It's not . . . it's not mine."

**Lass. It is. But the elders are gentle, even as they are
horrible. They've given us a gift, too. You and I, we
aren't like the others. We retain the ability to think and
make some choices. And we are allowed, within some
small latitude, to choose mercy. My friend here will kill
this man in a painful and bloody way. Or you can do it
yourself, instead.**

". . . no, I . . . no." Her voice was tiny.

She made herself small, falling to her knees, bending low over the food. Her face came very close to Dick's and their eyes met. Dick had no idea what she might have found in his gaze. He saw only her dark energy.

The ever-burning fire!

We can wait for as long as you like. But that will just prolong Singletary's fear, won't it?

Her head moved, lowering her mouth to nearly touch the food. So slow. Dick understood being slow. It didn't matter—you got there in the end.

Nilla!

Rule Five: Everyone follows Dick's rules, eventually.

Q: I've heard there's a vaccine available but the government refuses to release it until it's been thoroughly tested. But we need it now!
A: In any time of crisis there will be rumors that defy easy debunking but you have to assume that if something sounds too good to be true it probably is. There is no vaccine. If someone tries to sell you vaccine, report them to the authorities immediately.
Q: My mother/brother/sister/lawyer was in California, in one of the relocation camps, on 4/8, the day they announced CA was overrun. How long will it be before we get some news out of the camps?
A: At the present time, we just don't know. Every effort is being made to resecure California but for now all we can do is wait and pray.
[FEMA "Straight Facts about the Epidemic" Web site FAQ, posted 4/9/05]

"They were civilians. You can't just pop American civilians in the head . . . it's effed up. He was saying before it was just a disease. That there might be a cure."

"Yeah, officers say a lot of things. You get used to it."

Bannerman Clark opened his eyes and saw his feet sticking up at the end of a cot, his feet warm and dry in his uniform socks. He saw the place where he had darned a hole in the left one, saw the angular protrusion of his large toe beneath the thin fabric, like something carved out of soft wood. It occurred to him that someone must have removed his shoes.

He sat up and saw them placed neatly by the side of his cot, lined up so that he could just step into them. They'd been polished and relaced.

"Some of them were kids! A lot . . . a lot of them were kids. They're asking a lot of us. First the draw-down, then stop-loss and mid-tour extensions and no freedom leave, and what happens next? Do we stay here and pull CQ duty forever? Do we live here, in a prison, when everybody else is dead?"

"You have someplace else to go?"

There were soldiers outside his door, trading gossip. As soldiers had for the last hundred thousand years, since war was invented. Clark didn't worry too much about their bitching. He'd had a staff sergeant in Vietnam, back when he looked to staff sergeants for his orders, who had smiled and showed a full set of very white teeth every time he heard a troop complain about conditions on the fire-base or about the jungle patrols or how hard it had rained the night before. "A soldier with time to bitch," he had told Clark, "is a happy soldier. It's when they don't talk at all you have to keep one eye on the back of your shirt."

Sergeant Willoughby, that had been the man's name. If he had a first name he'd never shared it with the likes of Clark.

He pushed his narrow feet into the shoes and tied them tight, his breath constricted in his chest as he doubled over. That was just age. He did not seem to be injured or sick. Standing up carefully to avoid a head rush he looked around for his cover. The boonie hat was gone—his peaked uniform cover was back. A message from Sergeant Horrocks. Trigger time was over and the platoon had been reassigned to garrison duty, which meant proper uniforms and a more rigid chain of command. Clark smiled at his hat. The elegance of the message appealed to him. A good platoon sergeant must be half Mussolini and half Martha Stewart and Horrocks was a very good platoon sergeant.

"They say troops are AWOL all over the Midwest. Going back for their families. Can you believe that? I thought about it in Iraq, I think everybody did—we used to talk about it after lights-out, made plans for it even. Nobody ever did it. You would have got shot."

"You still will, don't kid yourself. Keep your nose clean, keep your ass dry, keep your head down. You saw the bodies they pulled out of that conex. Man, don't talk to me about that shit. Don't even look at me while you're thinking it."

Clark's ears pricked up. Desertion? Had it come to that? Vikram would have more information. He buttoned up his uniform top and donned his cover. Time to get back to work. He felt strangely good, at least healthy—maybe all he'd really needed was a nap. He should feel shell-shocked, he thought. He should be wracked with guilt. He had just shot one of his own soldiers, and even if she was dead she had been—

Dead.

She had died, while he watched, and then she had gotten up and stumbled toward him. Of course, his rational side insisted, she had been infected, not dead. She had been covered in fluids and tissues from the infected man, the man whose brain Clark had, well, shredded, so obviously she had been infected, even if—even if he had personally seen her bleed out. Even if he had watched her die.

He needed to think about that. He needed to consider all the implications. He also needed to put it out of mind altogether if he was going to continue to function.

"Shh! I hear him moving around in there, get your foodhole shut, alright?"

Clark cleared his throat discretely and opened the door of the warden's office. In the corridor beyond the two MPs stood at attention against a steel wall painted in flaking tan. Their salutes were perfect.

"At ease," Clark ordered, and they relaxed fractionally. "You two head down to the DCAF if you're hungry. I'm safe for now, thank you." He turned the opposite way, toward the prison's nerve center.

On the way he passed a window and was startled to see it was dark outside. Had he slept that long? Normally he woke and slept like clockwork. In the prison yard soldiers with red lens flashlights were sweeping the open area between the fences. So far none of the infected—the dead?—had wandered into the prison's valley but it was inevitable. They might be out there even now, stumbling toward the warmth and the food trapped inside the fences. He couldn't see them in the dark, of course, so he hurried along. He came shortly to a nerve center.

Racks of server hardware had been crammed into the Assistant Warden's small office and the floor was a hazard of unsecured cables. All the equipment made it ten degrees warmer in the room. The body heat of the half-dozen specialists plugging and unplugging the modular components helped, too. The heat felt good to Clark's old bones.

At the far end of the room Vikram stood before a massive flat screen monitor. He was reading from a printout of an Excel worksheet while a specialist inputted coordinates on a wireless laptop. "Woods Landing, Wyoming. That will be, now, let me look, call it forty degrees thirty seconds north, one hundred and six degrees mark west, we do not need to be so exact, yes? Given our resolution? The date for this location will be March the Seventeenth. Oh! The day of Saint Patrick."

Clark's thin lips twitched in something reminiscent of a smile. His friend had a way of staying cheerful despite circumstances that had seen them both through many a losing battle.

"Still working tirelessly, I see, while the old man gets his beauty sleep," Clark said. The specialist on the laptop turned away and looked busy, knowing he wasn't supposed to be part of this conversation.

"It is the epidemiology data, Bannerman." Vikram handed him the worksheet and Clark scanned it.

"Sanchez mentioned it to me before she was killed," he assented.

"It was what she wanted to talk to me about when she called me down to the Bag."

"It was her crowning achievement." Vikram tapped the flat screen monitor to show Clark a map of the United States. "This is what she died for." Tiny dots covered most of the West in several different colors. Clark imagined he knew what they represented— every known appearance of the Epidemic. "She had learned, as did we all, that this is no virus, and no bacterium. So she went on the hunt for some other villain. And this is what she found."

There were too many dots. Bannerman stopped scanning the screen and looked down at the paper in his hand. Each incident was listed with a place name and a date, with even a time of day listed for many entries. He flipped to the bottom of the sheet, to the oldest data. "This can't be right. These dates . . . they go all the way back into last year, some of them. I arrived here in the middle of March, what was it, the eighteenth? No, the nineteenth. The Epidemic was three days old then."

"Lieutenant Sanchez thought not so much. She believed it started earlier but that we missed the signs. Her notes are maddeningly vague and of course we cannot ask her what she was thinking."

Guilt erupted in Clark's stomach like a bout of acid reflux. He choked it back down—there was work to do. "What about her crew?" Clark asked. "Were any of them epidemiologists?"

Vikram nodded. "Three of them, good doctors all, but military doctors. She gave them orders and they followed without any questions. She let them know nothing of what she was doing—and that is standard operating procedure only. That is not the mystery. She had them look up newspaper articles, mostly. You remember the outbreak of violence that had the media so excited?"

"Yes, of course. I mostly attributed it to anger over the election. That's what the *Economist* blamed it on, anyway."

Vikram nodded. "But that could not explain it all. I have seen the clippings. I have read myself a story about a dog that ate its owner before it was put down. About a mother who tore her babies to pieces. Missing children. Serial killers. Bad batches of the drugs like

PCP. Lieutenant Sanchez looked at these and many more and saw evidence of a larger trend." Vikram touched the systems specialist on the upper arm. "Please show him now."

The screen filled in with what could have been a spider web or the root pattern of an ugly tree. Clark felt his breath leaking out of him. This changed everything. He reached for his cell phone. The Civilian had to know about this. Everyone had to know about this.

"It's not a disease at all, I do not think," Vikram said, rubbing his beard. "It is more like a radiation. Or perhaps it is magic."

Clark shot him a warning glance and pressed SEND.

NO VACCINE, NO PEACE!!!! Sheriff's Office in Clark County has some according to insider eye- witness but no plan to distribute to the people! WTF!!!! If I was WHITE like YOU, could I have my innoculation then, OFFICER??? ["unDead Amerikkka" electronic newsletter, distributed via email 4/9/05]

Men with machine pistols and brown baseball caps patrolled Ter- minal Two of McCarran international airport in Las Vegas. They moved in teams of two or three. One of them led a pair of Dober- man pinschers directly past where Bannerman Clark sat, waiting for the next flight to Washington.

"They don't have any badges," Clark observed to the man sitting next to him in the cocktail bar. He sipped at his ginger ale—a little sugar always helped with his jet lag—and watched one of the dogs shove his snout into a trashcan. "No insignia. Is this new?" He had never been to Las Vegas before, and was only there now because it was the last airport in the West that hadn't been overrun. A military helicopter had brought him that far but lacked the range necessary to get him to the Capital.

The businessman sitting next to him hunched his shoulders, wrinkling his tweed jacket and looked at Bannerman with some sur- prise. "This is the only city in a hundred miles that isn't crammed full of dead maniacs and you're worried about identification? They're private consultants. We don't ask a lot of questions about them, and you shouldn't either. Excuse me, I have a flight to catch." He dropped a five on the bar and hurried off.

Who had hired the private consultants? The mayor of the city? Organized crime? It wasn't Clark's jurisdiction. Yet when he finally arrived in Washington twelve hours later (after an unannounced lay-over in St. Louis where he was not allowed to deplane) he found more private consultants at Ronald Reagan National, though at least these wore some insignia on the back of their flak jackets: KBR. A man in a KBR vest with a long, fluttering mustache checked his ID before he was herded into the baggage claim, even though he had no bags to pick up.

At least the driver of the car that picked him up at the terminal was military—a regular army corporal with a stubbled dimple on the back of his head. In Georgetown the corporal gave him a snappy salute and indicated the door of a building Clark had never seen before. It was not the same building where he'd met with the Civilian the first time, nor was it anywhere near the Pentagon. There was no sign on the door except for the street number.

Inside he found what must have been a cheap hotel at one point in its life cycle. It had been converted into office space, the rooms on the first floor broken down into cubicles, but it took Clark a while to find anyone inside. Finally a man in a buttoned-down white shirt led him to a conference room and knocked on the door. Inside the Civilian sat silhouetted before dust- and fly-specked Venetian blinds, a fresh box of Marshmallow Peeps on the table in front of him. "Mission creep," he said, and stuffed one of the treats in his mouth.

Clark removed his cover and stepped forward. "I have something I'd like to show you," he began, but the Civilian's eyes didn't move at all. He looked deep in thought.

"Mission creep," he said again. "Powell Doctrine. A million Mogadishus."

Clark stepped a half step closer. "Excuse me?" he asked.

"You'll have to forgive me, Bannerman," the Civilian drawled. "I'm coming down from my afternoon dose of hillbilly heroin. I have a bad back, you see. A really. Really. Bad back."

He did not ask Clark to sit down, nor were there any extra chairs in the office.

"It's a shame about Los Angeles. And, uh, Colorado, right? You're coming from Colorado, Mountain time. They had some nice scenery in Colorado. I really need to re-velocitize. Hold on. Marcy!" he shouted. "Not even an intercom in this office. Marcy! I need my pick-me-up!"

A young woman brought in a tray and set it on the desk. It held a glass full of ice and a can of Red Bull. The Civilian ignored the glass and drank straight from the can. "Good of you to come out, Bannerman. I appreciate the face time. Listen, there's someone I need you to meet. You ready? Need to freshen up?"

"No, I—" Clark looked down at his briefcase. "I'm fine, thank you. With your pardon, though, there are some papers I need to show you. This is crucial material."

"I know that, Bannerman. I heard what you said on the phone. Now come on. I'm counting on you for my dead cat bounce. Did you know you were the only military type to come out of Denver without losing a single troop?" He held up a hand for patience though Clark had not interrupted him. "That's right, you lost one of your under-wonks. It's definitely a shame about Sanchez. Read all about her, wish I could have met her. Come on. The person we're meeting for lunch will want to hear about your papers." The Civilian rose from the desk and headed out the door. It was all Clark could do to keep up.

He protested a few times that they should really talk in private first but the Civilian just smiled. Clark played along—he needed the man. He needed the authorization to put together the last two pieces of the puzzle. He needed satellite time.

And he needed to find the blonde girl. She would have information that he crucially needed. She would be the answer he sought. She had to be. He was more certain of it than ever. What had been a hunch before had become a crucial piece of the puzzle. What Sanchez had learned made it possible. At least feasible.

He really needed to talk about it but the Civilian wouldn't stop. They moved quickly through the maze of the dilapidated office building, weaving through rows of cubicles and passing through two steel fire doors. Finally they arrived at a corner office in the third floor of the building. A keycard reader had been installed hastily next to the door, the plaster underneath broken and crumbling. The Civilian swiped a card through the slot and they stepped inside.

An aged woman in an immaculate business suit rose from behind a desk and hurried toward them. Her face was a white porcelain mask, unmoving, so slack and bloodless that Clark reached for the sidearm that he'd left in Florence.

"I'm not dead yet, Captain," the woman said, her mouth an unmoving slot in the middle of her face.

"Botox," the Civilian whispered behind his hand.

"This is not a town that respects wrinkles, not anymore. Special Agent Purslane Dunnstreet," she said, and took Clark's hand. Her skin felt as dry as old paper. "Welcome," she said, waving one skeletally thin arm expansively, "to the War Room."

Clark looked around at the office, a cluttered room maybe fifteen feet by fifteen feet. Paper in every conceivable form filled the room, stacks of it on the carpet, rolled sheets like scrolls stuck into actual pigeonholes above an overloaded desk, bound volumes squeezed into overloaded metal shelving units. One wall was lined with dozens of old grey enamel filing cabinets. A row of laser printers sat on the floor by the window, wired to a beige desktop computer. Page after page rattled through their mechanisms, filling the air with the smell of baking toner and more paper being created by the second.

"Agent Dunnstreet, meet Bannerman Clark, my favorite metrosexual. Clark, Purslane here is an old spy, one of the original Cold Warriors. I've never met anyone who hates Communists more."

The woman's upper lip bent in the middle. It had to be a scowl. "Jesus has taught me," Dunnstreet said, her frozen eyes piercing

the Civilian, "to hate the sin, not the sinner. Communism is a perversion, a sick compulsion of thwarted self-hatred. Communists
are persons, and as persons they can be re-educated, re-oriented,
brought back into the flock. Most of them. The fact that this
country is longitudinally trending Republican should demonstrate
that much."

The Civilian nodded. "Yeah . . . anyway . . . she's been back
here since the sixties. She was, what, NSA originally? She was
funded up all through the Reagan years and then got funded down
under Clinton. We're talking zeroed out, her purse strings cut off
altogether. Except nobody bothered to check if she was still here.
She came in day after day, her very existence so heavily classified
the Dems didn't have a chance of rooting her out, and kept up her
lonely vigil. After 9/11 she surfaced again, or at least she chose to
remind certain well-placed individuals that she was still here. Her
particular field of expertise appealed to Homeland Security and
she was rolled up under Ridge and friends. Now we've reached a
kind of tipping point and she has become one of the most important people on the planet."

Clark frowned at the woman. "I'm sorry, but I don't understand.
What exactly do you do?"

Dunnstreet folded her arms across her narrow chest. "I'm an
imaginer. A prophet of the possible." The lip bent again but this
time, based on the twinkle in her eyes, Clark thought it must be a
smile. "A dreamer of disaster. I deal in abstracts, Captain, intangi-
bles that I keep in a ledger book and next to them I copy down
numbers, as I may. I'm a hypotheticals modeler, a what-if specialist. For the last forty years I have been thinking up one terrible sce-
nario after another and plotting ways to deal with them should they
ever arise. In specific I have been imagining a land war fought on
the territory of the United States. This is Warlock Green, my mas-
terwork." She gestured at the printers humming under the window.
"These are the operational parameters and legal instruments necessary to win such a war. It is a fail-protected strategy that I stand
behind one hundred percent."

The Civilian beamed. "Warlock Green is our protocol for the end of the world."

KEYS INSIDE. WE'VE GONE TO BIRMINGHAM "SAFE ZONE," JIM PETERS AND THREE BOYS. WON'T BE BACK—HELP YOURSELF IF YOU NEED IT, LEAVE IT FOR SOMEONE ELSE IF YOU DON'T [Handwritten note taped to an abandoned car in Jasper, AL, 4/10/05]

"I touched his face with these fingers. His skin like beaten copper. His eyes were terrible to look upon. The water that had frozen me and kept me from the worm, for two thousand years was like fire by comparison—there never was a thing so cold as those eyes." Even as he relived the memory Nilla could see the religious awe that gripped Mael Mag Och and twisted his spine rigid. His face was the blank mask of the trance state, his eyes wild under their beetling brows. "He wore a mantle so fine, so soft to the touch that it lifted as the cold water stirred around me. Teuagh, he was, the Father of Clans. The judge of men. And he was angered. *"Gheibh gach nì bàs!"* he told me. All must die. Lass, do you believe me, that I saw him, that we spoke?"

"Yes," Nilla said. She stood on top of an arch of red rock overlooking a million square miles of desert. Below her canyons twisted like the surface of the world had been rumpled up, bed sheets kicked sideways by the stretching, yawning upheaval of the Rocky Mountains. Smoke coursed out of tiny holes in the rock, black smoke, greasy and thick with soot. It rolled down the canyons in a flash flood of dark energy, from east to west, following the sun. It was so heavy it was nearly liquid and it flooded the canyons, kicked up great spuming sprays of darkness, pushed onward, ever onward. It would flood the world. She blinked and it was gone. She saw nothing but rocks stained the color of sunset.

She'd seen lots of things since she gave in to Mael Mag Och.

She'd seen her own reflection. She'd seen a world that hated her, and she'd seen why, and why she was allowed to hate it back. Why she was supposed to.

She'd seen how things really worked. How just anyone could fuck with you, any time they wanted. There was no safety from that. There had never been anything like safety—just illusion. The illusion that people couldn't hurt you whenever they wanted to. There was no stopping them and they could make your life hell. Make you do horrible things.

"Teuagh is moving us like the pieces in a game, and I doubt you like it much. I know I don't care for it. Yet it's a hard thing to move backwards on this board. It's a painful thing to break the rules. You see, don't you, how we're made for this? How his hand molded the clay of us for this work? We can't paint pictures, lass, not with these clumsy fingers. We can't write poetry. But we can kill. Oh, we are made to kill."

"Yes," Nilla said. They were moving, moving eastward. The armless dead man moved behind them, easily keeping up. They moved against the flow of the dark energy—Nilla could feel it growing stronger the farther they went as if they approached its center. Stronger and more angry. It raged against the world it destroyed, it bit and scratched and rent everything it touched asunder. It was inside of her, that darkness, and Mael Mag Och had become its emblem.

She was terrified of him. She needed him.

"There," he said. He pointed to a place ahead of them. A place where the twisting canyons had been dragged into a semblance of order, into straight lines: a grid. A flat place, flattened out amongst the ridges of stone. Streets marked out square plots of land, tiny houses in the desert all pointing the same way. The city glittered on the dull desert plain.

It occurred to her that Mael was manipulating her. Maybe he was putting thoughts in her head. Maybe he was just using her the way people had used each other since the first dawn. But like a dream that feels so vivid when you hold it in your head, only to flee in every detail when you consciously try to recall it, she couldn't make the connections.

"There she lies, the fortress citadel of Las Vegas. She's stood longer than most, and I admire her for it. But all worlds must end some time. My world ended when I plunged into the dark water, a human sacrifice for the good of my folk. Yours ended with teeth in your neck. You know what you need to do, lass. For me and the Father of Clans."

"Yes," Nilla said, and headed down into the city of Las Vegas alone.

can u help?!? Got 3 ded outside, more on way. Plz, B4 2 18!!1 [SMS spam message, Evergreen, OR, 4/11/05]

An old chart laid out in grid squares flapped across the wooden table, stirring up dust motes in the wan light of the office. "Here, gentlemen, you see the Potomac River. It is so wonderfully fitting that my new Army of the Potomac will be turning the tide on this menace. I've thought often of that irony, especially in draft revisions five and six, which seem to fit best with the current situation. Revisions seven, eight and nine assume an insurgence of anarchists from the Mexican border. I don't feel that applies to us now, no."

Purslane Dunnstreet's botulin-paralyzed face couldn't show the years of tiny strains, the pockmarks of decades spent crouched over situation papers and classified troop strength analyses and ordnance maps, all the years of being ignored in her fly-specked pigeonhole where the light coming through the window was the color of old tobacco stains and even the radio got bad reception. The frozen contours of her eyes couldn't demonstrate the obsessive nature of her task, or the million slight frustrations the years must have brought her. The mental enervation of planning and planning and revising and re-envisioning and drafting and rewriting and compiling five hundred page reports guaranteed to be only glanced at before they were filed away in the Pentagon's back hallways, in the White House sub-basements, but most of all, the sanity fatigue of just *working at it,* spending every waking moment obsessed with one singular idea that *no one* else ever took seriously—that strain could not manifest on her face.

Instead it came out in her fingers.

She touched her neck and sighed happily. "Honestly I was beginning to doubt the Dunnstreet Maximum Faith-Based Provisional Order of Battle would ever need to be invoked. I suppose the Boy Scouts had it right after all. 'Be Prepared', it really is the most essential thing." She waggled her digits in the air and Clark's stomach churned.

Thin, white, worm-like appendages, extruded lengths of flesh that twisted around one another in complex patterns. It was not enough to say that she wrung her hands in excitement as she laid out her Big Idea on the table before them. She tied her pasty fingers in knots, cracked the knuckles with a sound like mice being trodden underfoot, drummed her fingertips on the table so fast her French manicure blurred while Clark watched it dance.

"The New Citizen Army will sweep through here, and up through Georgetown, cutting off any advance. The city will be secured. And then it's onward to New York." A new map clattered across the table, blasting cool air into Clark's face.

He shook himself awake. He'd been so mesmerized by the fingers he'd lost almost all the details of the plan. He had the gist of it, though.

Purslane Dunnstreet's foolproof plan would have worked marvelously—against an invasion of Nazi stormtroopers. She wanted entire columns of armored vehicles stationed on the Beltway. She wanted to draw in every element of the military—regulars and reserves—that could make it in time to create a single overwhelming force to protect Washington while the rest of the country was left defenseless. She wanted constant overflights of D.C. with nightly bombing runs. She had provisions against insurgencies by Fifth Columnists and a contingency for providing disinformation to any spies who cropped up. She wanted commando raids on enemy strongholds and a network of resistance fighters to sprout up in the occupied territories.

Not a single part of her plan made any sense when applied to a horde of mindless, unarmed civilians who outnumbered the military units a hundred to one.

The infected didn't send spies into your camp. They didn't hold strongpoints or even beachheads. You could bomb them into paste and others would just flood in to take their place.

Clark glanced over at the Civilian, who was paring his fingernails with a tiny nail clipper attached to a keychain. The Civilian must have understood the look on Clark's face. He shrugged in reply.

When Dunnstreet finally finished her presentation she went to the printers and handed each of them a hefty document, still warm and redolent of ink. Clark leafed through his, finding hundreds of pages of information on how to deal with looters in a time of martial law.

"Your Operational Parameters Document, gentlemen. Please do not lose it. That would be a grave breach of national security. It outlines the powers you will assume and the tools and equipment you may requisition in the defense of freedom."

"It's like the Sharper Image catalog," the Civilian gleamed, "except with more nerve gas."

Clark flipped to the back of the document. A hefty chapter covered when he was and was not justified in using lethal force against healthy civilians. Basically whenever he wanted, he gathered. He just needed to know which three-digit code to use when he filled out his after-action reports later. Clark placed it neatly on the table, square with the edge.

He cleared his throat. Time to get back to reality. He forced his mind clear so he could make the jump. "Thank you very much for that presentation, Agent Dunnstreet," he said, rising from his chair. "I have some information I'd like to show you myself." He clicked open the latches of his briefcase and took out the papers Vikram had prepared for him.

"I do so love raw data," Dunnstreet announced, writhing her fingers together at her shoulder until they flew apart with a dry snap.

To: DarkGothKiller14@hotmail.com
From: xxXHomerclesXxx@battle-net.com
Re: Mom's Okay, just Scared
So stop calling all the time, k? No word from dad/
step-whore but will let you know. Don't come here,
coz Ohio is bad, according to the tv. Stay put and
safe, bro.
Peace out
ted
[Undeliverable email stored on server mail@battle-net.com, 4/12/05]

Clark laid a sheet of 11x17 paper on the table. It showed a map of the United States with Vikram's spider web superimposed on top in various colors. "Our epidemiology studies produced this. A woman lost her life for it." He met Dunnstreet's gaze, then the Civilian's. They had to listen to this very, very closely. It could change everything. "Originally we were working on an infectious disease hypothesis. That is, that the Epidemic is a pathogen spread by close contact with bodily fluids of infected individuals. We believed it began in the prison at Florence, then spread to California by way of a vacationing staff member. The chain of evidence looked good and we believed we understood how this thing works."

Of course he had looked for a pathogen. It was what he was trained for: biological terrorism. He remembered how he had upbraided Assistant Warden Glynne for letting the prison riot go three days before calling it in. Glynne had assumed he was looking at a new and especially pernicious drug. Drugs were a major problem at the prison, so drugs were what he looked for.

Shame pushed up out of Clark's collar and spread across his cheeks. He should have been more flexible, more open to other possibilities. Countless people had died because he had made the same mistake, because he assumed the Epidemic had to be a disease.

"Then some very smart people thought to actually put the data into a spreadsheet and see what came out. What we see now is that this isn't an infectious disease at all. Whatever it may be instead is spreading in a radial pattern, something no biological agent ever does. Instead it propagates like sound waves or radio waves, only far, far slower." He pointed at some blotches on the map, places separated by hundreds of miles but which had been overrun by the infected on the same day, the same hour. "It's emanating from somewhere here in the Rocky Mountains and spreading outward in every direction like a ripple on a pond. Nothing stops it, nothing can protect against it. Wherever the leading edge of this wave arrives, the dead come back to life and attack the living."

"The dead?" the Civilian asked, glee lighting up his face.

"The dead." Time to face facts. Desiree Sanchez had finally proved her point to Clark, and all it cost her was her life. Enough! Guilt wasn't going to get him what he needed. "I don't know what's here." He stuck his finger on the spot in the mountains that had to be the epicenter of the apocalypse. "But I know it's causing this disaster to happen. And I believe that given the right opportunity," he stiffened his spine and stared into the middle distance. "Well. If something can be turned on, perhaps it can be switched off."

"You think you can stop the Epidemic? You want to stop it?" Purslane Dunnstreet asked, sounding dismayed.

"Stop it altogether? The dead just fall down and don't get up again, nobody else rises from the grave, we get around to the long and painful process of rebuilding?" the Civilian asked, no-bid contracts glinting in his eyes.

Clark folded his arms behind his back. "Yes."

Yes.

He had said it. He had suggested that maybe there was a way back. A way back from Armageddon. This was it. The last best chance for humanity and it could be done in his back yard with a handful of men.

He waited quite patiently for their response. It was a lot to believe all at once.

"So you're saying," Dunnstreet said, very, very slowly, "that you don't want to participate in the Defense of the Potomac." She went

to her charts. "I had a company picked out for you, especially,
Captain. A company all your own."

Clark's face fell. After decades of keeping his feelings to himself,
this was too much.

"Purslane, I think perhaps we've covered enough for today," the
Civilian said, rising from his chair.

"Captain," Dunnstreet said, ignoring him. "I can understand if
my battle orders frighten you. I can, truly, I know what it is like to
quaver before a grand duty. I hope you will reconsider. Before you
leave, though, will you do one thing for me? Will you pray with me
for our nation?"

Without taking her eyes off of him she sank to her knees on the
floor. She wove her fingers together into a tight, bony ball and
looked deep into him with dewy, innocent eyes that sat in the porcelain face like raw oysters on a dish.

"Well, you two?" she asked.

The Civilian grumbled and got down on his knees. He glared
up at Clark, still on his feet. "Get down here, you idiot," he hissed
in a low whisper. "Do you want to get branded as being Religiously
Incorrect?"

**FILL UP— NO REFUGEES. No food, no water,
no drugs, no money, NO TRESPASSING NO
SOLICITATION. Sorry, we're closed! [Painted on
the front entrance of a DiscountDen superstore
in Springfield, MO, 4/11/05]**

As she wriggled through the gap below a chain link fence on the edge
of a golf course a sharp point of steel stuck into Nilla's back. She
felt her shirt tear, then her flesh. She grimaced—there was little
pain, but she knew the wound would look terrible and she needed
to pass for human. At the very least she would need a new shirt.

There was nothing for it but to press on. She squirmed in the dirt
and crawled through onto immaculately maintained bluegrass. She
kept low and moved quickly across the green, knowing that if she

were caught she would be slaughtered on sight. She was halfway to the clubhouse when a barking dog made her jump in her skin.

"Shut up!" someone yelled. "Shut up already! What the fuck's the matter with you?" The voice came from just over a low rise in the course. Nilla dropped to the grass on her stomach and stopped breathing. The dog appeared on top of the rise, ears strained forward, nose sniffing at the air. A German shepherd straining on its leash. She quieted herself as Mael had taught her and banked the fuming darkness of her energy. It was getting so much easier. She could hold the darkness down for longer and longer periods of time. There. She was invisible. The dog pawed at the ground and whimpered for a moment, then kept right on barking.

Damn. It could smell her. She imagined sinking her teeth into the dog's neck. How good it would feel. The animal's golden life glared in the darkness and she wondered if it was thinking exactly the same thing.

"There's nothing there, facewhore," the dog's handler said. A teenaged boy in a brown baseball cap and a tan windbreaker. He had his collar up to keep out the night's chill and a lit cigarette dangled from his fingers. "See? Nothing. Now shut the fuck up!"

The boy yanked at the dog's chain, viciously. The dog howled in pain but at least it stopped barking. Boy and dog both disappeared behind the rise again and Nilla let go of the death grip on her energy, sinking back into visibility.

In another minute she was at the front entrance of the golf course and she crossed the road with an unbearable feeling that she was being watched, that at any moment the boy would look over and see her running across the deserted blacktop. Her luck held out and she made it to the shadowy side of a house.

She was in. Excitement thrilled through her—or maybe that feeling was just fear. She crept to the edge of the shadow and looked out and down the length of a razor-straight road that intersected the famous Las Vegas Strip. The neon lights were still on. They filled the air around them with an incandescent haze, turning the night into well, not day, but something more like day than it was like night.

She couldn't stop shivering, though she wasn't cold at all. She was terrified, she realized.

Mael had a task for Nilla and she knew better than to resist. Singletary's death had taught her the penalty for refusing him. She had been sent to infiltrate a heavily guarded city, on her own, and bring it to its knees. There were rumors going around that Las Vegas possessed a vaccine against the Epidemic. Certainly the city had fared better than Denver or Sacramento or Salt Lake City. It was still full of the living, for one thing. She had been chosen for good reasons. The armless dead man that Mael called Dick couldn't perform this task. He lacked the necessary humanlike appearance. Mael couldn't do it himself because he was merely a psychic projection and had no physical form in Nevada. Nilla had both physicality and arms.

She looked down the street again, this time looking at the shadows. All the places she could hide in the midnight hour. She saw a doorway that had her name written all over it and she stepped into the moonlight, ready to hurry across the street as quickly as she was able. She got about three steps before she heard the dog whimper in pain again. She caught a flash of golden energy out of the corner of her mind's eye and whirled to face whatever had stalked her.

"Excuse me. Excuse me, Miss!"

The teenaged boy stood not ten yards away, one hand barely holding the dog down from jumping on Nilla and tearing her face off.

Nilla froze. Jagged spikes of violence tore through her brain. She knew what she was supposed to do. What she had to do. She didn't know why she was delaying the inevitable. Her muscles wouldn't obey her brain, though.

"It's after curfew, Miss. Do you have ID? A driver's license or something?"

Nilla turned slowly, a big, warm smile on her face. "I guess I left them in my other pants," she said, shrugging helplessly. If she weren't going to fight she would have to bluff her way out of this. Act stupid, she thought. Not very difficult—she'd just completely blown her cover. "I'm just on my way home now, I promise."

The boy moved to stand a few feet away and frowned sympathetically. "Look, Miss, you're obviously not dead, I mean they don't talk and all. I still have to see some ID, though. It's that or I lose this job."

"Well, I wouldn't want that," Nilla said. She stepped closer to him.

Ice filled up her body, ice cubes sloshing around inside of her like a cooler at the end of a long beach party. She felt her skin might just fall off, she was shivering so much. She stared deep into his eyes and saw that playing sexy wouldn't get her out of this one. He had a gun, and the dog, and he was going to kill her in a second when he realized his mistake. He was going to see her dead energy and make the connection. Still she couldn't do it. She couldn't attack. The mindless dead did it all the time—what was her problem?

He was only a foot and a half away. She could make out every pimple on his face; she could see the pulse beating in his jugular. He was exactly the same height as her, she realized. Then something happened. He got even closer and suddenly she wasn't looking at him with her eyes, anymore, but with the hair on the back of her arms.

His energy was so bright and so golden. It called to her. Something snapped inside of her. Some part of her heart breaking, maybe. More likely just a half-dead neuron firing long after it was due, a connection finally being made.

She could do it. Oh, yes. Everything else disappeared as his energy got closer and closer to her. His delicious energy.

She reached up and knocked his hat off, into the street. She could do this.

"What the fuck did you do that for, you stupid bitch?" he demanded as he bent to retrieve it.

"I didn't want to get blood on it," she said, and grabbed him around the neck.

From: BIGSkyPILOT (Moderator)
Re: Tips for Keeping Water Clean and Potable
There's so much government spam now, isn't

anybody real still posting? I've only got power two
hours a day now but I'll keep the server running on
generator as long as I can. [Forum post from
www.bigskypilot.net, 4/11/05]

"That woman is a lunatic," Clark announced, between panting
breaths.

The Civilian had recovered from the lethargy that had possessed him earlier and was leading his wonk through the crowded
streets of Washington. His stated intention was to buy Clark dinner at "a really amazing titty bar I know just around the corner."
Apparently the Russian waitresses barely spoke English and didn't
yet know you weren't allowed to touch them. Clark was looking for
a way to gracefully bow out but in the meantime he had to hurry
to keep up with the Civilian's long strides. Compared to the (erst-
while) laid-back streets of Denver, everyone seemed in a hurry in
Washington.

"Purslane? Oh, she's nuttier than the combined scrotums of the
Boston Red Sox. She's also a close personal friend of the Second
Lady. The Veep loves Purslane Dunnstreet and when the Veep
loves somebody the SecDef loves them too, and as for me, well, I
love everybody. Hating people is such a timesuck. Come on, last one
there buys the lap dances."

Clark followed the Civilian into a dark, smoke-free den of
booming techno music and strobing lights. A skeletal woman in a
tight dress printed with hammers and sickles handed Clark a plastic martini glass. "O, *Kapitan*, my *Kapitan*," she sighed, and dug her
fingers inside Clark's uniform shirt to touch the skin above his
solar plexus.

Clark was paralyzed by the sudden contact. He hadn't thought
it possible for anyone to get that close to him that quickly. The Civilian crammed in between the two of them. "You're wasting your
time, sweetheart. He'd rather be cleaning his own weapon, if you
know what I mean." He led Clark to a bar at the back of the room
where a number of suited men sat deep in conversation. A woman

wearing nothing but panties and a Russian fur hat swayed back and forth listlessly over their heads.

Clark recovered himself, slowly. He grimaced and tried again to convince his benefactor of the danger. "I assure you, the plan we just heard will fail," he shouted over the music. The Civilian waved a finger at the bartender. "I've seen how these things fight. I've shot them myself. Dunnstreet's ideas are useless to us."

"Harsh words, Clark, from the great hero of Denver. You proved it's possible to prevail against the dead, didn't you? Not one man lost. You should be more proud of your accomplishments."

The lights in the strip club dazzled Clark. He looked at the martini glass in his hand—it was dry to the touch.

"You're supposed to fill it up at the bar and bring it back to her. That means you want to take her upstairs to the Martini Room."

"What happens in the Martini Room?"

"Many men wish to know exactly that," the Civilian barked. "But only the rich ever find out." His smile fell when he realized Clark didn't understand. "They fuck you, Clark. For money."

Clark set it carefully on the bar, out of the way of the dancer. He suddenly and pangfully missed the Brown Palace's restaurant, with its nineteenth-century decorum and its perfect slabs of beef. Gone now, most likely forever. With the rest of Denver.

"If anything," he said, quite careful of his word choice, "I proved that it is possible for the most heavily-armed, best-trained veteran warfighters in the world to *survive* in the midst of these things, and that's assuming they can bug out when things get too hot."

The Civilian scowled at him, a cold, reptilian look that made Clark's skin feel filthy. Clark had the sudden and repugnant thought that he was finally seeing the Civilian's true face, the one behind the epoxied-on smile. It was horrible to behold. "You're talking as if there were an alternative."

"There may just be! And anyway, anything would be better than that Dunnstreet's battle orders! How can you take her seriously?"

The Civilian gestured for a woman wearing a Soviet tank commander's soft helmet to come and sit next to him. She pulled her dress up over her head and he leaned into her breasts, rolling his face in her skin, inhaling long and hard. "Well, now, there is actually a good reason for that."

"I'd love to hear it," Clark replied.

The Civilian nodded as he sucked at his drink. "Because it's the only plan we've got," he said, slipping a fifty dollar bill into the woman's thong. "Nobody else has ever thought it through. I'm serious. No policy group, no strategic envisioning team, nobody at the Pentagon or West Point or OpFor or anywhere else has ever bothered to really sit down and figure out how to fight a war on American soil. It has always been unthinkable."

"Nobody?"

The Civilian gulped at neat vodka while he answered. He seemed almost desperate to get as much alcohol into his system as humanly possible. "There have been war game scenarios published, where Canada invades New York State, say, or France attacks with nuclear weapons. It's all Dungeons and Dragons shit and meanwhile Purslane Dunnstreet was toiling in solitude waiting for her big day, making the right friends, playing the game. Bannerman, sometimes you have to drink the Kool-Aid. You've just heard what we have planned. It's time for you to decide which team you're playing for. Listen, I gotta go piss away all the Red Bulls I drank this morning. Keep the girls warm for me, will you?"

The Civilian got up and pushed his way through the crowd. Not without some difficulty Clark ordered a scotch and soda from the bar and sipped it in morose quietude. He studied the crowd with his eyes—he'd never been in a strip club before and he was curious, well, mildly curious as to what sort of person patronized them. Studying the customers was less embarrassing than looking at the staff, though. The sight of so much naked flesh made Clark blush.

He was not the only uniformed officer in the club, nor was he the highest ranking, but the vast majority of the men wore the black suits of career civil servants. He recognized several, or thought he did—he couldn't see clearly more than a few dozen feet in the strobe-shattered darkness.

Despite the general chaos Clark managed somehow to be surprised when a young woman dressed like a Colonial era town crier walked into the club ringing an enormous hand bell. She had a clipboard under one arm and she read from it without much enthusiasm as she rang her bell. "Hear ye, hear ye, good people, it's time to get your bets in. All bets must be placed by midnight tonight. Today's dead pool is for Cleveland, Ohio. Double your money if Cleveland is overrun before midnight tonight! Hear ye, hear ye!"

Clark had blushed before. Now he blanched. He put his drink down on the bar and shoved through the patrons, needing to get out into the clean air. A completely naked woman with a red star tattooed on either of her nipples grabbed him around the waist but he wriggled free.

As he bumped past the reveling wonks of Washington he finally looked a few of them in the eyes and he realized what was going on. These people weren't just jaded cynics willing to sacrifice the country for their own self-interest. They were suffering from threat fatigue, just as they had after September Eleventh. Too much horror that required your full attention, all of the time. Too much demand on one's sense of *gravitas* and it broke, snapped, fell to pieces.

That wasn't a good enough excuse, he decided. They needed to regain their composure and get back to work. But he wasn't the one to tell them as much.

Out in the evening air he breathed deeply and stared up at where the stars would be if they weren't obscured by the light haze of the Capital.

The Civilian spilled out of the door behind him, a dewy can of beer in his hand.

"There's so little time left—did you hear? Cleveland is about to fall," Clark told him, his hands tight fists in his pockets. "I have no doubt the Epidemic has already spread to Asia, across the Pacific. It will be in Europe soon enough and then it will have covered the entire globe."

"A very wise man said something to me once. 'Laddy,' he said, 'time's only valuable to them that are counting it.' I guess that means the dead don't need watches. This is it, Bannerman, the big D, the big A maybe."

Doomsday, the Civilian meant. The big A was either Armageddon or Apocalypse—you could take your pick. Clark shook off the idea. He had one more card up his sleeve. "There's a girl out there somewhere. In California, maybe, though I imagine she probably got out in time. She's dead, but she can talk."

The Civilian popped open his can with a noise halfway between a fart and a gunshot.

Clark went on. "Denver was lost because the dead somehow managed to organize their behavior enough to get over a ten-foot fence. Disease spread through the relocation camps far more quickly than any of our models can account for. There's a deeper game at work here than we think."

"There always is," the Civilian told him.

"Don't you understand? We know how it spreads now. If we find the girl we'll know even more. It's a long shot, but we have to take it!"

"You want me to back your play? I'm truly sorry," the Civilian said, pausing to hiccup, "if you feel like you're being shorted here. But tell me, how much should I trust a by-the-numbers Captain of the Guard who comes busting in here telling me that he and he alone can save the world? Come on, walk a mile in my shoes. Hmm." He looked down. "I could use a shine, actually. Get 'em shined while you're walking in them, willya?" He giggled and nearly choked on another hiccup. "Come on. I know a place where they jerk you off into hot towels. My treat."

Bannerman could barely work up enough revulsion to shake his head. He stared down the alley. The people he'd seen inside—the wonks and the generals, the policy-makers and the people who knew all the secrets. They didn't have a plan. Not a real one.

He did. He had to make the Civilian see it. His benefactor saw him as a token in a broader game. He saw him as a way to cover

Defense's collective ass. No matter how bad things got the Pentagon could claim they'd been doing everything in their power—and Clark would be the symbol of that wasted effort.

It was time for Clark to become a player in that game, instead of just a pawn. He summoned up every bit of resolution he possessed. "We can save the world but you have to believe in me," he said.

The look on the Civilian's face was completely sober. It was a look of cold calculation. "Because some Californian blonde wasn't quite as stupid as the usual brand of dead people."

Clark understood just how serious the question was. "Yes."

The Civilian wiped at his face with his big hands and pushed back his hair. "Alright. But what am I supposed to tell the President?" he asked.

"Well," Clark said, feeling his heart pound in his chest, "you can remind him I am the Hero of Denver."

Light spread across the Civilian's face like a rush of blood. His eyes went wide and his mouth fell open. "George Fucking Washington's ghost!" The Civilian held his beer out toward Clark in salute.

"I take it that's a yes," Bannerman said, sighing in relief.

"Hells, yes. We can send you back West tonight. And you know what? I'm coming with you." He smirked when he saw the look that brought to Clark's face. "You think—hic—I want to stick around here and wait for Purslane to get us all killed, too?"

SOS DAUGHTER SICK HELP ANYBODY [Message mowed into a field of corn in Iowa, 4/12/05]

It had happened so quickly, Nilla hadn't really thought it through. Blood was everywhere. It had pooled beneath the boy, ruining his clothes. He stirred with a spasmodic movement beneath her and she felt his dark energy like an ice pack pressed against her flesh. Nilla recalled waking up in a puddle of her own blood, not so long ago. She wondered what he felt, if anything.

Behind her the dog barked up a cacophony of irritation. She wanted to enjoy the feeling the boy's energy gave her, the feeling like she was alive again. The dog wouldn't let her do that. She reached for its collar, intending to shut it up, and stopped herself.

Mael might own most of her soul, she decided, but not all of it. The dog had done nothing to hurt her. She wouldn't kill it just for being annoying.

Still. The damned animal wouldn't stop barking. Someone would come looking to find out what was going on. She had to leave before then.

She got up and she moved on, taking the boy's brown baseball cap with her. She thought it would shade her eyes and help hide her face. She moved quickly, almost running—faster than she'd been, more nimble than since the day she died. The boy's life energy thrummed through her, his gold coursing down the wires of her nerves. She stuck to the shadows, trying to look inconspicuous whenever she passed through a patch of streetlight.

Behind her in the darkness the dog stopped barking. She heard gunshots and thought of the boy. They had found the boy she'd eaten, what was left of him, and put him down like a rabid animal. She only hoped no one had recognized him before they started shooting.

She felt an irrational urge to go back and check. Stupid, she knew. She kept moving, though she spared a glance over her shoulder to see if anyone was pursuing her. Nothing there but dim shadows and the watery reflections of streetlights in dull windows, the orange pulse of a DON'T WALK signal that suddenly turned white. She turned around to get moving again and—

"Hey! Hey, you, come over here!"

Nilla froze in place.

Three men wearing brown caps stood at the back of a panel truck. The letters LVCC had been stenciled on the driver's side door. Two of the men wore surgical masks and latex gloves. The other one was staring at her with hot eyes.

"I fucking told you, get over here! I'm not waiting around all night while you figure this one out, asshole. Come on."

Nilla moved toward him. He had scars from a childhood illness all over his face and very long eyelashes. He had a gun holstered at his hip. If she didn't act fast enough, if she didn't strike hard enough he was going to kill her and even then, even if she took him down she had to worry about his two friends. This was it—the chain-link fence at the end of the dark alley. Endgame.

Before she could attack, though, he stepped toward her and held out his hands. "Here," he said, and shoved something at her. A mask and a pair of latex gloves. "You're on Plague Patrol tonight. I don't care what you were doing before, I'm three men short and I've got a schedule to meet."

Nilla had no idea what was going on but she pulled the mask over her mouth and nose. Maybe he wouldn't be able to see what she was through the thick paper. She fumbled with the gloves but managed to get them on somehow.

"Okay, up there, the balcony there. You take units B through G. It looks like it's going to be a bad one, tonight." A feathery thin layer of sympathy in his voice startled her. "St. Rose Dominican Hospital is already full up. We'll need to take this bunch all the way out to UMC." Nilla looked up and saw a split-level apartment complex with a red tile roof. The doors looked close together, each separated from the next by a single rectangular window. Blue flickering light came from most of the windows—probably the wavering campfire glow of television sets.

"I—I've never . . ." Nilla stammered.

"Christ, you've never been on Plague Patrol before? Well, it's pretty simple. You go in there and you see somebody who's sick, you drag them back down here and they go in the truck. They give you any trouble and I'll shoot them for you. Think you can handle that?"

Nilla nodded, knowing she couldn't handle it at all but also knowing she wasn't being given an actual option. She turned away without further comment and started up the stairs to the complex's second level.

"Jesus Fuck. The Chamber will take anybody these days, won't they?"

He wasn't talking to her. Nilla approached a door marked B and knocked. There was no answer but she could hear the television set inside blaring away so she knocked again, much louder. Finally she tried the knob and found the door unlocked. She stepped inside onto sea foam green shag carpeting littered with twists of paper tissue. Blood flecked some of them a dark red.

The TV played an old cowboy movie. John Wayne or somebody shooting two-handed from the back of a horse. Its ghostly blue light was the only illumination in the room.

Nilla moved through a filthy kitchenette—dishes in the sink full of dried-up rice grains, refrigerator chugging unhappily—and down a short hallway toward a bedroom. "Hello?" she called out. No answer, of course. The bedside table was covered in plastic bottles of over-the-counter medication.

Mael Mag Och had mentioned "poisoning the waters" with Dick. Was it really this bad, that armed thugs had to cart off the sick to avoid massive outbreaks of disease? Nilla could think of few things worse than the dead coming back to life to devour the living. A widespread pandemic of disease might fit the bill.

She turned back the sheets of the bed, half-expecting to find a dead man hidden there. Nothing. She turned around to head out of the apartment. Maybe there would be somebody in the next one. Maybe she could slip away while nobody was looking.

Someone sneezed right next to her left shoulder. Nilla wheeled around and threw open the door of a linen closet to find an enormously obese man wedged inside. He wore a white T-shirt and a pair of striped boxer shorts and a look of abject fear. He also had a ten-inch kitchen knife in his hand, raised over his head as if he was about to bring it down and slice her forehead open.

Nilla froze—no time to subtract herself from the equation, no time to hide, no time to think. Her hands were up, open, empty and he seemed to notice that fact.

"You," she said, the words bubbling out of her like swamp gas, "have got the drop on me, mister."

He didn't say a word. Just stood there staring at her. With his knife.

Nilla nodded reassuringly. "Tell you what. I'll run away now. I can't go out the front, though. Is there another way?"

"Maybe." He looked down at her. His knife hand didn't move. "If you're skinny."

A narrow little window in his bathroom opened over a back courtyard. It was a good ten-foot drop but there were piles of trash bags down there. The obese man helped by pushing her through the narrow opening, his hands pushing hard on her back and her buttocks until she went flying out into the darkness. Nilla landed with a meaty thud and rolled away. In a second she was up, collecting the brown hat that had fallen off her head in mid-flight.

The hat had fooled the man out front, the one organizing the Plague Patrol. It had terrified the obese man. The hat was more than just a way to hide her face, she realized. It was a badge that allowed her to be out past curfew—and something that would scare the hell out of everyone she met. She adjusted it carefully, low over her forehead, and headed back out into the night.

I have about THREE days worth of food. We WERE starving before but with only my MOUTH left to FEED . . . if you find this I guess that means I'm probably DEAD . . . if you don't find this I guess that means we're ALL dead, and this is really IT for the HUMAN RACE [Diary inscribed on the circulation desk of the Harold Washington Library, Chicago, IL, 4/14/05, emphasis as per original]

The Civilian took a handful of valerian root capsules as soon as they boarded the military flight back to Las Vegas. He fell asleep with his mouth open minutes after takeoff and snored obnoxiously the rest of the way. When the captain called back over the intercom to say they were being kept in a holding pattern above Las Vegas, Clark woke up his patron to give him the news.

Still half-asleep the Civilian nodded and looked out the window. "What's the hold up?" he asked. Before Clark could answer that he didn't know the Civilian offered to get on the radio and bully the air traffic controllers into submission.

"I don't imagine that's necessary," Clark told him, and tried to get back to the paperwork he had called up on his ruggedized laptop.

Eventually they put down and were met at the gate by a team of men in brown caps with carbines slung on their backs. Both of them were forced to submit to having the inside of their cheeks swabbed and tested on the spot.

When the results came back one of the men looked down at his shoes and offered Clark his hand. Clark took it, out of simple courtesy. "I am truly sorry for the inconvenience, Captain, but we can't take any chances right now. One of ours turned up dead— dead and walking, I mean—earlier today. Half his face was chewed off. It's not the first time but this one's a little weirder than usual and it's got us all spooked."

"Weird? How?" Clark asked.

"Well, there's no sign of a forced entry anywhere on the perimeter fence. And when you get dead people chowing on security personnel you expect to find a bunch of them—these things move in packs, mostly—but from all signs this was just one guy, or girl, or whatever, and our guy was armed to the teeth. Then there's the fact the kid was just about naked when we found him. Like somebody took his uniform for themself. It feels like they're trying to infiltrate our ranks or something. Impossible, yeah, I know. They don't have the brains for that."

All seven bones in Bannerman Clark's spine went rigid at once. The girl: the notion tore through his brain like a howling wind. "At least one of them does. They've shown organized behavior before, too— that's what happened to Denver. Listen, I'm way out of my jurisdiction here, but I think maybe I need to talk to your superiors about— "

"Yo, Bannerman, hold up there." The Civilian moved in with practiced ease. He switched his overcoat to his left arm and got his right hand on the brown cap's shoulder. "I'm sure these fine fellows have this thing under control. You guys work for, what, sheriff's office, state bureau of investigations, what?"

"The, uh," the brown cap stammered, "the Chamber of Commerce."

"Small business is the backbone of the nation," the Civilian intoned, putting every spare watt of power he had into the look of gravitas on his face. "Carry on, good man, carry on." He reached for Clark's arm and pulled him away. When they were out of earshot of the brown cap the Civilian hissed at his wonk. "We are so out of here. I'm not a very bright guy but I know one thing: when the local troopers start talking about weird and unexplained deaths, it's a short walk to doomsville. Las Vegas is going right down the shitter and I am not sticking around to watch. Is that clear?"

"The girl may be here," Clark protested.

"Yeah, and Wayne Newton might be doing three shows a night but you will not put me in danger for your personal obsession. Don't cross me on this, Bannerman."

Clark frowned. He could not afford to make the man an enemy. "Alright," he said, after a moment. "Our chopper is waiting in the other terminal. I suppose we should get back to Florence."

He had his orders. He didn't have to like them.

mike oppenbach, fought gators and bears in his life but this was too much. he was a good man to have with us when it hit the fan. real handy with a gun and a machete and he never complained. guess that's all i got to say [Eulogy written on a makeshift grave marker, Emeralda Marsh, FL 4/16/05]

"Step right up, folks, this is no time for the bashful. All the money you give tonight funds further research; we also take medicines and pharmaceuticals in trade. One to a customer, it's all you need. Guaranteed to keep you dead."

Nilla sat on a bench outside of a CVS pharmacy and watched what was happening in the parking lot with a critical eye. She was in the right place, the main distribution point for the vaccine in Las Vegas. Her informants—a couple of teenage kids out after curfew and easily scared by her brown cap—had not steered her wrong. Yet she couldn't believe that something so crucial could be run by people like this.

"He that believeth in me shall not live forever. Step right up. This little pill, this red and perfect ellipsoid, is the cure to what ails modern man. Thank you sir, please, tell your friends. One quick jolt and you're safe forever. Step right up." The barker stood six and a half feet tall and he was as wide through the shoulders as a professional wrestler. The waxed ends of an enormous mustache drooped from his face: up top he was going bald. He wore a stained baja shirt with bandoliers crossing his chest, sealed film canisters stuck in where rifle cartridges should be.

His associates weren't as outlandish in appearance but they had their own eccentricities. They worked out of the back of a passenger van airbrushed with stars and moons and galaxies. Two men. One as thin as a rake and twitchy, his head moving from side to side constantly as if he expected to be attacked at any time. The other pudgy and withdrawn. The former took the money from the block-long line of people waiting in the parking lot while the other handed out thick capsules of something sparkling and red.

"One to a customer, no greedy folk need apply. This is the love, the love you've been looking for. Who knew it came in pill form. Maximum love, step right up!"

Nilla rose from her bench and stepped into the sodium vapor glow of the parking lot's lights. In the line of waiting people her appearance made soft explosions of whispering panic but nobody fled. It was the brown cap. It masked her dark energy wonderfully. People saw it and they *knew* why her very presence seemed wrong and frightening. She was one of the jackbooted thugs who ruled Las Vegas with an iron fist.

"Do not be alarmed, folks, everything is under my personal control." The barker placed an enormous hand across his chest. In the orange light his flesh looked like cured ham. Nilla's presence was a signal and he was receiving it calmly but with all due attention. She could see his shoulders come in slightly, his stance changed to one of wary readiness. It felt like she was walking to the gunfight at the OK

Corral. "I will not rest," the barker continued, "until each and every one of you is satisfied."

The people in the line stared at her with open faces. Various fears chased each other through the furrows of their foreheads. They kept their hands shoved resolutely in their pockets. They looked like they were hunkering down against a dank and chill wind though the night air of Las Vegas was dry as a bone and late-spring warm.

"I'm from the Chamber," Nilla announced, to back up her one weapon in this showdown—the brown cap. "Who the hell are you?"

The big man placed a hand across his belt buckle and bent slowly toward her in a graceful bow. "I am he whose name was writ in water. I am the very model of a modern Major General. Some call me the space cowboy, while others refer to me as the gangster of love."

Nilla squinted her eyes. "Fuck this. I can shut you down with one phone call, jerk. In fact I might just do it on principle."

"Then call me Mellowman, the stoned superhero. I'm here to bring a little peace of mind to these benighted people. May I ask who you are, young filly?"

Nilla shook her head. "I'm from the Chamber. That's all you need to know. You people, get out of here now. Don't you know there's a curfew?" She ran at the scared people in the line and they scattered like pigeons. "Now. I want to see your operation here. I want to know just what the hell you think you're doing." The bravado act she was putting on made Nilla's nerves sing. She was no longer capable of getting an adrenaline rush but something ice cold and lethal blossomed inside of her and she liked it. Sure. For the first time in her death she actually had some power.

"Right this way, miss." Mellowman or whatever the hell his name was gestured for her to follow him. "Welcome to the Space Van, my home that gets up and goes when the home I got is got up and gone."

"You're selling vaccine, right? Does it actually work?" Nilla stepped around to the open back of the van to look inside. Brightly upholstered plush interior, crammed full of boxes and a pair of narrow folding cots. Apparently Mellowman and associates slept in their mobile drugstore when they weren't hawking pills.

"How about a free sample? Find out for yourself?" Mellowman picked up a box and slung it under his arm. Revealed below sat a jar full of the sparkling red capsules she'd seen handed out.

"Hey, dude, come on, let's not do this," one of his associates said, the thin and twitchy one. Nilla speared him with a glance. When she turned back Mellowman had one of the capsules in the expansive palm of his left hand.

Nilla wondered what would happen if she took it. Would it kill the virus or microbe or whatever it was that had reanimated her? Would she collapse in a lifeless heap? Probably it would do nothing. She picked up the jar and shook it. The capsules inside rattled with a satisfying noise. "Is this all you have?"

"Until we make some more. My *aide du medecin* over here, we call him Morphine Mike, is the man with the magic recipe."

Wow, Nilla thought. This was going to be so easy. Trash the pills, kill the guy who made them. Mael would be satisfied. Maybe he would even let her go. She put the jar back inside the van and turned to announce that she was going to arrest them all.

She found herself looking into the twin barrels of a sawed-off shotgun. It must have been in the box Mellowman had grabbed. The black OO of the muzzles looked like the symbol for infinity.

"You stupid bitch, who do you think sent us out here? I'm on the steering committee of the goddamned Chamber of Commerce. I don't know who you are, thinking you can come in here and rip us off, but you have made one truly dumb mistake."

She had time enough to turn herself invisible but she panicked and couldn't remember how to do it. She screamed instead. His finger jerked on the weapon's two triggers and she heard a noise like hell cracking open.

{fursuit19} is somebody there
{fursuit19} hello
{fursuit19} hello
* fursuit19 HAS LOGGED OUT *
[AOL Instant Message transcript, 4/18/05]

The Blackhawk came in low and slow over the juniper-studded arroyos that surrounded the prison. Clark touched the Civilian's arm and pointed out Pike's Peak. As they drew closer he said, "Let me officially welcome you to the Big One." He felt strangely proud of Florence-ADX though he certainly had not built the prison, nor did he particularly like it. It had become his headquarters, however, and in a sense his home.

The Civilian looked excited. "Is it true you've got Pineapple Face there? You know, Noriega? And the Unabomber?"

"All the prisoners were removed in the first days of the Epidemic."

The Civilian looked disappointed, yet as they circled around for final approach it was Clark whose expectations were truly shattered. When he'd left the prison had been a safe, discrete structure, hidden carefully behind its multiple layers of impregnable fencing.

In his absence it had turned into a shantytown. Tents and primitive shacks of corrugated tin had been erected in a wide semicircle around the side of the prison facing the road. Narrow alleys ran between the ramshackle housing units and these were full of people in civilian dress. More than a few waved at the Blackhawk as it roared overhead. They looked healthy enough. There were children, too, and some animals: dogs, sheep, even a few horses. A stretch of rolling hillside had been cleared of vegetation and turned into a parking lot for dozens of vehicles. Not just the buses and vans of the convoy Clark had personally lead from Denver but smaller passenger cars, too, motorcycles and bicycles and a smattering of single-engine airplanes.

The Blackhawk set down on a pad in the main prison yard where Vikram and Sergeant Horrocks were waiting to meet it. Vikram had his iron bracelet on and had added a new accessory, a strangely curved knife long enough to qualify as a short sword. Horrocks had dressed up in full uniform as if he expected Clark to demand an immediate inspection of the troops. Clark introduced the Civilian around and then gestured at the small town that had sprung up outside the gates. "Word gets around, I suppose. When did this start?"

"It is only a very recent phenomenon," Vikram assured him. "But more come in every day. We do not let them inside of the fence but they don't seem to mind. They say they have come for the protection of the Hero of Denver. We could hardly turn them away, you know."

Clark shook his head. He was famous, now? He didn't want this new burden. "This means new security issues, a whole new perimeter to keep secure, not to mention the health problems they'll face without proper sanitation. And we can't offer them any kind of medical care. We don't have enough supplies for our own people."

The Civilian grabbed his arm. "Come on, already, sunshine. You've earned this."

He led Clark to the main gates. Horrocks ordered for them to be opened and they swung out to reveal a gathered throng of people who pressed up close to the entrance as soon as it was clear. A man in a tattered business suit rushed up and grabbed Clark's hand.

"Captain, I'm Jim Jesuroga. I've got to thank you—my family couldn't make it on our own."

"Let me kiss him!" a woman shrieked, a middle-aged matron with dyed maroon hair. She wrapped her arms around Clark's neck and pecked at his cheek. She stank of body odor and artificial lavender. Her children came up behind her, their eyes bright with hope, while others moved in, all of them wanting to get close, to touch him, to speak with him if only for a moment.

Clark spent nearly an hour among them, listening to their stories. What he learned shocked him. So few people had survived, so very many had died and reanimated. It was bad, bad all over and the only way to survive seemed to be to get out, to get east. Since that was turning out not to be such a great idea (the dead were already in New York and Atlanta was overrun, he learned), the last resort seemed to be Florence-ADX.

When he was done meeting with survivors, when he was too exhausted for any more, he retired to the prison. The gates closed again and the Civilian came up beside him. "Feels pretty good, doesn't it? Being the hero and all."

"I . . . suppose it does," Clark admitted.

"Yeah, so you better not fuck up and get all of these good people killed."

Clark blinked in shock. Something to keep in mind, he told himself.

PART
FOUR

The new study in angiogenesis holds some
promise . . . stem cell therapy could be the key.
I palpated the neoplasm today and it was the size
of a robin's egg. Mood: Cheerful, though she
refused to eat. [Lab Notes, 9/12/02]

DICK COULD HEAR voices and he knew food was nearby.
But now was not the time to eat. He hid himself, as best he could,
and waited.

"Jesus! What is that smell?"

"Hell, I don't know, but we have to get out of here!"

"It's like month-old tuna or something. Cat piss sealed in Tup-
perware to let it mellow."

"They're going to get in here. I don't think you understand.
They're at the gates right now and we didn't have time to lock them.
They are going to come out onto this runway and then we won't be
able to take off."

"Huh. Alright, alright. French cheese left sitting on a radiator?
Help me get this door closed."

Darkness slid across Dick's hidden form. He wriggled deeper
into the packing material inside his crate. He hungered, oh, how
he hungered, and there was food just inches away but the Voice
had made it clear. There was still work to do.

His whole body vibrated as the military cargo plane jumped into the sky.

I won't accept this! No hope, they say. Keep her comfortable, they tell me. Enjoy the time you have left. No! I am a scientist and I believe all problems can be solved given adequate study and application. I am a scientist and I refuse to accept the inevitable. [Lab Notes, 9/20/02]

Outside, beyond the fence, construction crews were working nonstop installing plumbing and streetlights in the shantytown. Bannerman Clark watched a backhoe sinking its teeth into the yielding earth for a while and then turned back to the one-way mirror behind him to listen to another story.

"We had barricades across the roads but they just came up through the sewer. They came up out of the storm drain—covered in shit, um, pardon my French. Covered in sewage and they didn't care. You could see their eyes but it was like . . . God, do you know what I mean? Those aren't eyes anymore. They aren't people."

If he couldn't allow the survivors inside the prison walls Clark intended to do what he could for them. He could give them a healthy environment—Vikram had loved the idea of building infrastructure out there, it gave the soldiers something to do other than contemplating their own mortality. An Engineer to the end, the Sikh Major had thrown himself into the hard, backbreaking work as if he were going off to a round of golf.

"My sister-in-law told us to keep the car running, that she would be out as soon as she found her passport. We waited and waited and waited . . . we burned through a quarter tank of gas before Chuck decided we had to get moving. I cried, I cried but I didn't try to stop him."

Inside the prison Clark oversaw another program. Each survivor was brought in to be registered—name and vital statistics entered in a proper database, lot number in the shantytown recorded, a cursory medical exam performed. Those who wished it could stay and tell their stories and have them recorded onto audiotape. All of them, it seemed, wished it.

"Six days in my office, and then the water stopped flowing. I was so hungry and I knew I couldn't make it without water. They were all over the parking lot, touching the cars, just, just touching them like they were trying to remember what they were for. I knew I had to make a break for it."

A row of narrow interrogation rooms lined the space beyond the one-way mirror. In each room a survivor sat with a uniformed interviewer and spoke into a microphone. The chairs were uncomfortable, the rooms cramped and dreary, designed for use by hardened inmates. None of the survivors seemed to mind. The experiences they'd been through were so traumatic and so huge compared to the banal routine of their previous lives that they needed to get them out, needed to purge themselves of what they'd seen and not a single one of them complained or ended an interview early.

"I was out at a fishing cabin on Lake Mohave, me and three other guys and they . . . they wanted to leave, to get home to their families. I couldn't say no, even if I knew we were safer there. We loaded up the truck, we had about sixty pounds of Stripers in the back packed in ice, figured we could eat those if we didn't find anything else. It just didn't matter. I was in the desert two days before this Immigration Services truck picked me up."

They wanted someone to listen. Clark was happy to oblige them. The more information he could get about the outside world the better, of course. And at first that was all it meant—information gathering, intelligence in its most primitive form. As he listened in on the interviews, though, from his hidden roost in the administration building, he found he couldn't turn away. He needed to hear the stories, as much as they needed to tell them.

He needed to know it was possible to survive. He needed to know that people who weren't soldiers still had a chance to live.

"So we got to this one town, and Charles was in pretty bad

shape, and I stopped and there were dogs everywhere. I mean whole bunches, um, packs of them, you know? I guess when the people left they couldn't take their dogs with them. They were everywhere just smiling and wagging their tails, I was worried at first but they were so cute. They were hungry, though, you could tell. I tried feeding them but there were so many. I found some dog food in this grocery store. It was pitch black in there but I figured it was safe. If the dogs were just running around and okay then there couldn't be any dead people. I found the dog food and I was looking for a can opener when I heard this noise. It wasn't a scream, and it wasn't dogs barking. Okay, I mean, all the dogs were barking, they were always barking. That was kind of a nice sound, they sounded happy. This was different though. The dogs were going *crazy*. Somebody was really in trouble."

Clark pulled up a wooden chair and leaned his elbows on the railing before the mirror. The girl in the interview room had long dark hair stained with blood—how on earth had that happened, and why hadn't someone let her into the shower room? Perhaps she had refused the offer. He'd seen stranger behavior from the survivors. Many of them slept sitting in chairs, or in their cars, too accustomed to constantly moving to ever lie down again. Some of them wouldn't use the facilities without someone else standing guard outside. Hell had come to them and they had learned to live in hell.

"I came around the corner and the dogs were everywhere, and they were jumping up and down, biting at the air. Really upset. I tried shushing them but there were so many. Then I looked and I saw they were all over our car. The back door was open and Charles . . . I don't know what he was thinking. I guess they don't, you know. Think much. They just get hungry and wander off. Charles had tried to get out of the car but he got snagged in his seat belt. The dogs." The girl fell silent for a while. "The dogs."

"Go on," the interviewer told the girl. A female soldier, maybe five years older than the girl across the table. She poured a glass of water and handed it to her subject.

The girl had her arms curled tightly around her stomach as if she were feeling nauseous. She didn't even look at the water. "The dogs tore Charles apart, I guess. They tore him, well, to pieces. I tried fighting them but they didn't care about me, they just ignored me. They could tell, somehow. They could tell Charles was dead and they hated him. I used to like dogs, you know? I did."

The girl wasn't crying but she wiped at her face anyway. Maybe it was hot in the interrogation room and she was sweating. "I wish I didn't make Nilla get out of the car," the girl said. "She could of helped me, maybe."

"Nilla?" The interviewer asked. "Who's Nilla?"

The girl's face hardened into concrete and she stared at the interviewer with blazing eyes.

For some reason—a hunch, perhaps, a stab of intuition—Clark leaned closer to the glass.

Chemo isn't helping. Laetrile, interferon, gene therapy, mega-antioxidants: nothing. Soon I'll be down to dried tiger pizzles and psychic surgery. [Lab Notes, 10/30/02]

She never actually lost consciousness. She couldn't even faint.

The pain squeezed her down to a narrow field of view, like peering through the slats of a set of Venetian blinds. Solid black filled the rest of her vision. When she closed her eyes energy buzzed and crackled and spat all around her.

Mael, she thought. Mael, I didn't betray you. I tried to do what you asked.

Nilla, he replied, but she could barely hear him. **Nilla, what's happened to you?**

Her body felt like a torn-up rag. Ridges and threads of pain dug through her midsection, flesh and bone torn away from each other, organs punctured and deflated. Her stomach muscles hung slack and useless. She could not have stood up even with assistance.

Under her head the constant burr and rattle of the Space Van's wheels on pavement hurt her teeth, turned her eyes to bruised jelly.

Even her brain hurt. She couldn't breathe—not that she needed to, but it would have felt infinitesimally better to be able to exhale a long and lugubrious moan.

"You cut her to pieces. There's no pulse, Rick. No breathing. She's dead!"

"If she was one of them she would be up and at our throats. Just keep her alive long enough that we can dump her outside of city limits. I'm not taking the heat if it turns out she really was from the Chamber." Mellowman stepped into her field of view. Looking down at her his face turned bunched-up and porcine. "Listen, my little Muffin. If you die in my van I will shoot your corpse," he said.

"Get back, alright? It's hard enough doing this while we're moving. Jesus—could we slow down a little?" Something sharp slid into the flesh of Nilla's bicep. A hypodermic needle. Of all the pointless things. She tried smiling a little and found to her surprise that she still had a little control over her facial muscles.

"Dead my ass, look at that." Mellowman stared deep into her eyes. "She likes it, she likes whatever you just put in her arm."

"Just a reflex, Rick. Don't get excited."

Mellowman shook his head. "Who are you working for, lady? Who sent you? Playing dead isn't going to save you from a beating. Talk to me, fucker!" He leaned very close until she could smell the stink of garlic sausages on his breath. "I know you can hear me, you stupid cow!" When she failed to respond he pursed his lips and let a dollop of drool dangle out of his mouth, right over her face. It wobbled back and forth, yellowish and full of bubbles. It filled up her vision and instinctively she tossed her head to the side to avoid it.

He sucked it hurriedly back into his mouth. "I got you!" he screamed, and then he started punching her.

She went limp, as best her savaged muscles would let her. The pain kept booming away in her side, as rhythmic and powerful as the surf coming in. Her body jerked like a dog on a leash every time he hit her.

Eventually he stopped.

Nilla—it's hard for me to find you, where are you, lass?
She could hear Mael calling her but through the pain his voice
was a little light floating far out on a foggy ocean. She lacked the
resources to answer.

Nilla! I can barely sense you out there, talk to me!
Later, but still long before the dawn. She could see darkness outside of the window in the van's rear door. Occasional arpeggios of
light as they passed under streetlamps, pizzicato flashes of red as
they passed a car going the other way, few and far between. Mike,
the one with the needles, had his arms around her, moving her back
and forth. Maybe trying to wake her up. He pulled a blanket around
her as the van slowed and pulled away from the lights. The back
door fell open and she was pushed and dragged out, onto loose dirt.
She could feel the van's exhaust farting against her leg, hot and dry.

The desert at night: intimate or claustrophobic, you take your
pick. The very opposite of the expansive emptiness of daytime. The
darkness, near total, pushed in close looking to share your warmth.
The few sounds were mournful and polite.

"Welcome to Arizona, Muffin. Home of fuck-all and plenty of
it," Mellowman bellowed at her, his face very close to her ear. She
couldn't stand on her own. If Mike let go of her she knew she would
fall. "I'm going to shoot you again. In the head this time. If that still
doesn't kill you we're going to bury you in a shallow grave. If you
dig yourself out of the grave then I will come back and shoot you
again, until it works."

Just . . . just go invisible, Nilla thought. But that was beyond her,
way beyond her. She lacked the energy for it. She lacked the energy
to scream.

Mike set her down, leaning up against the side of the van. The
third guy, the fidgety one—had be been driving the van? He must
have been driving the van—leaped out of the back holding a shovel.
"Alright, Termite, you get to it," Mellowman told him. He moved rapidly out of Nilla's field of vision but she could hear him digging, quite
close by. "You know why I call him Termite? Nah, you couldn't
know. See he likes to go fast, our friend Termite, and when he's going

fast enough his teeth kind of grind together. You heard of meth mouth?" When she didn't reply he kept going. Clearly there was some time to kill before she was shot. That just made the fear worse. "So Morphine Mike, our famous physician friend, he figures the best thing to do is to put a piece of wood in the Termite's mouth when he's speeding. Otherways his teeth will just grind away to dust. We three look out for each other, you understand? So this idea of Mike's works great except for one thing. The first piece of wood we put in there, he just bites through it. So we get a chunk as big as your thumb. It was gone in a day. Most of it was just missing, ground away to sawdust. Mike said maybe we should stop but I figure, well, fuck. The son of a bitch needs the fiber!"

Mellowman burst out in an explosive laugh at his own joke. He knelt down near her and took one of the film canisters from his bandolier. He popped it open with one thumb and a complex, earthy, skunky smell came out. A vegetable smell. He dug out a finger's length of leafy green material and rolled it into a cigarette. He lit it and blew smoke in her face. "Not much longer now. You feel like talking?"

She let her eyes go lax in their sockets. No point in looking at anything. There was nothing in this little tableau that could save her.

"I don't expect you do. Some people like to talk when they get to this point, is all, they like to confess to things like I was a priest or somethin'. I've been out this way before, you see. I've had problems like you before. Not so much it's become a habit. You want a puff on this? Or maybe some water? Maybe, um, well, maybe, Muffin, you, you want to know what it's like to be with a man. You know, one last time."

She focused her vision on him again and was surprised by what she found in his face. He looked genuinely interested.

How was that even possible? She was dead, for one thing, and beyond that half of her body had been destroyed by his shotgun blast. And he still wanted her sexually. She recalled the time she had silently begged Charles to touch her, to want her. This should feel good, or at least comforting. But of course it didn't. She was afraid,

afraid that nobody was left to save her. That the end of her world had finally arrived.

She could plead for her life but that was beyond pointless— someone like Mellowman wanted her to suffer, to beg, and the more she did it the more he would want. She could ask for what she really wanted and maybe, just maybe she would get it. "Huh, huh," she snuffled. "Hungry." It came out on a long exhalation.

Mellowman shrugged. "Yeah, whatever. Then I guess a blow job is out of the question." It was a joke, whether or not she found it funny. Apparently he had been serious about granting her last request, though, or perhaps he just didn't care. Mike went into the van—she felt it rocking against her back as he moved around inside there—and emerged with half of a sandwich. Corned beef, judging by the smell. He held it near her mouth but she couldn't use her hands, couldn't even lift her arms. He had to feed it to her, disassembling the components, tearing the meat between his fingers. His motions around her were respectful, almost gentle. Maybe it would have been different if he knew the shreds of lunchmeat were far less appetizing to her than his fingers were. She managed not to bite the hand that fed her. When she was done eating Mellowman ordered Mike to pick her up and carry her and his hands grabbed her forcefully under her armpits.

Nilla.

Mael's voice in her head sounded distorted, fuzzy on the low end. It irritated her, itched in one corner of her brain, the left side high up. She felt the buzz in her teeth.

Nilla, Dick's on the road to you but I doubt he'll arrive in time. There's something else I can try, but no guarantees, lass. Do you understand? It may be as I can't get you out of this one.

She understood. She was grateful he was with her there at the end.

Mike and the other one, the twitchy guy, lowered her into the grave, a hole maybe three feet deep in the sand. The half of a sandwich she'd eaten had given her a little strength back, enough to sit up anyway.

Mellowman broke open his shotgun and loaded in a pair of shells. When he sighted down the barrels at her his free eye was wide with excitement. He was going to enjoy this, she saw, and she was certain by the way he looked at her, that and no other evidence, that of all the people he had killed and buried in shallow graves before none of them had been women.

Mellowman placed the end of the shotgun against her forehead and braced himself against the recoil. Nilla had been in that position before. Go invisible, she told herself, but she couldn't. The sandwich hadn't been enough, it hadn't bolstered her energy enough to let her do that.

Her mind kept working, though, no matter how fatigued her body felt. Her mind kept scratching and begging and pleading. It kept asking her one question: what if the bullet didn't kill her, but they buried her anyway? What if she got to spend the rest of time buried in a shallow grave, unable to escape and far worse—unable to lose consciousness?

Mellowman put his finger through the trigger guard of the shotgun. He started to squeeze.

Then he stopped. There was music playing somewhere. Muffled, deepened as it came wending its way through the fabric of his denim jacket, music floated up out of Mellowman's chest.

"Aw, fuck no, aw, not now," he whined. "Nah, not that ring. Goddamnit! The Chamber can wait five fucking minutes, can't they?"

He lowered the shotgun and took a red-white-and-blue cell phone out of his inner jacket pocket. He stared at it as if he were holding a coprolite in his hand. Something exotic and bizarre and loathsome all at the same time.

He flipped it open and started to talk.

Bad result from the nephrectomy but codeine was made for nights like these and the swish of the dialysis machine is perfect white noise. She's sleeping peacefully, now. Wish I could say the same. [Lab Notes, 11/1/02]

Vikram tapped in a password on his keyboard and a window opened up on the main monitor. Satellite imagery of the Rockies, received in real time from the OSR's newest and most sophisticated birds. The current view showed a composite image with the false color data from an infra-red Landsat run through a codec that matched it up with the standard footprint imaging of a Keyhole-class spybird.

"Amazing—you're telling me these pictures are how old?"

"Only a second or two, and that delay comes from the time it takes the computers to process and render the images. We have a Lacrosse-class satellite coming over the horizon in a few minutes and then I am promised we'll be able to start constructing stereoscopic images. Three dimensional views."

Bannerman Clark shook his head. He could hardly believe this. The last time he'd seen satellite data had been in Desert Storm. Back then images from the birds had to be developed—they came on actual photographic film, downloaded over a span of hours and then processed in a lab. And that was assuming the satellites were where you wanted them to be. Sometimes it took hours to get an image, or even days if the footprints weren't right. "How did we come so far so fast?" he asked.

"Advances in computer technology," Vikram suggested, with a shrug. "For the most part. Also there are very many more satellites now than before. They say five of them are passing over your head on any given day."

Clark shook his head. "We're still looking for a needle in a haystack, though." A map of Colorado had been tacked to one wall near the monitors. Desiree Sanchez's epidemiology data had been plotted on the map as a series of vectors pointing back towards the epicenter. Theoretically it should have been all they needed to triangulate the position—to find the locus where the Epidemic had truly begun. Unfortunately Sanchez's data were thin on the ground and some of them contradicted others. Some were almost certainly wrong, either due to faulty reporting or they might just be false positives, random violence that had nothing to do with the Epidemic. They had narrowed their search parameters to a narrow corridor high up in the mountains, a zone varying between three and seventeen miles across and about a hundred miles long from Steamboat Springs down to Florence. That left them with fifteen hundred square miles of rugged terrain to look at. An area a little larger than Rhode Island. And they didn't really know what they were looking for.

Clark nodded in anticipation and rubbed his hands together. "How do we start?" Clark sat down next to Vikram and the master processor box. The ruggedized computer had so many cables and patch cords emerging from its back end that it looked like the head of a squid. The monitors, the keyboard and the mouse were all wireless, which still looked wrong to Clark, as if someone had installed them incorrectly. "How do you aim the camera?"

Vikram smiled cheerfully and launched another program from his start menu. "This camera aims itself." Vikram keyed in a search request for point sources of heat above one hundred and fifty degrees Celsius. The laptop chunked and grumbled for a moment and then windows started popping up all over the monitor. Vikram maximized one and together they looked at a rendered view of a car fire, the chassis blazing away in super-high-contrast black and white. The camera wheezed in and out of focus as it tried to stay locked on to the wavering flames. Vikram discarded that image, moved on to another.

Together they paged through the windows. At first each picture was a new and exciting toy, a present to be unwrapped. The story they told, however, grew rapidly depressing and then more depressing. The images looked to Clark after a while like microscope slides, layers of horror meticulously dissected and mounted on slips of glass. A sprawling, out of control forest fire on the Western Slope had the appearance of a vicious amoeba attacking a stomach lining. Oil tanks exploding in colossal fireballs in Colorado Springs looked like alveoli bursting inside a collapsed lung.

As horrific as the metaphors might be they hid a worse truth. Colorado, the state Bannerman Clark called home and which he had sworn to protect, was dying. He'd seen plenty of chaos in his march south to Florence but chaos was what you expected on the battlefield. Soldiers rarely saw what came after, the all-crushing descent of entropy and decay. There were few people in the satellite images. Those few who did show up were already dead and still moving only out of sheer perversity.

"Time for a break," he said, after about an hour. They had finished with the high-temperature images and had moved on to those targets that displayed movement above a certain threshold. He had looked at far too many pictures of packs of ghouls milling aimlessly through the abandoned streets of tiny mountain towns, seen more than his share of cars racing away from undead hordes. "I need to hit the head."

Vikram nodded, not bothering to look away from the screen. He collapsed a window and the next one underneath showed the linear, no-nonsense buildings of a military base. The Buckley ARNG base, to be specific. The dead had swarmed through its main gates and were clustered on the parade ground, swarming over each other, clambering on top of each others' limbs and torsos and faces like a scrum in a rugby match. Clark wondered what must be at the bottom of that heap to make the ghouls so desperate and so active. Food, of course, that was their prime motivation. Whether said food was or had been human or not he decided he didn't want to know.

He headed down the corridor and pushed open the door of the men's room. Trash littered the floor, transparent cellophane and pieces of yellow cardboard. He could hear the Civilian inside one of the stalls talking on his cell phone.

"Yeah, well you will do nothing of the—um, umgh—nothing for the fucking sort until I give you the word. No, nobody gets shot. I don't care what she did to you, it doesn't justify . . . look, even I answer to somebody. You have to do what you're told, yeah, but this time you get something in return. You can write your own ticket, is what—anything that's in my power. I dog you today, and it is worth so much to you. Umhumuh, ugh, gah. It's the beauty of capitalism, everybody gets a turn pissing down somebody else's neck. Fine, then, fuck you very much too. I'll see you there in thirty-six hours."

Clark relieved himself and washed his hands carefully in the sink. He saw the stall door open in the mirror and the Civilian emerged with yellow foam dripping from one corner of his mouth. He had a half-finished box of marshmallow peeps in one hand and his cell phone in the other.

"Looking good, Clark, looking good. I might have something for you in a while. Keep yourself ready," the Civilian said. His eyes looked like they'd been frosted and there was sweat on his forehead and on the tip of his nose. He left the bathroom without further comment.

Clark didn't know what to make of that.

Back in the control room Vikram had narrowed his search down to three images he wanted Clark to see. The first showed the prison itself, thronged with motion—human, living human motion out in the shantytown beyond the walls. There were a few spots of extreme temperature Clark couldn't identify. They weren't located near any of the exhausts from the HVAC systems, nor were they anywhere near the generators. "We'll need to check those," Clark said. "I think we can safely say that the epicenter isn't right underneath our feet, however. What else have you got?"

Vikram switched to a second image. A complex of buildings near Clear Creek Summit. An abandoned but functional ski resort, judging by the constantly moving chair lift. "This looks like a hardened facility," he told Clark. "Look, here, these doors on the main building. They've been reinforced with welded steel. Over here, this looks to me to be a machine gun nest, what do you think?"

"I think you're right. They have power so we can assume there are people inside. Of course right now there's no reason to think they're bad guys. Anybody sane would reinforce their doors right now and a machine gun for perimeter security is one of the better home improvements I can think of. This definitely belongs on our short list, though. What's this?" he asked, pointing at a minimized window near the bottom of the screen. The third candidate for the site of the Epicenter.

Vikram opened it without comment. When he saw the image Clark sat down carefully and folded his hands in his lap.

"This one gets my vote," Vikram said, and Clark had to agree.

"What are those? Dinosaurs?"

Sheldrake is a crackpot, of course. Canalized pathways? Morphic resonance? It's all chemical! I don't know why I waste my time with this nonsense. Cell differentiation stimulated by a biological field that can't be directly detected? Come on! [Lab Notes, 4/9/03]

Up through Nevada, deep into denied territory. Nilla traveled farther in one night in the Space Van than she had since her re-awakening. Hundreds of miles. There was no traffic.

"Why are we heading east? Things were good in Vegas. We had an operation," Mike told Mellowman once. Nilla had nothing to do but listen to the two of them bicker, that and stare out the back of the van at stars and night. "We had some protection. This road leads to . . . I don't know, hell. Hell on earth."

"Here be dragons," Mellowman agreed. "And some people like dragons. Some people will pay anything for just one quick gander at a dragon's left butt cheek." He shifted in the back of the van, duck-walking across Nilla's field of vision. His eyes were bright red, almost glowing, which wasn't surprising considering the ratio of pot smoke to oxygen in the van.

"Where are you taking me?" Nilla creaked.

Mellowman seemed to have found a new method for coping with her refusal to die, it seemed, and that was simply to ignore her. "Besides," he said, but not to her. "Vegas is on the way out."

"What are you talking about? The Chamber is keeping people safe!"

"The Chamber," he told Mike, his tone growing imperial, "is made up of assholes like me and I know I'm running out of ideas. More people getting sick every day—more of these things getting loose. No. Vegas is on its last legs. If we want to make something happen, something real, the east coast is where we need to be. Maybe we even need to go further. I bet they'll just love our act in London. You ever been to Paris? It's the City of Lights. I can take you there if you'll just shut up and do what I tell you."

"You think it'll stop here? You don't think we'll take it to Europe with us?"

"I'm doing what feels right. I'm going on instinct. That's what I've got, which is what has taken me this far and let me survive and even build something in a world that wants to kill me every time I turn around. And you know what, Mike? Lately my instinct is talking to me about heading east, and how I can do that. Lately it's been telling me I got to travel light. That I gotta trim the dead wood. How do you like that? I will include you in my plans because you know how to brew up the shit. Assuming you stop arguing with me."

There was a long pause before Mike answered. "You want to get rid of me, huh? So you can be all alone with the Termite," he finally said, sounding like he had surrendered something. "Well, shit, he does what you say, that's for sure. He's a hell of a driver and he digs graves faster than anyone I know but he's not much for conversation. And then there's the question of what he's going to do when you run out of scooby snacks. You think he's tweaking now . . ."

Mellowman laid down on one of the folding cots. "You got a point there, I suppose. Now shut up. I want sleep. Mellowman wants sleep!"

"Sure. Sure thing," Mike said. Nilla couldn't see his face from where she sat.

Silence after that, for a long time. The sound of wheels on concrete, which is really no sound at all once you're used to it. Nilla started listening for the jingle of the keys in the ignition, or the sound of Mellowman's heavy breathing. He never snored, though occasionally he muttered something dark and foul in his slumber.

She wasn't allowed to sleep. She wasn't allowed to just zone out. It seemed that whatever fate had let her live through so much wasn't in the business of being kind.

She heard Mike come across the floor toward her just fine when the time came. When he was sure that Mellowman was fast asleep, most likely. He spoke to her in a dry whisper. "I know you're dead. Undead. I know you're not like the others, though. What the hell are you?" He didn't seem to expect a straight answer from her. Perhaps he thought that she would refuse to give him that kind of information. If she'd known, though, she would have told him everything.

"You have some friends in high places, I'll give you that. Getting you out of that shallow grave like that . . . it had to take some serious incentive. Or some serious threats. Somebody wants you really bad if they can talk Rick out of a thrill like that. Care to tell me about it?"

She shook her head, gently so as not to dislodge the bones of her neck. The vibration of the moving van made her feel as if she would fly to pieces at any moment. "I don't know," she said. "There's this guy, he's dead, but like me. His name is Mael Mag Och. He said he would try to help me. That's all I know. He talks to me . . . he sends his thoughts into my head, it's like telepathy, and he told me he would try to help."

Mike sat up and looked down into her face. "Mael Mag Och? What kind of name is that?" He leaned closer. "Do you think—I mean, what kind of a deal is he making with us?"

Nilla squinted. "Oh, he would never make a deal with you. You're the one who makes the vaccine. You're trying to stop us."

Mike's face folded in half down the middle. "The vaccine? No, that's not . . . well, I guess you don't know." He looked over at the jar of iridescent red pills. "That stuff's just a placebo. Sugar pills." He stared into her eyes looking for comprehension. "It's worthless, it doesn't do anything. This is all a scam that Rick came up with. I have a degree in environmental chemistry, I knew how to make them. Them, and the stuff that keeps the Termite marginally sane. It was Rick's idea to sell people vaccine. He called it a psychology experiment at first, he wanted to see if coming back from the dead was all in people's minds. Either that or he was bullshitting me from the start. Listen. I need to get away from him. You need to just get away. Maybe you and I can make our own deal. Maybe we can help each other out."

She lacked the strength to turn herself invisible. She lacked the strength to sit up for very long. She couldn't imagine any way in which she could help him but she knew this was her big chance, her one long shot at getting away from Mellowman and the Space Van. Mael Mag Och would never broker a deal with a living human, of course, but maybe if she just lied, made something up . . .

In the end she lacked the energy to think up a convincing lie.

"I . . . I'll try," she said, finally, her voice very small.

Mike's face froze, expressionless and cold. "I would advise that you try hard. Rick's not like other people. He's violently insane."

He slid back across the floor of the van and didn't speak to her for the rest of the night.

In the morning, with white light coming through the van's window, pummeling her with its heat, the van slowed down and went off road. Nilla felt it jounce and shudder and throw her around like a rag doll before it finally came to a stop. When the door opened and she could see outside again she was looking at the entrance to a cave. Warning signs covered the entrance: JUKEBOX CAVE. OFF LIMITS! A barred iron gate covered the entrance sealed with chains and a heavy padlock.

Mellowman stretched and groaned as he got up from his narrow bed. He stepped out of the van and reached deep into the front of his pants as if he was playing with himself. Eventually he pulled out his hand and revealed a steel key, which fit the padlock perfectly. He wheeled the gate open and the van backed into the burnt orange darkness of the cave. This, Nilla realized, must be their destination.

Darkness collapsed on top of her as the van pulled further inside.

This smacks of Vitalism but . . . I can't deny those results. Repeatable, if you follow the extended lab instructions . . . teaching the cells to grow? The force that makes the grass run green? Come on. I'm looking at magic here, plain and simple. Somebody bring me my pointy hat and my wand. [Lab Notes, 7/21/03]

"We're about five miles from the old Air Force base at Wendover. Just across the border into Utah." Mellowman stood silhouetted against the bare purple light at the mouth of the cave. Inside wasn't total darkness—a Coleman portable lantern painted a rough circle of yellow on the floor perhaps a dozen yards away. Nilla's eyes weren't in great shape, however, and she couldn't make much out.

"Back in the day," he went on, "the airmen used to come up to these caves with girls they picked up in town. Every girl loves a man in uniform, right? But they didn't want their daddies seeing what they were doing. These caves offered some cheap privacy. It got to be such a popular pastime that they brought in a cement mixer and put down the floor you're currently drooling on. It's tough to really enjoy yourself with stalagmites poking you in the back. Somebody else figured they'd give the place an air of legitimacy by rigging up a jukebox in here, and that's where the name came from. Jukebox Cave. They had some great parties, my grandpa used to tell me. He was one of those guys. I've always loved this place. Can't you feel it, the vibe in here? The feeling, that low-down, dirty feeling. This is ground zero for getting it on. This is fuck heaven. I brought some girls here myself when I was a young Mormon, back when I used to have ninety-nine sex. You ever had a ninety-nine? You know what that is?"

She didn't dare answer.

"Ninety-nine percent. That's everything but. That's when you do every last bit of dirtiness you can to the girl, short of squirting up her skirt. No, if you spill it on the ground well that's not adultery, no ma'am, that's just the sin of Onan and that has got to be at least one percent less sinful, now don't it? And sometimes one per cent is all it takes to get you into Heaven." Mellowman laughed maniacally. "Shit, there was a time when crap like that actually mattered to me."

"Are you . . . going to . . . rape me?" she asked. It was just a question. Her injuries wouldn't let her summon up the rage she needed to turn it into an accusation.

Mellowman's face fell all the same. "Aw, shit," he said, and scuffed one boot on the floor. "Aw, c'mon, Muffin, you really think I'm like that? Me and Mike, we're the laid-back type, real gentlemen, the two of us. We don't pay for pussy, and we don't beat up women just to get laid. Consensual sex is the best kind, we know that."

He laughed for a moment, the sound banging off the roof of the cave.

"On the other hand, the Termite is probably too far gone to know the difference. And he's taking the first watch. You have yourself some pleasant dreams, now."

He strode away, leaving her there in the dark.

She had plenty of time to work out what she was going to do next. There was little she could do except think. She managed to roll over on her side and crawl a bit, just enough to get closer to the lamp. Not actually get into its light. It took her far, far longer than she expected to halve the distance. It took more energy than she thought she had left.

She was doomed, she understood that much implicitly, though she had no idea what was supposed to happen next. Whatever Mellowman had in store for her in the morning it wouldn't be good. Maybe not as bad as having her brains blown out, perhaps not as bad as being buried in the ground and being unable to die. She wouldn't like it, though, that much she knew.

Mael, she called out with her mind. *Mael, help me*, she screamed silently, but either the walls of the cave were blocking her telepathy or she was took weak and he just couldn't hear her at all. There was no response.

She started crawling again. Managed to get far enough that the light played on her face.

She was on her own. Only one thing left to try.

"Hey," she shouted. At least she tried to shout. What came out sounded more like a wet wheeze. Maybe she'd broken something while crawling. Maybe her body was just done. "Hey, somebody! Termite!"

That was all she could muster. She waited, waited to regain enough strength to wheeze again.

Something moved in the darkness. A flittering, skittish motion.

Like the feelers of a cockroach feathering over a dried-up piece of potato chip.

It came again, this time followed by a noise like feet being dragged across rough concrete. Nilla thought she could see a blur of paleness in the distance. Soon enough it resolved into a shape, a humanoid form. It was the Termite.

"Y-y-you sh-sh-sh-ut up," he said. He rubbed at his nose and his left eye. "J-j-just shut up." He rubbed his eye again. Then his nose. In the dark he positively glowed, his skin translucent and shiny under the grime. The splayed and broken brown palisade of his teeth looked like the mouthparts of an insect. With his wrist he smoothed back his hair, which was greasy enough to stay put. "I've got my orders."

"What is he going to do with me?" Nilla asked.

"Sh-shut up, stupid."

Nilla sucked on her lower lip. Fear was filling her up. Not fear of what was going to happen. Fear that what she tried next wasn't going to work. If it didn't—then she would only make things worse. Much, much worse. If he didn't take the bait, if Mellowman thought she was trying to escape, what would he do to her then?

The Termite's eyes flicked downward. Into the shadows of her cleavage. She knew she still had a chance, then.

"Just sit and talk with me, please," she said to him. "Are you going to hurt me?" she asked. She put what emotion she had left into the words, twisted them. Made them dirty. Like she wanted to be hurt but only in a very special way. Nilla licked her lips. There was no room in her soul for being disgusted with herself. This was just like when she'd eaten the boy on the golf course. Exactly like that. Sheer survival.

"Aw, no, n-no, I c-c-c, I *can't do this*," he whined, his body curling around the negation. He ran both hands over his scalp, tearing at his hair, clawing at his cheeks. He rubbed his nose and his eye again and turned away from her, only to turn around again quickly.

"But I want it so much," Nilla said. And she did. She made herself want it. Want him to come closer. To touch her.

The Termite blinked his eyes rapidly. He rubbed at his nose, at his left eye. He reached over and grabbed her breast, hard, hard enough to make her gasp in pain.

It was the best she was going to get. She reared up like a snake and sank her teeth deep into the flesh of his arm. She aimed for the vein there and found it without trouble. He screamed, screamed like a stuck pig, screamed for help, for his mother, the pain in him lighting up the cave like neon. He screamed and screamed and reached for something on his belt. Something dangerous. A gun. He screamed and brought up the gun and started firing wildly, more noise, light in huge orange flashes, and still he screamed, and fired, and fired, and fired until his gun went dry.

It didn't matter. Before he got off his first shot Nilla had already stolen enough from him. Enough life. She banked her energy. Made herself invisible. It felt like it wasn't going to work but combined with the darkness in the cave it was enough. None of the shots hit her.

She struggled upward, up onto shaky feet, moving toward the entrance of the cave. Behind her the Termite kept screaming.

At the entrance she found Mellowman. She had hoped she would. She had hoped he would come running. Maybe he was smarter than her, though. He was going to ruin all of her plans by doing one smart thing. He had heard the screams and the gunshots—how could he not—and he looked deeply concerned. But not panicked. Instead of rushing into the cave, guns blazing, he was pushing the gate closed. He already had the key to the padlock out and ready. He was going to do the smart thing and seal her inside the cave with the Termite.

Had she wasted a moment more on the Termite, had she stopped to take more of his life force, she wouldn't have made it. She pushed and stumbled and snagged herself badly as she squeezed into the narrow opening left in the gate. Mellowman grunted and she knew by the way he tensed up that he could feel the resistance her body made. He could feel that something was holding the gate open, even if he couldn't see it.

"Muffin?" he asked. He started to grin. There was a brilliance in him, a malign genius. Had she underestimated him too much? If she had it would all be over in a second. He had grasped immediately the strange particulars of the situation. She could see the figures adding up in his eyes: crazy girl, probably undead, who knows what she can do? Maybe she can make herself invisible. He stepped into the gate, blocking her escape, knowing that if he didn't stop her at that moment she would probably get away.

Still the Termite screamed.

Nilla thudded against Mellowman's chest, the coarse weave of his baja shirt rough against her cheek. He smelled like stale pot smoke. His arms went around her, tentative at first, then closing with sudden conviction, trapping her.

"I've got you, Muffin. And I'm never going to let you go," he said. He wasn't looking at her—he still couldn't see her—but it didn't matter.

She would have preferred it if he was looking at her. She wanted him to see her. But it didn't matter.

He was almost a head taller than her. Nilla's face fit easily into the crook of his neck. Her lips could feel the pulse of his jugular vein—it was right there.

She tore his throat out and drank the blood that poured down over her mouth.

Subtle energies, discrete communication. So many months gone to this foolishness. Am I just looking for a way to keep my mind occupied? The neoplasm is an ostrich egg, we can see it right through the skin and here I am growing bluegrass in Dixie cups. The world's most expensive high school science project, I . . . I need some rest. [Lab Notes, 1/1/04]

She came trudging out of the cave to find the Space Van pinging softly in the starlight. Folding patio chairs had been set up around the open back and a tiny hibachi gave off a cheery glow from the tailgate. Morphine Mike was drinking a beer, his back up against the dusty metal of the van.

Mellowman's energy popped and crackled inside of her. She felt like an overdone potato in a microwave. She hadn't felt so strong since she'd eaten the bear.

The tight muscles across Nilla's stomach rumbled for a moment and something tiny and metallic squeezed its way out of her skin. The puckered exit wound it left behind closed up and healed over as she watched. She bent down and picked up the piece of buckshot. She was full of them, still, and her body was rejecting them one by one. She would probably be shedding them for a week.

It didn't matter. Mellowman was dead and she . . . wasn't.

Mike was agitated. He wanted to get in the van and rocket away, just get out of there and head back to Las Vegas. She could tell by the way he kept looking at the road. He would have heard the screams, of course. He would know what was happening.

She stepped closer to him. Into the red light of the hibachi. She let her energy flow back into her, spread through her limbs like tingling warmth. He yelped a little when she appeared in front of him with no warning.

"You're . . . you're dead," he said. It might have sounded like wishful thinking but that wasn't it. It was merely him completing a line of reasoning. One that Mellowman had worked through in the space of a heartbeat. Morphine Mike, with his degree in environmental chemistry, was just now figuring it out. Not all dead people are alike.

"Yes," she said. The darkness inside of her coiled and bent. It was laughing, laughing at him. Laughing at the living.

She had so many people inside of her now . . . literally, and figuratively. Jason Singletary was in there. So was Mael Mag Och. It was as if by losing herself, her memory, she had made herself a vessel to be filled up by others. Like being possessed, perhaps, or suffering from multiple personal disorder. There were many of her now. This Nilla, the one who stepped closer to Mike and leaned in, pushing up hard against the envelope of his personal space, was not the darkest of the lot. But it was close.

He swallowed a gulp of beer. Dropped the can onto the sandy

soil where it fizzed noisily for a moment like a flame going out. "Mellowman? The Termite?"

She smiled, showing him her teeth. Were there flecks of skin and meat stuck between her incisors? She didn't care. She contemplated telling him to go see for himself. Tricking him, locking him up in the cave with the Termite. Let them starve to death and see which one ate the other first.

The dead don't drive, though. She still needed a chauffeur.

"They're not going to be problems for us anymore. Can we go, or do you need to sober up, first?" she asked. She put a finger under his chin. It was necessary, she knew, to establish the hierarchy here. He had to know who was in charge. She found the pulse point of his neck and tapped it rapidly. In time with his heartbeat.

She felt so good. So strong. When he asked which way to drive she fastened her seat belt and told him to go east.

They were fifteen miles down the road, well on their way to Salt Lake City, when a helicopter flew by so low over them that the Space Van rocked on its wheels. "Shit!" Mike squeaked, the curse spurting out of him as he struggled with the steering wheel. He slammed on the brakes and pulled them over onto the shoulder.

"What are you doing?" Nilla demanded. "Get back on the road."

"They saw us!" Mike bit his lower lip. "Maybe we can abandon the van. Maybe we can go into the desert on foot—it's cold at night, though, so we'll show up on IR. Shit!"

"What are you talking about? That was just a helicopter. They probably have bigger things to worry about than us."

Mike shook his head. "Look, you have got to understand what's happening. This was Mellowman's plan. The military is offering to pay for your capture. Fifty grand, but only if you're alive. That's the only reason he didn't kill you back there. He was supposed to meet some guy from the Pentagon back at the cave and collect the bounty. I don't know if they just showed up for the meet and found his corpse or maybe they had the place under surveillance already. Either way they are not going to just let you go."

The military had a price on her head. She would have no chance at all if they caught her. Nilla remembered the man in the Army uniform, the one who had nearly supervised at her execution. She only had one good trick and he'd already seen it—they would be ready when the lady vanished. "Get back on the road," she said. "Turn off the headlights. There won't be any traffic."

"No fucking way! We're already caught. All we can do is surrender and hope they don't shoot us on principle."

She grabbed his forearm and put his wrist in her mouth. She crunched down, hard, but not hard enough to break the skin.

Mike got the message.

They burned out onto the highway accelerating as hard as the Space Van could, rolling from side to side like a boat. Without the headlights the van might as well have been plummeting forward into interstellar space. Nilla grabbed a map out of the glove compartment and studied it by the illumination of a Zippo lighter she found underneath it. "Okay," she said, "okay, we can do this—I've outmaneuvered them before. North of here is the Bonneville Speedway. Sure—the Salt Flats, right?" She remembered that. She could remember the rocket cars setting land speed records, but she couldn't remember her name? She would dwell on the disparity later, she decided. "There have to be some buildings there. Something with cover. Take a left up ahead."

"Where? I can't see anything!"

"A left!" she shouted when he started to veer into the right lane.

He turned hard, perhaps thinking she'd seen a turn he had missed. The Space Van left the road with a massive lurch. The Zippo touched the map and the map went up in flames. The van lost traction and listed over to one side. They were going at least sixty miles an hour, probably more.

The Space Van rolled at least once as he panicked and she screamed but she couldn't have said later how long it took for the vehicle to skid and slide and rock to a stop. She felt her soul leave her body, much as it had when she was restrained in the hospital bed, back when she thought she was still alive. She felt her soul careen back and forth inside the van, a bean inside of a maraca, one of a pair of dice inside a gambler's hand. She saw bits of flaming map dance in the spinning cabin, saw Mike's face turn to look at her, his mouth moving, forming words but she didn't hear them.

Go limp, she told herself. Her limbs turned to loose rubber as she bounced around inside the van. Her body shook like a doll. *Go limp.*

Then the van smacked the ground hard and slid about a hundred feet on its side, showers of sparks flying up every time it grazed a rock. It finally came to a stop. Nilla bounced a little inside the protective embrace of her seat belt, but she was okay.

She stared out at the starlit desert beyond the shattered windshield. Everything had stopped. She looked down, down at where Mike sat in the driver's seat. He wasn't there. She searched her memory, trying to figure out how that could happen. She remembered he hadn't been wearing his seat belt. There was a hole in the windshield, a jagged aperture dark with dripping blood.

Carefully, trying to avoid the piles of broken safety glass that seemed to be everywhere, Nilla unfastened herself and climbed out of the wreck. A helicopter shot by overhead very fast while she stood there, craning her head back and forth, looking for Mike. She walked out into the dark and the salt crunched beneath her feet.

Eventually she found him.

He had been thrown through the windshield in the crash and his body had gone skidding over the crunchy, perfectly smooth salt rime for over a hundred yards. Judging by the broken depressions in the soil he must have skipped like a stone on the top of a pond.

He wouldn't be coming back. Shards of glass stuck out of his head like a bloody crown. Nilla felt her shoulders fall, a certain tension dripping away from her.

From behind she heard the sound of heavy trucks roaring toward her. Overhead two more helicopters came in slow and circled around her, their lights stabbing the desert, missing her entirely.

Nilla was still flush with energy. She went invisible.

The books I ordered from Amazon last week (on a whim, just a silly whim!) have arrived. I should just

**send them back. This is plain dumb. I didn't even
think about it, just grabbed everything on the list
with one-click. "The Lesser Key of Solomon?" The
Greater Key was on back order. "The Alchymical
Wedding of Christian Rosenkreutz?" Huh? "Magick
Without Tears?" Well, we could use a few less
tears around here, though I could do without that
superfluous "K." Jesus. To save her I have to stop
believing in anything that's ever mattered to me.
I have to unlearn everything I thought I knew.
[Lab Notes, 1/9/04]**

"I've been looking for this girl since the Epidemic began," Clark
said. "Now you find her and you forget to tell me for most of a day?"

The Civilian stared straight ahead. He was strapped so tightly
into his crew seat that maybe he couldn't turn his head. "I can be
a wrathful god sometimes, Bannerman. But sometimes I throw my
favorite pet a bone. You don't ask questions, not of me."

Clark knew to back off. This fury was new—he was used to the
Civilian's cynicism but the anger was new. Clark kept silent. Unfortunately that left him with his own thoughts for company.

So close—and something had to go wrong. Well, something
always went wrong, that was the general rule of warfare. Clark had
even made room for something going wrong in his plans, bringing
along far more men and materiel than he should have needed to
pick up one prisoner. Still.

This was a monumental cock-up.

The Civilian had presented Clark with the opportunity of a life-
time. An individual associated loosely with the Las Vegas Chamber
of Commerce had captured the girl. He was willing to turn her over
to Clark in exchange for free passage east—with a military escort—
and fifty thousand dollars. The Civilian had set everything up.
Those were all the details Clark had and all, it seemed, the Civilian was willing to give him. It should be enough, the Civilian
insisted. He wanted the girl and now he could have her.

Only when they arrived the girl was gone—having apparently murdered all of her captors. They didn't know how long it had been since she'd escaped. They didn't know which way she went. They didn't know where she was headed. But she knew they were coming for her and would therefore be on her guard.

"There's two dead in here, sir," a troop said, leaning in through the open door of the helicopter. Clark closed his laptop with a click and nodded. He looked past the soldier and saw the entrance to a cave. An iron-barred gate swung open on its hinges. "One of them looks like a drug overdose," the soldier continued. "The other body is partially consumed."

Clark breathed out a long sigh of dissatisfaction. To get so close . . . "I take it there's no sign of any females." The soldier began to reply but Clark held up a hand to stop him. "That's not a question that needs an answer." The girl had literally been right there, right there no more than an hour prior, probably even less. Clark was almost ready to stage his offensive on the mountain location, the Epicenter. He had the troops, he had the supplies. Until he understood the girl's place in the Epidemic, until he knew what she meant, he would never be psychologically ready, though. He wouldn't understand the terms of the engagement. He wouldn't have a frame of reference to know what he was getting into. The girl was the key. "You don't have any good news for me, do you? She didn't leave anything behind that might help us find her?"

"No, sir," the soldier responded. No one had expected there would be. "Except . . . permission to add something, sir."

"Granted, of course."

The Guardsman bit his lower lip. "There's no vehicles here, sir, and we're a long way from where anybody lives. I don't know how these two bodies could have got here without a vehicle. Maybe somebody dropped them off, but I wouldn't want to be stuck out here so far from town without a way out. Not with dead people wandering around loose out here, and all. Sir."

Clark actually smiled at the young man. Not very professional but he couldn't help it. He jumped down from the helicopter body, slapping the Guardsman on the shoulder, and jogged into the area of operations. Soldiers were busy sealing up the bodies in type II human remains pouches and sifting through the sand looking for forensic evidence. This had been a standard mopping-up exercise following a failed rendezvous. It was about to turn into something quite different.

He came up on a group of soldiers near the cave mouth and asked if any of them were hunters. One of them was, an eighteen-year-old female from Littleton who used to go hunting with her grandfather. "Do you see any tracks around here, the kind a vehicle might make?" he demanded. It wasn't necessarily the kind of thing a deer hunter would know how to look for but he needed data right away.

She took a while to check. Clark waited, trying to be patient. "Maybe, sir, I guess . . . there are some tire tracks, they're pretty vague, right through here, sir," she said, and waved back and forth with her hands. Indicating a path between the cave and the highway. At his nod she trotted downfield and then came right back, slightly out of breath. "It looks like somebody peeled out. There's rubber on the road, headed east."

"Sergeant Horrocks," Clark shouted, and the Platoon Sergeant lifted his shaggy white head to look. "Get these people ready to move out—we have a target to chase." He didn't stick around to observe as his staffer made order out of chaos. He needed to be back in the helicopter—back where he could be on top of things.

A car or a van or a truck—a ground vehicle. It would stick to the roads and there was only one road nearby of any consequence, a major highway. The bodies they found in the cave had still been warm, even on a cold night.

They still had a chance.

Ten minutes later and a hundred feet up in the air The Civilian upended a tiny silver flask into his mouth and peered out through the helicopter's windows at the darkness below. "I can't see ass," he said, irritably.

The copilot leaned back to face the two of them. "Sirs, we had visual confirmation of the target vehicle on the highway but it's gone now. It must have gone off-road, sirs."

"Get the ground teams in place. Sweep this area with infra-red and image enhancement." It wouldn't find her, of course. She was dead and wasn't generating any body heat, so IR imaging would be useless. As for night vision goggles, well, they helped you see things in the dark but not things that could make themselves invisible.

Thank God he had an ace up his sleeve. This was going to be next to impossible as it was.

Adrenaline shot through the muscles of his back, making them ache a little. He hadn't been this worked up since the fall of Denver.

"So what exactly is she going to give you once you find her?" the Civilian asked.

"I'm hoping she can tell me that." An imaging window opened on Clark's laptop, piped through from the infra-red cameras. "Put us down at this location, specialist," Clark said, pushing forward between the crew seats of the pilot and copilot. "It looks like the target vehicle has come to a complete stop." The van lay on its side, dressed up in false colors where it was warm and cold. It looked wrong, broken. Flames danced in its windows.

When the helicopter's passenger door slid open the cold night air of the Utah desert bit at Clark's face and hands. He ignored it and stepped out into the darkness. He threw a hand signal at the pilot and listened to a flare being shot from a vehicle maybe half a kilometer away. One of his Hum-Vee's. A few seconds later the desert lit up with sizzling white light that reflected dazzlingly from the abandoned van's crumpled roof.

The vehicle was cooling rapidly in the night air. Its engine pinged from time to time. There were piles of broken glass around the windows, mounds of black charred foam rubber from the fire that still smoldered in the interior. Clark looked down and saw footprints in the sand heading northeast—the same direction the van had been traveling. He peered out into the harsh light of the flare and saw something out there. It looked like a body. He prayed the girl hadn't been killed in the crash.

He took a crowd-control bullhorn from his belt and switched it on. "Nilla," he said, and the name rocketed around the desert, bounced off hills a kilometer away. "Nilla, I know you're here somewhere. You have to stop running."

All around him in the shadows his vehicles were spreading out, taking up position. They could form a pretty tight perimeter when they were deployed properly. But did it matter? If she was invisible she could walk right past any barricade they made.

"Nilla, I know you're afraid of me. I know the last time we met was traumatic. Believe me, it scarred me, too." A Stryker rolled up behind him and came to a stop. Soldiers fanned out on his hand signal, scoured the desert ahead. A pair of soldiers with their M4 rifles at the ready reached the body he'd seen and threw back a thumb's down. So at least it wasn't the girl.

"Nilla. I only want to stop this thing. I want to stop the killing, the violence."

One of the soldiers screamed. He jumped up and down, grasping his arm. Clark was too far away to see if there was any blood but he knew what it meant. The soldier's battle buddy dropped to the ground and waved his rifle around but the girl was invisible. If she was an enemy, if she was too scared to listen to reason—it would be simplicity itself for her to kill one of his men.

He had to complete this before anyone got hurt. He turned to wave at the Stryker and his secret weapon stepped out of its rear hatch, escorted by two of his biggest troops. Beside them and their bulky body armor the teenaged girl looked even smaller and younger than she actually was.

The troops brought her to him and he placed an arm around her shoulders. This would be the tough part. "Nilla, I'm sure you remember Shar. I don't want to hurt anyone. But I will if I have to." He removed his sidearm from its holster and placed the barrel a few inches from Shar's forehead. It took real effort on his part to point the weapon at a civilian but he managed.

"Please, Nilla," Shar screamed. She wriggled under his arm and he held her closer.

Nothing. Another of Clark's soldiers cried out but not because he'd been attacked. Something had brushed against him. Was Nilla making a run for it?

Clark cocked the pistol. The sound of the spring drawing back echoed in the still desert night.

"Don't," someone said, no more than a dozen yards away. "Please."

"Show yourself," Clark demanded.

She did, not so much fading into existence as suddenly standing out where before she'd blended into the shadows. She looked different from how Clark remembered her—healthier, strangely enough, as if she had prospered while the country suffered and died.

Soldiers fell on her like a well-drilled football team, securing her hands and face, knocking her feet out from under her. She tried to make herself invisible again but Clark had warned them in advance and they didn't let go.

"Oh, Jesus," Shar said, sagging against him, her arms around his waist.

"You did very well," Clark told her. He carefully lowered the hammer of his pistol, mindful of accidental discharge even though the safety was on. "I promise, that's the last thing we'll ask of you."

"Yeah. Okay," Shar said. "Just—don't make me ride in the same car with her, okay? I never want to get this close to her again."

McDougall was a scientist, a real scientist. Surely I can trust his notes. The mice in the control group have reached the inevitable negative result while the experimental group . . . some minor side effects, dermatitis, hair loss but you expect that with radiation (not that this is any kind of radiation Roentgen or Curie would recognize). But they're alive, damn it, they're still alive. This could be something. Or not. Trying to stay scientific about this: lather, rinse, repeat. [Lab Notes, 1/18/04]

They gave her some clean clothes and let her take a long, hot shower. They fed her a couple of hamburgers that came on a biodegradable brown tray. She ate the tray, too, when nobody was looking. A female soldier wearing riot gear offered to help her fix her hair and her makeup if she wanted. She declined. They were all very polite and kind and they never got closer than six feet to her.

At all times they kept her chained to a wall.

She didn't know where they'd brought her, but she could guess a little. They kept her blind-folded, gagged, and hog-tied for the entire ride to their base but one look at the flaking paint on the walls, the endless series of locked doors, the narrow windows holding shatterproof glass suggested either a mental hospital or a prison. There were tie-downs and chain staples in every room, restraints built into every cot. Security cameras lurked in the corners and the doors all came in pairs so that she had to be buzzed through twice every time she moved from one room to another.

Eventually they locked her down in a staff lounge and left her there. Two long Formica cafeteria tables almost filled the room, leaving only a little space for a bar made of dented chrome. The carpet was burnt orange and speckled with tufts of hard plastic where prior occupants of the room had dropped their cigarettes, fusing the artificial fibers together. Horseshoe-shaped fluorescent lights buzzed down on her from a ceiling of crumbling white acoustic tile. Behind the bar someone had nailed up a line of wooden bubble letters:

YE OLDE ENGLISH PUB

There was a neon Coors sign near the door. In one corner of the ceiling a blank-faced motion detector clicked and displayed a green light every time she got up from her seat and wandered around the room. Eventually she got bored enough to try an experiment. Banking her energy down to nothing she stood in the middle of the room, quite invisible, and waved her arms.

Click. The green light flickered a little but it burned strong and bright after a moment. Clearly her best and only trick wasn't going to get her out of the room.

A door opened on the far side of the room, near the bar. The head asshole, the one who had asked her what her name was so very, very long ago, the one who had claimed he would kill Shar if he had to, walked in. He looked like he had a stick up his ass. He looked like he daily removed said stick, polished it, and reinserted it.

He sat down at one of the cafeteria tables at least six feet away from her and put his hat on the seat next to him. He looked at her without saying anything. He had brought a briefcase with him— now he put it on the table and flicked open its latches. "Do you drink, Nilla? We have a wide selection of canned beers to choose from. Soft drinks as well."

Nilla stared back at him. If he was going to treat her like an animal in a zoo she was damned if she would talk to him. She wanted to channel the personality she'd had before, the dark Nilla who looked on humans as food and who found the end of the world ironically amusing, but that Nilla was gone. No, she'd pretty much blown that act when she demonstrated she still cared enough about Shar to save the girl's life.

She wasn't about to go soft, though. She made a hard line of her mouth and didn't move. Tried to look as dead as possible. The world hated her, people like this man had gone out of their way to prove it. She refused to let them see whether or not she cared.

"I'm not a big drinker myself," he told her. "I do like to come down here from time to time, though. It's nice. Cheerful. It lets me forget for a few minutes what's going on out there. All the people dying. All the parents losing their children, all the children who are so afraid. I am trying to stop the Epidemic, and I will do everything in my power to advance that aim. But even I need to relax sometimes. To get away and pretend it all doesn't exist."

Nilla could feel her eyeballs drying out but she refused to blink.

He stood up and took something out of his briefcase. He walked closer to her, only hesitating once he came into biting range. She reached under the table and grabbed the chain that anchored her to the wall. He dropped a piece of heavy paper on the table before her.

With a flick of the wrist she smashed her chain against the underside of the table, making a noise like a gunshot. She bared her teeth at him, bugged her eyes out. Hissed.

He didn't jump, which she had to admit impressed her. His nostrils did flare a little but he didn't jump. He didn't exactly waste his time about retreating to the far table, but he hadn't jumped.

She had met so many weak people. He wasn't one of them.

"Please look at the picture in front of you. I don't have as much time as I would like, so if you could stop playing games with me I'd appreciate it. Look at the picture and tell me what you see."

She looked at him, not the picture. Eventually he sighed.

"The place in that picture is where it comes from. The Epidemic. In a couple of days I'm going to lead a raiding party up there and we're going to storm it. Maybe blow it up. I'd like to think that will be enough to end this. I'd like to have some confirmation, and I'm hoping that you can provide it. Do you recognize the place in that photo?"

Alright, she thought. *Give him an inch, see how much he takes.* She looked down. She'd never seen the place in the picture before. It meant nothing to her. It looked like a cluster of one-story buildings—too big for houses, maybe hunting lodges or something—on top of a mountain. There were strange shapes, animal-like, maybe reptilian, scattered around the building. Sculptures. Sculptures of dinosaurs, in between snow-covered peaks.

Snow-covered mountains . . . the fire.

She looked again.

A perfectly semi-circular expanse of ground around the buildings stood out, because it was empty. Beyond a certain limit the picture was full of bodies. Thousands of them, dead bodies, standing, facing inward. It was as if the undead had gathered to storm the buildings only some magical force was keeping them at a distance.

A place up in the mountains. A guilty man. A fire that would burn the world.

Jason Singletary had seen this photograph. Or he'd seen what it depicted. He'd tried to force his vision on her.

"You say it started here? How?" she demanded.

"We don't know. I'm gathering intelligence from every source I can find—including you. I saw a look of recognition on your face just now. Talk to me."

There was definite steel in his voice but Nilla didn't know what to tell him. "I've never been there. I don't know what you'll find. But . . ."

It was his turn to wait without speaking.

"I think I'm supposed to go there. Maybe you're supposed to take me there. I'm the only one who can do it." Singletary had been very clear on that last point.

"I see."

"No, listen, I was chosen for this. Maybe I was created for this, I don't know . . ." she considered telling him about Singletary and about Mael Mag Och. She knew it would sound crazy, though. She grew agitated as she thought through her options. She picked up her chain and stood up abruptly. "You have to take me there, or, or you can just let me go, and I'll go there myself."

He nodded at her and then quickly, methodically, closed his briefcase with a double click.

She felt as if she'd been sleepwalking. No, she felt as if she'd been in a bad dream, a dream where she'd forgotten something horribly, terribly important, something she had to do and that she had forgotten and now it was coming due. When Singletary had been trying to tell her about this she'd been distracted, she'd wanted to find her name so badly. Now she realized she should have paid more attention.

"You have to let me go," she said.

"Not a chance." He stood up and headed for the door. "I saw what you did to those men at Jukebox Cave. You'll never be free again, not if I can help it."

He didn't slam the door shut behind him but he might as well have. Nilla stared at it, at the door, for a very long time. Then she yanked at her chain, trying to get loose.

Not a chance.

They brought her another meal—pork chops—a little later. She ate them, of course, but they didn't really taste of anything. She was still sucking little bits of the grayish-pinkish meat out from between her teeth when the lights went out.

Oh God, she thought. *Lights out.* She didn't want to sit there in the darkness all night. The soldiers didn't know that she didn't sleep. Or maybe they did know and they just wanted to torment her, to force her to abide by a normal human day/night schedule. But then the room's emergency lights came on, a pair of wan halogen bulbs tucked away in a corner of the ceiling.

Nilla stood up and tried to reach the door, intending to signal to her captors that something was wrong. The chain wouldn't let her reach, though.

Hello, lass, Mael said, startling her. She looked to her left. He was reclining on top of one of the cafeteria tables. Naked, hairy, tattooed. He looked out of place in the Olde English Pub, to put it mildly.

"You—what did you do," Nilla sputtered. She looked up at the emergency lights and then back at her benefactor.

He winked in reply.

**It's growing . . . the mass is growing, on its own . . .
so like a cancer but . . . coherent, self-organizing . . .
so beautiful . . . Happy Valentine's Day, love.
Maybe . . . maybe this won't be the last one.
[Lab Notes, 2/14/04]**

Clark clipped the NODs over his face and switched them on. Peering out through a four-inch-wide window he could make out a little of what was happening. Out by the main gate of the prison a crowd of survivors had gathered. They were beating on the gate with their fists, their mouths wide with shouts and pleas that he couldn't hear. The dead were out there and the survivors were helpless. Someone screamed—a real, *in extremis* scream—but it was far away and it didn't trigger his fear reactions. It sounded like someone was watching a slasher film on a television in another room. "Let them in, of course," he said, because Horrocks had asked him what the soldiers at the gates should do. "They don't have a chance out there on their own."

Horrocks hurried away, taking his troops with him, leaving Clark alone in the observation balcony above the interrogation rooms. He could still hear the screaming.

Calm. He had to stay cool, calm, collected. The prison's emergency generators were up and running. Lighting in the corridors and pods was at a reduced level but it was holding up.

The first thing to do was to establish a secure perimeter.

Easy. The supermax prison was one of the most hardened facilities on the continent. He remembered Assistant Warden Glynne's introduction to the place. There were ten thousand doors in Florence-ADX, he'd been informed, and all of them could be remotely controlled.

There was a master shutdown switch in the operations room. Simple. Get everyone inside that he could, save as many of the people from the shantytown as possible, then hit the switch. Seal the prison off. Then he could worry about why the power had gone out. Then he could worry about what happened next.

Get to the operations room, and hit the master shutdown switch. Easy.

He forced himself to start walking.

He flipped open his phone and dialed for Vikram. Told his old friend to meet him in the Ops Room. He had a feeling they should stick together at this point. He called the Civilian as well but got no response. He made another call, to the MP station, and told them to secure the girl. He had a sneaking feeling she had something to do with the power outage. Why? Why did he think that? She was chained to a wall—she could hardly have sabotaged the prison's main generators from inside the Pub. She had abilities, though, and resources he didn't understand.

He'd made a lot of mistakes and gotten a lot of people killed for not thinking things through far enough. It was time to get rational again. To think like an engineer again.

Fine. He could fall back on logic. Logic dictated that the generators hadn't gone down on their own. Logic dictated that the prison was under attack. He could still hear screaming. Was it closer?

Vikram was already in the Ops Room when he arrived, looking concerned, his beard matted to one side where he'd probably been sleeping on it. He had a sidearm strapped to his belt. Clark's hand involuntarily went to his own weapon.

"The troops are letting in the people from outside. The story they tell is not good," Vikram told him. The Major started up one of the computers. It would drain emergency power but it would let them see what was going on. Vikram called up some views from surveillance cameras around the facility. The main courtyard was clear, swept by searchlights that showed nothing. The helipad on the roof looked fine.

The western fence was mobbed by the dead.

Their faces were blanks in the low-light view, their hands pale blobs that picked and tore at the barbed wire. Clark couldn't see their wounds or their blank expressions but he recognized instantly the way that they moved, the slow, remorseless march, the dragging but unrelenting way their arms lifted and fell and pulled and ripped and beat.

"Where did they come from? How did they gather so quickly? We expected a few of them at a time, not an army. The dead don't surge, Vikram. The dead don't surge. That takes conscious planning." Which normally the enemy didn't have. Yet they'd shown some measure of it when they escaped the detention facility in Denver. The girl locked down in the pub showed plenty of it herself.

This was a directed attack—a raid. The dead were organized.

"Get some men with crew-served weapons up on that wall. I don't think the infected can get through the wire but I don't want to give them time to try." Clark rubbed at his face. "Get the Stryker crews mobilized, I want to cut this off from the rear before it can turn into something significant. Are all of the survivors inside the gate?"

Vikram peered into a computer monitor and puffed out his cheeks before answering. "Yes. All of them that still live. That is about half."

The numbers would only distract him. He'd done what he could. "Fine." Clark went to a boxy terminal bolted to the wall by the door of the room. It looked like an antique next to the ruggedized laptops and industrial strength cabling that Vikram had installed in the Ops Room. It was the control terminal for all of the prison's facilities and systems. There was an identical machine in every part of the prison. Clark booted it up and paged through a main menu until he found what he wanted, glowing on the screen in flashing letters.

!!!CLICK HERE FOR EMERGENCY LOCKDOWN!!!

"Step away from that door," he called. Vikram was a good ten feet from it but he stepped away anyway, like a good soldier. Clark hit the ENTER key and an alarm sounded throughout the entire prison for two seconds. Moving silently on electromagnetic servos the door swung shut and clicked three times. It was locked tight. The clicking seemed to go on for minutes as nine thousand, nine hundred and ninety-nine other doors throughout the facility shut themselves and locked automatically.

For a long time Vikram and Clark just looked at each other and waited for something to go wrong. Nothing did.

"There. We're safe," Clark announced. "Now we just have to decide what to do next."

The two second alarm sounded again and the door of the Ops Room ghosted open.

Clark's heart started beating very fast. Too fast.

"Bannerman," Vikram began, but Clark held up a hand for patience.

He studied the terminal in front of him. He hadn't touched anything. He called up an activity log and saw that nineteen seconds after he'd given the order to lock the prison down someone else had given the order to release the doors again. All of the doors, including all the gates. Even the exterior gates. There was nothing to stop anyone or anything from just walking into the prison.

It could have been a glitch. He knew it wasn't.

There were security terminals all over the prison, and any one of them could have undone Clark's lockdown but it wasn't just a case of someone pushing a random button on a terminal because they needed to get out of a sealed room. It wasn't just a simple matter of a few keystrokes to undo an emergency lockdown in the system. It required someone to input an authorization code and then to manually set all the prison's systems to "all clear." You had to know how to do it and you couldn't do it accidentally. Clark checked the activity log again. "Someone's in the infirmary. Someone who wants the doors open."

Vikram chewed nervously on his lower lip until it looked red and sore. "Perhaps," he said, his eyes very wide, "perhaps we should go there and discuss this with them."

It was the worst idea Clark had ever heard. He couldn't think of anything else to do. "Right," he nodded. He removed his weapon from its holster.

Mars is a snowball, Venus a boiling pot of sulfuric acid. Everywhere we look in the universe we find sterile rocks and dust but not here . . . Earth is special, a special case. Lovelock's hypothesis is all but proved, life regulates itself, but through what agency or process? The morphogenetic field . . . the field is real, it's real and it can be manipulated. This I believe, now. I have no choice. [Lab Notes, 2/15/04]

"What the hell are you doing here?"

Mael Mag Och raised his hands in mock exasperation. "Saving

your skin, lass. You got yourself in a bit of a pickle, didn't you? That big fellow, the one with the vaccine, he was going to do your head in. So I did the only thing I could, which was to bring you here. Now I'm making it possible for you to get out of this place. Show me some love, lass. Show your best friend in the wide dark world a bit of love, won't you?"

"I almost talked my way out of here on my own. I could have, if you'd given me a chance." Nilla pulled and tugged at the chain that secured her to the wall but there was no give in it at all. She tried folding her hand, touching her pinky to her thumb, but still it wouldn't fit through the manacle around her wrist. "Now they'll probably just shoot me because they assume I'm the one who cut the lights."

Mael Mag Och swung his legs over the side of the table and got to his feet. He walked behind the bar as he spoke to her. "I'm here to rescue you, lass, but that's not the only reason I came to your side in this dank prison. This repressed lunatic of a soldier of yours is against us. And he's a smart one."

"You're afraid of him?" Nilla asked. It was impossible. But if it was true . . .

Mael laughed. He ran one hand over the bar as if he were wiping it with a rag. "He's not a threat. Our victory is assured. He could set back my plans by a few weeks, perhaps, if he put his shoulder to the right wheel."

Nilla strained against the manacle. It started to come off but it looked like it might take the skin of her hand with it. *Jesus, that would suck*, she thought. When you were dead you had to be careful about these things. "How did you manage this, anyway? Is Dick around here somewhere bashing in electrical panels with his face?"

"Dick's close by, but no, lass, this was an inside job."

She sat down and tried to relax. She had gotten herself out of bondage before. At the hospital, back when she thought she was still alive, she had crawled out of four point restraints. She looked at the manacle. Studied it. Maybe . . . maybe if she twisted her hand thusly while tugging gently, like so . . . . "An inside job? You were able to infiltrate somebody dead into this place?"

"Oh, ho, lass, now that would be a treat of a thing to do. Yet perhaps not all my good servants are dead, hmm? At least, this one wasn't, not until a few moments ago."

"I hate it when you get all cryptic," Nilla told him, her eyes narrowing. The manacle fell to the floor with a noisy crash. She was free.

The Hindu notion of the oversoul is obsessing me today, it sounds so much like the photon monobloc. Everywhere and everywhen, eternal and omnipresent, creating of itself a new definition of time and space. I roasted a chicken tonight for dinner, though she wouldn't take any. I saved the bones for the lab, for the . . . ceremony. Has it really come to that? I suppose it has. [Lab Notes, 3/16/04]

The dead came lumbering through the halls of Florence-ADX and they devoured whatever crossed their path. Soldiers unable to get their weapons up in time. Survivors, defenseless, who could only raise their arms across their faces, who could only crouch down, trying to make themselves small, trying to hide.

Sergeant Horrocks lead a surgical counter-offensive deep into the heart of the prison, looking for a defensible position from which to start pushing back the enemy. He had twenty years of experience running raids and building firebases. He set up barricades of heavy furniture, filing cabinets, anything that wasn't bolted down. He designated free fire zones and detailed squads to maintain various positions and hold them to the end.

Clark listened to the preparations on his cell phone as he and Vikram crossed the prison from one end to the other, headed for the infirmary. "Will they stand a chance, do you think?" Vikram asked. He had his pistol in his hand, low but ready.

"These kids are young but Rumsfeld plugged them right into hell in Iraq with nothing but the uniforms on their backs and they made it. They up-armored their own vehicles and they wrote whole new chapters in the book on guerrilla warfare. If anyone on earth can survive this, it's my company." Clark gritted his teeth at the thought of not being beside them. It was no foolish urge toward heroism, but instead a deeply inculcated and endlessly reiterated desire to protect his troops. No officer could function without that drive. He forced himself to accept that by securing the prison terminals and locking the doors down he was serving a higher purpose than he would if he waded into the fray and got himself killed.

Of course if he couldn't go to help the troops, he couldn't ask them to come assist him, either. Clark and Vikram were on their own.

"It's just up there," he said, drawing to a stop a dozen yards from the infirmary. What he expected to find inside he just didn't know.

That was no way to run an operation. He gestured for Vikram to head down a side passage, to a side door. A classic flanking maneuver. The Sikh Major nodded his understanding. For all of Clark's failures it was good to know that one person on the planet still trusted him implicitly. He watched Vikram Singh Nanda's turban disappear around a corner of the hallway and then he pushed forward to the open door of the infirmary himself.

Inside long shadows lay draped across a double line of beds. Over each cot a set of ballistic nylon restraints hung down from the ceiling, the buckles undone, the Velcro catches dangling open. The aisle between the beds was packed with wheeled carts full of supplies and equipment. The far end of the room was an enclosed space walled in glass—an intensive care unit. Clark thought he saw some motion there. He kept low, crouched down to avoid anything that might jump out and try to devour his face.

Something was definitely moving behind the glass. Clark found the door of the ICU room, found the brushed aluminum handle, tried pulling down on it. It started to move, gratingly, but then stopped. Out of ten thousand open doors he'd found the only one that was locked.

Or perhaps barred. He slowly straightened up to his full height, intending to peek through the glass and see what was obstructing the handle.

An intercom unit squealed into life. "Hey there, wonk," the Civilian said.

Clark slipped the safety back on his pistol. He stood up and looked at his patron through the glass. The DoD man looked pale but unhurt. The Civilian's sudden appearance had surprised Clark, but it shouldn't have. The ICU looked like it would stand up to undead attack pretty well. If you were going to hide somewhere it made a great choice.

"I'm glad to see you're safe. I tried to call you," Clark suggested.

"Yeah. I was busy." The Civilian turned around and went to sit on a surgical table. "Have you got anything to eat?"

Clark frowned a little. Why was the Civilian wearing a hospital gown? And what was wrong with his wrists? They were wrapped in thick gauze. Had he tried to commit suicide in some oxycontin-fueled haze? "We'll sort out provisions later. Right now I need to lock down the prison. I'm assuming you were the one who overrode my original attempt."

"I'd congratulate you on your detective work if you, me and Singh Nanda weren't the only ones with the authorization code." He studied Clark's face. "Yeah, this is going to be a hard sell, but you and me, we're loyalty oath types, right? Tried and true, red state good old folks to the core. So when I tell you the doors have to stay open you'll just get in line behind me."

"I'm not sure you understand. People are dying here, right now. Every second those doors are open somebody else dies."

Instead of answering the Civilian stared hard into Clark until he felt as if he was pinned in place, transfixed by that gaze. He tried to laugh it off, surely this was just some trick, some kind of hypnotist's trick but laughing didn't help. Clark had trouble breathing. He tried clawing at his uniform collar but it didn't help. He had a hard time standing up. Unable to really stop himself, he fell down on the floor, hard.

"I'm inside of your head, Bannerman. He told me there were incentives and wow, he did not lie. This is so goddamned cool."

"He? He who?" Clark gasped.

"This dead Scottish guy. His name wouldn't mean anything to you. He's like, the C-in-C of the dead or something, and I'm going to be his SecDef. Pretty cool, huh? He taught me how to do this to you."

The Civilian's eyes were lit up like two lighthouses spearing out light at Clark through a sudden fog that had come up out of nowhere, a buzzing, rattling fog that got inside his head, he couldn't think, he couldn't, he couldn't stand up there was nothing, there was nothing in the world except those eyes, those glowing eyes and the Civilian's voice . . .

"I literally have the power to cloud your mind, do you get it? It's easy. It's the easiest thing I've ever done and you have no defense against it. I'm squeezing your life energy right now, that's all. I'm cutting off the force that makes you alive. This is what dying feels like."

Instantly the fog was gone. The Civilian looked as he always had and the room, while dimly lit, was clear of haze.

"Okay. I think this pissing contest is over, and I think I got a mandate. Do you want a recount, Bannerman?"

The fog started coming back.

"No," Clark said. "No, I don't think that will be necessary."

What will it be? Waddington's chreode, inspiring some kind of Platonic human form on everything it touches? Or just a ministering angel with eyes like flashing gold? I need to know before I bring it to the surface—the potential negative consequences are truly chilling. [Lab Notes, 6/2/04]

"There are some victories that cost more than defeat," the Civilian lectured. Wearing only a hospital gown and a thick bandage around either wrist he should have looked absurd. Pathetic. His newfound power to strangle Clark's life force probably helped allay that appearance. "Then there are just plain old defeats. I never got that shit about captains going down with the ship. Even the rats aren't that stupid, right? So back in the first days of the Epidemic, when this Druid guy came to me and said, look, humanity's a done deal, it's gone, finito, a real non-starter, but maybe, just maybe there was a way for me to save my own neck, well . . . You know you have to listen to that. Look, give me your gun. I'm going to have power over the dead. He promised. You know, fuck dental, ruling the undead with an iron fist is the ultimate fringe benefit."

Clark handed over his firearm. He had little choice. The Civilian could kill him before he could get off a single shot.

"I was a little leery when, you know, he said I had to die and then crawl my way back from the grave. That's going to have a chilling effect on most negotiations. Turns out it was the easy part. I was going to come back anyway. Staying sharp, though, holding onto my faculties the way your blonde girl did, that took some work. It's all about maintaining oxygen flow to the brain."

"The girl," Clark said, still kneeling on the infirmary floor. He could feel his calves ping as they complained about their cut-off circulation. "What does she have to do with all this?"

"Surprisingly little. God am I sick of hearing about Nilla! My new boss is obsessed with her, too. What is it, the blonde hair? The tits? No, Bannerman, she's just a pawn in this game. A pawn that everyone thinks is a queen. Fuck her, alright? Let's stay on-message here." The Civilian smiled warmly at him. "I like you, Bannerman. I like you a lot."

"I . . . like you, too," Clark tried, warily.

The Civilian pulled away the chair that had been barring the door to the ICU. The door slid open silently and snicked against the magnet on the far wall, sealing itself open. The smell of blood and death billowed out of the enclosed room. "No you don't. Nobody likes me, and with good reason. I'm an asshole. Because I have to be to help preserve freedom. My country needed me to be an asshole. You, on the other hand, are likeable. You're honest, and dependable, and smart, and you try to do your best. Always. That's so commendable. It makes people trust you. No way am I going to just throw away a resource like that. So I'm going to take you with me, as my servant or something, right? I'm even going to hook you up to a respirator when I kill you to make sure you don't lose that beautiful brain of yours. Not all of it, anyway. I can't really let you be smarter than me, that wouldn't make a lot of sense. You'll probably experience some slurred speech and you won't be operating any heavy machinery, but you won't be one of these drooling slobs you see all over, either, and that's something. So come on. I have the bed all ready for you—the ventilator's hooked into the emergency power. We're going to live forever, Bannerman. You and me, side by side, wonk and wonklord." The Civilian stepped out of the ICU and held out a hand for Clark to take.

"No, no, I don't think that's going to happen," Clark said, slowly rising to his feet, shaking out his numb legs.

The Civilian rolled his eyes and lifted one hand as if he planned on choking Clark from afar. Before he could use his power Vikram Singh Nanda shot him twice in the back of the head. The Civilian collapsed in a tangle of limbs, completely dead.

There was a good reason why the flanking maneuver was considered a classic.

"Are you alright?" Vikram asked, picking up Clark's pistol from where it had fallen when the Civilian dropped it.

"I'm fine." He looked down at the corpse between them. "Thanks." It was all he needed to say, for the time being. He stepped over the body and into the ICU. The equipment there looked ready to use, just as the Civilian had promised. Clark ignored the waiting hospital bed and found a security terminal. He paged through the menus and re-activated the emergency lockdown. An error message appeared when the screen refreshed.

INVALID OR OUTDATED PASSWORD ENTERED

He tried again but he hadn't made a mistake, he knew it. The Civilian had changed the password and it had died with him. There was no way to shut the ten thousand doors.

Running out of options made it very easy to see what to do next.

Clark flipped open his cell phone and called Horrocks. The phone rang twelve times before it was answered.

"Sir," Horrocks reported, "I'm pinned down in a sally port and we're seeing heavy action right now, we have—have—please hold on a second, sir." Clark heard gunshots on the other end. "I have taken significant casualties. I cannot hold this section of the D Wing for very much longer, sir."

"I want you to break contact as soon as possible," Clark ordered. "We've lost too much time. I want you to retreat to the roof, to the helipad. We're going to abandon the facility. I will see you there and provide further orders when we arrive." He ended the call once Horrocks had confirmed the order and turned to face Vikram. "I suppose we should get out of here before the walking dead show up."

Vikram agreed.

The malignancy—oh, for the days when I could call it a "neoplasm" with a straight face!—is like a football now, or some horrible fetus growing inside her. Some nights while she's sedated I place a hand on its smooth edge and imagine I can feel it kicking. I've been working for so long with no result . . . I should take a break. [Lab Notes, 8/17/04]

A dead girl, maybe fifteen years old, pushed down the hall, one side pressed up tight against the cream-painted cinder blocks. She left a trail of blood behind her, blood that had soaked through her hair, ruined her clothes. She didn't seem to care.

Nilla balled her hands into fists and then let go of them again. The pain in her left hand—she wondered if she'd broken it while getting out of her manacles—brought her into perfect focus. Time to take stock.

There was shooting everywhere—it came to her from every darkened corridor, every pool of emergency lighting. Smoke filled one hallway. She was pretty sure the prison was on fire.

The dead moved through the prison like they owned the place. And she was one of the dead. She walked as calmly as she could past the dead teenager—the girl didn't even reach for her, didn't waste a moment's energy on Nilla—and stepped through a doorway.

The armless freak blocked her path.

He didn't look all that great. Skin had peeled away from most of his naked chest, long strips of it dangling around his waist. His face had puffed up and turned black with rot and his eyes looked like frosted glass. The smell of him would make animals run away.

He wasn't quite used up, though. He grinned down at her in the darkness, really grinned—how was that possible? There wasn't enough left of his brain to feel any satisfaction in intimidating her.

The grin slid into leering territory as she studied it.

"Fuck off," she told him. Something cold and sharp throbbed in her chest—maybe her dead heart going into cardiac arrest. "Just . . . leave me alone. Get out of the way."

The grin opened and he made an obscene sucking noise. "Nnnnnuggghhh," he told her, and she took a step back in extreme shock. He coughed and tried again. "No," he said, finally.

The explanation leapt to her mind and she felt foolish. "Mael, stop playing games."

"Fancy you saying as much," Mael said through Dick's mouth. The words were slurred, turned sideways by the corpse's swollen tongue and pulverized in his broken teeth but she understood him just fine. "You, who's been playing me for a fool this whole time. I have plans for you still. I think we have a real future together, but for just now I think it's best if you sit tight."

"Bullshit. This place is going to hell—I want out!" Nilla exclaimed.

"If you were to be hurt, I would feel just—" he said, but he didn't finish. She had started to duck under and around Dick's left side and Mael had to lean over to try to stop her. Which was exactly what she'd wanted him to do. She brought her feet up and slid across the monster's craning back and was behind him before he could even straighten up again.

She didn't waste any time after that. A corridor opened up before her, long and straight and pierced with pencil-thin windows. She dashed down it, or rather lumbered with as much alacrity as she could muster. She could feel the weight and mass of Dick behind her as Mael propelled his stolen corpse in pursuit, she could sense him back there with the hairs on the back of her neck but she refused to turn. She reached a doorway at the far end of the corridor and skidded through. She tried slamming the door shut behind her only to find that it was held open by some kind of magnetic stopper. While she tried to figure out how to release the mechanism she heard Dick smash into a wall not ten feet away.

She turned to head deeper into the maze-like prison but had to stop in her tracks. A soldier was standing in the doorway just ahead, staring at her, breathing hard. His eyes were very wide.

"Ma'am, it's alright, I can protect you," he said. "I promise we'll get out of here together."

Dick stumbled out into the hallway and wobbled on his feet for a second, trying to get his bearings, perhaps. The soldier raised his rifle to his eye and fired three rounds in one quick burst. The noise was huge in the narrow corridor, the muzzle flash blinding. Holes popped open in Dick's chest and neck and face and he spun around and fell to the floor.

The soldier was smart enough not to head over to Dick's body and check it for signs of unlife. Dick lay crumpled, his head down and away from the soldier, his legs splayed out before him. The soldier took aim again and unloaded half a clip into the dead man's back. "Shit," he screamed, and fired again. In the shadowy hallway he couldn't seem to land a head shot.

He stepped closer, then closer still. He raced up and kicked Dick's remaining boot and then danced back, but nothing happened. Licking his lips he stepped closer until he was looming over Dick's collapsed form. He raised his weapon to his face, ready to blow Dick's head off once and for all. "Ma'am, stay back," he shouted at her.

Dick sat up with enough force to knock the rifle butt right into the soldier's eye, making him scream loud enough to hurt Nilla's ears. Not half as loud, of course, as when Dick sank his incisors into the soldier's thigh and tore off a thick gobbet of flesh.

Nilla didn't stick around to watch.

If I only had more time to be sure. What am I screwing with here? I pinched the field for almost three seconds this morning. I could feel it bunching up, the heat of it on my hands. Warm, pleasant. Invigorating. This is crazy—I'm crazy! I'm not a scientist anymore, I'm a witch doctor, painted red and shaking rattles at the back of a cave. Except . . . it works. [Lab Notes, 9/4/04]

In a disused kitchen full of dust and spiders Nilla tripped over a fat woman whose legs had been gnawed down to splayed fragments of bone. The corpse kept trying to get up, to pull herself up to a standing position by grabbing at a table above her. She would get a few inches off the ground and then fall back again with a sputtering creak, only to try again, and again.

Nilla picked up an institutional-sized can of beets and bashed the dead woman's head in. Then she sat down on the floor next to the twice-dead corpse and tried to think of what to do next.

She was having trouble understanding what was happening. At least part of that had to do with the light. The emergency lights in the prison were everywhere and they were bright enough to let you see where the doors and exits were. The light came at weird angles, though, and it was dim enough that as you approached someone in the halls they looked like nothing more than a dull shadow. It was impossible to know if they were alive or dead.

Nilla. Nilla, talk to me. I can get you out of here if you'll talk to me.

She sat up, suddenly paying attention. Mael's voice had softened. Once his intrusions into her head had been buzzing, clattering torrents of noise. Now they almost sounded like her own thoughts. It was hard to resist him, harder than it had ever been before. He was figuring her out, learning her buttons, her triggers. He was going deep inside of her mind and she wasn't sure she could extract him anymore without hurting herself in the process.

And was that such a bad thing? She had to wonder. She was pretty sure he was crazy, but at least in the middle of his insanity there was a place for her.

Why do you hide from me, lass? I thought we were finally getting on alright. Just say something, will you? Say something so I can figure out where you are. Then I can get you to safety.

She kept her mouth shut. She just wasn't sure, yet. There was so much of her, so much she couldn't find anymore. There had been a complete human being, somebody with a personality all her own, with likes and dislikes and beliefs and attitudes and, and, and . . . memories. There had been memories and now they were hidden from her. That person had just stopped. When she died, that person had stopped functioning. Those memories had been barred from her, hidden behind a wall she couldn't seem to break down.

Were those things lost forever? Would she ever get her memories back? Mael promised her a name. He had implied there was more. She wanted so much for there to be more. She needed to know who she'd been. If she knew, for instance, whether she'd been a good person, a kind person, or if she had been a little wicked, a little mean. If she knew that maybe she would know what to do next.

Lass. Don't you know I'm your friend? Don't you know it by now? I've done so much for you. Is this how you repay me?

Jason Singletary could have told her the truth but he was dead now. Twice dead. She and Dick had devoured his brains between them. It was the closest thing to mercy that she had possessed to give him.

She thought maybe that she had started over. That dying had relieved her of the burden of having a past. Or maybe it gave her a duty—a duty to build herself from scratch. Maybe she had been brought back for a reason, but not for Mael's reason. Jason

Singletary had certainly thought so. She was the only one, he'd said, who could go to that place. That place in the mountains, that place at the end of the world. The place Captain Clark had shown her, in a photograph. Too bad nobody could tell her what she was supposed to do there.

She stood up slowly and dusted off her pants. She left the kitchen. She took the next left turn just because she seemed to remember that when you were lost in a maze you were supposed to take every left turn.

The corridor beyond was long and dark and cold. At its far end she saw a rectangle of pale light. She moved toward it. She was drawn toward it. "I'm here, Mael," she said out loud. Because she owed him that much. "I'm going to find my own way for now, though, if you don't mind."

Nilla—finally! I'd thought you must be dead. Well, I blasted well do mind, actually. We have things to do. Turn right at the next junction, lass. That's an order.

"I don't know about this," Nilla said. "I've seen what your dead people do to the living people. It looks pretty cruel to me. It looks pretty unnecessary. If he just wanted to kill them all off, why didn't your god Teuagh just melt the ice caps or set off all the nukes or whatever? Why raise the dead? It's so messy, so inefficient. Are you telling me he couldn't think of anything better?"

I don't question His ways.

"Which just means you don't know."

Mael's voice returned a little louder, a little harsher. She had gotten to him, she decided. If only just a little. That was a kind of victory in itself. **If you're going to tell me now that you don't believe in the Father of Clans, I wish you would just save your breath.**

"It's not like I'm going to need it for anything else. Mael, I need some time to think. Some space. I want you to know, it's not you. It's me."

His reply smacked into her ribs hard enough to make her squeak in surprise and pain. Something—something dead had come at her hard and fast. It wasn't Dick: it had arms, arms that wrapped around her waist, hard, unfeeling arms that would crush her if she didn't do something.

Nilla did something.

Twisting to her side she dropped to the floor like a bag of flour, slipping down through the ring of those crushing arms. At the same time she kicked out with one leg, crushing a kneecap with the heel of her shoe. Unfeeling, the dead thing came at her again, surging through the darkness, broken and stinking and ragged, torn and ravaged muscles convulsing, striking, descending to smash her to pieces.

Nilla reached up, felt hair, and grabbed. The dead thing swiveled and scratched and struck at the air but Nilla held it away from herself and avoided the worst of its attack. Heaving and grunting she hauled the dead creature toward the doorway, toward the light. She had to be fast and she pushed her muscles to obey her, to give her some kind of coordination as she pulled on the blood-matted hair. She got its head under her armpit and heaved one more time and shattered its skull against the doorframe.

The dead thing's skull cracked open and all animation fled from its flopping limbs. Nilla dropped it and stepped into the light, her body screaming at her, every muscle in her arms and back wrenched by the exertion. Then she looked down at the thing.

Shar looked back up at her.

It was her, it was definitely her. How the teenager had died Nilla had no clue. It really didn't matter. She had died and come back and Mael had been clever enough to make her one of his puppets. Nilla pressed one knuckle against her upper lip, trying not to vomit. When she stopped shaking she looked at the ceiling. As if he were there, somewhere, in the sky. The way someone else might have looked up to talk to God.

"This is it, isn't it. It's all you have to offer. Dead things struggling in the dark. Hurting each other. Well, fuck you. I'm done."

He didn't speak to her again. Maybe he knew better, or maybe she'd switched off whatever part of her brain listened to him.

Beyond the doorway stood a stairwell that led upward. At its top a door opened onto black air. When Nilla's eyes finally adjusted she saw stars. Clouds. The night sky. To her left a whirring, chuffing noise. She looked over and saw the spinning blades of a helicopter.

You can't see it but you know it's there, you feel its presence. Through the wall I can feel it . . . life, in the glorious abstract. In the middle of this morning's test run she started vomiting blood and by the time I had her cleaned up and sedated the extrusion should have collapsed but . . . it didn't. Right through the wall and I knew it somehow, I whispered it to her. It's self-reinforcing now, I think. I smashed all the fetishes and the instruments but . . . it's still there, the sensors show nothing of course but . . . I can feel it. [Lab Notes, 11/6/04]

"He's going to come out of there any second now," Clark promised, but he knew he was wrong. Together with Vikram he stared at the stairwell hatch leading down into the prison. Sergeant Horrocks was supposed to be emerging from that door at any moment, leading what was left of the troops.

It had been seven long minutes since his last call. There had been a lot of noise back then, a lot of shooting and screaming coming up from below. All of that had since stopped.

"Any second," Clark repeated, and Vikram muttered in acquiescence. Behind them the Pave Low helicopter spun its rotor uselessly. There was only so long that they could wait. Fuel for the aircraft was at a premium.

"Ah, Bannerman—here he is," Vikram announced, as a human shape appeared in the stairwell door. "Nothing to worry about, I—" Vikram fell silent for a moment, then let out a terrified shriek. He raised his sidearm and fired three rapid shots into the doorway. The bullets collided with dead flesh and sent the figure there spinning.

"That was unnecessary," the shadowy figure said.

It was the girl. She stood up and stepped onto the starlit helipad. A bullet hole in her neck oozed crusty powdered blood, dried up so long ago it wasn't even shiny. She prodded the wound with one undead finger.

It was so easy to forget that she wasn't one of the living. That she wasn't exactly what she appeared to be, a helpless, innocent survivor of this horror. Clark had to remind himself from time to time that she was part of the Epidemic, not a victim of it.

"What did you do with Sergeant Horrocks?" Clark demanded.

The girl shrugged. "I don't know who that is. I didn't find any living people on my way here. I saw some soldiers but they were already gone."

Horrocks must be dead, Clark realized. The good sergeant, the excellent soldier, could not survive against the Epidemic. No one could forever, not even the Hero of Denver. "I think we can assume he won't be joining us." Clark stood up straighter than before and stared at her with his best command face. "So. Are you going to eat us now, or did you have something else in mind?"

The girl's face soured and she threw him a mock salute. "I thought we would get in that helicopter and fly out to that mountain you were so excited about. You know, what we were supposed to do in the first place."

"You don't honestly expect me to take you with us," Clark sputtered.

"I think you need all the help you can get. Listen, Captain—I don't know anything about military tactics or politics or epidemiology or anything. I lost whatever expertise I may have had when I died. But I do know my destiny is up there. I'll walk if I have to, but I'd prefer to catch a lift with you two."

Clark felt a sinus headache coming on. He had no answers. He had no information. His chain of command was broken and his direct superior had turned against humanity. According to every order of warfare that he knew that meant it was time to fall back and call for evac. Yet fate had put him in this position and demanded that he come up withy something new, something not covered in any technical manual.

"Oh, hell," he said, sounding prissy even to himself. "Mount up already. We've got no time to lose."

It was all too true. Their destination, Bolton's Valley, was nearly a hundred miles away even as the crow flew. The pilots assured him they could reach the Epicenter with the fuel onboard but it would be a close thing. Once they had completed their mission they would have to find alternate transport out of the area of operations.

Assuming they survived. Clark doubted they would. It was all right, though. As long as they got close enough to the switch, as long as they managed to turn this thing off, that would be enough.

That was how he imagined it—the Epicenter—as some kind of science fiction death ray contraption. A big telescoping ray gun with fins and flanges and control panels sticking out of a hatch carved into the mountain. He imagined it had two buttons that controlled it, conveniently labeled ON and OFF. He imagined pushing the latter and then going back to Denver, to the Brown Palace, and finally having that juicy, rare steak that fate had stolen away from him. He imagined taking a room upstairs, a room with tasteful wallpaper and gauzy curtains on the windows and a big, soft bed with a white coverlet. He imagined going to sleep for a very long time and then waking up to find that humanity had rebuilt after the dead stopped rising, that while he slept everything had been cleared away, tidied up, made whole again. He imagined that the population of the United States would have replenished itself and that there would be no one left who even remembered the Epidemic, that there would be no wounds anymore, no physical scars, no emotional traumas. No nightmares.

Except, he knew, that he would still remember. He would remember the face, and the name, of everyone who had died. He would remember them for the rest of his life.

Perhaps it was better if he didn't come back after all.

"It is still a lovely world, is it not?" Vikram asked, jolting Clark out of his reverie. He hadn't even noticed the helicopter lifting away from the prison. He hadn't realized that they'd already swung way out across the mountains, that they were running fast, about a hundred feet up, following a ridgeline that probably marked the Continental Divide. Maybe an hour had passed and he'd been lost in his own thoughts. So close to the end and he'd wasted all that time.

He looked down, though, and saw trees clothing the rugged sides of the mountains, aspens and firs and loblolly pines. He saw mirror-colored water snaking between the peaks, the stars wavering in the depths of creeks and rivers. Oh, Vikram was so very, very right. It was beautiful. It was still beautiful.

Then he looked over at the girl. She sat very still in her crew seat, buckled in and motionless. Her chest didn't move with breath, her eyes didn't blink. You could tell she was dead if you paid attention. If you actually looked. She had the waxy skin of a corpse. She had the eyes that didn't really focus anymore, not on anything in particular.

She turned her eyes to look back at him. "What if we can't stop it?"

Clark couldn't stop looking at the girl. "At the very least I can perform the final duty of any soldier who watches his country die."

"What's that?"

"I can take our communal revenge on whoever did it." Enough. Clark wanted to change the subject. "So who told you about the mountain?" Clark demanded of her. "Who said you were the only one who could go there?"

She shrugged and looked out the window. "A man named Jason Singletary. He had a gift, a kind of a power. He was psychic, if you have to hear me say it."

"Psychic," Clark said. The word came out of his mouth and hovered in the air like a grim little cloud. It sounded a lot like other words he knew now. Like "undead," or "magic." It sounded like one of the things that had gone wrong with the world.

The pilot broke the silence that followed. "We're approaching the site," he said. "The valley should be visible in a few minutes."

Before he'd even finished his sentence the hatch to the cargo compartment started rattling.

The copilot unstrapped himself and came aft, walking with the motion of the helicopter, one hand on the ceiling to brace himself. "What have we got back here, just rations and some light munitions, right?" he called back to the pilot. "Anything that might come loose?"

It was like a dream, a particularly horrible dream, where you know what is about to happen but you are so plagued by self-doubt and general anxiety that you don't dare open your mouth to say it, because that would make it real.

The copilot reached for the handle on the side of the hatch and even before he had turned it all the way the hatch exploded inward, spilling two hundred pounds of meat into the crew compartment. There was blood, and torn flesh, and screaming, but in that first awful second Clark couldn't connect the dots, couldn't make sense of what was happening. Only when he heard Vikram calling his name did he really know.

A man. A dead man. A dead man with no arms.

A dead man with no arms, his torso riddled with bullet holes, his face distorted by damage and hunger, his body as dry and tough as beef jerky, had stowed away aboard the helicopter when it left the prison. The dead man had killed the copilot in one incredibly swift, incredibly brutal motion and now he had his teeth deep in Vikram's calf. Some of the blood slicking down the floor belonged to Clark's best friend.

The dead girl was up and standing on her chair. She looked horrified and Clark felt a quick irrational burst of desire—he wanted to comfort her. To tell her everything was going to be alright.

A better plan came to mind a moment later. He was standing next to an exterior hatch with an emergency release. He pulled up on the red handle and the door fell away into blackness, cold air bellying in at him so fast and hard it knocked everyone down. The dead man slipped away from Vikram. The girl fell off her crew seat. Clark grabbed her arm and hauled her up to stand next to him.

The dead man didn't bother getting up. He just got his teeth into Vikram again and kept chewing. Vikram drew his weapon and started firing at the dead man's head but the helicopter was rolling, pitching, yawing—nobody could fire accurately under those conditions, and Vikram was no marksman.

The pilot kept looking over his shoulder, shouting something back at them. Questions. He wasn't paying enough attention to flying the aircraft. "Soldier!" Clark yelled at him, "see to your duties!" Then he turned to the girl.

"This psychic," he said to her. "He told you—you were the only one. The only one who could go to the Epicenter. He told you that, he was sure of that?"

The girl's eyes were very wide. He grabbed her by the shoulders and shook her and finally she nodded. It was what he needed to hear.

Grabbing her by the arms he yanked her forward and shoved her out of the helicopter, out through the external hatch, out into the roaring sky.

Poor mood, no appetite, continued angiogenesis inside the deforming body. But she's alive. Fuck you, God, fuck you, Death, fuck you, fucking Cancer. She's still alive! [Lab Notes, 1/16/05]

The crash happened so quickly he missed most of it. He was facing the wrong way to see it happen. He lost consciousness for a while and then he woke up again. Something was burning—Bannerman Clark felt the heat on his leg. He felt the hairs there crisp and curl and melt. There was only a little pain, in his chest. He looked down and wished he hadn't. A jagged piece of steel transfixed him, held him down to the side of the broken helicopter. He was like a butterfly mounted in a case. Best to not try to move, he decided. Best to just wait it out. The heat on his leg kept getting more intense and he could smell his flesh burning, but still, there was no pain.

There had been a moment after he pushed the girl out of the hatch, a single moment when it looked as if the pilot might actually get them down safely. It had looked like Vikram might actually kill the armless dead man. It was a possibility that they could continue the mission.

Something slithered nearby, lit up by the flames.

There had been a moment and the moment had passed. The pilot had started screaming and then he had unbuckled himself from his seat, trying to get away, trying to get away from the murderous corpse. It had only taken a few seconds after that for the helicopter to smack into the side of the mountain.

The slithering thing drew closer. Clark opened his eyes, though he didn't want to. He had some idea of what he was going to see. A dead person, a hungry dead person coming to eat him. He just wasn't sure who it would be.

It was Vikram. The Sikh Major's face was crumpled in on one side and he was missing an eye. His turban was gone and his long, long hair draped casually on the ground. One whole side of his body didn't seem to work. He didn't say a word as he hauled himself closer. His mouth was open, his teeth very white.

Vikram had a knife on his belt. A *kirpan*, more of a short sword. It was one of the religious objects he was supposed to keep on his person at all times. Vikram didn't even seem aware of the weapon— he had teeth and fingernails and that was all he needed. Clark thought he could take that knife off the belt and destroy his friend's brain with it. That was the very least he could do.

Assuming he could lift his arm. Assuming that Clark wasn't completely paralyzed.

Vikram dragged himself an inch closer. Almost in range. Time to find out.

Something's out there . . . I saw it today, again, working its way through the trees. I called out but it didn't answer. Something is climbing up the mountain but I don't think it's human so what is it? What is it? [Lab Notes, 3/21/05]

Nilla stopped screaming. She opened up her eyes. She was lying in something wet, something cold and white.

Snow.

Her neck could be broken. She'd hit the side of the mountain pretty hard. Sitting up could be the worst thing she could do for herself—she might tear her spinal cord.

Of course, it wasn't like anyone was coming to rescue her. Clark hadn't been trying to kill her. He'd been trying to save her. He knew the helicopter was going down. Nilla had heard it crash and clatter and fall and slide for what seemed like hours while she lay inert on the hard, cold ground, looking straight up.

She sat up.

Her bones still worked. Her ribs hurt like a motherfucker, but her legs, and her arms, and yes, her neck were all still intact. She had fallen a hundred feet out of thin air to collide with the stony limb of a mountainside and it looked like she had made it okay.

There were some benefits, she guessed, to already being dead.

She tried to get her bearings. Trees surrounded her on every side, conifers with a dusting of snow on their needles. Straight up between the treetops she could see stars and the faintest sliver of a crescent moon. If there was a way to know which way was north based on the position of the moon Nilla couldn't remember it. She was lost. Lost and alone in the middle of the wilderness at the middle of a continent full of dead things. If her neck had been broken she couldn't have been in worse shape. She sat down and tried to think about what to do next.

That was when she noticed the light. It wasn't normal light, of course, or she would have noticed it right away. It was more watery, more indistinct. She could see it better with her eyes closed. Well. There you go. It was the same kind of light she saw when she looked at living people. Golden. Perfect. Pretty much every fiber of her being was agreed. Getting closer to that light was a good plan.

Her mind, strangely enough, concurred. For maybe the first time in her admittedly short memory something actually felt right. She had come to find the Source of the Epidemic. The energy that kept her from dying like she ought to. She was one hundred percent sure that this ethereal light that radiated right through the trees was it, the Epicenter, the Source.

She got back to her feet and started walking. Climbing, in places, her hands clumsy but strong enough to grab at rocks and exposed tree roots. Her feet dug into the slippery ground, kicking through a rime of years-old snow, through the accumulation of fallen pine needles beneath and into frozen dirt under that. She hauled herself bodily up slopes, then ran, headlong, recklessly, down the other sides. She clambered over ridges of bare rock carved knife-thin by eons of wind. She crouched under endless tree branches and smacked her forehead on those she didn't see and had bushel after bushel of freezing snow dumped down the back of her thin cotton shirt.

She should have been exhausted after the first quarter mile. Every step should have been harder, a brand new agony. But it wasn't. If anything the mountaineering got easier. Her body felt better, stronger, healthier with every step she took. At one point she felt her neck spasm and shake and she thought maybe physical collapse had finally caught up with her but no. It was the bullet, the bullet the Indian soldier had fired at her on the prison's rooftop. Underneath it the muscle fibers and nerves and blood vessels wriggled as they wove themselves back together. The inert leaden mass of the bullet popped out of her neck with an agonizing little sputter and fell to smack her hard on the bones of her wrist. She yanked her arm back in pain but even the pain disappeared after a second.

The light that came through the trees—it was better than heroin. It was better than sex with a loving partner. It was better than a drink of water after three days of wandering in the desert. She could even vouch personally for that last one.

It was nearly morning when she came out over a final lip of rock and saw the valley below her and the Source beneath it. Cold blue light the color of hallucinations lit up the sky over Bolton's Valley, the place Captain Clark had shown her in a photograph. The place Jason Singletary had shown her with his mind.

She wasn't the only dead person to have found the place. A crowd of them—maybe two hundred in all—stood below the ridge. Their battered and torn bodies looked relaxed there. Their ragged faces were turned upward to catch the light. It was tempting to join them. It was even more tempting to move closer, to go into that flaring beacon.

Nilla found herself elbowing through the crowd without really thinking about it. When one of the corpses coughed and cleared its dry throat she wasn't even surprised.

"Lass. Please don't go any farther."

Nilla turned to face what had been a middle-aged woman. She had been plump, with chin-length hair pulled back in a simple black band. She had very little skin left on her face and no eyes in her skull. Nilla understood, looking at her, that she could still see the light of the Source.

It was Mael who spoke through the woman, of course. "Why?" Nilla demanded. "Are you worried that I'll go up there and turn this thing off, like Clark wanted? I haven't actually decided what I'll do yet. I haven't decided who I am. Good Nilla, bad Nilla. I kind of want to find out, though." Nilla closed her eyes and felt rays of sparkling warmth shoot through her, healing her, feeding her. Oh, she wanted to find out so very much. "I've got more important things to do."

"Indeed, lass? And what's more important than the end of the world? Answer me that. Or don't. I've little left to teach you, but there's this: don't go another step."

"Christ, next you're going to tell me your god doesn't want me up there."

The woman shook her head. "Teuagh is no god. He is my father. He is the father of us all. When I was alive, children did what their fathers told them, without question. I used to think I was like a father to you."

"Really? Because I thought we had more of a love-hate romance thing going. Wow, now that I think about it that's kind of creepy. Well, listen, you can't stop me. If I want to go up there I will."

"You don't ken it yet, Nilla. I'm not trying to stop you because I'm afraid of what you'll do. I'm simply afraid you're going to hurt yourself. There's so few of us now. You, some fellow in New York who figured it out on his own. A lad in Russia who doesn't even know where he is. I'm just trying to protect a very scarce resource, that's all."

Nilla opened her mouth to rebuke him but then she saw charred corpses in the broken field ahead of her. She took a step closer and felt the warmth of the Source grow hot. Another step and it was painful. "Oh," she said. She understood immediately. The same energy that fed her could burn her to a crisp if she got too close. Yet moving forward meant getting closer.

But then she just had it, as if her body knew what to do even if her mind was oblivious. She banked her energy—subtracted her darkness—made herself invisible. The one thing she could do that nobody else could manage. The one thing that set her apart. Instantly the warmth was gone. She stepped forward, and again, until she was even with the burnt and disfigured bodies sprawled across the rocks.

Nothing happened.

Singletary had been right. She was the only one who could go to the Source, out of all the dead. She started to climb.

It was a far easier ascent than what had come before, though every step knocked loose showers of pebbles and dirt, eroded bits of hillside that went skittering down, pattering, pittering away from her. The handholds were stable, if the footing wasn't. In a few minutes she had reached the top of a ridge. A green-painted stegosaurus stood watch there, sculpted out of concrete. Just as Singletary had shown her.

Dinosaurs. Statues of dinosaurs. A tyrannosaur loomed over the site, while human-sized velociraptors leered out from around corners. In the middle of it all stood a dilapidated building with a sign posted next to its door.

DINOSAUR EXPERIENCE
—HALL OF FOSSILS—
PROPRIETOR DR. N. VRONSKI
OPENING OCTOBER 2006

The door opened and a man stepped out. A living man. He was mostly bald, with tiny, intense blue eyes. Nilla walked over to him and took the hand he extended. He had no trouble seeing her, even though she was invisible. She must be invisible—if she let her energy show, even for a moment, she would have been incinerated. But he could see her, just as Jason Singletary could.

She understood, then. The vision Singletary had shared with her hadn't just come full-formed out of the ether. It had been a communication, live and in real time, between this new man and the psychic. He had called out for her. He had summoned her.

"I never truly imagined you would actually come," he said, because he could read her mind. He didn't seem as sensitive to her thoughts as Singletary had been. "Please. We should go inside." He led her into a dark building full of glass display cases. Some of them were empty and collecting dust. Others held dark fossils half-buried in matrices of brown or red stone. Educational plaques hung on the walls.

"Are you Dr. Vronski?" Nilla asked.

"I was," he told her. "I mean . . . I was a paleontologist, before all this, well, you know, started. I'm the one, by the way. I'm the moron who killed off the human race."

Nilla didn't know how to reply to that. "You're psychic," she said.

"Not originally. I had to become certain things—I had to make certain changes to myself, to complete my work. Come on, please, this way." He frowned. His eyes fixed on her and moved slowly from left to right as if he were reading something written on her face. "It's funny. I can't seem to figure out what you want here."

That made two of them.

"But you're going to kill me, right? Kill me and eat me? It's far less than what I deserve. Here." He led her to the top of a stairwell. "Maybe you'd like to see it first, though. The, um, the eruption. Or maybe . . . something to eat."

Nilla looked down the stairs. There was someone else down there—or maybe two people, standing very close together. They moved into the light and her mouth fell open in true horror.

"This is my wife, Charlotte." He looked at her eyes and whispered, "please don't say anything about her appearance. She's very sensitive."

Unexpected side effects, all over the news I . . . I did this? I can't believe it spread so far . . . I did this? I did it for her, only for her . . . forgive me . . . [Lab Notes, 4/2/05]

"I'm sorry that it's dead. I know you would prefer it alive."

Vronski put down a plate in front of Nilla. A dead rat lay on its side there, one glazed eye pointed in her direction. She ate it without thinking too much about it. She was too busy trying not to look at Charlotte.

The paleontologist had prepared a Lean Cuisine for himself. Apparently Charlotte didn't eat anymore. Instead he had placed a vase full of cut flowers where her plate should go. As Nilla tried not to watch Charlotte slowly and methodically tore the petals off the flowers and crumpled them between her fingers.

Charlotte was still alive. Vronski had assured Nilla of that fact. It was hard to believe him. Boils and eruptions covered the skin of her one remaining arm that emerged from under a pendulous roll of ill-defined flesh. When she moved Nilla could almost make out the shape of a human woman in the mass.

The paleontologist's wife had been a lawyer, once, he had told her. Now she was an abomination. Pancreatic cancer had blossomed inside of her, spreading to every part of her body. It should have killed her. Vronski had kept her alive at the cost of apocalypse, but he couldn't make her healthy again. The Source had been created to keep her going, to give her body the strength to fight off the tumor. Unfortunately it didn't discriminate. It made the tumor unnaturally healthy as well. The two of them lived on, in their way, even as the world died.

The cancer outweighed what was left of Charlotte, probably by a factor of three to one. Its abstract tissue draped over her back and down her sides. It dragged on the floor behind her. It obscured her breasts and hips and it completely hid her face. It mostly looked like fat tissue covered in thin, translucent skin but in places it had tried to form itself into pieces of a human being. A row of forty or fifty perfectly formed teeth emerged from the smooth expanse where Charlotte's shoulder must be. Patches of hair had broken out here and there on her back and there were fingernails growing in places that weren't fingers. A single closed eyelid could be seen on her stomach. It never opened but sometimes it twitched as if there was an eye underneath trapped in the endless swimming motion of REM sleep.

A thick bundle of black cables drooped from under the roll of flesh and snaked its way out of the room. It connected Charlotte's nervous system directly to the Source. Without those cables, Vronski explained, she would die instantly. The energy had to be introduced directly to her various bodily systems. The tumor seemed to draw its energy right from the very air around them.

"I kept her alive," he said, over and over. "She didn't die." She was the culmination of his life's work.

He had tried his best to give her back a face. To this end he had bought a porcelain domino mask—the kind found in little girl's bedrooms around the country—and tied it around where her head should be with a length of pink ribbon. From time to time it would begin to slip down and Vronski would patiently get up and readjust it.

He had not bothered to put any clothes on her, though Nilla imagined it would take a tent's worth of cloth to cover her swollen bulk.

"Is she even aware of us?" Nilla asked, dragging her gaze away from Charlotte to look at the thing's husband. "Can she smell us or something?"

"Please don't start," he hissed.

After dinner he agreed to take Nilla down to look at the Source. On the way she passed quite close by Charlotte. She noticed the mask had been broken at some point and very carefully glued back together.

Vronski led her down two flights of stairs into a room at the very bottom of the museum. It had been used once as a workshop and laboratory and it was still full of crates full of carefully packed fossils. Vronski offered to show her his best specimens—he claimed to have a nearly intact archaeopteryx—but Nilla was far more interested in the room's other contents. Namely, the Source.

Various items surrounded it. What looked like tikis carved out of wood and shrunken heads mounted on sticks formed a circle around it, while boxy scientific apparatus blinked and buzzed and hummed in the corners of the room. A complicated looking device collected the energy of the Source and sent it through the black cables to where Charlotte waited upstairs. Vronski tried to describe how that worked but Nilla didn't care at all. The Source demanded all of her attention.

It was difficult to say how large it might be—it radiated life energy so strongly that when Nilla closed her eyes it looked like a blazing star. She could feel its power, quite literally—it pushed at her. It blew her hair back. It was beautiful, far more beautiful than a dead thing like herself deserved. Probably it was more beautiful than anything on Earth deserved. It was constantly in motion, its shifting, shimmering rays twisting through the air as if they were threads of gossamer billowing in a pleasant breeze.

It was the beginning, the start of all things. You could feel as much, if you reached out a hand toward it. It made you. It shaped you. From a center that was also an edge it reached out to every cell, to every twisted coil of protein. It spoke the language of chemicals binding together and combining, recombining, a language that was more sung than spoken, and more imagined than sung. It knew your thoughts. It gave you your thoughts and your feelings.

"I'm sorry," Vronski said.

She looked up at him. "For what?" she asked.

"It's just— you've been standing there for fifteen minutes now and I'd kind of like to get on with things. If you don't mind. You can go back to looking at it after you've killed me."

Fifteen minutes? There had been no time when she was gazing on the Source.

"I'm still considering what I should do," Nilla said. And she was. She had choices, or at least a choice, for the first time since . . . well, the first time she could remember. She could kill the man who had started the Epidemic. In the process she would insure that nobody else could ever take the Source away from her—that her unlife would go on forever. Mael would like that. Alternatively, she could do what Captain Clark had wanted. She could shut this thing down. That would end her own existence, certainly. It would end all the death and pain and horror too.

She thought of the creature upstairs that Vronski called his wife. Vronski had started the Epidemic in order to prolong her life, long past the point where anyone would think she would want to keep it. Nilla's choice was sort of the same. Prolong her own, largely miserable, existence, or choose death. Actual death.

She stalled. "What is this?" She asked. "How did you make it?"

"It's a field, a kind of biological field. It's similar to the Earth's magnetic field. Life couldn't exist without it. I didn't make it. It was always there, I just let the Genie out of the bottle."

She glared at him. "You can give me the grown-up version," she said.

He nodded apologetically. "It's sort of like the Earth's magnetic field, except this is a biological field. The energy, the life force, is everywhere, all the time. It's in every cell of every living thing. What you think of as the golden energy."

He was reading her mind again. It didn't bother as much as when Singletary had done it. "Go on," she said.

"That energy is what makes cells divide. It's what makes organisms want to reproduce. It makes DNA strands spiral around each other and it carries some of the pattern of living things. It's the force that drives evolution. Without it living things would just die. Scientists have been trying to find that energy for centuries with no success. It's too subtle. You need other methods to see it— methods scientists, including myself, generally frown upon. Once you know it's there, however, you can feel it all the time. You can touch it—and you can mold it. I liberated some of the energy from that system, to keep Charlotte's body from failing. Unfortunately I liberated too much. You, and the others like you, are the result. The excess energy can't just dissipate into space. It has to go somewhere. It looks for things it can animate, things with nervous systems it can flow through. Dead things."

"I can't believe this. You fucked with the life force? Talk about playing God. What are you, some kind of mad scientist?"

Vronski shrugged uncomfortably. "I don't think 'scientist' is the right word for what I've become. You have to understand, though. I kept her alive. She's still alive." He raised his hands and lowered them again. "I would have killed myself a while back. I know what I did, and how wrong I was. But then who would look after Charlotte? She's always bumping into things and cutting herself by accident and she needs someone to tend to her little boo-boos. One time she fell down an entire flight of stairs. Back when she still had a mouth she almost ate some drain cleaner because she couldn't see what she was doing. I love her, you see. I love her so very, very much. I can't stand the idea of her going away."

He looked less human in that moment than his wife. He looked like a part of a person, an idea that never got thought over. A fragment of intention with nothing to back it up. He was a mad scientist all right, but not in the traditional sense. He wasn't some latter-day Prometheus plumbing the very depths of the secret cosmos. He was a scientist who was also mentally ill. That was all.

"Okay, enough." Nilla had made her decision. "I understand. But it doesn't matter—this can't go on. You and I are going to shut this thing down. I don't care how difficult that is or what it will do to her. Just show me how."

He looked up with a strange expression on his face. Incomprehension, coming from a man used to understanding things intuitively. "Shut it down?"

"Yeah. We end this, I fall down dead, the world goes back to normal. That's what I've chosen. How do I begin, do I do this?" she asked. She knocked over one of the tiki statues. She picked it up and threw it against a wall until it broke. "How about this?" She grabbed an oscilloscope off a wheeled cart and dropped it to crash in pieces on the floor. "Stop me when I'm getting warm." She found a hatchet on one of the lab tables and started breaking equipment.

"I don't think you understand," he told her. "This is a breach made in one of the most basic elements of nature. This is a self-reinforcing singularity. It provides its own power, it increases in size without any kind of input!"

"So?" Nilla shouted. "So what?"

"So you can't shut it down. That isn't physically possible. You can't stop it. You can't stuff the air back into a punctured balloon."

Nilla let her arm drop. She stared at him. Into him. He was telling the truth. He wanted someone to stop the Source. He needed it, though it meant losing his wife. But he knew of no way in which it could be done.

He turned away from her and picked up a fossil from a lab bench. A trilobite—something extinct and yet still beautiful. "I imagine you're going to kill me now, which frankly, I'm fine with. I mean I deserve it. I deserve worse."

"Yeah." Nilla thought of all the people who had died to get her this close. Shar and Charles. Mellowman, Morphine Mike. The Termite. Captain Clark and all of his soldiers. Jason Singletary, the boy in Las Vegas. The man who bit her on the neck, the man who killed her. Every single person she'd met since her reawakening was dead along with others, so many others, so many millions of others. What this man had done was beyond evil. "Yeah. You do deserve worse."

She picked up the bundle of black cables that ran across the floor. With the hatchet she cut through them all in one stroke.

They heard a tiny shout from upstairs, a sudden yelp of pain, but nothing like speech. Then something large and heavy collided with the floor.

Vronski's blue eyes quivered in their sockets and sweat broke out on his forehead.

Nilla dropped the hatchet and walked away, away from the scientist, away from the museum, away from the mountains.

She started walking east, toward New York. She didn't ask anyone living to help her. She saw very few living people anyway.

Somewhere in Kansas she stopped in the middle of a highway
because Mael was trying to talk to her. She turned around to see him
standing naked behind her, looking apologetic.

"Your name was Julic," he told her, and then he vanished into
thin air.

ABOUT THE AUTHOR

DAVID WELLINGTON was born in Pittsburgh, Pennsylvania, the hometown of George Romero and therefore the birthplace of the modern zombie. He attended Syracuse University and then Penn State where he received an MFA in creative writing. He currently resides in New York City.

For more information or to read other works by the author, please visit http://www.davidwellington.net.